FORGOTTEN HOLLOW
BOOK 1

# MISCHIEF IN A BOTTLE

## MARIE ANDREAS

**Other books by Marie Andreas**
**The Lost Ancients**
Book One: The Glass Gargoyle
Book Two: The Obsidian Chimera
Book Three: The Emerald Dragon
Book Four: The Sapphire Manticore
Book Five: The Golden Basilisk
Book Six: The Diamond Sphinx
**The Lost Ancients: Dragon's Blood**
Book One: The Seeker's Chest
Book Two: The Finder's Crown
Book Three: The Hunter's Chalice
Book Four: The Diviner's Scroll


**The Asarlaí Wars**
Book One: Warrior Wench
Book Two: Victorious Dead
Book Three: Defiant Ruin
**The Code of the Keeper- Continuation of Asarlaí Wars**
Book One: Traitor's Folly
Book Two: Destroyer's Curse
Book Three: Keeper's Tempest

# MARIE ANDREAS

**The Adventures of Smith and Jones**
A Curious Invasion
The Mayhem of Mermaids
An Intrigue of Pharaohs

**Broken Veil Trilogy**
Book On: The Girl with the Iron Wing
Book Two: An Uncommon Truth of Dying
Book Three: Through a Veil Darkly

**Books of the Cuari Trilogy**
Book One: Essence of Chaos
Book Two: Division of Chaos
Book Three: Destruction of Chaos

**Magic and Sorcery Chronicles Trilogy**
A Touch of Magic
A Slice of Sorcery
A Dash of Devilry

**Forgotten Hollow**
Book One: Mischief in a Bottle
Stand-alone prequel novella: Murder in a Bottle

# Contents

A cknowledgements

There's no way all of my weird adventures could ever make it out into the world without a lot of help.

A LOT OF HELP.

I want to thank my editors-beta readers: Lisa Andreas, Patti Huber, Lynne Mayfield, and Laura Schilling. Thank you so much!

Also, a big thank you to Barbara Elness and Sonia Manzo for your amazing insights and assistance—you rock! Thank you to Ilana Schoonover for excellent proofreading. Any errors or mistakes that remain are completely mine.

Thank you to all of you who have read, reviewed, talked about any of my books—I do this for you (and to get the stories out of my head, but mostly for you )

Thank you to Deranged Doctor Design for a wonderful cover and interior title page.

# Chapter One

I knew this wouldn't be a good day when a goat stood bleating at me from the foot of my bed.

And it wasn't my goat.

Rolling over and ignoring it seemed the best option until Lucie, the orange cat menace, ran across my bed, jumped on the headboard, tail in full puff mode, and hissed.

If I had access to my magic I could have sent both of them out into the barn where they could sort out their issues and leave me in peace. Unfortunately, being a paroled jinn trapped on the backwater planet like Earth meant that wasn't an option.

Of course, the humans of this planet were clueless about being a halfway house for paroled criminals. Nor did they know of the hundred worlds, loosely grouped as the Eltrisphere, hidden far beyond their solar system. Earth was just a joke to the advanced peoples of the Universe, and Earthlings weren't in on the punchline.

"Lucie, what is that goat doing in here?" I had a goat. Actually, I had a goat assigned to me. At this time in the morning, Tiberius was probably still passed out in the living room, drooling into the carpet, and not appearing at all goat-like.

Tiberius was also a jinn, a different line than mine, though. He didn't have magic at all.

He was also a former centurion and the one who brought me in for a crime I don't think I'd been involved with. There were complications after my hundred-year imprisonment in my bottle for said crime. So, two months ago, I was given probation on Earth to prove I was now a functioning member of society. Tiberius was sent along to keep me on the straight and narrow. Or to spy on me. That possibility was still in my head.

Here on Earth, I looked as I did normally, tall, slender, with long, black hair and green eyes. My skin was a dusky tan, so I said my people were from some place called India. Long ago.

In real life, Tiberius was about seven feet tall, broad-shouldered, blue, and had a massive wingspan. Those attributes only appeared now when he was asleep. Otherwise, he was a talking goat. Who fainted when startled.

He hated when Lucie or I pointed it out.

The goat at the end of my bed gave a soft bleat, folded its legs, and settled in for a staring contest with Lucie.

"Seriously, Lucie. Take your friend outside." A glance at the clock informed me I still had fifteen minutes before I had to get out of bed. I planned on treasuring all of them.

The large orange cat hissed once more—which the goat ignored—but stayed on the bookcase, which doubled as my headboard. "That's not my friend. None of them are. Get up and shove them out!" Lucie had been a companion of the jinn who'd sent me into lockup for crimes he pulled off. The creep had also been my late and unlamented ex-boyfriend. Lucie helped me resolve a few problems when I first came here, and as he wasn't an Earth cat, he decided to stay with us.

I started to roll over when his words caught up with my attempt at dozing. "Wait, *them*?" That got me up. "There are more?"

"Yes." Lucie flapped his tail. "At least seven more. There might be more outside. I came in here to get away from them."

I was in my robe and slippers in a flash. Tiberius might look like a goat, but he wasn't one. I didn't need a flock of real goats eating my furniture.

The goat on my bed looked up as I ran toward the bedroom door, but then snuggled back into the blankets.

I'd deal with it later.

The snores from the far corner of the living room told me Tiberius hadn't noticed his admirers. But they had noticed him. Not a single piece of furniture had become goat food. Not even the crocheted throw blanket Martha made me, which covered the back of my sofa.

But seven smallish goats were watching Tiberius with complete adoration. Even though, from the massive blue foot sticking up in the air, he wasn't currently in goat form.

I quickly shut the front door in case there were more coming. How it got open would be a question for Lucie. He stayed out last night, doing whatever it was he did. I told him I could have a cat door built that would let him come and go as he pleased. But he insisted on using his lock-picking skills. When he felt like it. Mostly, he scratched and meowed to make me open the door for him.

He hadn't shut the door behind him this time, and whatever he'd been doing, it involved a herd of goats.

"Okay, this isn't good. Not today." I ran my hand through my mass of unbound hair. It had a mind of its own, so I usually kept it in a high ponytail, even in bed. I'd been so exhausted last night prepping for the grand opening of my tea and spice shop that I'd let my hair go free. "Tiberius, get up. Slowly." The goats around him didn't look violent, but who knew what would happen when he transformed.

No movement from the blue foot.

"Centurion Tiberius, get up now!" I deepened my voice and shouted loud enough to make the goat from my bedroom come out to investigate.

The massive blue foot dropped, there was some muttering, and then a large goat with impressive horns appeared wearing a blanket.

He blinked at the smaller goats watching him, then at me, then back at them.

"Why are they staring at me? And why are they in our house? That's not sanitary."

I ignored the fact that *he* was a goat and spent most of his time inside. His glitching back into his real form when asleep meant sleeping outside was off-limits once night fell. "I have no idea. Lucie came running in with them."

"I did not! They followed me. I couldn't shut the door in time." Lucie came into the living room with his tail twitching furiously. He ignored the goats and jumped on the kitchen counter.

I'd tried to convince him the counter wasn't a good place for a cat to be—he ignored me. But the way the goats turned to look at him made me think it might be okay this time. The one formerly in my room hadn't reacted to Lucie much aside from staring. But the other seven were looking at him like he was goat food on the paw.

I knew goats were fairly open about their eating preferences, but I didn't think it extended to cats. Most likely, he'd annoyed them somehow. It was one of his skills.

Tiberius stalked through the goats to reach Lucie's counter. "What. Did. You. Do?"

Lucie's tail lashed so quickly it looked like it was about to fly off. His orange-gold eyes narrowed, and he gave a hiss-growl I'd never heard before. Even from the local cats.

"I did nothing. I was making my rounds, checking out the town, as I do. These followed me. Center of town, just a herd of goats out for a stroll in the middle of the night."

One of the goats came alongside Tiberius and leaned into him. He gave an alarmingly goat-sounding bleat and tipped over. Not only had the council changed him into a goat, but they also turned him into one that fainted. Tiberius scrambled to his feet and backed away from the other goat in a few seconds.

"They like you." Ignoring his faints was usually the best response. I pulled open the curtain across the front window. Yep, a few more goats were milling about the yard. "Someone has to be missing them. They look too tame to be feral." I was only allowed to travel twenty miles around Forgotten Hollow under the rules of my parole. I'd never seen any goats free-range.

"They need to go outside." Tiberius stomped to the door and waited for me to open it. Unlike Lucie, his hooves weren't good for opening doors. I would have said cat paws weren't much better, but I had a feeling Lucie had skills he wasn't sharing with us. He and I were both magic users, but our nice silver jewelry—two thin bracelets on my wrists and a matching collar of an odd, flexible silver on Lucie's neck meant we weren't casting spells.

Tiberius didn't have magic, but he got a collar as well. Supposedly, along with keeping Lucie and me from using magic, the collars and bracelets blocked other magic users from using magic against us.

Magic users who shouldn't be on this planet unless they were parolees as well.

I was reaching for the door handle, the goats were lined up behind Tiberius, when a sharp knock rattled my door.

I clutched my robe tighter and peered out the side window. I thought it might be Jack Lanclin, my local police detective. He'd been the first one to find me when Tiberius and I were dumped here. He also helped out when dead bodies showed up not long after.

I hadn't seen him much since then. Sadly.

To be fair, I'd been working on getting my teahouse, The Fainting Goat Tea and Spice, built and ready to open. But he could have stopped by just to visit. Honestly, it was almost as if he was avoiding me.

The man on my stoop wasn't Jack. His hair was blond and his profile was kind.

Just from what I could see, he was what my friends Betsy, Jamie, and Martha would have called a hottie.

And I was here in a bathrobe, wild hair, and a herd of goats. Nice.

The man knocked again. I couldn't take the time to change, fix my hair, or hide the goats. With a sigh, I opened the door a few inches.

"Yes?"

"Hello, I'm Camfield. My goats appear to have wandered into your yard." His accent was delightful. From my late-night TV binging, I recognized it as from somewhere in Britain. I would have known if someone like him had moved into town.

No matter how caught up I was in getting The Fainting Goat up and running.

One of the goats behind me bleated, and I opened the door further. "A few of them came inside as well." I didn't want this handsome, amazing-sounding man to think I was trying to steal his goats. "I have a goat with health issues. He comes inside sometimes, and I think they followed him. I woke up to find them here."

Tiberius narrowed his eyes at me, but he led the goats past Camfield.

"That is an impressive buck. No wonder my girls followed him." He laughed as Tiberius trotted toward the barn and all of Camfield's goats trailed after him. "I'm new to farm life, but never heard of a goat living inside a house."

"He has serious health issues, rare ones. It's better to give him his medicine inside. And he faints."

"Ah! I've heard of those. Are you interested in selling him? I could use a buck like him with my herd."

I swore I heard Lucie muttering behind me, but it was low enough that Camfield didn't respond. "I couldn't. He was left to me by my favorite great-uncle when he passed. Part of the family." Jinn couldn't lie if they knew the truth; it would literally make us choke, but we were great at crafting tales. The line was extremely thin, but one I fought to hold.

My official story concerning Tiberius was although my great-uncle did leave him to me, he was also the only good thing I got in an ugly divorce. As long as I kept my stories straight, I should be okay from choking.

He nodded. "I understand. Fainting goat, you wouldn't be Ceian, the owner of the new teahouse, The Fainting Goat?"

"I am. We even built him a pen alongside it. Namesake and all." I shoved my mass of hair aside and tried my most winsome smile.

Camfield sighed and looked back toward the barn. "It's been wonderful making your acquaintance. I apologize for any issues my goats caused you. But I should get them back to my yard."

"Anytime." I flustered. "I mean, they weren't any trouble at all." That time, I knew I heard Lucie muttering swear words. They weren't in any human language, luckily.

Camfield flashed a stunning smile, gave a nod, and followed Tiberius and the goats to my barn.

I took a step to follow them, but Lucie dropped down and rubbed my legs. It wasn't affection; he was pointing out my current attire.

I watched Camfield vanish into the barn with a sigh, then shut the door.

Sulking at my lack of a wonderful first impression with a new and very handsome man, I went to the kitchen, started warming up the kettle, and brought some eggs out of the fridge.

Lucie resumed his spot on the counter. "You have a crush. I thought you liked the cop?"

I tried ignoring the cat, but I knew it was pointless.

"*Detective* Jack Lanclin, his name is Jack. And I don't like him. He was interesting when we first arrived here and helpful in getting us through that mess. If I went to jail, you'd be on the streets right now. But he has other things to deal with besides me." I crammed tea leaves into my loose-leaf strainer. Probably more than required, but I felt a need for a lot of caffeine this morning. Things weren't off to a great start. "Camfield is just a nice man who isn't blaming me for you leading off his goats."

A knock at my door brought me stumbling to answer. Maybe Camfield had something else to say. I tried fixing my hair, but it was still a massive pile. Nonetheless, I put on my best smile as I opened the door.

To find three little old ladies staring past my barn. Betsy had her hand up to knock again, and I coughed before she could finish the movement and hit me in the chest.

"Oh! Sorry, Ceian. Just got distracted. That Camfield is quite the looker. He's already calling on you?" She grinned as I stepped back to invite the three in.

They were my only friends in Forgotten Hollow. People in town were nice, but they seemed to avoid getting too close. Possibly because of the dead bodies associated with me when I first arrived.

Not to mention, I'd been told they could take years to warm up to a newcomer. I was hoping my parole down here wouldn't last that long.

Martha and Jamie followed Betsy in, and all three stopped to say hello to Lucie and give him the required pettings. He purred, rubbed against their hands, then darted out the door before I could shut it.

"Stay out of trouble." I kept my voice light, but he needed to be more aware of what was around him.

"What brings you over this morning?" Without asking, I poured everyone tea and added some cookies. The ladies often dropped by, but rarely this early.

"There's been a murder!" Betsy's bright blue eyes were round as she beat the other two to the punch.

# Chapter Two

Only a few hundred years of drinking tea kept me from choking at her words. "A murder?" I put down my cup, but none of the three were slowing down in their drinking or eating.

Betsy nodded enthusiastically as she finished chewing her cookie.

"Yes! There was a police presence inside The Drunken Toad Pub. You know that new one that opened up when the fancy gastropub failed?" Jamie sipped her tea.

"Police presence?" I reclaimed my teacup. In the village of Forgotten Hollow, there were about ten uniformed cops, two other detectives, and Detective Jack Lanclin. Along with whoever was in charge.

There weren't enough people to create a *presence*.

"Okay, maybe just that new lady cop and the borrowed officer. But they were there for a while." Martha polished off her cookies and gathered more on her plate.

I remained in the kitchen in the hopes they would eat, drink, and leave, but finally gave up and joined them in the living room. "What new lady cop and borrowed officer?" I hadn't seen Jack in a while, but I felt a pang of concern that he might have moved to another town.

"That lady cop we're also borrowing. Tall, cute, short blonde hair, I can't recall her name. The other one is a guy nearing retirement. He came up from San Francisco a week ago. His bosses made a deal for him to have a cushy job until he could retire." Betsy grinned. "Not as cute as our British man, but he's not too shabby."

Jamie and Martha raised their eyebrows.

"Betsy has been nattering on about him all week," Martha said. "Gets that way whenever we have new blood. Be grateful you've been busy with your teahouse."

Betsy puffed herself up in an attempt to appear offended and imposing. Neither worked. "I have not. I simply find an older man who has kept himself up and might happen to be a widower who lost his wife over twenty years ago, intriguing. Ralph said he and his wife agree that the new cop and I would make a cute couple."

Ralph was Betsy's handyman and confidant. I took a sip of my tea and watched all three of them. "This is fascinating, and don't think I haven't missed hearing this information about the people of the town. However, you mentioned a murder?"

When I first met them, they styled themselves as sleuths who solved murders. The first real murder they ever ran across involved me. It happened to be my ex-boyfriend, the idiot who got me a hundred years of lock-up in my bottle. Like the vast majority of other people from the Eltrisphere, he shouldn't have been down here. Alive or dead.

Don't get me wrong, jinn mostly love our bottles. They embody our center of being.

Unless we're locked up in them.

My bottle was tucked away on the bottom of a full bookshelf. After a hundred years in it, I wasn't sure if I would ever go back inside unless forced to.

"Well, what else could it be? It was four in the morning, right in front of The Drunken Toad. No one was around. There must have been a murder!" Betsy managed to find a way to raise and lower her voice dramatically at the same time.

"But you three were downtown at four in the morning." It wasn't a question, and I found myself wanting nothing more than a nice, long shower and quiet breakfast.

I adored these three; they reminded me of various jinn aunties I'd had growing up. But it had been an odd morning at the end of a busy week. My teahouse opened in a few days, and I still didn't feel ready.

"We were making our rounds. There are things afoot, you know. Strangers are all over." Betsy held up her cup and I refilled it automatically.

"There are strangers because of all the new businesses." I put down the teapot on its trivet, held up my hand, and counted off. "Mine, The Drunken Toad Pub, which isn't finished, even though they opened. That gym at the edge of town." It was a monstrosity. There were maybe three thousand people living in Forgotten Hollow; the Max Gym looked like it could handle the entire town working out at the same time, plus a few hundred more.

For a town this small, that was a lot of activity.

However, unlike the three ladies before me, I didn't think there was anything wrong with new people in town.

"Ah, but something *is* going on." Betsy dug into her purse and waved a bunch of mail at me.

"Betsy, you can't steal mail." I almost added, 'Even I know it's a federal offense' but held off. Aside from a few close calls, none of these three, or anyone else in town, knew who and what I really was.

Let alone about Tiberius and Lucie.

"That's it, *we* didn't steal it. It was partially buried behind The Drunken Toad. Not well either." She sniffed at the incompetence of criminals and handed the stack of mail to me.

I leafed through the collection. "These are all different people and different days. So, there's a mail thief?" From what I could tell, it mostly looked like junk mail. Why would anyone steal unopened advertising and then bury it?

Before any of them could respond, although Betsy was the only one who appeared interested, my phone rang.

Not my cell phone, but my landline. Something few houses had anymore, apparently. I'd had to have one as a way for the council, which controlled all parolees, to contact me without giving anything away if there were humans in my cottage.

Hopefully, I was the only one who noticed that the landscape painting on my wall rattled with each ring. It wasn't an ugly painting, but I flinched every time I looked at it. My bottle was dutifully replicated right in the middle of a field.

I nodded to the ladies as I grabbed the phone. "Excuse me." I picked up the receiver. "Hello?" I pretended I didn't know who it was, but I wasn't surprised at the deep and annoyed voice on the other end. No one but Xieth ever called on that line. I warned him that the ladies were often here in the mornings, so he was doing better about using it instead of just appearing through the landscape painting.

"It's me. Who else would it be?" Xieth, my cherub jailer with a heart of obsidian. Exactly who I'd expected.

"Oh! Uncle Clark, it's been so long. Some guests dropped by, just give me a moment, please." I partially covered the phone and then looked over to the ladies.

Who were already getting to their feet.

"Oh, don't you worry, dear! Family first. Don't forget that we'll come to help finish things up at The Fainting Goat in a few hours!" Betsy left.

"Thank you for the tea!" Martha tottered out after her.

Jamie had her mouth full of cookies, but waved as she followed the rest. She was the skinniest of the bunch, but could put away almost as much food as Tiberius.

I followed them, locked the door, then hung up the phone.

Xieth's voice switched to the framed landscape painting, which faded and showed an extremely un-angelic-looking cherub.

"You need to stop hanging out with the humans. It's risky." He chomped on the end of his dusty cigar for an accent.

"It would be more suspicious not to speak to them. You and the council put me in this tiny place, but small-town folks watch people too closely. If I were in a large city, I would be less noticeable." Which was true. I originally regretted being dropped here, but after a hundred years in my bottle, I found I now enjoyed the space. "Not to mention, you ordered me to fit in. That means I have to socialize with humans."

"There were solid reasons for your location. Which I'm not going to discuss at this point. To be blunt, there's a problem."

I sighed. "What now?" The security around Earth and the other parolee planets was supposed to be top-notch. Yet my ex-boyfriend had managed not only to come down here but also to run a scam that could have endangered or killed a lot of humans. There had been others who shouldn't have been here as well—all discreetly removed once discovered. Of course, there was no explanation.

"I can't tell you." It was difficult to tell, but it looked like Xieth blushed. "The council just wants you to watch everything. Especially that cat."

I studied him for a moment. Calling me outside of my normal check-in times was supposed to be for emergencies only. Yet he called me to tell me he couldn't tell me anything?

"What's really going on?" I folded my arms and gave the most serious glare I felt I could safely do. Settling in and building a business had been Xieth's idea. Or at least an idea from the council members who were pulling his wings. They fronted the money and claimed it was important that I had a solid reason for being in town.

"Nothing you need to worry about." Whatever caused his concern and possible embarrassment before was gone now. And he was back to his normal snarly self. "Just get that place open, try not to be noticed, and report back on anything odd that you see." He started to fade out, but came back. "Anything that isn't *human* activity. No one cares about the humans." He gave a glare that wasn't up to his normal level, then let the screen fade back to the landscape.

I picked up my tea and slumped into one of the kitchen chairs. While events when I first was dumped here had been a bit alarming, things had seemed to settle down in the past two months. I spent time focusing on my new business; it wouldn't just be one of the cute teahouses with delicately stacked trays on each table, but a place for tea drinkers to sit and relax, along with simple lunch food. And I would be selling spices and bulk tea. I loved spices.

Betsy was coming on as my chef for baked goods and sandwiches, with Jamie and Martha coming in as needed.

This morning should have been filled with excitement at this adventure of building up this business from nothing. We were only three days from opening, and everything seemed to be moving along well.

Instead, there were goats, murder, and mischief. I paused. And Camfield. He was quite attractive and charming. Especially if he didn't blame me for his missing goats.

I'd been interested in Jack, as pointed out by my goat and cat. But after the spate of dead body issues when I first arrived, none of which were my fault, he'd taken care to keep his distance.

Camfield, however, was charming, handsome, and appeared interested in me. Or so I allowed myself to believe as I ate a quick breakfast, showered, and changed into work attire.

I looked down at my faded jeans and plaid shirt. Rather, my work attire for constructing a lovely place for people to gather, drink tea, nosh, and chat. I had already shopped for and ordered suitable attire as the hostess and owner of The Fainting Goat Tea and Spice Shop. Even found a matching tie for Tiberius for when we opened. I hadn't told him about it. Or the others I had on order. But it was all for the greater good. Reminding him that the more successful I was at establishing myself as a functioning member of this town, the faster we could all get back to living normal lives in the Eltrisphere was my go-to response to him disagreeing about anything.

Brushing and pulling my mass of thick, black hair up in a ponytail on the top of my head, which still dripped well past my shoulder blades, I found myself whistling. Things were going to be okay. Just a bit more to set up, move in the rest of the supplies, and my tea and spice shop would be up and rolling.

The sound of something slamming against the front door stopped my happy whistle.

"Who is it?" I didn't want to open the door. I shouldn't have even answered; maybe whoever it was would go away.

"It's me! Let us in!" Tiberius's voice was clear but low. We had a deal for all our safety, no speaking from him or Lucie when humans might hear.

Who else was outside with him?

I unlocked the door and stepped back. Tiberius raced in with Lucie, along with a mass of small dogs sprinting after them from across the yard.

"Shut the door! Now!" That was Lucie from the top of his cat tower. Tiberius kept running into my bedroom. Two of the small dogs dove inside before I could stop them. One ran after the goat, the other stayed under Lucie's cat tree and whined.

# Chapter Three

They appeared to be small lap dogs, but then I realized they were black and tan puppies. Ones that were looking at Lucie and Tiberius with a combination of admiration and something that looked like hunger. And they had massive paws. A glance out the window showed three more tumbling around the yard.

"Where are you two finding these animals?" I held up my hand. This needed to be finished, but I had work to do at my teahouse. "You know what? I don't want to know. Puppies, thank you for coming by, but you need to leave. *Now*." I couldn't use magic, but I had great command of my voice. The last word would make Tiberius's former centurion leaders proud.

The puppies backed down from Tiberius and Lucie and followed me to the door. I paused with my hand on the doorknob. "There's nothing else out there aside from more puppies, right?" I'd assumed that Lucie and Tiberius were running away from the puppies, although they looked far too cute to be any problem.

Neither Tiberius nor Lucie spoke, but they both shook their heads. That was odd. They hadn't been worried about speaking in front of Camfield's goats, but they were both refusing to speak in front of two harmless puppies.

Nope, not something I was worrying about today.

I opened the door and gently nudged the puppies. They went tumbling out and then took off after a rabbit on the far side of my yard. The other three puppies raced after them.

My money was on the rabbit with the way those puppies kept flopping over their massive feet. They were small now, but that wasn't going to last for long.

I shut the door and again held up my hand before either Tiberius or Lucie could speak. "No. I need to get into town and get things going. You two are staying here until I come back."

"But—" they said at the same time.

"No. Not a word. Now pretend you're normal Earth animals and nap." I grabbed my bag, then opened, shut, and locked the door before they could regroup.

Riding my bike into town was normally a peaceful endeavor. I hadn't been a bicycle fan when I first arrived here, but now I have found riding often clears my head.

At least it did when nasty drivers didn't come racing over the hill behind me and send my bike and me into a clump of bushes. It was one of those huge, dark SUV things with tinted windows.

They didn't even slow down.

I felt a flash of anger. Whoever that driver was, they were lucky that I didn't have my magic. That flash of fury wasn't a warranted reaction to the situation, and had I had magic, it might have resulted in an incinerated SUV.

That was something I hadn't thought of when I'd been locked up in my bottle. I'd been focused on earning my freedom and regaining my magic. But magic users had to train to stay in control. For a hundred years, I hadn't had to worry about that, as my magic was fully blocked.

What would happen with my magic once I was free? Flashes of irrational anger fueled more magic disasters than anything. And meant a fate far worse than lock-up. I shoved that thought to the side, dusted my bike and clothes off, and returned to my travel.

The trip into Forgotten Hollow was much nicer than coming back up due to the gentle slope into town. It was all small boutique farms, spas, and wineries where I was. Restaurants and cute shops appeared on each side as I rode. All were aimed more at tourists than locals.

Then the town proper appeared. Neat rows of houses, larger ones further back or near the cliffs that overlooked the ocean, surrounded the town. More shops and restaurants filled the center.

Forgotten Hollow was by far the smallest place I'd ever lived—aside from my own bottle. My preferred planets were filled with large and exciting cities. The closest to them that I'd seen in my online searches were places called London or New York.

Neither of which would the council condone transferring me to. I wasn't sure if there were other parolees from the Eltrisphere in those places, or if they felt I was too dangerous there even with my magic block.

Or Xieth was just being more of a jerk than usual.

But after two months, I found I was becoming used to the way of living in a forest.

"Get out of my way!" A loud horn and swearing, followed by what looked to be the same SUV that had run me off the road earlier, rushed past me. Luckily, I wasn't riding, but pausing to sort my thoughts. I didn't get knocked over this time.

"I hate this time of year." A cop car rolled up next to me after the SUV, and the blonde woman inside gave me a friendly smile. "Are you okay? I don't think we've met. I'm Officer Flannigan. Just transferred back here to help out for a bit. You're Ceian, right? Jack told me about you." She smiled. "I'm happy to help out, but I should have realized what time of year it was. I would have put up a fight not to come." She shook her head and glared in the direction the SUV had gone.

"I am her. As long as nothing bad was said about her." I smiled. I didn't think Jack would say anything, but we had an odd relationship. Or an odd non-relationship. "Nice to meet you, Officer Flannigan. I'm fairly new here. Just what is this time of year?"

I spun as I thought I heard another SUV. Luckily, it was just a pickup driving at normal speed.

"There's a big group of business bigwigs from New York. They come here once a year for a business retreat, but they're all jerks and hate it here. The retreat is supposed to help them relax. It gets worse as the week goes on. Just make sure to be off the roads as much as possible for the duration, you'll be happier."

"Thank you for the warning, officer. I'll stay on the bike trails. Where are they staying?" I hadn't seen a massive influx of SUVs until this morning, but they could be hiding. Forgotten Hollow wasn't large by any standards, but it did have a few hotels for tourists. If I were lucky, it would be one of the ones at the far end of town.

"They're always at the Grasshopper. The owner of the company is buddies with the widow Helen, who owns it. And please just call me Alice." Her smile was friendly.

I let out a sigh of relief. I'd seen the Grasshopper once from a distance. I decided I needed to see the entire town a few weeks ago. The Grasshopper was the closest thing to a fancy hotel here, at least fancy according to the search I did online. And it was as far from my little cottage as possible.

"Oh, that's nice." I stopped myself from saying that was great. Alice didn't seem like she was fond of the business group, but better not to alienate anyone. Being nice wasn't required for the parolees here on Earth. But as fitting in was, it made life easier.

Not to mention, with Jack gone off wherever, I might need a cop I knew on my side. Just in case I didn't fit in as well as I hoped.

"It would be if they stayed there. Most of them feel the need to stomp around town daily. Just in case we forget how superior to us they are. I think they're clones. No matter what color skin, height, weight, or gender, they all act the same." She started her car up. "If you're lucky, they won't notice your cute teahouse when it opens. This round at least. Have a great day." Alice headed into town.

I got back on my bike for the final hill into town. It would have been nice for Betsy and her gang to have warned me, but unless it was a mystery to be solved, they didn't notice a lot. Or they forgot that I was still fairly new here.

It was early enough that there wasn't much activity in town beyond two small delivery trucks making their rounds. I gave a deep sigh as I took in the view; I could have been paroled in worse places. Then coasted down toward my business.

Or what should be my business. The building was solid, fully inspected, and was currently being covered in some massive striped tent as I rode up. "Excuse me? What are you doing?" I asked relatively nicely as I secured my bike to one of the six bike stands I installed in front of my place.

"Eh, the owner said they have bugs, so we're taking care of them." The man didn't even look up as he answered.

"*I* am the owner. There are no bugs, I never called anyone, and I'm getting ready to open in a few days." Again, the flash of anger hit me. This was just a mistake, but for a moment, I felt as if I were in the stadium getting ready for a gladiator fight.

That wasn't good.

He shrugged, but continued to adjust the ugly tent. "It was a guy who called, Chuck. Gave us the address and everything."

I got out my cell phone. "Chuck who? I need the number." The hand holding my phone was shaking so badly with the need to strangle someone that I switched hands.

"I don't have it on me; it's at our office." He walked over to another part of the tent and pulled it down.

"Stop doing that! Was your company called out to do an inspection? Because I've had them all done, and you don't look familiar." The level of bureaucracy involved in starting a simple business was something a cherub would love.

"We can't stop; we have orders." He glanced up at that, then quickly away.

I almost snapped my phone in half, and a film of red filled my eyes. It was a good thing I didn't have my magic.

A moment later, an unnatural wind kicked up, and the striped, non-secured fabric covering my tea and spice shop flew into the air and dropped over the busiest intersection in town. A few blocks away.

The screech of tires and colliding metal pointed out that while it was early, it wasn't early enough, and there was traffic in the area.

I looked at my magic-blocking silver bracelets. They seemed secure; my magic should be effectively contained.

Maybe that was just a freak wind.

The laugh in my head at that thought sounded like Tiberius. Somehow, I used magic. And might have caused a serious car collision. Or a few of them from the continuing sounds.

The workers in front of me were now running around, yelling, and throwing their things into the trucks.

And not going after the escaped fabric.

"Don't you need to get that back?" I pointed toward the intersection. The buildings around me blocked visibility, but while I still heard horns and yelling, there were no sirens yet.

"Nope. Not our problem." The one who'd initially spoke to me peeled off the coveralls he was wearing, then pulled a magnetic company sign off his truck. The others did the same, and both trucks took off before I calmed down enough to take photos.

I ignored the commotion down the road and walked toward my teahouse. What were they up to? At five hundred and eighty-seven years old and after dealing with cherubs most of my life, I was excellent at following government details. Everything had been completed and properly documented.

What if I hadn't come down here this morning? The odds of that were slim, but no one around town would question one of those bug-fumigating tents.

I shoved down the little voice in my head screaming that something was seriously wrong with the bracelets and that using magic down here could get me locked up for a few hundred years, or worse.

I needed to see if they'd done anything to my teahouse.

The door appeared locked, but since the door wasn't fully shut, it wasn't. Sharp marks around the keyhole showed where the lock had been picked. If they'd shut it completely, I wouldn't have known someone went inside.

Nothing seemed out of place until I walked back into the kitchen. I was originally going to mostly sell bulk tea and spices, but having seen the coffee shops doing food, I'd included a decent kitchen to accommodate sit-down teas or lunch.

The kitchen now had a large plastic tub filled with what could only be explosives in the middle of my formerly pristine floor.

# Chapter Four

I wanted to run but needed to know what was happening, so I crept forward. I still wasn't certain how my magic managed to slip out from the bracelets that I wore, but if this thing exploded, my magic better kick in again.

Being caught using magic on a parole world was better than being blown up.

I didn't see anything that looked like it was designed to be a timer or detonator for the explosives. Also, no connecting-colored wires, which made me feel better. Too much late-night TV had left me with a healthy fear of having to cut the right color wire.

I leaned lower; in the movies, there was always a ticking sound to bombs. I had no idea why someone would want to blow up my teahouse, but these shouldn't be here.

No ticking. Just a pile of what appeared to be unconnected small explosives. I was still holding my phone, so I took photos from all angles. Then stopped. Who would I send them to? My three nosy friends? Alice the cop?

The sound of knocking at the front door made me scream. Okay, it was a muffled scream as my throat closed up, but still. I sent the photos to Betsy just in case whoever set this up was coming to kill me, and went to the front door.

It was Camfield.

"Hello, Ceian. I thought I'd see how the setup is going." His voice faded as he peered closely at me. "Are you okay? You're quite pale."

"There's a tub of explosives in my kitchen. And strange men were covering my teahouse with a bug tent, but they changed clothes and drove off." My words tumbled over each other, and I doubted he got half of what I said.

"There's a bomb in here?" He grabbed my arm and started pulling me outside.

Okay, he caught part of it.

I pulled back. "I need to save my teahouse. There's nothing to make the bombs explode."

"What?" He calmed himself down and marched past me into the kitchen. "They're not connected to a detonator. There's no detonator at all. What did you say those men were doing?"

"They said they were bug exterminators and had to fumigate my teahouse. Which is a lie, because we passed all of our inspections a week ago."

Camfield continued to glare at the explosives. "You should call the police and have these removed by professionals. They're useless like this, but could still be dangerous." There was a flash of anger as he turned back to me, but he quickly shook it off. "Let's go outside to call, though."

We went to Tiberius's pen outside the shop, and I called the police station to report the problem. Forgotten Hollow didn't have a bomb squad; the closest one was twenty minutes away in Ghoston. But Alice was a former bomb squad member in a larger town, so they would send her over.

I thanked them and hung up.

"Are you going to be okay?" Camfield gently put a hand on my back. "You look odd."

I took a step away, but tried to make it seem like it wasn't because his touching me freaked me out. A good-looking man comforting me shouldn't do that. I knew why I looked weird—there was something seriously wrong with me.

"It's a creepy thing to find a bunch of explosives in my kitchen a few days before opening." I tried to smile, but it felt weak even to me. "It's been a long time to get here, and I'm a little overwhelmed." The rest of my fumbling, trying not to lie but also not telling the full truth, was mercifully cut off as Alice's patrol car and a motorcycle cop pulled up to my teahouse. Alice was alone before, and I'd never seen a motorcycle cop outside of TV, but both were serious as they gathered at Alice's trunk and brought out equipment.

I jogged over the moment Alice motioned for me. Camfield stayed a few steps behind but followed.

"How large an explosive are we looking at?" Alice was all business as she put on the bomb gear. The older officer behind her nodded to me and Camfield but remained focused on getting his gear on.

"It seems to be a bunch of pipe bombs." That was what they looked like to me. At least based on my late-night cop show fixation. "But there wasn't anything that we could see to make them explode. They're in an open storage tub in the middle of the kitchen." Then I explained about the suspicious men trying to tent my place, their running away when I confronted them, and their tent flying away. There was no way they wouldn't have seen the tub of bombs, which meant they were in on them being where they were.

The other cop nodded. "That was a mess. That tent of theirs caused three accidents. They're going to be hard to find if they took the company panels off their trucks, though. But we will find them." His voice was low and gravely, and the scowl he flashed spoke badly for the men behind this once he caught them.

I'd stopped them in time, hopefully, but that was too close. Xieth hadn't completely blamed me for the dead bodies or issues that happened when I arrived on the planet two months ago, but he made enough noise about the council that I knew I was being watched carefully.

Earth wasn't the Eltrisphere, but it was a lot better than going back into my bottle. If the council felt I wasn't fitting in, they could rescind my parole.

Alice and the still-unnamed motorcycle cop double-checked their equipment and dragged a large metal tub out from the back of her car.

"Please stay here, we'll take care of this." Alice gave terse nods to Camfield and me, then the cops marched into my teahouse.

"It'll be okay, I'm sure of it." Camfield's soothing British accent worked like magic, and my shoulders crept down from my ears.

"Thanks. I'm glad you were here." I forced a better smile and watched as nosy townspeople came closer. Two cop vehicles with lights flashing were a bigger excitement than cleaning up the accidents the tent had caused. Interestingly, the three I'd expected to see—Betsy and her cronies—were nowhere in sight.

Especially odd since the cops were at The Fainting Goat Tea and Spice, and the three had been popping in daily during construction and set up. The Fainting Goat was built on the remains of the Coffee Time Perks coffee shop, but there had been few things that could be salvaged in the rebuild. Most of it was burned too badly to be safe.

"Is something wrong?" Camfield asked as he turned to look at the gathering crowd. "Do you see the men behind this?"

"No. Sadly." I unclenched my fists. Just the thought of seeing them made me think extremely magical retaliation thoughts. Not good. "Just wondering how long the crowd will gawk." I noticed three people in sharp black suits, two men and a woman, watching, but making sure they remained away from the crowd.

Must be some of those business people Alice mentioned. If I were lucky, this event would keep them from visiting The Fainting Goat.

Providing this didn't slow down my opening in three days. Something I sadly doubted.

Camfield looked at his watch and swore. "I hate to leave a lady in distress, but I have a business call in ten minutes that I can't miss. I work from home, but I still need to be on time." He handed me his card. "Please call me if there is anything I can do to help." He smiled briefly, then all but ran off the moment I accepted his card.

Weird. But not as weird as Betsy and the crew still not coming around.

It didn't take long for Alice and the other cop to walk out with their tub. They secured it in the trunk of the police car and then turned to me.

"You were right, there were no detonators on any of them." Alice's frown deepened as she glanced back at my teahouse. "However, if those men had connected the fumigating equipment, it could have blown the entire block up. We have a part-time sketch artist in town; I'll call him to come into the station and see what you can tell him. Could you be there in an hour? We need to know who we're looking for."

I knew enough about crime shows that the explosion that could have happened—if those fake bug guys got the teahouse set up—would be blamed on a faulty connection or something.

I started shaking.

Alice dropped one hand on my shoulder. "Are you okay?"

"Yeah. No, not really. But I just realized that a lot of people could have been killed. Who would do that just to stop a tea and spice shop from opening? It seems extreme." I barely knew anyone in this town, and any enemies were dead or locked up.

"That's going to take a while to sort out." Alice waved a gloved hand around at the rest of the block. "Your shop might not have been the actual target, but rather a convenient place to focus on since it's not open yet. If you hadn't come down here when you did, this could have ended badly." She took out her paper pad, then swore at her heavy gloves and removed them before grabbing her pen. "Was this a planned visit? Did anyone know you were coming down this morning?"

I tried to think through things. I'd been coming in later in the day as the work was finished. This visit was more out of excitement and final touches than anything planned.

Betsy, Jamie, and Martha knew I was coming here. But aside from the oddness of them not coming to snoop out what happened with that tent, there was no way they were involved in this. I finally shook my head. "No. The last few days, I've been coming in later." A bit of a stretch, but not a lie. "You think there's a chance this wasn't aimed at me or my teahouse?" There was too much hope in my voice, and Alice frowned a bit.

"It could be. We need to catch the perps and question them about who hired them. Your shop would have been destroyed whether it was the target or not."

"I know. But my uncle financed me on this. He wanted me to leave Forgotten Hollow when those bodies showed up a few months ago. He might force the issue if this was aimed at me specifically." Again, close enough to the truth to keep me from choking. Xieth could pull me from here, and he was biologically closer to me than any of the humans.

Alice nodded, jotted a few more notes, and flipped her pad closed. Her lack of interest in my mention of the prior murders meant she'd read the files already. "Head to the station once you secure your teahouse. The sooner we know who we're looking for, the better. The odds are that they weren't locals, but I'll send their information to the surrounding towns. Call me directly if anything else happens." She handed me her card, then she and the motorcycle cop turned off their lights and left.

The three business people in black suits took that as a cue to leave and turned as one and walked toward the center of town. The rest of the crowd watched me for a few moments, then also dispersed.

Still no Betsy, Jamie, or Martha.

# Chapter Five

I stalked around the entire teahouse, but there wasn't so much as a chair out of place. I made two more laps before triple-checking the locks and leaving. I could ride my bike to the police station, but it was becoming a lovely day, and I needed a walk to shake off the creepy feelings from what had just happened.

Before my unfortunate lockup a hundred years ago, I had mostly drifted around the Eltrisphere fighting for prize purses as a gladiator. I was one of the best lower-weight gladiators on the circuit.

Until my late and unlamented ex-boyfriend set me up for a crime and left me holding the bottle.

I didn't age the way humans did, but my aching muscles were pointing out that some fight training might do some good.

The walk to the police station was peaceful and relatively calm. The accidents caused by the tent were cleared up, and most people had already left for work. I did see a different group of black-suited people enter the A Lotta Joe's coffeehouse. Three women and one man. All of them walked past people as if they weren't there.

The Forgotten Hollow police station wasn't an imposing building; like most of the town, it was cozy. I suppose that might change if you were being dragged in for a crime. But most criminals got sent down the mountain to Peek's Valley, a larger city about an hour out.

Alice was at the front desk and looked up as I walked in. "Perfect timing. Keith is in the back room getting set up. Just give him the background of what you saw and as many descriptions of the men as you can. Oh, and the trucks, too. Most people wouldn't have noticed them when they came in, but might have seen their signs."

"Which would be useless once they removed them."

She nodded. "True. Can I bring you anything? Coffee? Tea?" She waved to a kitchenette in the open office behind her.

"Tea would be lovely. Black, please." Not all black teas were the same, but I'd found that non-tea drinkers had no clue.

"I have Assam or Darjeeling."

I smiled. "Darjeeling every time. Thank you."

Alice went to prepare my tea after showing me where the room with the sketch artist was.

Keith was a tall, slender, aging hippy, at least that's what I'd heard people like him called on TV. His gray hair was almost longer than mine, but tied back in a thin braid. His blue eyes were so light they seemed to almost glow. His grin was contagious as he wiped his hands on his pants to shake off pencil dust and jumped to his feet. "Ceian! Sorry, I've heard so much about you from Jack that I feel like I know you. I just got back last week, so I missed your prior adventures." His wink might have seemed odd on some men, but it fit him. "Please sit, and here's our tea. Thank you, Alice."

Alice came in with two large mugs and a huge plate of snacks from a vending machine. "You're welcome to these as well, Keith needs lots of fuel when he works." She grinned and mostly shut the door behind her when she left.

Keith opened a bag of potato chips and sipped his tea. "Better. Now, start from when you first rode up to your shop. I know what the report said, but I do better to hear it directly."

Around an excellent cup of Darjeeling, not always an easy thing to pull off, since it could be fussy, I explained approaching The Fainting Goat, confronting the men, their tent flying away, the men stripping the identifying logos off their trucks, and then fleeing. As well as finding the bombs after they fled.

Keith had been nodding and sketching even though I hadn't gotten to any of the men's descriptions. He paused and tilted his head when I mentioned the flying tent. "Ah, yes. I heard the call about that on my scanner at home. No one was clear on how it got loose. The ties on it were still intact."

I took a long sip of my tea and tried to come up with a plausible non-lie. "I'm not sure. I was busy yelling at the men to remove it. Maybe since they don't seem to have been real extermination experts, they had the lines tied, but not around anything?" I opened a bag of corn chips and followed that thought. "It wouldn't matter if the tent stayed over the shop or not; once the poison was released, it would have blown up."

Keith continued to watch me for a few moments, then his bright smile came back. "Could be the truth of things. Go through what the first man you saw looked like."

It took a bag of corn chips, a pack of cookies, and another mug of Darjeeling for me to finish describing the men that I recalled. It was funny, but maybe the sugar and caffeine helped; I recalled more of what they looked like than I'd thought I would.

There had been more of them than I could recall; at least three more, but even in my caffeinated state, I couldn't mentally pull up what they looked like.

"These are them?" Keith turned his sketch pad around and flipped through the pages.

"Yes, wow, your art is amazing." Ten men, ranging in build, hair color, and skin tone, but I knew the moment I saw the drawings that they were accurate. He even did a detailed drawing of The Fainting Goat with a striped fumigation tent on it. "This detail is stunning." I didn't want to relive today, but I almost wanted to frame the art.

"Thank you. I've been at it for a long time. Alice said they'll probably be sending feds in to help; the explosion they could have triggered would have been worse than she originally thought. We'll make copies of these to give to them as well as the nearby towns."

I got to my feet. Nothing I'd planned had gotten done today, but all I wanted to do was go home and lock myself inside. "Do you know where Jack went?" That hadn't been what I meant to say at all, but he had mentioned that he knew Jack, and the words popped out. I blamed my mental stress.

And that Jack had spoken of me. Considering how our first encounters had gone, I wasn't sure that I wanted to know what he'd said.

Keith's grin reminded me of a cherub trying to hit some poor saps with his arrows. Even though he was far too tall, slender, and human to be one.

"He had to go to Canada, something to do with family. It wasn't planned, but I figured he'd be back by now." His grin faded a few levels. "I've been remiss; he asked me to keep an eye on you if he was gone more than a week. Which he has now been gone. Consider me now keeping an eye out for any further problems."

Part of me was flattered, for a moment. Then I put my hands on my hips. "Just what did he say for you to keep an eye out for?"

He shrugged and gathered his supplies, including the unopened vending machine snacks. "He said that you were trouble. A lot of trouble. And that he didn't like the idea of you being left alone in his town." He winced. "That sounded worse than I'm sure he meant it."

I folded my arms. "No, he meant it that way. But he's wrong. If bad things happen to a good person, is that person bad?"

Keith shook his head. "Not at all. And now that I've met you, I will make that abundantly clear to Jack when he gets back. I promise."

I wanted to be mad, and I was. But it wasn't Keith's fault. "Thank you. I'm going home now. Thank you again for helping with my case." I forced a smile and stomped out of the room.

There was an older man, one of the retirees who helped sometimes, at the front desk. He gave me a curt nod as I marched through. Probably trying to figure out what crime I'd been accused of as I left.

Shaking out my hunched shoulders at my annoyance at Jack, I marched back to my teahouse and my bike. I did another thorough walk around the entire thing, testing all the doors and windows. Still no sign of Betsy, Jamie, or Martha. I hoped they weren't getting into trouble, but right now, the urge to go home and have a pint of rocky road ice cream was more what I was up for. They'd gotten into things and out of them without my help long before I came here.

The Eltrisphere didn't have ice cream, but it was rapidly becoming one of my favorite things on this world. Maybe once I got off parole, I could open a chain of ice cream shops on different planets.

My ride home was wonderfully uneventful, and I was almost humming to myself as I rounded the corner to my cottage.

Humming turned to swearing. My front door was hanging on only one hinge, and the large picture window was shattered.

# Chapter Six

I let my bike fall and ran toward my cottage. It wasn't much, but it was all I had. I darted inside, expecting to see my few belongings destroyed or missing—but aside from the door and window, everything appeared to be where I left it.

I *was* missing an orange cat and a centurion goat, however.

A closer look at the door and window indicated that the door had been kicked out, but the window had been broken in from the outside.

There were multiple goat hoof marks on the wooden door.

"Tiberius? Lucie?" I walked around my small place calling for them. Nothing was out of order, but they weren't here.

If I had my magic, I could have fixed both the door and the window in a blink, but that wasn't an option. Although I wasn't certain that I hadn't broken through the spell blocking my magic when I sent that fumigation tent flying. The fact that there should have been no way for me to do that was a topic for a later panic.

I did a quick check of the yard and barn, even calling for them in case they wandered off once they escaped. I walked a block away in every direction, still calling, but no sign of either Lucie or Tiberius.

Nothing.

I needed to call the cops. I hated to do it so soon after the attack on my teahouse, but this was also a crime. I sighed and dialed the station. The bored dispatcher promised to get someone out. Eventually.

I knew cops liked to see the damage in its unaltered form, but I was postponing my date with my ice cream. Which I now needed more than before. However, I wasn't going to sit in my house, polishing off a tub, with my door hanging by a broken hinge and my curtains flowing in the wind.

I was about to go to my barn and find tools and wood when an annoying chime came from the landscape painting.

Xieth. If I weren't having a uniquely bad day already, I might have been surprised at two calls in one day.

"I'm here." I watched as the landscape changed into Xieth's unattractive face.

"Are you alone?" His eyes were always beady and narrow, but he was twitching around with a look of panic in them now.

"Yes, but someone broke into my cottage. My door and front window are busted open."

"Who did it?" That was pure terror.

"I have no idea. I just got home. Someone tried to blow up my teahouse, and I had to go to the police station."

I didn't think his eyes could get wider than an annoyed squint. I was wrong.

"They tried to blow you up? And broke into your house? This has gone too far." He waved his right hand, and in a moment, my door and window were as good as new. The goat prints were even gone.

I wondered if he'd been drinking again. Or smoking. Or taking a lot of various illegal potions. I also didn't like his suggestion that the attack on my teahouse was aimed at me. I'd decided to favor Alice's theory that my teahouse might have simply been a convenient location.

I nodded toward his magicked repairs. "That's great, and thank you. But the police have been called. I was just going to cover them both with wood until then."

He waved his hand again. They went back to busted, then suddenly had rough wood covering over the window and a rudimentary door. "You're okay, though, right? And Tiberius?" He didn't ask about the cat, but Lucie wasn't Xieth's concern.

"I'm fine, but Tiberius and Lucie are missing. Like I said, I just got here."

"There's something seriously wrong down there. I knew they were up to something! Anything else? Any strange...puppies?"

That was too specific to be comforting. I told him about the puppies who followed Tiberius earlier and then left. "But they were harmless. You know, *puppies*."

"Not harmless, but not sure what they are. That Eltrisian dog belonging to the human idiot trying to sell magic mind-controlling coffee with Darius's help escaped down there. She was pregnant. Someone was running an off-world dog breeding market down there—she was an escapee. This is not good. His words drifted off as he started muttering to himself.

"What should I do?" I still seriously doubted those little puppies were the cause of the destruction of my door and window, or my teahouse, but an Eltrisian dog having magical babies on an embargoed planet was bad for many reasons. The dog had been called Brutus by her late human owner, but I helped her escape when he was killed. Something there was no way I was telling Xieth about. Ever.

"Don't panic," Xieth said in a tone of pure panic. "We'll sort this out. Stay calm. Everything is normal. Make everyone believe that."

"My animals are missing, my house was attacked, and so was my teahouse. No one is going to expect normal."

"True, true, true. Has anything else gone missing?"

"No. Well, three of my friends, but they're human." I didn't add that they were probably off on an adventure. I hoped.

"That's not good, even if they're only humans. Okay, talk to the police, try to find Tiberius, but only on your property. Sorry about your friends, but you can find more. Do not leave your property tonight. The spell will fall in the morning." He cut the call.

I stared at the landscape with the image of my bottle on it for a few moments in shock.

Xieth was scared. There were theories that cherubs couldn't be scared—ever. And before this, Xieth had been the most annoyingly non-scared cherub I'd ever met.

But something about what was happening to me here was causing him to be seriously terrified. I should be scared, too, but the day had sort of beaten it out of me.

The rocky road was calling my name, but I needed to look for Tiberius and Lucie first, at least on my property. I'd felt a magical command spell hit me at Xieth's demand that I not leave here today. But I could check my barn and yard again. Just in case.

There wasn't much in my yard; it was designed for farm animals, but I hadn't wanted to get any. I grabbed the flashlight I kept right inside the door of the barn and hit the light switch. The flashlight was needed because the barn was dim no matter what type of bulb I used.

Still no sight of a cat or goat in the barn. It did look a bit tossed about, but that could have been just regular roughhousing. I searched everywhere; things had been hidden in my barn before, but there was nothing this time. I left the barn door open in case Tiberius and Lucie came back in the middle of the night, then stomped up to my cottage.

Alice's patrol car came up my drive as I reached the front of my cottage.

"You're fast. Nice work as well." She had her phone out and took photos of the front of my house.

"Thanks, I didn't like it open. I know you would have rather seen it as it was, though. The dispatch person made it sound like it might be a while before you got here." Had I thought about it, I should have had Xieth let me take a few photos before he changed things.

"It would have been handy, but I doubt it would have helped me find who the culprits were. Nothing was disturbed inside?"

I opened the plank door for her. "No, but you're welcome to check. My cat and goat escaped, so I'm a bit rattled." Jinn couldn't lie, but the painful truth of my statement hit me harder than I expected. Tiberius and Lucie were both assholes if I was honest, but they were *my* assholes.

Alice nodded sympathetically as she walked into the front room. "Do you have photos of the animals? I can get the word out."

I started to say that I didn't, when she stopped in front of my landscape painting. A pair of pictures of Tiberius and Lucie, nicely framed, sat on the shelf below it. Ones I'd never seen.

"Do you mind if I copy these?" She gave me a sympathetic smile, mistaking my confusion for sorrow.

"Ah, no, go right ahead." Xieth must have made those photos when we were out front. Which meant he was listening in even when the screen was down.

Something he supposedly couldn't do.

Another issue to deal with later.

The photos were nice and looked like them. Alice clucked over the cuteness of both as she copied the photos, then put them back.

The search of my place was short as there wasn't much to search. Alice agreed with me that it didn't look like anything had been taken or disturbed.

"Was the shattered glass inside or outside of the window?"

We were back in my front room, so I hoped that Xieth was still spying on me in case she wanted to see the glass or the busted door.

"Inside. Sorry, I shouldn't have swept it up. The door was swinging outward because of the broken hinges when I got here. It looked like they forced it from the inside."

She raised an eyebrow and looked closer at what was left of the doorframe. "That's odd, they could have just unlocked it."

"Right? I thought so too. Why break the window, only to bust out through the door?" Alice seemed cool, but trying to explain that my talking goat kicked the door out wasn't something I was ready for.

She finished taking photos of the interior and then went outside. "Do you mind if I look around the barn and yard?"

I nodded. This was all a crime scene after all; she could go where she wanted. "Mind if I tag along? I went down there looking for my pets earlier, but maybe we'll see more together."

Xieth's freak out about all of this, even my missing human friends, was hitting me. I felt like I was being watched.

She shrugged. "It's your place."

We trooped down to the barn with a few side trips through the yard, but I didn't see anything.

"Sorry, there are tracks, but they look like deer and not fresh." Alice patted her notes, "But I have the descriptions and photos and will make sure a few more patrols come out this way for the next few days and nights. If you need anything, call." With a reassuring nod, she went back to her patrol car.

"Thank you. I plan on locking myself in for the night."

We'd only been in the barn for a few minutes, but there was a note stuck in the rough plank door when I got back up to my house. I looked around, but there was no one in sight.

A chill hit me, and I took the note inside to open it.

"I have your companions. If you want to see them alive, bring the Stone of Zalianthia to The Drunken Toad Pub at midnight tomorrow night."

I swore as I stared at my cellphone. I wasn't sure if the person had my human friends, if they were missing and not just investigating something, or Lucie and Tiberius, but this was bad no matter what. The Stone of Zalianthia was a powerful and extremely well-known jewel of the Eltrisphere.

No one on this planet should have heard of it, let alone think I had it.

# ChapterSeven

I reread the note three times, then stumbled to the landscape and grabbed the button on the frame that would call him. "Xieth? XIETH! I need you!"

"What now?" Xieth's voice came before the landscape image fled. He sounded and looked as freaked out as I was.

And he hadn't heard about the note yet.

"Someone here knows who I am, or at least *what* I am." I held the note up to his image. "What is going on and why am I in the middle of it?"

Xieth remained silent even after I lowered the note. Pale green wasn't a good look on most people, particularly cherubs.

"I can't comment now." He waved his chubby hand, and a wave of magic flowed around me and my cottage. "I've increased the prior command spell and have sealed everything until daybreak. Do not try to break out, no matter who you think you hear. It won't be your friends."

Before I could protest, he vanished. The landscape didn't even reappear; the entire image turned into a brick wall.

"I...I need ice cream." I dropped the note on my coffee table, made some tea, grabbed my rocky road ice cream tub, and the largest spoon I had.

There were so many bad things going on at once that my brain was refusing to interact with any of them. Tea and ice cream were an odd combination, but they both soothed me. With my steaming decaf and tub of sugar, I went to my favorite chair. It was only then that I noticed Xieth had reinstated his completely repaired door and window. There was also an extremely serious spell glow outside of the window as I closed my thicker curtains.

Any magic user would notice it, which I figured was who Xieth was trying to warn off. Which, while comforting, reinforced that I was up against a magic user. Lovely.

How did my life get this messed up? When I'd been locked up in my bottle, all I could think of was getting out and having a normal life.

Now I was seriously contemplating jumping back into the thing and staying there indefinitely.

I'd fallen asleep in my chair, clutching my empty and extremely soggy carton of ice cream, when the voices started outside. Betsy, Jamie, and Martha all spoke after each other quickly. The voices sort of sounded like them, but the words weren't ones they would use. All three were begging for me to save them. My upper lip curled once I woke up more. A simplistic spell that any teenage student of magic could do. The good ones used the same speech patterns, but these weren't even close. Even if Xieth hadn't warned me, I wouldn't have believed those were my friends.

Then came a cat's meows and a goat's bleat. Even weirder. The person or persons behind this were from the Eltrisphere, but didn't know that Tiberius and Lucie could talk? Speaking animals weren't shocking on most worlds within the Eltrisphere.

I waited for more, but only a lone wind whistled around my house, so I gave up and took a shower.

Afterward, I sat in bed and tried to figure out what the connections were. Jinn were naturally good at puzzles, but I had a feeling being in my bottle for a hundred years hadn't helped my cognitive abilities.

I pulled out the pad of paper I kept next to my bed when I'd been in the planning stages for the teahouse. Then I itemized the entire weird day and prepared to look for connections.

Yeah, nothing.

I'd originally put, 'out on an adventure' next to Betsy, Martha, and Jamie. I scribbled that out and wrote, 'taken' instead. That thought sat unhappily in my gut and turned to rock when I added Lucie and Tiberius to the missing list.

Someone tried to blow up my business, kidnapped my only friends, and my animal companions. Whoever they were, they were from the Eltrisphere, had magic, but weren't very talented at it.

After the prior criminal and unauthorized incursions to Earth came to light when I'd first been brought here, Xieth said the Council had tripled the security around the planet. Whoever was behind this probably had been here longer than me.

I tried to think of any reason someone would think I had access to the Stone of Zalianthia. Until an alarmingly short time ago, I'd been living in my bottle under guard. Then I was here. Not much opportunity for a major crime spree.

I dredged my brain for what I knew about it.

Neither search came up with much. Rather, who might think I had something like that was no one. Information about the stone itself was murky at best. It was only a rumor among anyone who wasn't in the ultimate top tier of our society. Not only was it supposedly a diamond the size of my fist, but it was also a container for questionable and dangerous magic. In the long-ago dark ages, victims of tyrants were slowly drained of all magical powers and their life forces, which were fed to the stone.

Or so it was said.

It happened thousands upon thousands of years before I was born.

I glanced at my plain-looking human computer. Earth websites wouldn't have a clue as to what it was, but the infinity web that Xieth had installed on my machine would.

The infinity web was the internet of the Eltrisphere. It made the one on Earth look microscopic. It also had an actual functional search engine.

With a sigh, I started to climb out of bed. Then froze. Xieth had been seriously freaked out about most everything that happened to me today. But he'd been terrified about someone thinking I had the Stone of Zalianthia.

Which meant going onto the system that was connected to every world in the Eltrisphere and calling up a search for it might be an extremely bad thing.

If I had access to my magic, I could shield my search on the infinity web. With the magic blocking bracelets on me, all I'd be doing is waving an electronic flag to whoever was looking for the stone.

Just the fact that it was missing and somewhere other than where it should be was bad enough. I didn't need more people thinking I knew where it was.

I slipped back into bed and glared at my computer. Eventually, I fell asleep, but my dreams were chaotic. I woke up feeling less rested than when I started.

***

I put on my robe, stumbled out to start the kettle, then poured food for Lucie. I was about to ask Tiberius what he wanted to eat when the events of yesterday hit me. Hard. Tiberius had been my prior captor, and Lucie was a nuisance in the best of times.

I missed them both enough that my chest hurt.

After that performance last night, there was little doubt that Betsy, Jamie, and Martha had been taken as well.

I cut off my panic attack with a cup of extra-strong Pu-erh tea. It was closest to the teas that I'd grown up with, but I didn't have it all the time because it could be a bit strong.

That caffeine kick was needed now.

I ran back to my bedroom and grabbed the pad of paper, then sat down with my tea, a lot of bread, and pretended I wasn't the one with kidnapped friends.

I jotted down the times that my missing beings were last seen. Betsy and her crew's tendency for mysteries was well known in the town, so the weird bit with suspiciously missing mail might have been a trap. I knew the last time I'd seen Lucie and Tiberius, but the house could have been broken into anytime within a few hours of my leaving.

I added a note to check with Alice about mail thieves and what she and another cop were doing out that night at The Drunken Toad Pub.

Camfield made my list for his missing goats. Had someone used his escaping goats to get to me, Lucie, or Tiberius? Then I wrote down 'puppies'. But, regardless of what Xieth said, I had a hard time believing those adorable furballs were evil. I put Brutus next to them on the list. If she was their mother, they weren't of this world. I had no idea where she'd been the past two months, but I needed to find her.

I knew that if anything came in about the men who tried to blow up my teahouse, I'd hear about it from Alice.

Unless the feds really did get involved. I'd seen enough TV shows not to trust them. They'd question me like a suspect, then leave me without information. I needed to check with the police again.

I blamed the lack of sleep, fear, and my current intense focus on the resulting high-pitched scream when my cell phone rang.

I grabbed it after the third ring when my heart stopped crawling out of my chest.

"Ceian? Am I speaking to Ceian Lasinaria?" The voice was older and male, but could be anyone.

"Yes? Sorry, you caught me at a bad time."

"This is Officer Jones; we met yesterday when Alice and I took out the pipe bombs from your teahouse."

My brain kicked in. "Ah, yes. Any news?" My thought process had been focusing on my missing friends, but all of them might be connected to the people who tried to blow up my teahouse.

"Sorry, nothing yet." He dropped his voice. "Alice and Keith are trying to get as much done as they can before the feds take over. We're a low priority for them, and those pipe bombs were amateur. But nothing so far." He spoke louder. "I'm calling because we have the last effects of your cousin, Cyber Kondle. I have here that you called him Darius. A shipping crate arrived a week ago from India, with his name on it. Sorry it took so long, but the boxes have now been scanned and are ready for pickup."

That snapped my brain around. I didn't want or need whatever that rat shipped here. I'd gone through what junk he'd left from the hotel he'd been staying at, and it mostly went in the trash.

He'd used me, set me up as the fall girl for his crimes in the Eltrisphere. Then ran a bunch of scams here. The words 'no thank you' were almost out of my mouth when I caught myself. "Thank you, Officer Jones. Since I won't be able to open The Fainting Goat until everything is cleared, I can come up today and pick them up." Xieth's shield and compulsion spell against my leaving the property fell at sunrise. And there was the slimmest chance that something Darius left could be tied back to the Eltrisphere. But going through his things wasn't going to be fun.

"Excellent. Um, you ride a bicycle, right?"

"Yes." I didn't like the tone of his voice.

"Do you have any friends with cars? There was a lot of stuff in that crate." He paused. "Hold on, Keith wants to speak to you."

The phone shifted. "Hi, Ceian. I was just at the station to pick up some copies of the sketches. If you can be here in the next hour, I can take you and your cousin's effects back to your house."

I'd been on the fence about taking Darius's things originally, and I wanted to say no now that I knew they needed a car, but I was trapped. Not to mention, Xieth would lose his mind if there was a chance of Eltrisphere junk being in town. "Thank you, Keith, that's extremely kind. I'll get ready and be there soon."

"See you then." He hung up.

The odds of most of the junk Darius had being only helpful to fill a dump were strong. And he wasn't connected to my current problems.

I screamed again when the landline rang a moment later.

Xieth appeared on the screen immediately, looking frazzled but less freaked than yesterday. "Any news?"

He had been less worried about me when dead bodies were dropping everywhere in my first week here.

"No. Well, the police want me to pick up some stuff that Darius had shipped here from India. I'll probably send it all to the dump next week."

"No!" Xieth coughed when the word came out as a screech. "I mean, we don't know what's in there. Darius had a lot of contraband with him; you need to search everything extremely carefully. Then store it somewhere safe. Too bad the cat isn't there—he'd be useful for once."

I wasn't going to defend Lucie to Xieth, but he had a point.

"Fine. But there are a lot of boxes coming in. Is there any way you could help speed things up in searching them?" I raised my magic blocking bracelets as a reminder. "I'm looking for my friends, have no idea who tried to blow up my teahouse, or who thinks I have the stone. I'm running out of options and time." There was no way he'd agree to let me have my magic back, but I had to try.

He paused. I might have overplayed my hand. What I was asking for was access to an extremely low-level searching spell. That I might use it to also help find my friends wasn't something I was going to tell him. Magic might not be allowed on Earth, but that hadn't stopped others—including Darius.

I also had no intention of ever telling Xieth about my possible magic slips.

He scowled. "I'd have to limit it. You wouldn't be able to do other magic." He drummed his chubby fingers on the desk in front of him and watched me through narrowed eyes. "I'll see if the Council will clear it. They need to be aware..." He let the rest of his thought drop. "I'll see what I can do. Keep me updated." He ended the call, and the landscape reappeared.

I sat for a moment in shock. I was glad he was going to try and get approval for the searching spell, but terrified at how messed up everything was for him to consider it.

Xieth was the type of cherub to deny a glass of water to someone dying in the desert out of spite.

# Chapter Eight

I needed to get to the police station before Keith left if I was going to bring the stuff home today. I didn't want Darius's stuff in here, but the barn was good for storing things. Within twenty minutes, I was showered, changed, and locking my front door.

A chill wind blew across my back, a foreboding one as my grandmother would have said. But aside from five tiny dark shapes vanishing under my fence into the abandoned lot next to me, nothing was around.

Were the puppies and their mother living over there? Brutus had been there with some criminals once she escaped. But they'd been picked up by Xieth and crew, and there was no sign of the large dog when the place was searched.

The lot had remained suspiciously vacant since then. Another thing to ask Xieth, which he might or might not tell me.

The day was gloomy and gray with a wind coming in that seemed to be moving more thick clouds our way. I normally loved rainy weather, as long as I was home with a fire going. Bringing home a carload of boxes in a downpour didn't sound appealing. Neither did opening my new shop. Although the rain might drive some folks in for tea, it wasn't an auspicious beginning.

Or wouldn't have been if I'd been able to open on time.

I started to get my bike from the barn, then locked it up instead. I had no idea how much room Keith had in his car, but my bike might be pushing it.

I went to the narrow bike lane that skirted through the coastal woods, looked around, and started sprinting. It wasn't magic; it was just part of my subset of jinn bloodline—I was fast. I hadn't taken a chance using my speed since I'd been here, as I was faster than any human, but I needed it now.

There would be no way to explain my speed if anyone saw me, so I stayed within the trees. It felt good to let loose.

Living in a bottle had far more possibilities and room than most people would think, but a wooded trail at a full run wasn't an option.

I heard a pair of hikers closer to the cliffs and zigged away from them. I slowed down to a walk right before the town came into view.

I wasn't even breathing hard when I walked off the bike path and onto the sidewalk. Luckily, the police station was closer to this side, so I wouldn't have to walk past my closed teahouse.

I didn't need to see the yellow crime tape they'd put up again. At least not until it was coming down.

A few people whom I knew, on sight anyway, waved at me as I walked to the station. I waved back and figured that at some point I needed to find out who they were.

A clump of five of the black suited crew were down Forester Street, arguing about something outside the camping and hiking store. They didn't wave. And I certainly wasn't going to.

The officer at the desk this time was little more than a kid. I knew I was a freak compared to humans at five hundred and eighty-seven years old, but this one looked like a baby.

"Do you need to report a crime?" He stood up, tall, but a faint breeze could send him airborne. My old gladiator master would have been bulking him up immediately. He'd also lowered his voice and adopted a stern expression.

"No, that's already been done. I'm here to meet Keith."

His big blue eyes widened. "You're Ceian. Nice to meet you. Detective Jack told me about you." He bobbed his head a few times, but it was impossible to sort out what had been said. I was getting annoyed at Jack telling everyone about me, then vanishing.

"That's nice. Where's Keith?" I prompted when the kid didn't do anything but stare. No one so far could tell me when Jack would be back, but I wasn't going to feed into his stories by asking this kid about it.

"Oh. Down the hall, grabbing a bunch of stuff." He shrugged and pointed in the opposite direction from where I'd gone yesterday. The station wasn't large, but at this rate, I'd have seen everything but the jail.

I could pass on that.

Keith was pulling a huge flat cart piled with boxes toward me. "Ah, perfect timing. My van's right out front. There's another load, but I think I can make them all fit, and you too."

"Thanks for this." I forced a smile. I'd figured there were a lot, but even this run was more than I'd imagined. What was in these things that he had them shipped on an incredibly slow boat from India? And Lucie said they spent some time in Canada, *after* India, before coming here.

I followed Keith outside and over to an ancient, brightly painted vehicle. I'd only seen one of these in movies and wondered how I hadn't seen Keith's in the two months I'd been on the planet. It was unique with stickers that reflected the 1960s.

A Volkswagen Vanagon.

The good thing was that it appeared to have a lot of room in it. The bad thing was that Keith believed we would need all that room.

"I know what you're thinking—these babies haven't been made since the early 1990s." Keith patted the side door of the purple, orange, and green vehicle fondly. "It's a labor of love to keep her running. But worth it."

"She's quite interesting." I'd almost said lovely, but a lie like that would have made me choke.

Keith laughed. "She is indeed." In a flash, he had the boxes off the cart and next to the large open door. "If you can get these inside, I'll bring out the rest."

"Sure." I waited until he was out of sight before touching the boxes. I knew the cops had scanned them, and these were probably just things to hold his stuff. But if Darius had left anything strong behind, I might feel it.

I shouldn't, not with the magic blocking bracelets on, but having two magically adjacent reactions yesterday made me wary. It would be hard to explain if I suddenly freaked out while moving a box. Especially without lying.

I moved the boxes inside the van with no reaction. I had to say the van's interior was immaculate.

Keith came out with a much larger load, and together we got them crammed inside. I thought I felt a faint tingle from one small box, but I ignored it after I made note of which one it was.

Keith ran the cart back inside and then jogged out. "Do you mind if we stop at the diner first? I'm famished."

I was starting to feel the reaction of my sprint and lack of actual breakfast, so I nodded. I told myself I wasn't delaying dealing with the boxes. Food was important.

Hannah's Diner was small, cute, and tucked down a tree-shaded street. I'd just started going there the last two weeks when I was working full days at my teahouse.

After a hundred years of having food brought to my bottle, it was nice to make food at home, even though I wasn't a great cook. I had to admit that the diner cooks made much better food than I did.

We were there after the early breakfast crowd, but before the lunch rush, so only a few tables were occupied.

Keith must eat there a lot; the tiny, older waitress on duty smiled and waved him over to a corner table.

She came scurrying over the second we both were seated. "Keith! You old charmer, glad you're back in town. Try to stay longer than a few days this time." She appeared to be the same age as him, but the wink she gave was friendly, not flirty.

Keith grinned and winked back. "I'll take that under advisement." He turned to me. "Do you trust me to order? I'm picking up the tab since your teahouse opening has been delayed."

I shrugged. "Sure? And thanks."

"Ah! That's who you are! I'm Hannah. Sorry about the problems with your teahouse." Her grin immediately made me feel at home.

"Thank you, I'm Ceian. Could I get an iced tea?"

"You got it. Two specials, one water, one iced tea." With a nod to both of us, she shot off.

"She seems nice."

"She's an old timer, like me. Although Hannah was born and raised here. I found myself adrift and landed here forty years ago. It's a good town." He looked up as the door chimed and a group of six black suits came in. Keith's smile dropped. "Most of the time."

All six went directly to a center table without waiting for Hannah to return or for the waiter coming out of the kitchen to acknowledge them.

"Is it just me, or are they creepy? Two of their SUVs almost ran me over yesterday morning, but they all seem like robots." They also made my skin crawl.

"That's not good, but sadly not surprising. They barely notice anyone else is alive. Hopefully, they should at least be in meetings most of tomorrow. And yes, they are extremely creepy." His face softened in concern. "I hope getting your cousin's belongings isn't bringing up bad memories."

I paused, building a partial lie now would lock me into it, and constantly skirting falsehoods wasn't fun. "Thank you, but I'm fine. We weren't close anymore. He was an ass." That felt wonderful to say. And extremely true.

Keith chuckled. "I have a few of those in my family tree. One of the reasons I hide out in this town."

Before I could ask him more about the town, Hannah showed up with two of the tallest and widest burgers with fried eggs dripping down the sides that I'd ever seen. Next to them was a huge pile of assorted types of French fries, onion rings, and hash browns. Breakfast and lunch in one meal.

The waiter ran in behind her and dropped off our drinks before going to the people in black.

"There you go. All sauces and condiments are on the table. Oh," she paused and whipped a bottle out of her pocket. "And ranch dressing. If you need anything else, just holler." With a smile to us and a glare at the black suited group, she darted back into the kitchen.

"I had no idea they had something like this here." I took a bite. Their food had been good when I'd come in, but this was beyond that. "That's amazing." I refrained from inhaling the entire thing in one move and nibbled on the fried foods. Also, amazing.

"Yup. And now that she knows you, Hannah will make it for you any time."

We remained silent for the most part and cleared our plates.

Keith finished with a sigh. "I hope you don't mind, I'm allergic to black pepper, so she keeps it out of my meals. She would have done the same to yours. I should have said something."

"Really? I usually ask them to leave it off. This was great." Another reason that I was more likely to cook at home—many jinn, and others from the Eltrisphere, although by no means all, didn't process black pepper well.

# Chapter Nine

I would have enjoyed sitting around chatting with Keith and Hannah, but the weird vibe from the black suited group was weighing on me. They never turned to us or acted like they even knew we were alive, but I felt like we were being watched.

Hannah refused to take any payment from Keith or me and made me promise to come in the next morning for breakfast.

"I feel like I'm just now meeting people," I said as we got in his van.

"I've seen you with Betsy and her crew; they're good people."

I must have frowned too loudly at that, as Keith turned off the engine and sat in the parking spot. "What's wrong?"

They'd only been missing for less than a day. And I couldn't explain how I was certain they'd been taken. The weird voices that I'd heard seemed distant and could be a trap. But from the worry in his eyes, Keith deserved to know something was wrong.

I'd just skirt some details. "I haven't seen them since early yesterday. They never came by when they were supposed to help with the teahouse, not even when the cops were there." Keith's eyes widened at that. He knew those three well.

"When I last saw them, they were investigating something. They'd found a bunch of hidden but unopened junk mail behind The Drunken Toad Pub and were going back to look for clues." I reminded myself to check with Alice as to what she and Officer Jones were doing there that night, or early morning.

Keith's hands tightened on the steering wheel. "That's not good. Did you talk to Ralph? He's Betsy's handyman. Well, everything around the house and yard man. He likes helping her out." He paused. "I'm going to drop you and your things off, then I'll go to Betsy's place. And Jamie and Martha's places, too."

I looked back at the boxes. Yes, Xieth was frantic about my searching them. But I needed to see if there were any clues as to who took my friends. "These will be safe in here, right?" The windows were dark, so it wouldn't be obvious that there were a bunch of boxes here.

"Yes, and I can make them even more so with my front window cover. Are you sure?"

I didn't have to fake the concern in my voice. "Those three are my friends. My first friends here. They went missing when my pets were taken, my house was broken into, and my teahouse was almost blown up. I'm afraid it's all connected." That was more than I'd intended to say, but it wasn't wrong.

Keith reached over and took my hand. "We'll fix this. I agree that those three are troublemakers, but no one in town would harm them. What are your pets' names?"

"Tiberius and Lucie, goat and cat." I thought I saw an odd look cross Keith's face at their names, but I was busy blinking my eyes not to cry.

"Interesting names." He smiled. "I bet there are some stories behind them. But you are welcome to come with me. I'm not sure what we'll find, but we can call in Jack if we discover any clues." He shook his head at my reaction and unspoken question. "Yes, he came back to work an hour ago."

At my distracted nod, Keith put his brightly colored monstrosity into gear and took off. Much faster than I would have expected. I'd heard these things were as slow as a drunken cherub.

I'd never been to any of my friends' houses; they seemed to prefer coming to mine. But when we pulled up to a lovely, well-gardened, bright yellow house on a slight hill, I knew whose it had to be. "Betsy."

"Yup, not all people reflect their homes or vice versa, but this is all her. I don't see Ralph anywhere, though. This is one of his days to work in the garden."

We parked and walked to the front door. When I first met Betsy, I assumed Ralph was her husband or partner. Then it was made clear he was married and just a dear friend.

Keith knocked on the door a few times, then scowled and walked around to the side gate.

"This shouldn't be unlocked. Even when someone is home, it's locked." He marched into the immaculate yard.

I wondered if Betsy kept it secured to keep people from stealing her flowers. It was like a magical garden in here.

Except for the pair of unmoving legs lying under a massive shrub.

"No!" Keith ran forward, with me right on his heels.

I'd been so focused on the fact that the creepy note said they had my friends that I didn't think they might have already hurt them. Or worse.

Keith pushed back the shrub to reveal a furious middle-aged man, tied up and gagged. Keith pulled him free of the shrub, then undid the gag and helped him sit up.

"Keith! You have to find Betsy; someone took her and ransacked her house."

"Take it easy, Ralph, let me get you untied." Keith nodded to me. "This is Betsy's friend, Ceian. She was worried about her."

"Ceian, she's said great things about you." Ralph winced when he moved once the ropes were free. "I've been there since last evening. I was worried about Betsy and saw the side gate open. They jumped me the moment I stepped into her house. But what I saw wasn't good. She's going to be furious."

I almost smiled. Not that Betsy's house might have been damaged, or that she was missing. But one of her closest friends was more concerned that she would be furious about what happened to her home.

I needed to channel Ralph's optimism.

With Ralph leaning on Keith, being tied up in a garden overnight didn't do a lot for circulation, we went inside her house. Ralph had been right; she was going to be angry. It didn't look like anything was broken, just tossed about. Since I'd never been there before, I had no idea if anything was missing.

"We have to call the police." All three of us said at the same time.

"Are you up for it? You are the victim." Keith gave Ralph a reassuring smile.

"Yes." He patted his pockets. "They didn't even take my phone." He quickly told the officer on duty where he was and what had happened.

I winced when he mentioned Keith and me. The police were going to lock me up just to keep things from happening in town.

Ralph listened to the other person, then handed his phone to Keith. "They want to speak to you and for Ceian and me to wait in the front yard."

I offered to help Ralph as Keith spoke to the police, but he shrugged. "Thank you, but I'm feeling a bit better." He paused. "Did you check Jamie and Martha's homes?"

Another knot of worry crawled in my gut. "Not yet, we came here first." I heard sirens and decided to wait silently. I needed to rescue my friends from whoever in the Eltrisphere took them, but talking about them was only going to make things worse.

Two cop cars came up the hill. A bit overkill in my mind, but I was grateful.

Alice and Officer Jones were in the first one, and Jack was in the second. Like when I'd seen him last, he didn't wear a uniform because he was a detective, but he often drove a squad car. But he was still handsome enough to make angels weep. About 6'4, thick, wavy black hair, deep brown eyes, and a chiseled jaw. He was stunning even when scowling.

Keith had been inside but came out when the police parked. "I took all the photos I could, but didn't move things, so you can try for prints."

Alice and Officer Jones were in front; Jack was looking up and down the narrow road, and glaring as if the houses were keeping secrets from him.

"Thank you, Keith. Ceian." Alice nodded to me, then turned to Ralph. "You need to go to the medical clinic." She raised her hand when he started to protest. "No option. You go on your own, or we'll take you. Jones can get your information, then go. We'll find her. I promise."

Ralph shrugged and nodded to me. "Keep me updated and have them check on Jamie and Martha." Then he followed Office Jones to the side of the police car.

"Are you okay?" It took me a moment of mental drifting to realize Alice was speaking to me.

"Yes, shaken, but we weren't attacked. Do you want my statement? It's not much."

Alice grinned. "You never know what will help." She looked up to where Jack was still stomping around up the street. "Let's go over here. Keith will work with Jack."

Probably for the best, I wasn't sure how I felt about Jack. Or how I felt about my reaction to seeing him.

I told her everything that wasn't related to the weird stuff.

"Your animals are still missing? That's not good." She grabbed her radio and called the station. "We need a car to go to Jamie Ghastlin and Martha Stone's houses; they might have been taken when Betsy was."

I waited until she finished her call before bringing up what Betsy and crew had been doing before they came over to my house yesterday morning. "They said they saw you and Officer Jones at The Drunken Toad Pub at 4 am."

"We'd gotten a late call about some trouble out that way. Supposedly, monsters roaming the streets. We didn't find anything, so we stopped to write it up and see if anything appeared. We never saw the three ladies." She flipped her notebook closed as Keith came out with Jack. "I'll let Keith take you home." With a pat on my shoulder, she went up into Betsy's house.

Keith said a few words to Jack that made both men look at me. Jack's frown faded, but then he shook his head and went back inside Betsy's house.

Fine, I didn't want to talk to him either.

"Let's get you and these boxes home. If you'd like, I can do some sketches of your animals. Alice said she had photos, but more versions sometimes help."

I smiled as we got into his van. "Thank you. This has been overwhelming."

We remained silent as he drove to my place.

"Can you pull up to the barn? That's about the only place with room for these boxes. I ignored the tug I felt when no cat or goat came running over to see what was up.

"Good idea. Probably a good idea that you keep it locked too." Keith stopped the car, and I was stepping out when his words caught up to me.

"What?" I walked to the barn doors. Granted, after the events of two months ago, locking it would make sense. But I knew I hadn't bought a lock yet. "I don't have a lock."

"That's not yours? It looks like a combination lock. And there's a note?" He didn't touch anything, but nodded to the lock and note tucked into it.

I grabbed the note and kept my stream of swearing in my head with difficulty. It was written in Sihlia, a common Eltrisphere language. "It's a code of some kind. It's the combination."

It actually told me that I should be grateful that someone was watching over me, added 'you're welcome', then gave the code. I stuffed the paper in my pocket under the guise of needing to unlock the barn, but I was trying to sort out how to get rid of it without Keith seeing the strange language.

My swearing went external as I almost stepped on an unmoving black suited body when I got the door open. I jumped backward and bumped into Keith. "Not again."

"But you were cleared of the other bodies." Keith noticed the black suit. "Kind of figured it was only a matter of time until someone took care of one of them. But why dump him here?" He didn't touch the body but peered closely. "Looks like he was shot in the chest. The hole in his back indicates it was a through-and-through exit point."

I was trying to find a place to be sick when I saw movement further inside the barn. I hit the light and grabbed my flashlight.

Three humans, a cat, and a goat were in a pile, and one of them was twitching.

# Chapter Ten

K eith saw them when I did and tried to stop me from running in. But I was too fast.

Lucie was on top, gagged and tied like Ralph had been. They were all gagged and tied. Tiberius, Betsy, Jamie, and Martha.

But they were all breathing and slowly coming around.

I grabbed Lucie and removed the gag and rope, then did the same for Tiberius. Both animals appeared stunned but conscious.

"We should call this in," Keith said, but he still removed Betsy's gag.

"Yup, after we free them all. The cops can search the rope and gags; I'm not leaving them like this."

Betsy, Jamie, and Martha appeared unhurt after we freed them, but they were having a harder time waking up than Lucie and Tiberius. As it was, both cat and goat sat in the hay looking confused and blinking a lot.

Keith nodded as I adjusted my friends to make them more comfortable, and he called the police. From the other voice, it appeared he'd called Alice.

"They're coming with an ambulance." He kept glancing at Lucie and Tiberius with a concerned look. "Can your goat eat part of the note you got? You might not want anyone else to see it."

I figured it was because it sounded like whoever killed the man in the black suit was working with me. Then I remembered it was in Sihlia. My eyes narrowed as I watched Keith.

"He might be up for it, normally, but his eyes aren't focusing at this point. We just won't tell them about the note at all."

Keith sighed and rubbed the side of his face. "They'll be here soon. I had no idea who you really were; there was no chatter that anyone was coming here. I didn't read the note, but I know it wasn't in any Earth language. No one can be allowed to see it as it is, and we don't have time to discuss it. I can fix it. They might wonder how you got the lock open otherwise."

I went from freaked out to even more freaked out. Keith was from the Eltrisphere? And he wasn't a parolee. No one from home was supposed to be in Forgotten Hollow or anywhere near here. Then why did Eltrisian people keep popping up?

This was layer upon layer of bad. And the sound of approaching sirens meant that I should trust him, and my questions needed to wait. I handed him the note and moved closer to Lucie and Tiberius.

His words were short and nearly silent. Sihlia sounded odd whispered in my barn, but I felt the magic.

"Here." He sat on a bale of ancient hay after he handed me the note.

It now said, "I found your friends and the one who took them." Then it listed the lock combination.

That was an extrapolation, but to be fair, my reading of Sihlia might have been rusty. "Thank you."

He nodded but looked tired. Another thing to discuss. Later.

Alice was the first on the scene with two EMTs with gurneys running after her.

"I can't believe the ladies were here, and your pets!" Alice stopped by the animals to give both a scritch. They were still groggy, so neither responded.

"All of them were knocked out with something strong." I pointed to the dead body Alice had stepped around. "Except him. We untied everyone, but didn't touch him. Sorry, but Keith and I touched the note that was stuck in the lock." I handed her the magically changed note.

More sirens, more cop cars, and a second ambulance.

Jack stomped in, glaring around the barn. "The coroner is coming for him. No one touched him, right?"

I folded my arms but bit back my snarky response. I was so happy my friends were all back; even Jack couldn't get under my skin right now.

Jack's face softened. "You can take your pets inside. We'll question you after we take care of Betsy and the others." Then he ruined it by turning away before I could thank him.

"I'll help you carry them." Keith seemed recovered, but I still nodded to my wheelbarrow.

"Thank you, but Tiberius is extremely heavy." An annoyed snort from the goat was terrific to hear.

Keith and I got Tiberius into the wheelbarrow, I grabbed Lucie, and we went to my house.

Keith waited until I'd shut the door before speaking. "The note—"

"Will be extremely helpful, thank you for finding it." I didn't know what Keith was, or why he was here, but I did know Xieth had listened in before without me noticing. "If you can help me set them up to be comfortable, I'll let you go back to helping Jack."

Keith's eyes narrowed, but he gave a small nod.

I followed him outside after we got Tiberius out of the wheelbarrow. "I can't talk inside. But we do need to talk."

"Yes, we do. But I'd better fill Jack in on what I can. I'll come get you when we can move the boxes out of my car."

I'd almost forgotten about them. But, given my history with dead bodies and mayhem in this town, I was grateful Keith had been with me this time.

Lucie was on a pile of pillows on the sofa, furiously washing his face. We'd put Tiberius down on a pile of blankets on the floor, but he was up and stomping around, albeit a bit unsteadily.

"What happened? I feel like I was on the losing end of a gang grudge match." Right now, it looked like he wished he were still a seven-foot-tall centurion so he could go break some bodies.

Even though we had no idea who needed to be broken.

I grabbed some of his favorite food, a cereal called Cheerios, and put it in his bowl.

"I have no idea. I came back yesterday evening to find the front door busted out, the window shattered in, and you two missing. Betsy, Jamie, and Martha were taken at some point as well. Do either of you remember anything?"

Lucie stopped mid-lick and appeared to be thinking. I turned away so I wouldn't laugh at his tongue blep. "Yes...vaguely. You made us stay home. Then a massive wind crashed through the window—nice repair job by the way, Xieth, I assume? Anyway, couldn't tell who was riding the wind, but it tried to grab both of us."

Tiberius looked up from his cereal, nodded, then continued to eat.

"The goat kicked out the door, and we ran." Lucie scowled. "I don't remember anything after that until waking up in that barn and you untying me."

"We ran toward the empty lot. I figured it might be a good place to hide." Tiberius got the same annoyed and confused expression Lucie had. "That's all I recall. How long have we been gone?"

I refilled his bowl of Cheerios and put a full bowl of kibble near Lucie on the coffee table. "I'm not sure when you were grabbed. I came home about five and found you both were gone." I coughed to hide the emotion that hit me. I'd lived alone for a hundred years in my bottle, but less than twenty-four hours of these two and my other friends missing, and I was losing it. "Oh, and someone tried to blow up the teahouse. I stopped them, but it's under investigation by the cops. Who will also want to speak to me soon. You two can stay out here, but look sleepy."

Neither animal seemed terribly surprised at the teahouse almost being destroyed. And even without being afraid of Xieth eavesdropping, I wasn't going to tell Tiberius that my magic might have slipped. Lucie wouldn't care; Tiberius might be a goat now, but he was still a centurion at heart.

They'd finished eating and settled down to rest, which didn't appear faked, when a sharp rap came at my door.

Jack, Keith, and Alice were all there, and more cops were going in and out of my barn.

"Are Betsy and the others okay?" I noticed that both ambulances and the coroner's vehicle were gone.

"Yes, the EMTs just want to check them all. None of them remembers what happened. Keith has told us his story, but I'd like to hear your end." Jack was completely professional as he took a seat at my dining table. That handsome face showed no emotions.

I had no idea why the thought of wanting to run my fingers through his hair hit at a time like this, so I quickly took a seat at the table.

Keith and Alice sat on the more comfortable seats in the living room and cooed over the animals.

Jack's questions were to the point and blunt. He began with yesterday morning and the last time I'd seen Betsy, Jamie, and Martha. Then he politely asked about the animals. The questions went from the fake exterminators, going to the police, and coming home.

"Nice work on the door and window, by the way." Alice looked up and smiled.

Keith watched Tiberius pretend to snore, but grinned. "Thank you. I did it earlier. I had replacements of these sizes in my garage."

I forced myself to smile. "He's a miracle worker."

Alice looked like she wanted to ask more questions, but Jack moved the conversation to Betsy's house. "The other two houses were ransacked like hers was, but until they can all go home, we won't know what was taken." Then he leaned forward intently. "Was that dead businessman the one who ran you off the road yesterday?"

Alice frowned and gave me an apologetic shrug. She also glanced at Jack and shook her head.

"You think I'd kill someone for that? Nothing was hurt but my pride. Alice wasn't too far behind him; she saw the interaction. Not to mention, I didn't see the face of the driver, nor the face on the body that got dumped in my barn."

Jack held his impassive stare for a moment, then leaned back and shrugged. "I didn't think so, but we need to check all avenues. There was no ID on the body, so we'll have to take the photos to the Grasshopper and see who he was."

"As well as interview all of the people attending the retreat." Alice's sigh of unhappiness could have probably been heard by Xieth even without his eavesdropping equipment.

Jack flipped his notebook closed and got to his feet. "We'll keep you updated on news of your teahouse."

Alice left before he did, but Keith stayed seated as Jack stopped at the door.

"It is good to see you again." The look on his face was a cross between sincerity and fear—I think he wasn't happy that I was involved with a dead body again.

"You too." I kept my smile sincere and shut the door behind them.

Keith glanced around the room, and I nodded to the landscape painting. He frowned. "Where should we put the boxes? The front of the barn is still a police scene."

I looked out the window as Jack, Alice, and Officer Jones pulled away. That extremely unwelcome yellow crime tape covered the entrance to my barn, even as the remaining officers left.

"There's a spot in the back of the barn; it's separated from the front. Looks like it might have been another entrance for it at one point, but the previous owners boarded it up. Let's try there if the police didn't block off the entire barn. I do want to go through my cousin's things quickly."

I waited until we were trudging through the high weeds along the side of the barn before speaking. Even then, I kept my voice down. I was more than a little freaked about Xieth's eavesdropping. Sneaky cherub.

"I'm a jinn on parole. For a crime I didn't commit, but one I spent a hundred years in my bottle for. Tiberius is a centurion guard who got on the wrong side of some important people and was changed and sent here to watch me. Lucie is some weird cat criminal who'd been with Darius but not really on his side. Darius was the idiot who set me up for the crime and whose things are in your car."

Keith stopped walking at the words. "An honest jinn at that. Fair is fair, I'm—"

"Hello? Ceian? Is everything okay? I saw the police leaving." It sounded like Camfield was in front of the barn; he must have seen us go down the side. The weeds were over knee-high. I didn't blame him for not wanting to trudge down here.

I gave Keith a shrug. "Yes, I'm fine. A friend and I were just checking barn security." I winced; that sounded stupid. But I felt weird about more people knowing about Darius. Or maybe it was just Camfield knowing about how messed up my life was. I couldn't deny he was a handsome and charming guy.

My weakness.

"We're coming back that way, hold on."

Camfield looked impeccable as usual, and a glance down pointed out that I was wearing a lot of plant debris. The long, dark hair strands waving about wildly on either side of my face pointed out that a lot of it had pulled free of my high ponytail.

So much for wooing Camfield with my beauty.

"Hi, Camfield, thank you for checking on me." I paused. I had no idea who I could say what to. "This is Keith, he's with the police and helping me."

Keith stepped forward with a wide grin. "Nice to meet you, I've seen you in town, but we haven't met yet. I do sketch work for the police. I was here to ask Ceian if she had any other memories pop up from the attack on the teahouse." He laughed. "Then we thought we saw something go around the back of the barn."

Camfield shook his hand. "Ah, yes, the one with the van. I have seen you walking around town. But your van is truly remarkable. Any news? Is that why the police were here?"

I still felt odd about saying anything. Jack hadn't said that I couldn't, but I didn't want to let too much information out, and for the person or persons who kidnapped my friends to get away.

"They found a body in her barn! Can you believe that? Not sure how or what they know, I'm just a part-time sketch artist." Keith jumped in, and I felt a soothing energy coming from him. I was a jinn, and it immediately settled me. Camfield practically melted.

"How horrible! Everything was okay, though? Do they know who did it?"

"Not that they told us." I was grateful for Keith stepping in. Lies by omission could be tricky sometimes.

"That's so scary, right after the attack on your teahouse," Camfield swore as his phone began chirping. He glanced down and swore more. "Sorry that I can't stay. Business things are blowing up. It was nice to meet you, Keith, and please take care, Ceian."

He barely waited for either of us to nod before running toward his car.

"That was interesting." Keith watched as the sleek Lexus drove out of my yard.

"So was a certain sketch artist's soothing magic." There were a few Eltrisphere member races who could use empathic magic. Jinn were one of them. Keith appeared human, but so did I.

"Caught me." He grinned. "Your friend was extremely anxious about something, and I felt that getting him out of here calmly and quickly was a good idea. Don't worry, I don't scan or influence my friends unless it's absolutely necessary. I've been on this planet for forty years, and I don't want to have to leave."

"Are you a slanaigh?" They usually appeared taller, thinner, and more mythologically elf-like. But he had the empathic magic down.

"Yes, indeed, although it's been a long time since I heard that term. I'm not an escaped criminal. I was exploring forty years ago, found this town, and stayed." He frowned. "Who is your parole guardian?"

"Xieth. One of the most annoying cherubs...." I paused as Keith's scowl grew nasty.

"I know him. Or knew him long ago. Whining, self-centered...he's my third cousin. My true cousin. I haven't seen him in over a hundred years and was hoping to keep it that way."

I'd been counting on more help from Keith; it was nice having another Eltrisian here. But I couldn't risk Xieth catching his cousin on Earth. I knew how that would go, and it wouldn't be good for Keith.

"Don't worry, now that I know about him and his spying, I will make sure he doesn't know it's me. I can probably also create something to block his spying completely. He'll still be able to get through normally, but none of this sneaking about. I can't believe he became a parolee guardian. He never was good for much." Keith dropped into his thoughts for a moment, then shook his head. "Shall we continue our search for an entrance?"

I was happy that I had someone to talk about home with and who knew and hated Xieth as much as I did. "I do need to go through those boxes. Let's see if this will work."

Keith had a hammer and a pick that he'd brought from his van to pry open the wood covering the old side entrance. Quick work, but only to find out there was literally no way in from this side.

Unless I could go inside the barn from the front and haul out a few years of junk abandoned by prior owners. I'd seen some stuff back there before, but mostly, I avoided the barn.

"Where else?" Keith put the pieces of wood back.

I knew he'd take me anywhere I said, he was a good guy. "I have an extra bedroom. I didn't want those boxes in my house, but I also don't want them too far away from me. Who knows what's in them?"

"Gotcha. Let's get them moved. If anything in them causes a problem, call me and I'll contain it. I've found plenty of questionable objects in the past forty years; I have a small secure holding area on my property."

I wanted to ask him about the things he'd found as we trudged back. But it was better not to know at this point. I wouldn't have to lie about what I didn't know.

"Thanks. Hopefully, it's just all junk." I sent a short prayer to any deity out there that there was nothing dangerous in the boxes.

We each grabbed a few boxes and lugged them into the nearly empty guest room. Tiberius and Lucie were snoring loudly, but their food dishes were both empty.

Like with the sleeping, I didn't blame them at all.

We got the boxes into the guest room, and Keith glanced over at Lucie. Tiberius was hidden under his blankets behind the sofa, but snored like a true centurion. "I'm glad they're safe. If I hear anything about *anything*, I'll text you."

"Thanks again for bringing my stuff. And brunch."

"Not a worry. And don't forget to drop in on Hannah, she runs a good diner." With a glare at the landscape painting, Keith nodded and left.

# Chapter Eleven

I regretted having finished my rocky road ice cream yesterday, but made do with a turkey sandwich and iced tea. I was fine until I grabbed a bag of potato chips. One crunch and Tiberius was in full goat form and at my side, licking his lips.

"They aren't good for you." I grabbed a handful out of the bag and dropped them into his goat chow dish.

"Not good for you either." Anything else he said was lost as he chomped his way through the chips. I couldn't find anything about goats and potatoes, but Tiberius had a love of potatoes that was terrifying.

"Who was the skinny guy? A bit old for you, right?" Lucie stretched as he jumped off the sofa and wandered over. He often ate non-traditional cat food; he loved yogurt, but he didn't like potatoes.

"He's a friend. His name is Keith." I twitched when I said the name near Xieth's landscape. But it was fairly common, and I doubted Xieth knew his long-lost cousin was on the planet.

"He's a part-time sketch artist for the police and has been helping me with the attack on the teahouse. Plus, whoever grabbed you two. How are you both feeling?" They seemed more like their old selves, aside from sleeping and eating a lot more.

"I'm good. Pissed, but okay. But when we find who did this, I'm shredding them." Lucie flashed his claws to make his point, then rubbed around my legs for more kibble. Which, of course, I gave him.

"I agree," Tiberius said around a mouth of more goat kibble. "Just let me have my real form back for ten minutes with them." He didn't have claws to accent his point, but the glare on his face was far more centurion than goat.

I finished eating and was working up enough energy to at least go through a box or two when my phone chirped. It was Alice.

"Hey, what's up?" I probably sounded more cheerful than I felt simply because I had a temporary reprieve from box duty.

"Betsy and her friends are awake now. Hungry like a bunch of dock workers, but the doc says they're fine. She doesn't have a clue as to what knocked them out, though. She's sending their blood out of town for more tests, but she warned us that whatever it was, it was disappearing fast. We might never know what was used."

That was both good and bad news. Unless they had a relapse of some kind, I couldn't risk bringing Tiberius and Lucie to a vet. They might appear as normal animals, but they weren't anywhere near that. The idea of Tiberius falling asleep and changing into his true self at a vet's office was horrifying. It was amazing that whatever had knocked him out didn't create that reaction as it was.

"Can they have visitors yet?" I'd been terrified for my friends. Seeing them groggy was better than not at all, but I'd rather see them healthy and awake.

"Only official ones. But Betsy has informed Jack that you're an official one, and if he doesn't bring you in to see them, they're getting out of there immediately." She gave a low laugh.

"I take it you're nowhere near him right now?"

"Nope. He's still trying to interview the three, and they're still keeping quiet until you show up."

I could imagine the three troublemakers. And it brought a massive grin to my face. "Let me change. I was dealing with weeds. Then I'll be right down."

"Excellent. I think Jack will be extremely glad to see you." Alice laughed again and hung up the phone.

Even knowing that Jack's being glad to see me was based on trying to get information from Betsy, Jamie, and Martha, it still gave me a warm feeling.

I finished a lightning-fast shower and changed into something less plant-covered when my landscape painting chimed.

I controlled my muttered swearing as I walked over just as the landscape vanished and Xieth's round face appeared. "Where were you? I've been trying to reach you." We'd already spoken recently, so I wasn't sure what his issue was.

"There's been a lot going on." I gave him the condensed version of the past few hours, leaving out details that he didn't need to know. "So, I need to get going to find out what Betsy and her friends know." I gave him my best earnest citizen smile.

"Why? You need to go through those boxes immediately. What happened to the humans isn't important." He wasn't happy, but it was a weaker reaction than I feared it would be.

"Because whoever brought them back left me a note in Sihlia." In my haste to keep things tight, I might have forgotten that. "It said the writer of the note killed the one who took them."

I expected Xieth to blow up, but he sat there looking like an old cherub. "That's not good. Go see what they can tell you. But unless you have something important, don't contact me until tomorrow morning, your time." He nodded, and his image vanished.

"That was unlike him." Lucie was curled up on the back of the sofa, cleaning his tail. "I do need to make my rounds outside tonight."

I shot him a glare.

"Okay, given the recent circumstances, I can spend another night inside." He flashed me a cat's grin and moved on to cleaning his legs.

"I agree, something is disturbing Xieth. Never fear, we will guard the house." Tiberius was a true centurion through and through. He adjusted his position on his blankets to watch the door and the picture window.

Before anything else could stop me, I ran out the door, locked it out of habit, more so than thinking anything could get through Xieth's spell, and hopped on my bike.

The hospital wasn't large and seemed almost cheerful. I'd only seen it once, during my full tour of the town.

I locked up my bike and jogged inside.

"Can I assist you?" A staunch middle-aged woman sat behind the reception desk. She had a look that would have served her well in the fighting arenas that I used to frequent.

"The police requested my presence. Three of my friends are here."

"Ah. You're Ceian, correct? They're on the second floor." She nodded to the elevator and almost smiled.

I did smile, never knew when someone in the medical field could be handy. Although, like Tiberius and Lucie, I probably shouldn't be examined by any human medical professional. I made a note to ask both Xieth and Keith about that for future reference and jogged to the elevator.

Officer Jones stood guard. Well, he was sitting between the elevator and the stairway, reading a newspaper. He smiled when he saw me. "Good to see you again. The ladies are driving Jack crazy."

"Not surprising. Thanks for guarding them." Another smile. Officer Jones might be in Forgotten Hollow only to run out his time until retirement, but he seemed like a good guy.

The room was cheery, a light yellow with large windows. Betsy, Jamie, and Martha silently glared at Jack from their beds when I came in. Alice sat just inside the door, fighting a grin.

"Ceian! Thank you for saving us!" Betsy gave me her widest smile, but didn't move to get out of bed. All three of them looked exhausted, and I had a feeling their earlier threat of walking out of the hospital was a ruse.

"Thank you, Ceian, for coming so quickly." Jack's smile was thin, and there was a twitch hitting his left eyelid. "Now maybe we can get some information as to what led up to the kidnappings?"

"We were always ready to talk, Jack. We just needed our friend to be here. You're not always the most sympathetic to us. And we *were* found in her barn. There's some sort of connection going on." Betsy turned up her smile a bit. She'd originally thought that Jack and I would make a great couple and had been annoyed when it didn't happen. Then Jack left town, making things worse.

Payback was a tiny, smart, and feisty old lady.

"I...would you like a chair, Ceian?" Jack forced a better smile, and Alice brought over her chair.

"I should go back to the station, unless you need me?" Alice nodded to Jack. He wasn't her boss, but detectives usually took over investigations if they were involved.

"No, thanks. Tell Jones he can leave, too." Jack settled back into his chair.

"How are you doing, Ceian? We heard your teahouse was attacked?"

"Is everything okay?"

"When can you open now?"

Betsy, Jamie, and Martha almost spoke over each other's questions.

"And were we taken because of it?" Betsy gave a knowing nod and glared at Jack.

I wasn't sure why she glared, but it felt good that she had my back. I quickly filled them in on the details that Jack hadn't, which were most of them.

"Oh! Keith's back in town? That will be such a help. He's a good guy." Betsy's eyes lit up.

I hid my grin. I noticed that Keith was concerned about Betsy a bit more than the others. They'd make a cute couple.

Aside from the bit about him not being human. I shoved that aside for now. "He's been helping me with the police sketches and bringing in the things my late cousin left behind. That's how we found you three. And Tiberius and Lucie." My voice quivered a bit. They'd all only been gone a day, but it hit me harder than I would have thought.

"I'd like to say we remembered being found, but everything's a fog." Betsy didn't glance over when Jack coughed. "I *do* remember when we were taken, although I'm not sure why they took your pets." She leaned back in her pillows, took a long sip of water, and settled into her tale.

"The girls and I left your place yesterday morning, intending to meet you later at your teahouse."

Martha cut her off. "I do wish we'd been there, that must have been so frightening!"

"Yes, very." Betsy continued. "We were investigating the pile of suspicious mail we'd found behind The Drunken Toad Pub. We'd gone back there when Jamie saw a suspiciously small pile of dirt further into the woods. More junk mail. From many houses, and all were unopened." She gave a slow nod as if that were a telling clue.

I nodded back without having any idea why a bunch of stolen junk mail led them to being kidnapped.

The frown line between Jack's brows grew deeper.

"We collected those pieces as well. Then there was another pile of dirt and leaves just in sight and in the direction of the Old Hollow."

"I spotted that one," Martha said proudly.

Jack was taking notes on a pad of paper, but the grip on his pen was extremely tight. He also didn't look at any of us.

"Yes, yes," Betsy continued. "Now I'm sure by now you realize that we were being lured in. We knew it as well. But that deepened the mystery. Why would our finding discarded mail be a threat? We continued."

I listened through two more mail dumps, each one getting smaller, and leading them deeper into the coastal forest. That was great; they knew it was a trap. After this, we needed to discuss avoiding traps, not running toward them. Jack looked up at the same moment I did. And appeared as concerned as I felt. Then went back to his notes.

These three little old ladies spent years looking into non-existent mysteries in Forgotten Hollow. The locals thought it was charming and tolerated it. Aside from the issues stirred up by Darius and a few others a few months ago, this town had no major crime to speak of.

Who would want to hurt these three?

# Chapter Twelve

"After the final pile, or so we believed, we were well within the Old Hollow." Betsy gave another slow nod. "Which reminds me that you've never been there, Ceian. It's only known by us old timers, but it is a place of mystery and danger." She paused for dramatic effect.

Jamie and Martha looked suitably impressed.

I really felt that Betsy should be a professional storyteller. She would get rich on the storyteller circuit if we were in the Eltrisphere.

"And then what happened?" Jack finally asked as the pause continued.

"Rushing tales never helps. Especially when the tellers are older and have had great trauma." Betsy pushed back on her pile of pillows and put one hand across her forehead as if having a swoon.

"I do apologize." Jack lowered his voice. "The three of you were attacked, and things could have turned out far worse than they did. It's my job to find who was behind this and make them pay." His dark eyes flashed, and he looked like a knight of old.

Betsy held her pose for a few moments, then smiled. "True. And we need to see what was done to our homes. You do still have them under guard, yes?"

Jack gave a nod. "Of course."

"Very well." Betsy coughed, took some more water, and looked around the room. "The Old Hollow grew dark, and a wind came from the west. Then strong arms grabbed me from behind. A cloth was forced across my mouth before I could scream. Two dark shapes grabbed Jamie and Martha, and they collapsed. I fought as hard as I could, stomping back on my attacker's feet and kicking their shins. Alas, the substance on the cloth knocked me out."

Jack paused his writing and looked up.

"What else do you remember?" I spoke before he did, as he didn't look friendly.

"Waking up here. And the nice doctors and nurses making sure we were okay." Jamie spoke before Betsy did.

"Nothing else? Three dark shapes with cloths knocked you out. After you followed a trail that you knew was a trap." Jack was an extremely handsome man, and being angry didn't take away from that.

Not much anyway.

"That sums it up quite well." Martha smiled and nibbled on a vending machine candy bar. "Can we see our homes now?"

Jack got to his feet but seemed to be taking long, slow breaths. "Once the doctor has cleared you, yes. Obviously, report anything missing from your homes to Officer Jones, and leave a message for me if you recall anything else about the attack." He looked up as someone came to the door. "Ah, perfect timing, Keith. Do you mind escorting the ladies around to their homes? If there is any indication that any of the houses are unsafe, we'll find accommodations." With a tight nod to Betsy, Jamie, and Martha, Jack stomped out of the room after Keith nodded.

Betsy laughed once he was gone. "I don't know what happened to him when he was out and about, but he's even more prickly than before." She hit a small button next to her table. "We've got a ride, what say we blow this popsicle stand?"

The others laughed, and my late-night TV habit caught the dated reference. "Do you mind if I join?" I felt incredibly responsible for the attack on them. Who knew what would have happened if the mystery savior, who could write in Sihlia, hadn't done what they did? The person who took them knew what I was and thought I had the Stone of Zalianthia. Or rather, persons. At least three people attacked the ladies. Only one was now in the morgue.

Keith and the ladies nodded in agreement about my joining them.

"I now have a bike rack on my van, so we're all good." Keith shared his grin with all three of the ladies, but he definitely lingered on Betsy more.

"Is anything wrong? Do you need anything?" A tall young man with a long black ponytail and a nurse's badge stuck his head in to answer Betsy's call.

"We're ready to leave now. If you could speak to that lovely doctor for us to make it official?" Betsy gave her best little old lady smile. "I do so worry about my home. We all do."

He started to shake his head, then sighed. "I'll see what Dr. Lopez says."

Arguing with Betsy was an exercise in futility. I'd noticed that even though the other two were often silent, things became more set in stone if Jamie and Martha were with her.

"Dr. Lopez is such a lovely person. And she has the best bedside manner." Betsy had been lingering in her bed, but after the nurse left, she hopped out and gathered her things. "The cops claim the mail is evidence, and kept it, but we might not need it to sort things out. We will need to go through each house as a group, carefully, to make certain there are no clues missed. Anything missing or damaged must be noted."

Jamie and Martha followed suit, each also shoving a bunch of snack packages in their purses.

"We have no idea what damage was done to our kitchens; snacks are important." Jamie grinned.

"Women after my own heart." Keith bowed to all three.

The nurse came back quickly. "As long as you all sign out, Dr. Lopez says you are free to go." He held up three clipboards but didn't lower them to the ladies. "But you must promise to check in if there are any unusual issues." He paused and focused on Betsy as the leader. "*Anything*. She could bring you all back in if she feels you're injured."

"We promise to report anything unusual." Betsy flashed him her best smile until he lowered the clipboards.

Smart man. I didn't doubt that if he remained between Betsy and her escape, he was going to be extremely unhappy. Regardless of being twice her height.

All three quickly filled out their paperwork and handed the clipboards back to the nurse. He glanced at the pages, then stepped out of the way as Betsy led the escape.

"Thank you, dear boy!" Betsy marched into the hall.

Keith and I went last.

"She needs a scepter." I shook my head as everyone moved out of her way as she went to the elevator. "Or maybe not."

"True, Betsy is imperious enough."

The three ladies chatted about the hospital staff, all favorable, on the short elevator ride down, then turned toward Keith's van.

"I'll get my bike." I could have left it secured in the hospital bike rack, but the way things were going lately, I wasn't sure about leaving anything anywhere.

As Keith secured my bike to his van, I climbed into the back seat with Jamie and Martha, and we took off.

At some point, when we were alone, I was going to ask Keith what he did to change how this thing worked. Vanagons weren't supposed to move this fast.

Betsy's was the first house on the list, and the other two seemed fine with it. I was sure they were anxious to see their homes, but both agreed when Keith picked their first destination.

An officer whom I didn't recognize was sitting in his patrol car when we pulled up. Younger than Officer Jones, but older than Jack, he got out of his car as we drove up. He smiled when he saw Betsy.

"I'm so glad all of you have recovered from your ordeal. We've kept watch around the clock on your homes since we realized that you were missing. I'll stay here until things are confirmed inside."

"Thank you, Horace. Such a nice boy." Betsy reached up and patted his face.

He blushed a bit, then nodded to the rest of us.

Betsy gently unlocked the door and paused, almost as if she wasn't certain that she wanted to go in. She'd put up a fierce front, but that was crumbling now. Back in my arena days, I'd had my home broken into when I'd been off-world for a few weeks. Even though nothing personal was taken, it was a horrible feeling.

I squeezed her shoulder. "Take your time."

She looked at me and reached up to squeeze my hand. Tears were hiding in her eyes, but she blinked them away. "Thank you." With a deep breath, she marched into the house.

I'd seen inside her house briefly when Keith and I were looking for her. But now, imagining it through her eyes, it was worse.

Betsy carefully studied the spot in front of her, a small bookcase and tiny table in the foyer. Then she took some photos, picked things up gently, and put them back the way they should be. "Nothing is missing or broken from here." She gave a tight nod and moved on.

"The police took photos when they came here." Keith hung back.

"I would have expected them to. These are for me, just in case something was missed." She glanced around the front room. "This will take too long, and we still have two more houses. I will take my bedroom and bathroom. Martha and Jamie, could you handle the living room and office? Keith and Ceian, please take the kitchen and dining room. Photos first, then pick up. Keith and Ceian won't know what goes where, so just place things on the table and counters if you would." Her sorrow was still there, but so was her fury at whoever was behind this.

Keith and I headed into the kitchen with our cell phones at the ready. It was tiny, but cute with white paint and delicate green plants painted on the walls, along with a deep window full of real ones.

"Are my plants okay?" Betsy yelled from the back of the house.

"It looks like." I walked to them, but none of the tiny plants seemed to have been disturbed.

"How many are there?"

I shared a look with Keith. That was an odd question. With a shrug, I counted them. "Fifteen." How she got that many in that window, even a deep one like this, was fairly impressive.

"Fifteen?!" Betsy yelled and ran through the house. "Oh no. No, no, no. Can you get my step stool? It's under the table."

Keith grabbed the small stool and handed it to Betsy as she glared at her plants.

Jamie and Martha came in as well. They appeared worried. Betsy was pissed.

"They took them. All three of them. Bet they got the ones in your homes too." She turned and nodded to Jamie and Martha.

"What did they take?" I was a little confused as to why someone, probably from the Eltrisphere, would kidnap three old ladies, ransack their homes, and take some plants. I was still sorting Earth out, but that was weird for any place.

"Three vine clippings. Oh, I am so mad!" Betsy hopped off the stool and glared around the kitchen as if she could find the missing plants—or the persons who took them.

Keith studied the other plants, but looked as confused as I. "What kind of vine clippings?"

"That's it, we don't know." Jamie now looked furious, something unusual for her. "We found them on the edges of the old Coffee Time Perks location, right before the rubble was removed to build Ceian's teahouse. They were just growing along the edge of the cement. At a glance, they appeared to be simply Hedera Helix, a common English Ivy. But their leaves were oddly shaped. And there were tiny red flowers when we rescued them. Alas, the flowers vanished."

"They had quite a sweet smell, though. Not like anything we've ever had in the plant club." Martha looked around in case we'd missed them. "Do you really think they took all of them? Whatever for?"

I shrugged. I had no idea that Forgotten Hollow had a plant club, let alone that these three were in it. "Why toss everything if all they wanted were plants? I'm not a great grower of plants, but it seems to me that if that was what they were looking for, they would have only hit the kitchen."

Keith frowned, then shook it off. "Did you have any of the cuttings in your yard?"

"No, I was going to transfer them this week." Betsy watched Keith carefully. "You think they might have been searching for more when they attacked Ralph?" Her fists bunched up.

"They might have. But they didn't hurt him." Keith patted her shoulder.

"I won't be returning that favor. We know there are at least two more attackers at large. Probably an entire gang! *Here*, in Forgotten Hollow!" Betsy was ready to fight.

"Easy, there. We don't know much at all." I looked around the kitchen. "We need to get your place finished, then Jamie's and Martha's. Then we can look at plant gang warfare." I'd never heard of people fighting over plants, but the look that kept crossing Keith's face said we needed to talk alone.

"Excellent point." Betsy nodded like a tiny centurion. "Let's finish, then let's move on."

Once the three had returned to their duties, I moved closer to Keith and kept my voice low. "What do you know about those plants?"

"I'm not sure." He raised his hand before I could respond. "Not trying to be sly, I wouldn't know until I can see and test them. But they sound like something that shouldn't be here. In fact, if it's what I fear, it shouldn't be anywhere off the secure prison planet, Laxtunius."

"Dren," I blurted the TV show swear word louder than intended and froze, waiting to see if anyone would come to see what the shout was about. Laxtunius was mostly a giant salt mine, but had a few temperate areas. It was also the last place Darius had been before he escaped to Earth.

With Lucie.

# Chapter Thirteen

"I believe we will have much to discuss." Keith shook his head. "But let's finish this."

Keith wasn't a jinn, but he could almost move as fast as one. We had our areas picked up and displayed on the counters in a few minutes.

We walked out just as Jamie and Martha finished the front room.

"Nothing missing from here that we can tell." Jamie looked around the neat room with a nod.

"And we're here almost every evening," Martha added.

"Same for my rooms." Betsy had showered and changed clothes. Mostly, she kept to the same outfit when she wasn't in all black, skulking about. In this case, faded jeans and a plaid shirt over a wild t-shirt of a squirrel with a flamethrower. "Let's lock up and go to Jamie's, she's closest."

We trooped out to Keith's van, and Keith spoke to Horace. The cop nodded to all of us, then headed out.

The ride to Jamie's was far more silent than the one to Betsy's. The enormity of what had happened seemed to be hitting the three.

"I can't believe they took our mystery vines," Jamie muttered as we got out of the van.

They'd been stalked, kidnapped, knocked out by some unknown compound, had their homes trashed, but they were worried about some vines. I shook my head as we went into Jamie's home.

It might just be because Jamie had a lot fewer belongings than Betsy, at least at first glance. But her place seemed to be less disturbed.

All three ladies ran to the kitchen. And started swearing.

"My clippings are gone as well." Jamie sorted through the even larger collection of small plants in her kitchen window. "I'd like to do a walk-through, take photos, of course, but I can fix things later." She quickly processed things, then also went to shower and change.

We took the obligatory photos, then went to Martha's. Her home was a massive Victorian near the center of town. A style I admired, but really hoped we didn't have to do a full check-and-straighten on.

Three cars beside a retired police volunteer car waited out front, and five people came running out of the extra cars to hug Martha.

"Her family?" None of them spoke much about family.

"No, her staff." Jamie grinned. "But they're pretty much family. Martha doesn't act it, but she's rich. Her late husband left her a lot of money, and she already had plenty."

That was interesting. I liked all three ladies, but none of them acted affluent.

Keith didn't appear surprised at the house or the staff now linking arms as they escorted Martha up the steps to the front door. Then again, he'd lived in Forgotten Hollow for forty years.

The house was grand, even tossed about as it was; it was seriously impressive. We'd known what to expect, but Martha's crew didn't. All five gasped and ran into the huge front room.

"Hold up, please." Martha raised her hands. "We need full photos of everything first. The police took some, but you never know what might have been missed. My friends and I will be going to look at the greenhouse, then after a shower and a change, we'll be heading back out. I'll fill you all in tonight." She flashed them a warm smile, then led us toward the back.

We passed the kitchen and continued to an attached green-house, one that was about the size of my entire cottage. It was full of plants, along with tiny twinkle lights and statues of faeries, dragons, and other wee creatures. It also had benches and lounge chairs for relaxing.

I might just ask her if I could come hang out here for a while once we got through this. I grew up on a lush greenbelt planet. I hadn't realized how much I missed it until this moment.

Martha jogged past the tipped-over chairs to the far back, swearing under her breath as she did so.

Her swearing grew louder and far more inventive when she reached the far end. "They took mine as well. I will have my revenge if they've hurt them!"

Martha was the most kindly and grandmotherly of the three, but neither of those terms applied to her right now.

"We will get our revenge." Betsy laughed as her stomach rumbled. "But why don't you go shower? You'll feel better. Then I think we need to go to Hannah's Diner and get some real food. I need a meal, early dinner, late lunch, don't care. We can't fight back on hospital food and snacks."

Keith shrugged. "I'd argue about the snacks part, but agreed."

I was still full from my turkey sandwich from home, but I wouldn't say no to going back there. My appetite might kick in when I smelled the food.

The other two finally coaxed Martha away from the green-house, and we went into the front room to wait. Her staff had already moved to another room.

"This place is lovely." I settled in on a sofa that looked ornate but was extremely comfortable. "Nothing against your houses, or mine, but why don't you hang out here?"

Jamie sighed as she took over an overstuffed chair. "It is amazing, isn't it? Sadly, the ghosts don't always tolerate a lot of visitors."

"I'm surprised they didn't stop the intruders, to be honest," Betsy added.

"Ghosts?" Keith smiled. "I'd heard that rumor, but are you sure? Sometimes these older places shift and move."

"Oh, there are ghosts. At least two, possibly more. We tried to have a séance here years ago, to find out what they needed. Scared the psychic we brought in so badly he practically ran out of town." Betsy shrugged. "They aren't malevolent, just set in their ways. I do hope they are okay after the invasion."

Jamie and Betsy seemed so sincere that I didn't point out that ghosts weren't real. Then I saw Keith's scowl. It was far too akin to the one he had when we first heard about the vines.

Ghosts *were* real, and from his face, they weren't supposed to be on this planet either. Great.

I just wanted to run out my time here, clear my probation, and return to my normal life. Whatever that was going to be.

Martha came down looking much happier. "Let's go! I need some waffles."

Keith drove us to Hannah's Diner. Like this morning, a table right near the front was filled with black suits. Only five this time. I glanced over while we waited to be seated, but I honestly couldn't tell if any of them were the same ones from this morning or not.

Hannah came jogging out with five menus. "Ladies! I'm so glad that you're safe! Dinner for you is on the house today." She glanced at the five in black, scowled, and marched to the opposite end of the restaurant. "This is as far from them as I can seat you. But they should leave soon. They have important meetings tonight, you know." She sighed and handed out the menus.

"Is it always the same group?" Maybe it was just me who couldn't tell them apart.

"Yes...wait." Hannah scowled and leaned back so she could see the black suited people better. "No? Dang, I couldn't tell you, and up until this moment, I would have said I could. It's usually a similar number of them. Ten was the largest group, three the smallest. I think this is a different group from this morning."

"You could ask them to leave," Keith said. "This *is* your restaurant."

She sighed. "I know. And if they ever do anything besides annoying me by existing, I would. But I'm trying to be tolerant. They are always neat, pay promptly once the bill is served, and tip well. They just bug the heck out of me. And my staff." She glared at them for a few more moments, then turned back. "Drinks?"

Keith took coffee, the ladies and I asked for tea.

It was just before four, but whatever I didn't eat here, I could reheat later.

Hannah bustled out with water and the hot drinks. Then she leaned in closer to me. "I heard about your barn this morning. Do you think one of the ones who had been here this morning was the dead one?" She glanced toward the black suits.

"I'm not sure. Getting a good look at them is hard, and the one in my barn was face down."

Keith was next to me and gave a grim nod. "They're hard to tell apart. The body was of a blond man, but that still leaves a lot of them."

Hannah nodded. "I'll make a point of watching them more this week. Although one of my staff mentioned overhearing a group of them saying this retreat was being extended. Possibly another full week. Or longer." Her scowl made it clear what she thought of that.

And it was reflected by all the faces around me.

"They've never extended their time." Betsy nodded to Jamie and Martha. "Since we know that Jack won't be happy with us nosing around our case, maybe we should go up near the Grasshopper and see what's afoot up there." She turned to me. "Unless you want us to investigate around your place?"

I hoped my fear of that didn't show. "No, thank you. I really need to go through my late cousin's belongings. They're taking up my guest room." I'd rather the three weren't investigating anything, but if anyone tried to keep them away from the Grasshopper and the weird retreat going on there, they'd sneak out anyway.

Besides, I really did need to get Darius's stuff out of my cottage.

Hannah continued to watch the black suits as she took our orders—Betsy, Jamie, and Martha almost ordered as much as Keith. I felt like I might need to step up my food game down the line if I was going to keep hanging out with them.

Betsy was telling stories about the Old Hollow and was just getting into the spooky parts when shouting came from the front of the restaurant.

It was the group of black suits.

Three of them were standing and yelling at the other two. They were loud enough to cause attention, but not loud enough to understand their words.

"Traitor!"

That word was loud enough. It came from a woman with tan skin and short blonde hair who was standing and seemed to be aimed at a seated woman with deep red hair. Then the blonde woman spat at the red-haired one and ran out.

The rest got up to follow her, and a thin, dark man left a pile of money on their table before he followed them.

Hannah ran over, but they were gone. She took the wad of bills, and her scowl deepened. After a few words to her busboy, she came over to us, still holding the money.

"They paid it exactly, tip and all."

Keith tilted his head. "Isn't that good?"

Hannah shook her head. "They hadn't been given their bill yet. In a few seconds, that man calculated their bill, tax, and tip exactly. That's not normal."

# Chapter Fourteen

We looked at each other at Hannah's comment. Then she gave a nod and marched back to the kitchen.

"That's odd, right? I know I couldn't do that, and I was pretty good at math." Jamie shook her head. Betsy had told me that Jamie was a master electrician, well, a retired one. I knew enough about this world to know that meant she definitely had serious math skills.

Keith looked over to the table the black suits had been seated at, but the busboy had already cleared all of the dishes. "That's extremely odd. But then everything about them is odd. Do you three mind if I join you on your surveillance after we finish here and drop off Ceian? I would like to see what's going on."

I had a feeling a few more items just went onto the need to talk to Keith in private list.

"Actually, I'm fine with riding home. I could use the workout with all I've eaten today." I grinned as Hannah and a waiter brought over massive piles of food. "And will eat."

"That's what I like to hear. Healthy bodies and a healthy appetite." Hannah waited until we started eating, then smiled and went to seat a couple.

Betsy smiled up at Keith. "We would be honored to have such a charming escort."

I smiled at the two. "Have these business people always been this troublesome? I know Alice said she might not have agreed to come up here right now if she'd known they were here."

"They're always obnoxious," Jamie said and waved her fork around. "But usually they come through town, remind us that we're just bumpkins, and go back to their hotel. This time it's like they're looking for something in town. And for one of them to turn up murdered? That's going beyond their normal behavior."

"And what was their connection to you all being kidnapped? Or at least the one who turned up dead?" I didn't mind a mystery or two, but this one was hitting me on many levels.

Martha nodded. "And your cat and goat. I do hope they're both okay?"

"They're fine, thank you. Did they grab all of you, my pets included, then one of them turned on the others, the dead body guy objected, he got killed, and they dumped you all in my barn?"

Betsy looked toward where the black suits had been. "It seems ridiculous, but those ones were fighting about something. I doubt most high-level business people spit on each other. At least not in public."

"They do seem more intense this time. I think us going to the Grasshopper is a good idea." Keith turned back to me. "Are you certain you'll be okay biking back?" The tone said something far more than just worry about my bike ride. He knew what my silver bracelets meant. If someone from the Eltrisphere was targeting me, I couldn't fight back magically.

"I'm fine. I'd like to swing by the teahouse on the way home. I know we're stalled until the investigation is done, but I just want to make sure that nothing else has happened to it." I figured enough had happened that a little yellow crime scene tape wasn't going to get to me.

"Oh! We should go too!" Jamie grinned. "I didn't get to see the recent updates. And if some nefarious person has returned, it would be better with more of us."

I sighed. From the looks around me, arguing was pointless. Even Keith shrugged.

"That would be fine, but we're just popping in, not a long visit." I turned to Keith; I'd seen on those cop shows that they didn't like their crime scenes tampered with. But this was my crime scene. "Will they mind?"

He winced. "Technically, yeah. If the feds were here, definitely. But they aren't here yet, and might not be coming from what little I heard. And you might have left something valuable or important in your shop. Your friends are helping you find it." He grinned. He might work for the police, but he wasn't one.

Hannah came by for any last fill-ups, then hugged all of us, and we left.

"I can drive everyone." Keith stood near the small diner parking lot.

"We're supposed to be less noticeable, right?" I nodded to his van. "You might want to think of parking a bit away from the hotel later as well."

Betsy smiled and patted his arm. "It's a lovely van, but everyone knows it's yours, and it's hard to miss. I won't insist on us going in disguise, but I agree with Ceian. We'll park a ways off at the hotel when we go and walk to the teahouse now."

He shrugged, and we continued down the block.

"Why do you think the feds might not be coming?" Betsy kept her voice down, but few folks were on the street right now.

"Unfortunately, I'm not privy to that and only heard a vague reference. I do know those pipe bombs were extremely crude. Probably below the fed level of concern, although they appeared to be sneakier bombs originally. And from what I also heard, no news on the men behind it. One of the trucks was caught on a security camera down in Larkspur, but they didn't get a full license plate."

I sighed. "They didn't seem bright, but it could have been a ruse. Still, they've most likely all left the area. I just wish I knew if there was a connection to you three being grabbed along with Tiberius and Lucie. I don't want everyone I know to be targets. Especially since I don't know why."

"Oh, we're prepared now." Betsy was far too cocky for me not to turn around.

All three of them pulled out chunky little keychains. Two items hung on them instead of keys.

"An alarm and pepper spray. No one is grabbing us again. And Ralph is putting an alarm on my house and will do Jamie's next." She reached into her other pocket. "And I have these, if I need them." She held up a pair of brass knuckles.

"I'm having my alarm updated. My housekeeper said it was triggered when they ransacked the place, but the call didn't go to the police." Martha scowled. "I am extremely glad that the crew had the day off."

"You all still need to be careful. Especially around any of those black suits. We don't know who's behind this." I knew Betsy thought she was fierce, but she didn't know what they might be up against.

Betsy's smile dropped. "You be careful too. They went after your friends and your teahouse, but they could be targeting you directly next."

"Or they're different attacks." Jamie shrugged. "Just no way to know, really."

The conversation dropped as we saw my teahouse. 'The Fainting Goat Tea and Spice' sign that made me so happy before all of this just made me sad.

Betsy grabbed me in a tight hug. "This will be okay. You're not the reason for these attacks. Someone might be targeting you, but there's no way that you did anything to deserve it. Trust me, I'm an excellent judge of character."

I opened my mouth to argue, then shut it. I had far too many examples of my own lack of good judgment to even think of arguing. "Thank you."

With that fortification, I marched up to my teahouse and ducked under the yellow crime tape. Everything outside looked as it should this round, and I was sure that given enough time, I wouldn't be sad when I saw the sign. I unlocked the door and hit the lights. I might have held my breath in case there were more problems.

"See? Looks just fine." Betsy darted in and scurried to the kitchen. "Everything is fine here!" She yelled out through the swinging door. That was going to be her domain once we were cleared to open. I'd take her word on the state of things.

I went over to the spice shop side and frowned. Jars weren't broken on my wall display, but they were in complete disarray. Had they been this way before and I hadn't noticed? I had been in a state of shock at the time.

Keith might not mentally spy on his friends, but he was a strong empath. "Were they like that before?"

"I don't know." I stomped to the shelves. All of my neat rows were messed up. Nothing appeared broken, but it would be a while before I noticed if anything was missing. "Who breaks into a shop to mess up their shelving? Right before they try to blow it up?" As much as I wanted to sort them now, I knew us being here longer would be pushing things if the cops showed up. Or with my luck, Jack did a drive-by.

I straightened the jars enough to pull them from the edge, then we searched the rest of the place. Everything else looked ready and waiting.

Betsy came out of the kitchen as we finished. "We will need to wash everything before we open. Who knows what the dishes, pans, and surfaces were exposed to when those men were here."

"Agreed." I was surprised I hadn't thought of that immediately. Betsy had once owned a small deli before she moved to Forgotten Hollow.

I did one final pass through the entire place. I had a small office in the back, but nothing was touched that I could tell. Then I triple checked the back door and all of the windows. Finally, I nodded to my friends. "*Now* we can go." As I locked the door, I contemplated asking Betsy if Ralph could alarm the teahouse and shop. It might be a good idea to do my house as well, but there was so much weirdness there that I couldn't let him or anyone on this planet know about.

We all seemed lost in our own thoughts as we walked back to the diner. Keith took my bike off his van, and I turned to the three ladies.

"Stay out of trouble, you three. I need everyone to stay safe for a bit." There were way too many bad things happening; I needed to know they were protected.

"You too. You're not invincible, you know." Betsy gave me her sternest look. "We'll keep you updated if we find out anything."

The concern that flashed through my mind at her words, alarmingly similar to what she said before she and the others were kidnapped, must have shown on my face as she ran over for a tight hug.

"We'll be fine." She pulled back to see my face. "Really."

"I'll make sure they stay safe. Promise." The seriousness of Keith's face spoke to his being willing to do anything, even risk magic, to protect these three.

I smiled at both of them. Knowing that Keith was along and willing to risk everything to guard them made me feel better.

"I'll be home going through those belongings from my cousin." As much as I wanted to get those things out of my house, going on an adventure sounded more appealing. But leaving Tiberius and Lucie locked up for much longer probably wasn't the best idea.

And with my luck, Darius had something that would explode in the boxes.

That definitely sped up my bike ride once I was out of sight of the town.

I slowed down as I approached my street, and I slowed even more when I saw a car with red and blue flashing lights in my driveway.

# Chapter Fifteen

I knew that cop car, Jack Lanclin. But why the flashing lights? Then they turned off. A moment later, back on. The siren blurted out, then stopped.

I got off my bike and walked down the driveway.

Jack was pissed. From his focus on his car keys, it wasn't at me. "What's wrong with your car?"

He gave a few sharp swear words and hit more buttons. "I have no idea. It was fine until I pulled up here. We have some information about the attack on your teahouse. I'll drop my car at the shop, then come back tomorrow."

My right hand twitched toward his keys. "Can I see? Sometimes gizmos like me." True in my universe, but not demonstrated at all here. Yet my hand kept twitching. And I wanted any information on my teahouse now, not tomorrow, when he might get too busy.

He shrugged. "Sure. But it's not..." He cut himself off the moment the keys were in my hand. The alarm had been warm to the touch, but cooled and quieted immediately.

I thought I felt a slight nudge of magic, but again, my bracelets were still secure. "Here ya go. Probably still want to check it out. What news do you have?"

He glared at his keys and his car, then dropped his keys in his pocket. "Can we go inside? I feel conspicuous with the noise it was making before."

"Sure." I sounded more confident than I felt. Tiberius and Lucie had been locked up for hours. "Due to circumstances, I left the animals locked up. The house might be a mess. But they're both housebroken." I added the last as I sent a silent prayer and unlocked the front door. "Please come inside, Detective Lanclin." It felt stiff, but I wanted Xieth to know I had company. Just in case he was eavesdropping. He'd been so twitchy, I didn't want him blasting Jack by accident.

"Even the goat?" He sounded dubious at that.

"Yep. He came to me that way." Just easier not to explain it.

Jack nodded but didn't push it. I knew I'd explained it to him, probably awkwardly, when we first met; luckily, he recalled it now, or didn't care.

The front room looked neat and animal-free, and my landscape painting was in place. Not that it meant Xieth couldn't eavesdrop. I hoped Keith could find a way to block the spying soon.

"They must be asleep. Let me just check, have a seat." Normally, I wouldn't go looking for them. But a trigger of panic hit me right after happiness at the living room not being trashed.

Both of them were in my bedroom, but neither was asleep. Tiberius had dragged his blankets in and was on the floor, and Lucie had taken over my pillows. They opened their eyes when I walked in.

Tiberius opened his mouth to speak, but I quickly shook my head and pointed to the living room. "It's fine, they're both asleep," I called back to Jack. I nodded to them and slightly shut my door.

Jack raised an eyebrow. "You let them sleep in your bedroom?"

I got a glass of water for myself; Jack waved off one for himself. "They usually have the second bedroom, but it has those boxes in it." I sat and gave him my best hopeful look. "Please tell me there is good news about my teahouse?"

Jack's eyes went wide, and he seemed transfixed. "Have your eyes always been that amazing shade of green? I feel like I could fall into them." His voice was so soft that I barely heard him.

I pulled back and started blinking rapidly. I didn't feel a surge of magic that time, but that was an extremely unnatural response for Jack.

He gave a few blinks himself and leaned back. "Sorry, I'm not sure what I just said."

There was enough confusion on his face that I believed him. Whatever misfiring spell hit him, it took away the memory as well. I hoped that Xieth hadn't been listening in, or if he was, he couldn't pick up on Jack's soft words.

That I heard them was disturbing enough.

"I didn't hear it. Maybe it was about your car?" I gave him a less beguiling smile; jinn could charm people. Some of them. My charm abilities had never been strong, and nothing should have gotten through those bracelets. I touched my right bracelet. Nope, felt cool like normal.

He smiled. "It could be. I think I will have that glass of water, if you don't mind."

I wanted him to tell me about my teahouse, but I had offered the water. I filled it and slid the glass over, making sure our hands didn't touch. I normally wouldn't worry, but he'd been hit with a charm spell from somewhere. "About my teahouse?"

"Still no luck on finding the men behind it, or who hired them. It's believed that they're long out of town at this point. None of *them* were locals."

"But you believe that whoever hired them for the job is local? Who would hate me enough to do that? I barely talk to anyone, and my teahouse isn't competing with anything else." There was a sterile-looking, high-tech coffee shop in town, A Lotta Joe. But it wasn't anything close to my teahouse in what they served or ambiance, aside from we both would be serving warm beverages.

"I know. And we haven't found any indication as to who was behind it. But it's felt that it was someone local. They might not have even spoken to you before."

"You think someone wants my teahouse gone?" As much as the recent drama had distracted me from the bottom line of my life here, the fact was that I needed to fit in. Be a functioning member of this world, and then I'd win my freedom and could leave.

Losing my teahouse would cause some major problems in that. My throat went dry. Was that it? Someone besides Keith knew who I was and why I was here. Could they be trying to make sure that I never finished my parole? If this business didn't work, I could be locked up in my bottle again.

"I have no idea, nor does anyone else. The feds decided it wasn't a case for them, but made a file for it. One of their analysts did say they believed the person behind it was local. The good news is that you can open a week from today. They want to give it a few more days to make sure nothing pops up. We'll be taking the crime tape off tomorrow."

I was happy, but also dismayed at waiting another week. I sighed. "They don't think we'll find who was behind it."

He shrugged, but the look on his face said he agreed with my statement. "There's no way to know. We keep track of all cold cases. You might want to invest in an alarm on the teahouse, though, just for your own peace of mind."

"I was going to ask Betsy to have her handyman install one." I wasn't happy at all about someone in town going that far to try to destroy my teahouse and then remaining free.

"What's wrong? I expected you'd be happy."

"I am, thank you. It's just going to be weird walking down the street, shopping, eating out, not knowing who it was. And wondering why they hate me or my teahouse."

He finished his water. "I get it, even in a small town like this, police aren't always people's favorites. Until they need us. But most of this town is good, don't forget that." He got to his feet.

"Thanks. And thank you for coming out here to tell me. I should go through the boxes from that storage crate. My animals need the room back." I walked him to the door. "Oh! When is my barn going to be cleared?"

I hadn't gone over there when I came home, but the yellow tape was now gone.

"Now." Jack flashed a grin. "You're welcome. The body was confirmed as one of the visiting businessmen staying at the Grasshopper, and it was clearly a body dump in your barn. His bosses said he'd been having some money issues and might have been involved with the wrong people. The murder is still under investigation, but there was nothing else forensics could gather from your barn. There was also no connection to the kidnappings." He paused in the doorway and turned. "Call me...if you need anything." The odd pause indicated he'd intended to say something else. "I'd better drop my car in for a checkup. Good night." He practically ran to his car. This time the alarm stayed silent.

I left the front door open for Tiberius and Lucie. I still didn't want them leaving the property, but they'd been cooped up for a while.

That was weird. Someone cast a charm spell on Jack, a delayed one would be my guess, as I knew that I hadn't done it. I wouldn't lie; I had a crush on him when he first caught Tiberius and me on our unceremonious arrival two months ago. But then he took off for parts unknown, and I realized the last thing I needed here, aside from people attacking my teahouse, my friends, or my pets, was an ill-fated love interest.

I walked into my bedroom and opened the door. "He's gone, and the barn's open again. Go out and play, just please stay on the property tonight."

"Thank all!" Tiberius tore past me and out the front door.

"You can go too," I said to Lucie, who was casually cleaning his left front paw.

"I think I'd rather see what that jerk Darius had in those boxes. He made sure I didn't bring anything I found in India along when we left. But he had a storage container? It's a good thing he's already dead." He jumped off my bed and stalked to the closed second bedroom door. "Shall we?"

I was going to ask Lucie about the missing vines that Betsy and the other two found that Keith said were from Laxtunius, but I'd rather wait until I had more information. Not to mention that it fell under the 'not talking about inside the house' rule.

My mental list of those items was getting longer. Keith needed to block Xieth's eavesdropping before I slipped up.

"He packed all of these things, shipped them to Canada, and then forwarded them here, all without you noticing?" Cats, even Eltrisian ones, didn't always take action if it didn't suit them, but they noticed a lot.

Lucie's tail lashed about violently, and he nudged the door shut. "He was using magic to keep me from noticing. Said he was just working some low spells on the locals. Which I knew was wrong. But I now believe he was spelling me. *Me*!" He took a swipe at his collar.

Another thing that I wanted to speak to him about, but outside the house. Shutting the door was a good idea, but we had no idea of what Xieth could still hear.

"Well, hopefully you can tell me if anything in here is dangerous." My theory was that Darius had been gathering things to sell, most likely in the black markets of the Eltrisphere. Lucie might not have known about the shipment, and forwarding from Canada to here, but he probably had seen many of the items that Darius packed.

There wasn't any labeling or system to the boxes that I could tell, so I grabbed the first box in front of me. It was sealed with enough tape that it took a bit for my box cutter to work through.

"I thought the cops went through these?" Lucie stayed far enough away to watch and still be out of any mishaps. I wasn't sure if he was worried about possible explosives in the boxes or my wielding the box cutter.

"They said they scanned them, but not for what." A weird, multi-international shipment that arrived after the sender had been murdered, and was the suspect in another murder, and the cops didn't open the boxes? "Maybe this tape is from the cops. I don't see Darius being this thorough." The tape finally surrendered.

"True. He was a slacker and a con man. Plus, we'd had to leave India pretty quickly when whatever scam he was working blew up." Lucie leaned closer to the box.

"That's him all right." I pulled out the first thing in the box. A sealed, magical missive. Even if the cops had opened this box, they wouldn't have even known this was there. My swearing switched into the ten languages I knew when I saw the name it was addressed to.

Me.

# Chapter Sixteen

"Ceianthia Da Hithjan." Lucie peered at the envelope. "That's kinda short for a full name for a jinn."

"We don't let most people know our full names. This was what Darius knew before I realized what an ass he was." I stared at the envelope. "How long ago were you in India?" Part of me wanted to destroy the letter without reading it, once my mind started putting things together.

Destruction that I couldn't do without magic. Even burning a magic missive like this would simply cause it to come back in pristine condition.

Lucie looked up as he muttered out loud, counting off time. "I've been here for a little over three months. We were in Canada for about four weeks, more or less. So, four months? Maybe five? Something like that." His tail started lashing as he made the same connection that I had.

"I wasn't even out of my bottle lock up at that time."

"How did he know you'd be here?"

We both spoke at the same time.

"This isn't good. How did that lousy, cheating con man know that I would be getting paroled before I did? And to where? No one is supposed to know where the parolees are until we're granted freedom. After the parole." Panic collided with Xieth's recent odd behavior, and that someone on Earth knew who and what I was. "What should I do?" If I told Xieth, either he was in on it and he'd lock me up or have me killed. If he wasn't in on it, he'd pull my parole so fast I wouldn't know what hit me.

"Ceian? Ceian? Hello?" Lucie was almost shouting as I envisioned another hundred years, or longer, in my bottle.

"What?" I spun around.

"I know without magic you can't destroy that thing, but you could end up not being able to read it soon."

I glanced down. I'd twisted the envelope so badly it looked like a piece of rope. I tried to fix it. "It's a bit better. Thanks for stopping me. I guess I need to open it and worry about why he thought I would be here later." Not going to be as easy as I made it sound; I currently wanted to get gloriously drunk and just forget everything.

My hands shook as I touched the edge of the envelope to let the spell sense it was me. There were a bunch of papers inside, and a note on top in Darius's annoyingly neat handwriting. I started reading.

"Out loud, please. I need to know how screwed I am, too." Again, Lucie's tail lashed about violently, and his ears were flat.

"Fine. Dear Ceian," Just saying that almost made me ill. "If you're reading this, then it means I'm dead. I was planning on meeting you once you got here and making everything up to you. I have a cat with me, Lucie. He will find you, as I told him to protect you."

"What?! That stinking rat bastard never mentioned you once! Never! He didn't send me, he ditched me a few days before you showed up—probably was dead, but I didn't know it then. I followed you because cats have keen noses; I knew you were a jinn." His tail was now puffed up, and his back was arched.

"Don't worry, I believe you. I don't know what Darius's plan was, though." I sighed and continued reading out loud. "There are dangerous games taking place in the Eltrisphere, ones that could shake the entire empire. I came here for answers and to rescue you. I never meant for them to believe you were involved in the robberies. But I wasn't able to save you." I looked at Lucie, and he made a hacking motion like he was coughing up a hairball.

"He's so full of it. Even reading this is making me ill." I flipped the paper over; it was only halfway on the other side. Thank the goddess. "Oh, ick."

"What now?" Lucie leaned closer.

"He signed it with 'love and adoration, your Darius'." I shivered. "I need to get my magic back so that I can destroy this thing."

"Agreed. I can't wait to have this collar off my neck. Maybe you should finish reading the note so we can move on to the stuff?"

My visions of how I would destroy the letter, the closest I could get to killing Darius now that someone beat me to it, were put on hold, and I flipped back to the front of the letter.

"While waiting for your arrival on this planet, I searched to find you gifts that might remind you of home. Lucie and I had grand adventures in a land called India, as well as a few side trips to a place called Egypt."

"Wait, what? *We* never went to Egypt. I asked him to go a bunch of times. They used to worship cats there—some of that mojo has to still be around. But he did leave me for days at a time. Bastard."

Only his tail tip twitched now; I figured the rest of the tail was exhausted at this point.

I tilted my head to make sure he was done, then continued. "I know that your heart is broken, both that you spent so long in your bottle and that I am now dead." I almost choked on that one. "Only because that means I can't kill you myself."

"I would have helped you with that." Lucie settled down and hunched over his front paws. His ears were still flat.

"Things are happening in the Eltrisphere, as I said. Dark and dangerous things. I will tell you in the next letter, but I wanted you to know how much I never forgot what we had." I stopped reading and flipped the page. "The rest is a bunch of made-up stories about things we never did before I got caught." I looked at the pile of boxes that suddenly seemed much larger. "He must have another note in there somewhere."

"What are those extra pages?"

"Good point, it's been a really long day. I'm not thinking well right now." I flipped through the pages. All of them were documents or printouts from an Earth computer, but gathered from the infinity web, judging by the small code on the bottom of each one.

"Not a single one is from him. But he wanted me to have them, so they might tie into something." I put the papers and his note in the back of the small filing cabinet attached to the desk in this room.

Annoying papers out of the way, I dug into the box I'd opened. It was filled with chimes. There were at least a dozen, and all were different. I loved chimes, or I had in the past, but that might change now. And if tuned properly, strong magic users could make chimes become weapons. They could even kill.

"What was he planning on doing with these things?" I gently put them back in their box, carefully avoiding making them ring. Darius wasn't a strong magic user, but there was a chance that he'd already messed with these. I folded the box flaps over each other, taped them, dug out a red marker from the desk, and put a big 'X' on all sides. This was one box that I couldn't donate to charity. At least until I got my magic back and could verify that he hadn't spelled the chimes.

Lucie sniffed the closed box. "Resale off planet, as far as I know. He'd shown me a few things he said we could sell once we got back, but then implied he'd left them all behind when we fled India."

"Let's get this done." I moved the chime box over to a corner and sliced open the box that had been under it. It was a large box and had seen better days. It also had stamps from at least five countries slapped on it.

And it was addressed to Darius in India, or rather, to Cyber Kondle. I'd had to backpedal when I'd called him Darius in front of Jack the first time. I'd told him and Betsy that Darius was a nickname.

"Do you know what he ordered?" I'd hoped that Lucie would be helpful with this stuff. Unfortunately, like everyone else in his life, it seemed that Darius kept a lot from him as well.

"No. How did he get something that big delivered to our house without me noticing? Seriously?!"

"Magic, most likely. This is already getting old." I folded back the flaps. "An anvil? This box wasn't heavy enough to be an anvil. And why would he have ordered one?" I rapped my knuckle on it, but instead of metal, it was spongy. "A *rubber* anvil?" I'd figured on some weirdness in these boxes, but this was off to an impressive start.

"A rubber what?" Lucie peered into the box. He tentatively reached out a paw to it, smacked it, then pulled back. "Yup, that's what it is."

"Why? And this thing bounced around the entire globe for months, according to these stamps, maybe longer." I narrowed my eyes as Lucie began studying other boxes. "You know something you're not saying. What is this, who wants it, and why was it being mailed around this forsaken planet? Darius didn't know anyone on this planet; he couldn't have.... You and Darius weren't the only escapees from the Eltrisphere on Earth." It wasn't a question, and it tied in uncomfortably with my current situation. Keith wasn't a prisoner, and hopefully not a criminal. But it didn't mean that whoever had left me that note, and freed my friends, wasn't wanted by one of the Eltrisphere governments.

"Okay, fine. There's a secret passage to Earth used by people who might not want to be in the Eltrisphere for various reasons. Darius heard about it; he not only had the government after him, but a bunch of less-than-savory elements that he'd pissed off." Tail lash.

"Which he failed to tell me about until after we'd escaped the salt mines in Laxtunius, by the way. That is a magic anvil and helps protect magic users from being detected while they're on Earth. Once the user has gained the ability to block their magic on their own, it's sent to the next person on the list."

And they disguised it as a toy anvil? I closed my eyes. If I thought about everything in these boxes too much, I'd never get through them. "Who's next on the list for this thing?"

"No idea. Darius never figured out how to make it work when we were in India. According to him, he sent it away when we fled."

"So, someone, or someones, knows Darius had this last?" I didn't need a bunch of escaped criminals descending on Forgotten Hollow. Providing they weren't here already.

"Yes. Unless he told them he sent it away as well. Maybe the next person's name is somewhere in these boxes?"

I closed the box and sealed it. And added the red 'X' to it. "No. I am not mailing anything to any criminals. I am trying to finish my time here and leave."

He shrugged. "Moving on."

Lucie might not be worried about a bunch of criminals, possibly armed with magic, looking for us. But I was worried enough for both of us.

# Chapter Seventeen

After an hour of going through six more boxes, still having ten more to open, and shoving all but two of those boxes into the 'can't give away' pile. I was ready to go to bed.

It had been an extremely long day, and Betsy and her gang would be here early in the morning with the report of their investigation.

I needed downtime and a lot of sleep before then. However, while rest was good, mentally sorting some things out would be better. I was a professional gladiator, not a serious thinker. But right now, my brain was the only thing getting me out of this mess.

"Keep going, maybe there's something good in those." Lucie waved a paw at the remaining unopened boxes.

"We've found two boxes of unworn clothes, which are going to be donated, and a bunch of potentially dangerous junk that Xieth will have to do something with. Not to mention that anvil. I seriously doubt Darius had anything we can use or won't need to be destroyed by magic." I got to my feet, stretched, and almost fell over. It was later than I thought.

"But there could be riches." Lucie leaned toward the boxes with a paw raised and a single claw extended.

"No. We have tomorrow, and I'm exhausted. It's time for bed." That didn't mean much to Lucie; like most cats, he slept whenever he wanted.

I chased him out of the guest room and locked the door. Tiberius was back inside, so I locked up the house and went to bed.

***

I actually woke up feeling better. Until I recalled all of my current problems. With a sigh and a lot of grumbling, I let Tiberius outside, then showered, changed, and ate breakfast.

Then Lucie started scratching to be let out. He didn't leave, but Tiberius was running around the far side of the yard. Normally, nothing to worry about. With the way things were going recently, it could be a lot to be worried about.

Lucie followed me outside.

To see a fierce centurion being chased by five black and tan puppies. Then I realized that he was playing with them as they ran.

That was far more surprising than anything found in those boxes. I hadn't known Tiberius *could* play. It might get him booted from the Legion. Being a goat was letting new sides of him show.

Lucie stayed back, but it wasn't long before the puppies noticed him and raced his way.

"Nope!" Lucie tore back inside the house and managed to kick the door shut.

An odd, high-pitched whistle froze the puppies in their tracks.

All five froze, then answered back, and I swore I heard, "Coming" in Sihlia.

They turned to Tiberius, "Thank you!" Also in Sihlia. Then raced to the fence between my place and the abandoned lot next door.

"Making friends with the puppies? I thought they scared you?" I asked as Tiberius walked over to me.

"Ha." He snorted and tossed his head as if to remind me of his horns. "I wasn't scared of them; they simply startled me before. We talked this time, and they said you rescued their mother, and she said we were to be protected because of it." His smug look indicated that he'd done something to save Brutus. Maybe association counted in a centurion's thinking.

I'd figured Brutus, incorrectly named, was their mother. Unless there was a flood of huge black and tan Eltrisian dogs on the planet. It might be nice to have her as a neighbor if things went badly.

Or worse than they already were.

"Meet me in the barn, we need to talk. Let me get Lucie." I needed them to know about Keith, and Tiberius needed to know what we'd found so far.

He narrowed his eyes for a moment, then shrugged and trotted to the barn.

I hadn't asked if I could share Keith's information, and I probably should have. But these two were as close as I had to family right now. If something did happen to me, I wanted them to know who to go to.

Lucie was on his cat perch near the front window, lashing his tail.

"You know that tail is going to fall off eventually if you keep doing that, right?"

"I'll get a new one. Are they gone?" He still sounded cranky, but his tail slowed.

"Yes, we need to do some stuff in the barn. I fear that the cops left it a mess." A lie, but spoken as an unconfirmed fear, it couldn't choke me. It wouldn't be a great idea to say we needed to talk about things Xieth shouldn't hear. Right in the house he might be spying on.

"I have important things to do around town, you know." He paused as I tilted my head toward the landscape painting. "But I'm part of this group, so I'd better earn my keep, eh? Let's go!" His jump from his cat tower almost made it to the open door.

I followed and made sure to lock the door behind me. Paranoia was a good idea right now.

Tiberius was stomping around inside the barn, sniffing the areas the police had been examining.

"There's a bunch of chemical smells, but I also smell myself. Both as me and as a goat lying here."

"You were an unconscious goat when we found you. I'd hoped that meant you didn't change when they grabbed you." This could be going from bad to worse.

"Not likely." Lucie gave a few sniffs. "I smell him as both too."

Tiberius marched around a few more moments, then gave a goat shrug. "Maybe that's why they released us, they knew better than to mess with a centurion."

Lucie snorted with laughter and then jumped up on a rafter.

"You are quite impressive in your normal form, but I think they released you because someone killed the guy behind it all. Or one of them. And that someone already seems too aware of who I am, so now they know about you as well." Another thought bounced around my head. "I received a ransom phone call before you were all brought back. And they didn't know that you and Lucie weren't regular Earth animals. They also demanded the Stone of Zalianthia for your release." That was weird. They wanted a rare Eltrisphere gem, but didn't know what Lucie and Tiberius were.

"What? You have *that*?" Lucie almost fell off his rafter with his screech. "It's in that bottle, isn't it?"

Both Tiberius and I gave him the same look of annoyance.

"I don't have it. I have never had it, and do NOT think about trying to force your way into my bottle." Jinn bottles were sealed to only be entered by the jinn or people they brought in with them. But I didn't trust Lucie. At all.

"The bigger question, aside from fantasy stories from a cat who only thinks of himself, is who took us that knew Sihlia?" Tiberius settled on a pile of hay and mindlessly began chewing.

I'd say being a goat made him continuously hungry, but he was most likely that way as a seven-foot-tall centurion.

He didn't wait for either of us to respond. "I'd say that Keith character. I know he's helped you out a few times, Ceian, but there's something off about him."

"That's one of the reasons I needed to speak to you both out here. Xieth's eavesdropping in the living room, so we never know when he's listening." I took a deep breath. It made sense in my mind to make sure they knew, but I was second-guessing myself now. "First, you both swear not to speak of this to anyone beyond us three. And never inside the house." Even if we got the eavesdropping covered, I didn't trust Xieth, or the people he worked for, not to find a way around it eventually.

I waited until both nodded. "Keith is from the Eltrisphere." I barely whispered it and hoped he'd forgive me. Stunned silence from both told me they heard me.

"Eh, another one of us escaped criminals? What was he in for? Drugs?" Lucie nodded. "Makes sense."

At least Tiberius appeared surprised. Lucie already knew there were more Eltrisians on Earth than there should be. A lot more.

"Wait, there are criminals here who aren't on parole? We have to tell someone!" Tiberius scrambled to his feet.

"We can't. Not until we know more of what's going on and what Xieth knows. Xieth has been acting weird the past few days, and it probably has something to do with us. Or this planet. Either way, no, Keith isn't an escaped criminal that I know of. He just wanted somewhere new and has been here for forty years. Which does imply there are more vacationing Eltrisians here as well. My point is, I trust him. You two should as well. If something happens to me, find him."

Tiberius glared for a few moments, then went back to his mat of hay. "I'll have to interview him, you know. Out here, just for my own peace of mind. And, of course, for the tribunal that I'm sure will follow when we get back."

"Fine. But let me warn him before you drag him off. Last night, he, Betsy, Martha, and Jamie were investigating the group that might have been behind who grabbed all of you. He'll probably be driving them here soon. So, both of you, be good. Under no circumstances do you let anyone else know about us or him."

I wasn't sure how well I got through. Tiberius had a law-abiding streak longer than his natural wingspan, and Lucie would be looking for angles to play.

A moment later, the distinctive sound of Keith's van came down the driveway.

"Remember, you're a normal cat and goat. You're welcome to stay out here, but until we know for sure who was behind this, don't leave the property." I raised a finger as Lucie opened his mouth to protest. "No. There's a lot of bad going on right now, and I didn't want to admit this, but losing you two scared me badly."

Lucie jumped down from the rafter and rubbed around my legs. "Thanks. I'd miss you too. I promise to stay in the yard." He bounded out of the barn and around the side.

Tiberius looked embarrassed. If someone had asked me what an embarrassed goat would look like a minute ago, I couldn't have told them. But this was it.

"Thanks. You too. I'm going to stay out here. If the puppies come back, I'll send them home for now." He gave me a thoughtful look and went back to his hay.

That was about the best I could hope for at this point, so I left and mostly shut the barn door. He could get out if needed, but I didn't want any of the ladies looking for him.

Keith was opening the side door of his van to let the other two out as Betsy waved and ran over. "Good morning! Anything exciting in those boxes?"

"Sadly, not yet. So full of junk that I only got partially through them." Her face lit up at my words, so I changed direction. "But so emotional, it will take time and solitude." That was close. Even before digging into Darius's boxes, I knew Betsy and her crew had to be kept away—now I *really* knew.

"Darn. About like our adventure last night. But come along, I promised Keith tea and cookies as a reward for escorting us." She linked her arm through mine and we walked to my cottage.

Betsy went right to the kitchen and started putting together tea and scrambling around for cookies. To be honest, she bought most of them and stored them here for our meetings.

"Here you go." I brought the cups, saucers, plates, and cookies to the living room and put them on the coffee table. Betsy followed with two pots of tea.

I wasn't sure I had a second pot, but she knew. Or it was hers, and she smuggled it in when she brought cookies the last time.

"I must make bread for next time." Betsy poured tea. "Nothing against the cookies, you know."

"Your bread is the best," I spoke first, but the other three echoed with similar statements. It wasn't a lie. On my first day here, Betsy introduced herself with three loaves of freshly made bread. I'd been hooked ever since.

"Not to mention, I'm sure once we get open next week, the entire town will be coming in for your bread more than my tea service or bulk spices." I was counting on her baking skills to be a major support for the food and tea side of my teahouse.

"What? Your teahouse has been cleared?" Betsy was in mid-pour, but managed not to spill. "When did that happen?"

I'd forgotten about Jack's visit last night. I quickly repeated the interaction, ignoring the weird car alarm issue as well as Jack's reaction to my eyes. I did glance at Keith as pointedly as I felt safe. I needed to talk to him separately about a lot of things.

"That's wonderful! The tape is down now? I think we need to do some serious sprucing before our opening." Martha clapped her hands. "Oooo! I have a few Tiffany floor lamps that would look wonderful there. They're just sitting in the attic gathering dust. Oh! And one of those tall Turkish mosaic lamps with all the smaller lamps hanging on it."

I started to nod; we didn't have a distinctive element in the shop, and a collection of stained-glass lamps would be a great start. Then I recalled who was in Martha's house. "That's extremely generous, but are you sure there aren't any spirits attached to them?" I wanted to be unique, but a haunted teahouse wasn't it.

"Sadly, yes. The ghosts don't seem to be able to leave my house. We've tried before, and they pop back into the house the moment we cross the threshold with the item they've haunted. That would have been cool, though. A haunted teahouse." Her dreamy smile made me nervous.

I forced a smile. One person's fun was another person's terror. "That is too bad. But I think your lamps might be just what we need, thank you. I'd been so focused on just getting things open that I didn't do a lot of styling." I watched the four dubious faces in front of me. "Fine, none. I did no styling."

"How was your stakeout?" I had a feeling that the fact they weren't bubbling over with telling me about it meant it was a wash. But it was polite to ask.

"Useless." Betsy sighed into her tea. "Those black suits all trooped into the convention center of the Grasshopper, and then never came out. Four hours, and they never left. What could they be doing at that time of night?"

"We even moved in for a closer check after the first two hours," Jamie said. "Walked around the hotel grounds. Absolutely nothing. A few housekeepers were doing nighttime rounds, but they all simply said they loved it when their conference was in town. Full hotel, clean guests, and great tips. Boring."

Keith nodded. "It was a bit like that old movie The Stepford Wives, but it was both men and women." This time, he shot me a pointed glance.

Something was going on up there that was related to the Eltrisphere. "How long have the black suits been coming to town?"

"Eight years?" Martha suggested.

"This year is number ten. I've not trusted them since that first year. Snobs, elitists, jerks." Betsy shook her head. "I get it, that retreat probably keeps the Grasshopper running, but there must be other groups who could do the same."

"And they've gotten worse? They weren't always like this?" There was something seriously odd about this group.

"Much. For the most part, the locals ignore them." Keith polished off another row of cookies. It was a good thing that Betsy had recently stocked us up. "This year has been the worst, though. And that they might stay even longer? This isn't good."

"Do you think Hannah might know more?" In my world, the tavern keepers always knew the most about the town. Many of them were slow to speak of the real issues, but they knew what was happening.

"She might. She notices a lot," Keith said.

"We should invite her over for tea." Betsy clapped her hands. "Tomorrow. A small, informal, full tea run of the Fainting Goat Tea and Spice shop before the official opening. A test tea, as it were."

I knew the look on Betsy's face, even if I said no, she'd find a way to make it happen. "Sure, I just don't want her to think we're ganging up on her." A test tea sounded like a great idea, for my own peace of mind if nothing else.

"She won't," Jamie said. "She's often said she admired the three of us and our investigations. But it's hard to leave her diner at the last minute, so she usually can't join us. This is perfect!"

The discussion broke into what other cool Victorian, non-ghost items would be great to borrow from Martha's attic, and Keith finished another full pack of cookies.

I lifted my eyebrow when he went for another half-opened pack. He shrugged but looked guilty. Something involving him using magic happened up at the Grasshopper.

And I couldn't find out until he dropped off the ladies.

As much as I wanted to know, I also had a backlog of needed downtime. When I was stuck in my bottle, I had way too much of it, but this week had pointed out that a little bit was a good thing. Right now, I felt overwhelmed. As much as I loved the ladies, I needed a day to just think and sort. Especially before the grand opening next week.

"Shall we meet at Hannah's diner tomorrow morning? Have breakfast and invite Hannah to our secret test opening? Then we can go check out the teahouse."

"That works for me. I foresee a nap in my future today." Keith got to his feet and stretched. "Who knew spying was so exhausting?"

He hadn't been tired a few moments ago, and with all the sugar he had he should be bouncing off the ceiling. One more glance in my direction, and he headed for the door.

"All excellent ideas. We'll reconvene tomorrow at eight at Hannah's." Betsy was the second to rise and put both teapots on the counter.

Martha and Jamie got up at the same time. "See you tomorrow."

I waited until the group got into Keith's van and he'd driven away before I relaxed. I went back inside, leaving the door open for Tiberius and Lucie, and spotted a note stuck behind my sofa cushion.

Right where Keith had been sitting.

In Sihlia, it said, 'Call me in half an hour, urgent.'

So much for nothing happening on their spy trip.

# Chapter Eighteen

I didn't want to get involved in doing anything, like dealing with more of those boxes, before I spoke with Keith.

And I obviously couldn't call him when I was in the house. Xieth hadn't shown up yet, but he might have been listening when the others were here. I left and locked the house up again.

I wandered over to the fence where the puppies kept coming through. They could get in from the driveway even if I closed any gaps in the fence. That's probably how Camfield's goats got in.

The fence was in such bad shape that it would have to be rebuilt to stop the smallest puppy from getting through. A nice hip-high collection of tall, straw-like grass kept me from seeing how bad it was before.

That, and I honestly hadn't thought about it.

I'd never owned a home with a yard before. I moved around a lot as a gladiator, so I mostly just rented cheap apartments as I changed cities. Not to mention, if I had to, I could always rent a small locker and sleep in my bottle.

It was going to be a long time before I ever did that again.

I mentally made a note to see if I could get someone to come fix the fence, and maybe look into a gate across the driveway. Having an illusion of security might be nice.

I wandered to the barn. Talking in the yard wouldn't be much better than the house.

Tiberius was sleep-eating, and the only straw left near him was under him. Whatever Lucie had been doing was done now, as he had found a pile of straw of his own and was sound asleep when I first saw him.

But cats were cats, and he was awake and watching me before I even finished opening the door. "Took you people long enough. I want to sleep in my cat tower." He stretched and slowly walked over.

"You could have come to the door and meowed like an Earth cat."

"Gabba, gabba, gabba. Too much talking." He must have been watching The Incredibles again; he loved the Edna Mode character. He started to head for the house.

I followed him and unlocked the door, nudging Lucie to get inside faster.

"What's the rush? Got a hot date?"

"Nope, just need some quiet time." I kept my voice low and practically slammed the door on Lucie.

No Xieth popping in was a good thing. Then why did a tendril of worry crawl up my back? Me? Worried about my jailor? Bah, I must have had some bad cookies. I went back to the barn.

Tiberius was still asleep, but he would probably stay that way. I was halfway through Keith's phone number when it hit me—Tiberius was *asleep*, but wasn't a seven-foot-tall, blue, and winged centurion. He was completely passed out and all goat.

I ended my dialing and ran to the snoring goat. "Tiberius? Wake up. You need to wake up." I tried not to come upon him when he was asleep, as seeing him in his real form was exceedingly disturbing.

"Whaaa?" He yawned and opened his eyes.

That word sounded too goat-like for my liking. "Wake up and speak to me." I grabbed his face and shook it.

"Back off, Ceian, I'm awake. Are we under attack? Why am I lying on the ground? Where are my weapons?" He looked at himself. "Where is my body?"

I released his face as he scrambled to his hooves.

"I forgot I was a goat." He sighed and looked past me. "Your friends are gone now? No one saw me as I really am?"

I shook my head slowly. "Not even me."

"What? You must be mistaken, maybe I'd already changed, and I was a little awake."

"You were snoring. Hard. This isn't good." I didn't want to freak him out, but I was freaked out for him. Was he becoming a goat? The spell that changed him was supposed to be temporary; the stunt about changing into his real form when he lost consciousness was a revenge addition by a high-ranking Eltrisian official and wasn't supposed to be part of his time here.

"Did you piss off someone else in the Eltrisphere? Someone with a lot of magic?" His goat eyes were disturbing, even more so when they widened in terror as he made the same connection that I had. "Or maybe this is an unexpected side effect from whatever the kidnappers used to knock you out?"

He stood there nodding slowly. "I need to think some things through. You're staying in here?"

"Yeah, I need to speak to Keith. You could talk to him, too. He's a magic user."

"Not yet. I'll be on the side of the barn for a bit." He trotted out the barn door.

That was so not good. If he wouldn't talk to Keith, I would. Maybe not this round, but soon if Tiberius didn't do something.

I dialed Keith's number.

"Thank the stars, I was about to head back to make sure everything was okay." He sounded like he actually had been running.

"Just got caught up in looking around the yard. Do you know anyone who could build me a gate across my driveway?" I needed some mental distance from Tiberius and his possible problems.

"Sure, I could do it. But I don't think that's what those glances were about. And I need to talk to you about what really happened up at the Grasshopper."

"Do we need to meet somewhere?" I didn't want to leave my home today, but if something dangerous happened with Betsy and the crew, I needed to know.

"Better not to meet again today. I'm not sure, but I felt like I was followed after I dropped the ladies off. Only for a few blocks, but a small gray car was following me. It stopped when I pulled over. We can do this on the phone. You're not in your house, I take it?"

"No." I started with my possible magic slippage, both when the fumigation tent went flying and when I got pissed at the SUV driver and my eyes went red.

"That's bad, which you already know. I didn't get a close look, but the bands on you, Lucie, and Tiberius are top line—or were. Not sure about changes since I came to Earth. I felt the spell on the bands as you first entered the police station when we met. They're fully working. I'll try and get a chance to study them more tomorrow."

"Thanks. Then there are the things I've found in Darius's stuff so far." I started with the letter from Darius, and the fact that he'd known about my parole and where it would be, before it happened. Then I told him about the stuff. That took a bit longer as he kept asking questions, and I was going from memory. I had an extremely good memory, but it had been a trying couple of days.

"I need to see these things. And that anvil? I've heard of it, but it's low-level magic, nothing to worry about yet."

I had never been fond of the word, 'yet'. But I wasn't going to bring it up now. If I could ignore some of the mess that Darius brought into my life, I was all for it. "Thanks again—there's one more thing." I took a deep breath and told him about Jack's reaction to my eyes when he came by last night. It was hard to admit.

Keith was silent at this one. Then finally let out a long stream of air. "That is possibly the worst thing you've told me. You're a charmer?"

"Not really. I could be charming, no magic, just me, but I was never a charmer. And this was definitely a *charming*."

"I'd guess someone is messing with your magic and the bracelets. You don't know anyone else in town from the Eltrisphere?"

"Whoever brought back Betsy and the rest, and that could be more than one person. Oh, and Brutus and her puppies. They're Eltrisian. She was possibly working with Darius, as she stayed with the guy he was working a scam with. A human. Brutus is female and has five puppies. Pretty sure the dog family is living in the abandoned place next door to me."

Keith let out a low whistle. "Black and tan? Huge? Super smart? That's a hoxien wolf. I wanted one of those growing up. My parents said they were too dangerous. I thought Darius came here with your cat?"

"He did. And Lucie's never said anything about knowing the dog or wolf. She doesn't look wolfish, to be honest, but the rest matches. Oh, not sure if you ran into him much, but Brutus was with Norm Capper, the late owner of the Coffee Perk shop, before Darius and Lucie arrived. Xieth was concerned about the puppies, but wouldn't say why."

"Which would mean yet another Eltrisian invasion of this town. Another that I didn't notice.  There are too many things going on. I'm starting a spreadsheet of all of this. There must be answers somewhere. Who knows, Brutus could be connected to our black suits. They've been coming here long enough...."

I waited for the rest of that statement when he faded away, then finally prodded him. "You think those business people are from the Eltrisphere?" That terrified me far more than I would have thought. If they were all Eltrisians, we might be in serious trouble. "You think they're gomblers?"

Gomblers weren't the brightest species, but they could copy other people. There was usually a powerful magic user controlling them, though. And they were supposedly locked up on their planet.

There was a longer pause on Keith's side than I would have liked. "No, they can't escape their world. At least, they were secure forty years ago."

"I've been in a bottle for a hundred years. I have no idea what's been going on." I started pacing and kicking up the straw on the floor.

"True. But I seriously doubt that's who the black suits are. I'm sensitive enough that I think I would have noticed. And gomblers don't have that level of prolonged control over their assumed forms; those black suits are everywhere."

There was an unfortunate level of doubt in his words, but I'd ignore it for now.

"What happened up at the Grasshopper?"

"Nothing. And a lot of things. It appeared to be as Betsy and the others told you. What they couldn't tell you was the ten minutes of their memories that I had to push aside. Those memories will come back, but hopefully spaced out and diffused enough that they'll just seem like dreams. I hate doing that, by the way. But I panicked."

"Keith, *what happened*?" He sounded panicked now. I was already panicking, and there shouldn't be two of us doing that on the same call.

"Sorry. Just not used to things like this. I came to Earth to get away from intrigue." He took a deep breath. "Better. There was a *presence* in the convention center. It was noticeable when we'd moved onto the grounds once the black suits had been inside for a while. The entire place seemed eerily calm and normal, just a normal night. Then a wave of emotion hit, and I think I'm still reacting to it. The wave came from the convention center. Betsy,

Jamie, and Martha all froze, then marched to the main doors of the center. I grabbed them before they pulled the doors open, but it was a near thing. They kept saying they were being called and had to answer." He went silent again until I coughed.

"Sorry, I hit them with a blocking spell and relocated them to the edge of the grounds. Ten minutes later, they woke up with no memories of that brief time, and all of them complained that this was boring."

"That's not good. Humans shouldn't have anything that can do that. What happened to the housekeepers when the wave hit?" I'd hoped that Keith's call wouldn't add to the list of problems in my life, but it was a futile and stupid hope.

"Nothing. There was a pair of them in sight of us when the wave hit, and both continued with their work. I also saw a maintenance worker go into a room, totally unaffected."

"There's no way to confirm that the black suits aren't Eltrisians." Even just saying that made my stomach clench.

"I don't believe they are. However, there could be people behind this who are. I might be wrong, but the black suits feel human. Even if you didn't have those bracelets on, I would have sensed you being 'other' within a few moments of meeting you. I've run into more than a few of our black suits over the years they've been coming here, and none of them feel that way. Not to mention that the autopsy on the man from your barn didn't show anything odd. Human through and through."

"Then there's one of our people behind them?" That made me feel a tiny bit better, mostly because there were over sixty of the black suits. There might just be one or two rogue Eltrisians.

"After what happened in that center, I'd say yes. But who and what? No idea how to find out without risking people. They already know about you, or someone there does. I hate to say it, but we might just need to wait this out. We can't risk Betsy and the others."

I continued stomping around the area of the barn that Tiberius had been lying in and started swearing as more straw was pushed aside by my angry walking.

"We'll figure it out, I promise." Keith misunderstood the source of my swearing.

"I know we will, but that's not the current problem. There's a pentia spell carved on the floor of my barn. I don't know much about these, but there are symbols of a goat in between the words. That's why he didn't change when he fell asleep." Pentia were a group of powerful magic users who were mostly nature followers. That didn't mean that one of them couldn't have turned bad, or that one of their spells wasn't being used by someone else.

"That's not good. Wait, why he didn't change? Into what?"

I rubbed the side of my face. So much for not telling him about Tiberius. "I didn't want to tell you yet, in case Tiberius wanted to. I had to tell both him and Lucie who you really are, by the way. If something happens to me, you're the only safe one for them to go to." I was talking fast and continuing to kick away straw as I widened my circle of pacing.

"Tiberius turns into himself, a seven-foot-tall, cerulean centurion when he goes to sleep."

"Wings and all?"

"Yup. He pissed off someone, and they added that to his transformative spell when he was sent down here. Anyway, he hadn't transformed when you and I found them. I was hoping that it was because of whatever chemical was used to knock them all out. But when I came here to call you, he was sound asleep. And still a goat."

"That can't be good. Maybe I can run a—"

I cut him off with a scream as I uncovered more drawings within the spells. "They have me here too!"

# Chapter Nineteen

"How large is this spell board?" Keith sounded like he was running. "Never mind, don't touch anything else. Get out of the barn, keep Lucie and Tiberius out as well. I'm on my way." He clicked off the call.

The fear in his voice made me move at jinn speed to get out of the barn, without touching any of the drawings, and lock the barn door in record time. If I could have flown, I would have.

Tiberius heard me swearing as I backed away from the barn and jogged over from the side yard. "What's wrong? A spider?"

"No, worse, far worse." When I was much younger, a spider got into my bottle. Jinn and their guests shrink to enter their bottles. This spider just crawled in full-sized. Which meant he ended up being large enough for me to ride. It took an hour for me to get it out.

It was trying to eat me the entire time.

Tiberius used that fear to help capture me when I was set up for Darius's crimes.

I looked around for someplace safe to fill him in. Couldn't go inside the house, there was no way I was going inside that barn, and it might look odd for me to be standing in the middle of my yard, talking to my goat. "Come back around to the side."

I was really going to have to clean out these weeds and grasses if this was going to become a regular clandestine meeting spot.

Tiberius coughed to get my attention when I started contemplating pulling a few of them now.

"You're freaked out, why?" He nibbled on some of the weeds.

I told him about the pentia spells in the barn.

"What?! Burn it! We have to burn it! What have they done to me?" He twisted around trying to get a look at himself, as if being a goat wasn't enough trauma.

Nothing like a hysterically yelling goat to make things better.

"Easy there. Keith is coming over. Don't forget, my image was in those spells as well." Not a great likeness, but it was clearly me. Pentia spells were always in a circle; the image was the target, and the words that only a practitioner could read linked the image to the spell. The spell's effects remained as long as the circles were complete after casting and being activated.

We could figure out what Tiberius's spell was—not allowing him to change back when he slept. Which was good in some ways, but not good if it meant he was losing who he truly was.

I didn't want to know what the spell about me was.

"What about Lucie?"

I'd been so freaked out seeing myself etched into the floor that I'd forgotten the cat. "Don't know. Either the spell caster wasn't worried about Lucie, or it was further down the spell circle. Keith said get out, so I got out."

"Or Lucie is involved." His stumpy tail lashed back and forth like a cat's.

"I don't believe that, and neither do you. Lucie isn't as innocent as he pretends, but I also don't believe he's as bad as Darius. Xieth knows about him being here; Lucie's survival depends on ours." That was an interesting thought. I actually believed what I said. I'd seen Lucie as an acceptable nuisance up until he and the others were kidnapped. Now he was family.

Keith must have gunned it all the way here, as his van was now pulling up to the barn. It was interesting that he obviously used magic of some kind to make his van go much faster than its counterparts, but he hadn't adjusted the sound. Of course, the sound of one of those vans was distinctive.

Tiberius and I came out from around the side of the barn.

We met at the locked barn doors. "I told Tiberius everything. Lucie is napping in the house, but until we know if he has a spell in the barn as well, I'd like to leave him out of this for now."

Tiberius gave a smug goat snort.

"Not because I don't trust him, Tiberius. Because it might be safer if he doesn't know right now." I hadn't noticed anything odd about Lucie, so he might not be spelled.

"Let me see what I can tell. I studied pentia spells a few hundred years ago at a year-long magic retreat. Some of that information might still be relevant."

I handed the key for the lock to Keith and stepped back a few steps. Which might have actually been all the way to the front porch. It wasn't that I thought the spell was going to jump out at me if I got too close. I had no idea how long those things had been there, and I'd been in that barn a lot in the past two months.

But it was better not to take risks.

Keith went inside with Tiberius remaining outside the door, watching carefully.

I almost jumped up to the roof of my cottage when a scratching came from the other side of the front door.

Lucie had great dramatic timing sometimes.

I unlocked the door and he sauntered out. Not looking at all like he had been sleeping.

"What's going on?" He sat next to me and washed his face. Sometimes his choice of where and when to wash was just cleanliness. Other times, he was trying to make a point.

Face washing was usually his attempt at trying to gain trust. Or to appear sweet.

I didn't think that Xieth's ability to eavesdrop through the landscape painting extended anywhere outside of the house, but as I was a foot away from the front door, I didn't want to risk it.

"There are some weird things in the barn. Might be *bugs*. Keith's checking them out for me." I shook my head and pointed behind me when Lucie looked ready to argue. Obviously, any bugs, weird or otherwise, would have been eaten or chased out by him.

"Ah, gotcha. There are weird Earth bugs here." He gave a slightly disturbing and exaggerated, slow wink.

I expected him to go over to the barn, being a cat-like thing to do, but he just settled in next to my foot and waited.

It felt like Keith had been in there for hours, but a glance at my watch indicated twenty-two minutes.

Neither Lucie nor I had taken our eyes off the goat or the barn door.

Keith came out wiping his hands and said something to Tiberius. Tiberius looked toward Lucie and me, and then jogged over to Keith's van.

Keith locked the barn and started over to us, but then waved us toward the van, too.

"He might need to get some supplies. Let's go see what he found." I could be paranoid, but I locked the house behind us. Again. Locks weren't infallible, but they were better than nothing.

I thought we were going inside the van, and Keith did have the doors on the side facing the barn open. But he and Tiberius were just waiting for us.

"My van will block any observation, both visual and audible. The good news is that it's a low-level pentia spell. Most likely not cast by a practitioner, but skimmed from the infinity web. I might be able to break it. The bad news is that Lucie is shown there as well, and I can't be certain what any of the spells are supposed to be doing. Or even if they're fully active." He nodded to Tiberius.

"Aside from his. It's definitely a separation spell; if it had been stronger, it could have turned him into a goat for good already."

Lucie's tail went into high-speed flapping mode. "Where would Tiberius be?"

Tiberius gave a goat shrug. "Gone, I'd be lost to the void." If he was upset about that, he wasn't showing it. Of course, centurions were extremely stoic by training. And goats were just plain stubborn.

"No hint what it is supposed to do to me or Lucie?" I fiddled with my spell bracelets. "When was it cast?"

He looked at my wrists long enough that I stopped playing with the bracelets.

"No idea on the commands embedded there, I have some trusted sources to check with first. As for when? From the age of the spell, they've been there for at least three months, but were just activated a few days ago."

That was extremely not good. "Tiberius and I have only been on Earth for a little over two months."

Keith watched the barn for a few moments. "Obviously, Darius wasn't the only one who knew you two would be paroled here. And they knew Lucie would be with you."

Lucie looked back at all of us. "That's impossible. I was here with Darius, and if that idiot hadn't gotten himself killed, I'd still be with him. Unfortunately."

I leaned forward to look at him closely. I trusted Lucie, but he was a criminal, a con cat, and looked like he was lying about something. "What was the plan? Were you and Darius simply going to show up on my doorstep and say hi? How did he know I was coming here? You said that you didn't know."

"It's complicated..." Lucie dropped his voice as all three of us glared at him. He gave a quick lick of an imaginary speck of dirt on his left shoulder and sighed. "Darius didn't tell me much, not even your name. I was honest about that. I didn't know for certain that you would be paroled here. Darius seemed to believe so, but wouldn't tell me how he knew." He raised his right paw. "Honest!" He gave his best honest cat grin and slow blinks.

"And?" I folded my arms. His charms weren't working on me this time. Slow blinks could cover a lot of lies.

"*And* whenever you did arrive, he'd point you out. Then I was supposed to show up as a stray and win you over. After a few days, Darius would come by looking for me and find you." He dropped his head.

"What do you know about the spells in the barn?" Tiberius bared his teeth and stomped his front hooves.

"Nothing! If I were involved, why would I agree to a spell about me?"

Keith watched Lucie closely, but finally nodded. "He's telling the truth, or as much as he believes is the truth. Darius deceived everyone. As for the barn, the man who owned this place previously, Higgins, died two years ago; the cottage and barn were in shambles, and there wasn't a will. It finally fell to a real estate company six months ago, which quickly sold it. The rapid fixing up was the talk of the town for a week—until it wasn't. Everyone suddenly felt it had always been in good shape."

"Magic. They spelled the entire town?" I wasn't allowed to use even tiny spells, and Xieth's people cast one on an entire town? So unfair.

"That was my guess. It was subtle, though. Even though I have defenses against most magic, I should have felt it. I only saw the results."

"So, sometime after they sold and fixed the house, someone using a cheap pentia spell knock off, aimed at the three of us, cast it, but left it dormant. Then someone triggered the spell. And we don't have a clue as to what it's supposed to do to Lucie or me."

"Nicely summed up." Keith looked ready to say more, but dropped it after a glance at Tiberius and Lucie.

"What are we going to do with the barn? I happen to like it in there." Tiberius glared at the locked door.

"Like I said, I have built up resources during my time here who can help, and no, I won't tell you who or where they are." Keith gave Tiberius a small smile. "You are still a centurion."

Keith knew he was risking himself and the life he built here to help us, but he wasn't going to sacrifice others. I scowled at Tiberius.

"I...I appreciate your help for me and Ceian. What happens while we're here won't ever be reported." Normally, he would have crossed one massive blue arm over his chest with such a promise, but he couldn't do that, so he bowed.

"Thank you. I'll still keep my sources secret, both for their sake and all of yours." He looked up at the darkening sky; a storm was moving in. Unlike yesterday, this one looked like it was serious. "The barn now has a spell-dampening incantation on it to block the pentia spell until we know more about it. I've got a few things to check out today. I'll see Ceian tomorrow morning at the diner, and you two soon, I'm sure." He started to walk to the driver's side, then stopped and handed me a small cube. "Here. Put this on that shelf below the landscape painting. Unless he officially calls in and is visible, Xieth won't hear or see anything in your house."

I took the cube. "He couldn't have seen us before without our knowing, could he?" That was a disturbing thought.

"Probably not. See you soon." Keith nodded and left.

Since they didn't have the barn to hang out in, and I still didn't want Lucie cruising the streets creating kitty mayhem, Tiberius and Lucie joined me back in the house. I placed the tiny cube that Keith gave me directly below the landscape painting. It seemed too small to do anything, but it was all we had.

I'd just dug out a frozen meal for lunch—something with chicken—when the chime for Xieth's incoming call rang. Of course.

Lucie and Tiberius scampered into my room. The cowards.

"Ceian. I've been looking for you. There hasn't been any indication of anyone seriously looking for the Stone of Zalianthia. Nor is its location known. I'm sorry about your friends. Tonight was when you were supposed to turn it over and get them back, correct?"

There had been so many different things running around lately that it took my brain a few moments to cycle through to the stone—and the ransom demand.

"Sorry, things have been hectic. Someone dumped Tiberius, Lucie, and my three human friends in my barn yesterday. They're all fine. I haven't recently heard anything from the kidnapper, but the police believe he might have been the dead body left with my friends." I hadn't meant to bring up another dead body on my property.

"What? You should have notified me immediately. What dead body?" Those beady little cherub eyes were trying to bore through me.

I gave an extremely vague description of the body, and the fact that the cops knew I had nothing to do with his death.

"Was he human?" The fact that he asked indicated that he had a good idea that there were more Eltrisians here. He just wasn't going to talk about it.

"I believe so. The police said he'd been shot once, and nothing strange seemed to come up when they brought the body in to examine it." I couldn't tell him about Keith, nor did I believe Jack would let me look at the autopsy report.

"Then he couldn't have been working alone. No human would know of the Stone of Zalianthia. This is disturbing. Any updates on your place of business?"

That I could talk about. I explained that they hadn't found the people who tried to destroy it, but the belief was they'd been hired for that specific job and were long gone. And I'd be opening the teahouse next week.

"Finally, good news. You need to keep your head down, get your place open, and become a functioning member of that society. The high council is watching you." He gave a warped little attempt at a smile. "This is good. Carry on." With a nod, the image of the landscape came back.

It was good that Xieth wasn't as upset as he'd been before, but I was almost as concerned about his sudden joviality.

Tiberius and Lucie came out immediately, as if they hadn't bailed on me, and started eating.

I popped my frozen meal into the microwave, grabbed a beer, and sat. I didn't drink a lot, but this planet was making me do so. Or rather, the dangerous collision of Eltrisphere and Earth, with me in the middle, was doing it.

I was halfway through my exotic lunch when Lucie climbed into his cat tower and Tiberius settled in his blankets. I was surprised at their napping, but glad. I needed to think.

I grabbed another beer, a pen, and a pad of paper. I'd burn this list after I sorted things out, but jotting issues down always helped in the past.

I started with the last week of my bottle time, right before my appeal hearing. I couldn't think of anything weird that happened then—or honestly, anything odd that happened during the hundred years before it.

Being fairly close to immortal, some jinn were over five thousand years old, meant that a hundred years wasn't that big of a deal. But it was still mind-numbing. One decade flowed into the next with a slog.

Maybe go further back. Three months ago, someone had known I'd be paroled, where I'd be assigned, and with whom. Before I knew. I put down Darius first. He wasn't in Forgotten Hollow yet, but he knew.

Xieth most likely knew. He took great joy in knowing things that others didn't.

Who worked with Xieth? I knew the government had way too many people working in it, but mostly I needed someone close to Xieth.

Or Darius? I ran to look in the file where I'd put the documents that came with Darius's letter. Everything in the file was gone. Xieth had lifted things before, but he'd usually told me. He must have heard Lucie and me when I read the letter. "Xieth took the letter and documents." I didn't yell it, but both Tiberius and Lucie looked up. "Never mind. I'm just sorting some things out."

When I'd first arrived here and gone through some of Darius's possessions that he'd kept in his rented room, I'd found that he'd double-crossed a major player in an Eltrisian mob family, Elizabeth Rebecca Xlontg-Firesti. She had a hit out on him, but as far as I knew, she wasn't who finally killed him. Although the killers could have been working for the Xlontg-Firesti family.

Even though I knew I was going to destroy the list, I didn't even want to write that family name. Or speak it. I was a bit weirded out even thinking about it.

What if they *were* behind all of this? Even Xieth wouldn't be able to protect us; I didn't think he'd even try.

My hand was shaking as I wrote 'XF' down. I couldn't imagine them going after me for whatever Darius duped them on. Oh. Unless they knew about the transatlantic shipping container, they thought that whatever was rightfully theirs was in it, and they were aware of me.

And if they *had* been behind the ones who killed Darius.

My frozen meal picked a fight with my third bottle of beer in my stomach, and I finally shoved the list away.

Yes, I needed to sort things out, but I also just needed to relax. I burnt my list in the sink, grabbed some decaf tea instead of more beer, checked the door locks, and went to my room.

It was still mid-afternoon, but the darkening sky made it seem later. So did the two snoring animals. The beer seemed to be putting me to sleep. I'm not sure what Lucie and Tiberius's issues were.

I just needed to not do anything for a bit. There were no plans with the ladies until tomorrow, and I wasn't up to going to the teahouse. Or dealing with more of Darius's stuff. Plus, I couldn't stop yawning.

I'd once read that TV numbed your brain more than sleeping. I needed that right now; maybe some downtime would help me shake off this sleepiness. I hit the channel and watched the first show that came on.

# Chapter Twenty

The TV was still on when I woke up. I had heavy curtains on my bedroom window; a hundred years in a bottle meant I'd developed the need for pitch black to sleep.

Aside from the flickering lights of the TV, anyway.

I turned it off and stumbled to the front room. Tiberius and Lucie glared at me.

"What? It was on low."

"Not the TV, the food. It's morning." Tiberius nodded to his empty plate. "And I need out."

"It can't be morning." I trudged to the front window and shoved back the curtain. Yup, still overcast, but it was morning. This wasn't good. The annoying collars and bracelets were supposed to help block against another magic user hitting us with spells.

Now that I was awake more, I recognized a spell of sleep lingering around the edges of my mind. But how? And why?

"Were you both asleep the entire time?"

They both gave embarrassed nods.

I ran for my phone to call Keith, then saw a few messages from him. The first was a warning that his investigation of the pentia spell might have triggered a defensive reaction. And he needed me to call him. The other two were about the same, with the last one saying he was outside my cottage and heard snoring.

And for me to call him when we woke up.

"That spell in the barn knocked us out."

"What?" Lucie shrugged. "It would explain things, I guess. Best nap ever. Aren't you supposed to meet your friends soon?" Lucie was also wandering near the front door.

"I really need to go outside. Now. Shove the food out there before you leave." Tiberius was dancing in his need.

It was already half after seven. I ran to the door, let them both out, dumped a bunch of food for each into bowls, shoved those out, and ran back inside to shower.

I called Keith as I was locking the cottage.

"Ceian? Thank goodness. Are you all okay?"

"After our extremely extended nap? Yes. Is that going to keep happening?"

"Sorry. Been too long since I was around pentia spells. No, it shouldn't happen again. Long story, but the spell will settle down now."

I started riding down the bike trail, slowly, as I was still holding my phone. "Is the reason that spell got past the collars and bracelets because it was here before we got them?"

"Unfortunately, that would be my guess. I'll see you at the diner. Ride safe." He clicked off.

Great, any spell down here that was over two months old could hit us. And I couldn't tell Xieth how we knew.

The roads were easier to travel, but I could make up for my lost time on the woodland path by using my jinn speed. Not to mention that venting some of the tension flowing through me right now, *before* I met my friends, was a good idea. I wasn't going to lie, that extra sleep felt great. It was how it happened that was freaking me out.

I had to slow down briefly when I heard a group riding along an adjacent path closer to the ocean cliffs, but I was still the first one of us to get to Hannah's. I took some deep breaths to settle my still bouncing nerves, one of the things I learned during my bottle time, and then went inside.

The black suits weren't there. Maybe they had set meal times. It would fit with their other oddities.

Hannah came out from the kitchen and smiled as she waved me in. "Good to see you, Ceian. Just you for today?" She'd paused at a table near the front.

"Good to see you, too. Nope. Betsy, Jamie, Martha, and Keith this time. Somewhere away from others?" There were only a few diners there right now, scattered around the place. But that would change.

"Not a problem." She winked and nodded. "This way." It was a table back in the far corner that was mostly hidden by a half-wall dividing the areas. After I'd sat down, she placed some plastic cones on the floor between it and the rest of the restaurant. "There we go." She handed me the massive menu and scurried back to the front to help an older couple.

Betsy, Martha, and Jamie came in five minutes later, and I waved them over. I'd almost expected Keith to have given them a ride. Nothing in Forgotten Hollow was far, but sometimes having a driver was nice.

"Where's Keith? He said he'd meet us here." Jamie grinned as Hannah came back with their favorite morning beverages. And a cup of Darjeeling tea for me. Then she raced off to seat more customers as the diner crowd picked up.

"I don't know, I just got here myself," I told my overactive mind to calm down. Keith sounded fine when I'd spoken to him. He was still fine.

Right.

"What's wrong?" Betsy was on my right and tapped my arm as my mind drifted into horrible scenarios.

Unfortunately, I couldn't tell her that a magic spell, worked on by Keith, had knocked Lucie, Tiberius, and me out, and could be why he wasn't here. I appreciated Betsy, Jamie, and Martha, but there was no way I was going to pull them into whatever twistedness was happening in my life right now.

"Ceian! Ceian!"

I looked up to see Camfield waving enthusiastically from the front of the diner. Before I could respond, he was jogging over to us. The fact that he'd spotted me behind the half-wall was impressive. Until I thought of my high ponytail. Tied at the top of my head, it added more than a few inches.

I might need to reconsider my hairstyle if I were going to be sneaky.

"And Betsy, Jamie, and Martha! What a lovely surprise!" Camfield's accent was even more charming than usual, and his smile was top-notch. "Waiting for someone?"

"Keith is joining us today," Jamie said, almost drooling. "But you can join us too."

I felt Betsy kick her friend while continuing to smile.

Jamie blinked as she came back to her senses. "Or another time. That would work too."

"I'm afraid it would have to be another morning, but I shall look forward to it. I came in to get a take-away order and must get back to work. Just wanted to say hello." His smile was blinding now. He waved to all of us and went back to the front of the diner.

One of the busboys came out, presumably with his food. Unless I stood up, I couldn't see more than his head. A few moments later, Camfield left.

"Isn't he dreamy?" Jamie almost swooned, then blinked her eyes rapidly and frowned. "Um, sorry about that, Betsy, I wasn't thinking."

"Just be careful. As handsome and charming as Camfield is, and there's no denying that, he's not part of our group."

"And not being part of our group means they could be the enemy," Martha added. "Which would be a shame. I do think he and Ceian would be a lovely couple."

I laughed. "Thank you? But I'm too busy to deal with romantic entanglements right now."

"Anyone I know?" Jack's voice behind me at that point was not what I wanted to hear. So much for Hannah's traffic cones keeping people away from us. "Sorry, ladies, didn't mean to interrupt, but Ceian's ponytail is noticeable. Have any of you seen Keith? He's not answering his phone, and I need him to come to the station this afternoon for a sketch of a hit and run on Market Street."

I was glad my back was to Jack, as I'm sure my concern wasn't hidden. Keith was late to meet us, and not answering a call from the police? The other three looked like they were thinking the same as me; had something happened to Keith?

"No, but if we do, we'll tell him to contact you post-haste. Probably out in his garden and left his phone on the counter." Betsy smiled and waved her hands. "I do that all the time, don't I, ladies?"

Jamie and Martha murmured agreements, but didn't add to it. Probably better that way, if someone wasn't a great liar, or genetically couldn't lie, staying quiet was best.

"Thanks." He looked toward the front. "My food is up, see you all around town." He glanced down at me, but I simply gave him a polite smile and sipped my tea. He quickly left.

I wasn't sure of a plausible lie as to why I'd called Keith this morning, so I couldn't bring it up.

"Do you ladies want to order now or wait for Keith?" The diner was filling up, but Hannah made a detour over to us and then looked toward the front door. "Oh! There he is. I know his usual breakfast order, but if you tell me yours, I'll give it to the kitchen.

I was suddenly starving and ordered something called a Lumberjack. Betsy gave me an impressed look as the rest gave their orders. Hannah nodded to Keith as he walked up.

Keith waited until the orders were given before sitting down. His long hair was normally in an immaculate braid; it was in a loose ponytail this time, and gray wisps waved around his unshaven face. "Thanks, Hannah. We'd like to talk to you when the rush dies down." He smiled, but it didn't reach his pale eyes.

"You got it." Hannah smiled at all of us and briskly walked off.

"There's a group of ten black suits coming down the road; they were a block behind me." He smiled as a waiter brought him some coffee.

"Were you attacked?" Betsy asked before I could think of a subtler way to ask. I might not have known Keith more than a few days, but he was extremely un-Keith-like in appearance right now.

"No, just overslept and ran into some raccoons in the trash bins. They didn't want to leave." He gave me a nod. Something happened after I spoke to him. The oversleeping was a clear lie; he'd sounded fine when we spoke.

"Are you okay? We should get you to the doctor." Betsy was usually the calmest of the three women, unless she needed to fight someone. She wasn't right now.

Keith waved her off. "I'm fine, a little groggy and out of sorts, but caffeine should help with that."

Hannah and a waitress brought out our food. My plate was the same size as Keith's, which was massive.

"Our little Ceian has a healthy appetite!" Martha grinned.

Never mind that I was a good five or six inches taller than her and the other two. I knew something was messing with my metabolism. Even with the fact that I'd slept through dinner.

"I didn't eat much yesterday, but this looks lovely." I had to slow down to keep from inhaling the food. Nothing that I did yesterday should have made me this hungry. This was the way I'd eat when I was still on the gladiator circuit. Or had used too much magic. Or it was that pentia spell messing with me.

We ate in silence, driven mostly by Keith and me.

"Oh! Jack and Camfield came by." Betsy pushed her plate back. "Jack said he was looking for you and had been calling you."

Keith slowed down long enough to pat his pockets in concern, then pulled out his phone. "I don't have any messages or even missed calls. Did he say why he was calling?"

"He said he needed you this afternoon for an eyewitness sketch for a hit and run." Jamie's eyes narrowed as she looked at the phone in Keith's hand. "What's that on the bottom of your phone?" Jamie was the techie of the three ladies, and she glared at Keith's phone like it was a snake.

"What?" Keith flipped his phone over, swore, and handed it to Jamie. Then raised a finger to his lips as he looked to the rest of us.

Jamie looked like someone's athletic grandmother. But she didn't swear like one as she snarled and dug a small button off the bottom of Keith's phone. Then got to her feet and stomped on the bug a few times.

"You were bugged. Someone was listening in on us."

# Chapter Twenty-One

"Are we sure he was the only one?" I pulled my phone out of my jacket pocket and handed it to Jamie. Betsy and Martha followed suit.

Jamie was silent as she searched the phones, then held out her hand to Keith to get his back. She took them all apart, including her own.

She found three more bugs that she again stomped on. "There wasn't one in Ceian's phone. Keith only had the external bug, but the three of us all had bugs embedded inside the case." She snapped the phones closed and handed them back. "I would have liked to have examined them, but I don't want them to have any more intel than they already have."

"Them who?" Martha leaned forward.

"Those who kidnapped us and whoever is behind this, I would gather." Betsy put her phone away. "Better to be safe right now. Could the one on Keith's phone blocked Jack's calls from going through?"

"And Jack said he left messages." Now I was worried. Was that really Jack? Could someone have copied him? Even though Keith didn't think the gomblers were on Earth, that thought refused to leave my mind.

Jamie scowled, then nodded. "Modern tech can do some amazing things, so it might have diverted calls and voicemail to another phone. Again, no way I can examine the remains of those bugs."

"It's better that they are destroyed." Keith finished off his mountain of toast. "I get that you three probably had your phones bugged when you were kidnapped. But when did mine get hit? Unless someone knocked me out, broke in, bugged my phone...and? What?"

"They wanted to hear what we were talking about? Jamie, do you have one of those bug detectors I see on TV shows? Might want to sweep our houses. Even mine. Don't forget someone broke in when they kidnapped Tiberius and Lucie." I really hoped there wasn't anything in my place. If the people who planted the bugs were from the Eltrisphere, they heard things they shouldn't have.

They would have heard things they really shouldn't have heard, even if they were human. If Xieth found out that humans knew about the Eltrisphere, he would probably grab them all. Or worse.

"I can get some better equipment; mine is a little old." Jamie shrugged at Betsy. "Sorry, I didn't think we needed top-line stuff."

Betsy looked annoyed but shrugged it off. "Now then, what are we going to do about them?" She tilted her head in the general direction where the table of black suits was seated.

"At this point, just wait them out," Keith said. "I know you want to investigate them further, but there's not much more we can do. We're lucky the hotel didn't ask us why we were lurking around for that long."

I didn't believe him. Keith thought the black suits were humans, but someone was controlling them. Or at least influencing them. And most likely, *they* weren't human.

Hannah came over. "How are you all doing? Need anything more? I have some lovely lemon-blueberry pancakes." She looked at all of us, but focused on Keith.

"No, I couldn't...well, maybe a small stack?" He grinned.

Betsy lightly tapped my leg.

I'd almost forgotten. "Oh! And we're having a test tea run at my teahouse later today, and I would love to have you join, say one-thirty? I've been given clearance to open next week, but we need to test things first."

"Thank you! I would love to. I have a heavier staff than usual on for lunch today, and they are more than qualified to run this place." She leaned in closer to Betsy and dropped her voice. "Any discussion of a mystery afoot?"

"Tea discussions are often insightful." Betsy winked.

Hannah clapped her hands. "Wonderful! I'll see you all then."

Sirens coming our way made her look up. "What now?"

"Just add this all to my tab, Hannah." Keith got up and looked toward the parking lot.

"Consider it done, Keith. I'll see everyone at one-thirty." Hannah scurried toward the front of the diner.

We grabbed our things and followed her.

The diner parking lot wasn't large, but a lot of people walked or biked around town, so it was only half full.

Three cop cars surrounded the driveway of the diner, but didn't pull in. They kept their lights going, and Officer Jones started diverting passing traffic.

Pretty much everyone in the diner crowded to the front to look.

Except for the ten people in black suits. I glanced back at them, but none of them even looked up as they continued eating and looking over their data pads.

"Okay, that's not weird or anything." I stood next to Keith and tugged his arm to look over.

"I swear they're human, but they aren't acting it." His voice was low.

Betsy might not have heard what he said, but she noticed where we were looking. "What's wrong with them? That's not normal."

Suddenly, the cop cars pulled back to the ends of the block, and Officer Jones and Alice put up wooden blockades on both sides of the street.

Jack came running in. "We need everyone out of the diner immediately, but it's not safe to get out this way. Hannah, do you have a way to get out through the back?"

Hannah didn't even question him. "Yes, through the kitchen." She spoke to her staff and told them to start leading people out and down the side street behind the diner. Away from here. Once things were moving, she grabbed Jack's sleeve as he turned away. "What's wrong?"

"There are two bodies alongside the driveway. No idea how they died, but they're definitely dead. One has what looks like pipe bombs strapped to his torso. Alice and Jones will get into bomb gear, but until then, we have to assume there are more explosives under him." He looked into the nearly empty restaurant. "You! In the black suits, you have to leave now."

The black suited people slowly gathered their things.

"Not kidding, out of here immediately, or I'll call your bosses."

I blinked at that. The black suits were halfway to the kitchen immediately. They were more afraid of their bosses than of being blown up?

"Weird," Keith and I said at the same time.

"That goes for all of you, too. Take them with you, Hannah." Jack scowled at our group, as we were now the only ones remaining.

"Come on, ladies and gent, we don't want the detective to yell at us. Keep my place safe if you can, Jack." Hannah was closest to Betsy, so she grabbed her arm and jogged toward the kitchen. The rest of us followed.

"Oh, Ceian. Where will you be later? I need to ask you about something." Jack called out as I was almost to the swinging kitchen door.

"At my teahouse, cleaning up and decorating." He hadn't had anything to ask me when he was here an hour ago. Hopefully, it wasn't anything to do with the bodies and explosives out front. And also, that he hadn't been replaced by a gombler.

"Good, stay there if you would." He gave me a tight nod and went back to yell at people outside.

"What was that about?" Betsy asked as we went out the back door and down an alley.

"I have no idea. That man is weird." I still thought he was extremely attractive, but definitely odd.

We walked to the end of the alley and joined the cooks and staff from Hannah's diner at the cross street. The black suits were nowhere in sight, and only a few other customers wandered around waiting.

"What do you think Jack wants?" Martha asked.

"Who knows with him?" Betsy shook her head. "He's been peculiar since he returned."

I wasn't even going to guess, but I had a bad suspicion it had to do with the bodies, the bombs, or both. How did the two people die? Were they black suits? Hired assassins? The fact that one of them was carrying explosives and potentially heading into Hannah's place wasn't good.

After twenty minutes, everyone except us and the staff of the diner had left. After Hannah made sure the customers all understood that it was fine that they didn't get a chance to pay, even if they'd finished their food.

"I think I'm going to head over to my teahouse." Hopefully, no explosions yet were a good thing.

"We can go get the lamps and other interesting items from my attic." Martha was bouncing on her feet. "I'm so excited that these things will have a home!" She turned to Keith with a smile.

"I can help gather them, but until they clear the parking lot, I can't haul them."

"Oh, no worries, Ralph has a nice truck we can use. He's in the garden right now, but I'll ask him to come by Martha's and haul our loot." Betsy smiled.

They settled into a debate on the best direction to walk to Martha's house, and I waved goodbye. I spun back to Hannah as another thought hit. "I left my bike in front of the diner. I'm not sure if Jack will let me get it yet."

"Don't worry. I'll bring it with me when I come to your tea." If she was concerned about her diner having to be closed for a while, she didn't seem like it.

"Thanks." I went down a side street and meandered a bit until I got back on the main road. A bunch of black suits were outside the A Lotta Joe coffee shop in a line. Far more than just the ten who had been in the diner.

They were chatting as they waited, but it didn't look casual. I started to turn to walk past them, but a familiar handsome blond came my way, waving.

"Ceian! I'm so glad that you're all right." Camfield took my hands. "I heard there were bombs at the diner?"

The line at A Lotta Joe's moved forward, and the black suits went inside. I hid my sigh and smiled at Camfield. "Yes, we all got out. As far as I know, the bombs were being secured. I'm not sure if the diner will reopen today or not."

"Such a scary thing! I moved here from Los Angeles because I wanted a safer place, but I'm not sure about that now."

"I thought you were from England?"

"Originally. I move around a lot." He'd been facing me, but aiming his eyes slightly over my shoulder. Toward the diner. Suddenly, he dropped back to me. "Say, I'd love to take you to dinner tonight. No pressure, just two new friends getting to know each other." His smile was extremely impressive when he turned up the wattage.

I was going to say no. I should have said no. My life was already getting complicated, and I still needed to go through the rest of

Darius's things. "I'd love to." That just came out. Maybe a nice, harmless dinner between two new friends was just what I needed. That the new friend was handsome and had a wonderful accent just made things better.

That was my story, and I was sticking to it.

"Great! Shall we say 7 o'clock for dinner at Chez Champion?"

The only semi-fancy restaurant really in Forgotten Hollow, and one I hadn't been to. And even better, I could get down there on my own. Even though I was attracted to Camfield, I did not need a romantic entanglement during my parole. "Perfect. I'll see you there."

Camfield's smile was almost blinding when he squeezed my hands. "Lovely, until then." He took off at a brisk walk toward the diner.

I ignored the coffee shop and kept going toward my teahouse. It was doubtful that I would have heard anything useful from the black suits anyway.

It was nice to finally see my teahouse without yellow tape around it. But I also felt a lump in my gut as I unlocked the front door. Xieth demanded that this shop open and for me to become a functioning member of this society in order to be released back to the Eltrisphere.

What if the attacks and events that were slowing me down were related to stopping that very thing? Could I have alienated someone so badly over a hundred years ago that they followed me here to make sure I was never freed? That thought caused a nasty chill in my soul.

I opened the door slowly, looking behind it and hitting as many lights as I could, as that cheery thought continued to bounce around in my head. I couldn't think of anyone who would have hated me that much. Then again, I also had no idea that Darius had set me up to take the fall for his crimes. There was a good chance I was more clueless than I thought.

I pulled open the curtains and turned on all of the lights in the kitchen, shop, storeroom, and my tiny office. Even in the bathroom.

Everything looked fine. I went through my supplies and tossed anything that would need to be replaced as possibly contaminated. Then I went to the spice shop side. I didn't get a chance before to go through and really sort out the spice jars. I doubted that those fake bug guys stole spices, but it was a weird situation. And they had been messed up.

I looked at my clock, and it was barely ten thirty. I had plenty of time before anyone would get here.

I removed all the jars and sorted them as I put them on the tables. I used my stock list to check off the amounts. I didn't carry much back stock for these in the store room, so it was easy to go through. All of my numbers matched, and the bottles still had my seals on them. They hadn't taken anything? Just messed them up?

Until I found four jars in the back that weren't labeled with my handwriting.

And one of them was hissing.

# Chapter Twenty-Two

It didn't look like anything was alive in the four jars, but a definite hiss came from the nearest one.

I reached for it slowly. I couldn't leave it here, and I had no idea what it was or what the other three were. The names written on them weren't in any language I'd seen before.

I didn't think Betsy and the others should see them, even if one wasn't hissing at me.

Instead of grabbing it, I darted into the kitchen and came back with a pair of oven mitts to hold the jar with. Then I opened the kitchen door, cleared a path to the trash can, and flipped up the trash lid.

I went back inside, took a deep breath, and grabbed the hissing jar with both mitt-covered hands.

The hissing stopped, and I scurried to the back door. A massive jolt shot through the mitts and my hands, stopping at my silver bracelets. I threw the jar in the general direction of the trash can and slammed the door shut. A rattling sound hit the door, but I waited a few moments before opening it.

Tiny pea-sized seeds covered the ground around the trash can and the area between it and my door. I kicked one of them with my toe.

And jumped back with a scream when a green tendril shot from the seed and sprouted tiny, weird leaves as it reached for me. It looked suspiciously like the description Betsy and the others had given of the vines that had been stolen from their homes. The ones from Laxtunius, if Keith's guess was right.

I swore in Sihlia and locked the kitchen door. Hopefully, the rest of the seeds would remain dormant, but I had no idea what to do with them, nor if the other three jars were filled with them as well.

I went back to the three mystery jars. Now, another one of them was hissing.

Throwing it hadn't worked, but I didn't want them exploding in here either. I had two large freezers, neither even halfway full. I grabbed the hissing jar and put it in the furthest freezer.

No explosion that I heard.

I snatched the other two and put them in the freezer before they started hissing.

Now I just needed to keep Betsy from the freezer. And find a way to get Keith to verify the seeds without anyone else getting back there.

I grabbed my phone, went to the freezer, and snapped a photo of the weird writing. Then popped open the kitchen door and took a few photos of the vine. It looked like it might have moved, but I couldn't be certain.

I locked the door again. I needed something to keep Betsy and the other humans from going out there until we could sort out those seeds. I moved a task stool in front of the door, and wrote a sign saying the door was broken, and don't go out there.

Then I moved the two inside trash cans in front of that.

"What ya doing?" Lucie's unexpected voice, coming from behind me, made me scream and reach for a knife.

"What are you doing here? How did you get in here?" I held onto my knife—it had been that kind of morning.

"I came in when you did. It's not my fault you were too freaked out to notice me. I was napping in that chair in the corner of the shop." He sauntered toward the kitchen door, weaving around my blockade. His tail and back fluffed up, and he gave a drawn-out hiss. "Why do I smell laxiun weed? That stuff is deadly, addictive, and very illegal." He stayed puffed up and slowly backed away.

"Is it a weird, invasive vine that evil people might want to grow?"

"Yes. Yes. And get rid of it. Now." He backed into the tearoom.

I followed him out. "Was Darius smuggling it? I think it might have been growing around the former establishment here. And how do I destroy it? There were four jars of seeds hidden among my bulk spice and tea supplies. One exploded outside in the back. I put the others in the freezer."

"The freezer? What? Why?" His tail fur settled down. "Actually, that's a good idea. They grow naturally in the valleys of Laxtunius and need heat. That was good thinking. But you let one explode? There are active seeds out there?" His orange fur started rising again.

"I didn't plan on it. The thing was hissing, and then it shocked me. Wait, heat? Like an exploding teahouse? I think those jars were left by the crew trying to blow this place up. What would have happened if they succeeded with the bombs?" I was still upset about the trying to blow up my teahouse scenario, but adding these seeds made it far worse.

Lucie's golden-orange eyes went extremely round. "That could have taken out all of this town, and possibly the entire mountain. I'm not a deadly plant expert, but within a year, most of this part of the world would have been taken over by those things."

I stumbled out of the kitchen and collapsed in a chair. Whoever was behind this wasn't just trying to mess up my life; they were going after Earth. "But why?"

"Laxiun weed is extremely profitable. Darius might have been experimenting with growing it here, but he never told me. And unless there are more seed jars in his things, I'd say he only had a few clippings. Someone else has far more."

I dropped my head into my hands. I couldn't tell Xieth, he'd shut down not only my parole but probably wipe out all of Forgotten Hollow.

"What are you doing here? Thought you were having breakfast with your friends?" Lucie had mentally dealt with the potentially killer plants and was now washing his face on the window seat.

I wasn't as lucky. I quickly filled him in on the dead bodies and explosives at the diner. And that my friends were coming by for a test tea and strategy meeting.

"You're going to tell them about those vines?" He'd switched to cleaning a foot and left it hanging there in surprise.

"No. Besides, Betsy, Jamie, and Martha already had some clippings. They were stolen by whoever kidnapped you all. I need to enlist Keith to help me destroy the seeds. I'm thinking fire's not a great idea." That had crossed my mind before I spoke to Lucie. I couldn't keep them in my freezer forever, not to mention what to do with the mass of them out behind the kitchen.

"No!" Lucie shuddered. "I'm sure between Keith and me, we can come up with something. We shouldn't tell Tiberius, though. Centurion and all."

I agreed with that. In our current situation, I honestly liked Tiberius. That would change drastically when he was back to being seven feet tall, blue, with massive wings, and an even larger attitude.

"Okay, we can't do anything now. I need to get set up for their arrival. The tea is at one-thirty, but I know they'll be over sooner. I'm not sure what you can help with." I'd gotten to my feet and turned to Lucie, only to find him sound asleep.

There were times I wished I were a cat.

I dusted the shelves where the bulk teas and spices had been, then put the jars back up in order. This side of the shop wasn't as cute as the tea service side, but maybe if I brought in some non-killer plants and stands, it would help.

The picture window on that side looked over Tiberius's pen. I promised him he wouldn't have to be there all the time, but he was the namesake of The Fainting Goat Tea and Spice. And he had a stake in my fitting in here and both of us being released.

I was turning away when a cop car pulled up, and Jack stepped out. He'd been so cranky since he came back to town, not that he'd ever been a bundle of cheer, that I almost didn't recognize the slight smile as he approached.

Then he saw me through the window, and the smile dropped.

I sighed and walked to the door to let him in. Like Camfield, Jack was another potential messy situation that I did *not* need.

"Hello, Detective Lanclin, to what do we owe the pleasure?" I waved for him to come in.

Lucie gave an exaggerated stretch in his sleep, then curled up tighter.

Jack ignored Lucie and came in. "I have some reports that I was hoping you could help with. They have to do with the disappearance of your cousin's body."

"Darius is missing?" Honestly, I'd figured that once Xieth and his superiors realized that Darius was down here—and dead—they would have done their mojo to steal the body immediately. Some jinn might appear human on the outside, but we weren't, and an autopsy would reveal more than a few differences.

"Yes. There was a chain of command issue when he died, and everyone thought the other had done the autopsy. It became clear two weeks ago that no one had and there was no body. Unfortunately, I was gone and the report got filed and forgotten."

Maybe Xieth and crew did steal it, just a bit late in the game. I motioned to a chair and took the one across the table from it. "Would you like some tea? Water?" I felt like I should offer him something.

"No, thank you. Now, when was the last time you spoke to your cousin?"

That wasn't expected. "What? I thought you had questions about his missing body?" We'd gone over my weakly made-up relationship with Darius when I'd found the body. It had been a busy two months since then, and the likelihood of my recalling my story from then was thin. Since jinn couldn't lie, we had to rely on well-constructed stories.

"Whoever took the body also took all of the initial notes. My file simply had information that the body of one Cyber Kondle had been reported missing, along with all the interviews and photos. I get to rebuild the notes." It was nice to see his annoyance not directed at me.

I wasn't happy about him digging into Darius again, but I understood his frustration. Cherubs loved paperwork, dealing with it, making more, processing it, almost as much as they loved making two idiots fall in love. But most normal people hated it.

"Today isn't a good time to dredge this up. I'm having a test tea before the grand opening. And Martha is bringing over some lamps and tables to help cozy things up a bit." My brain was having to spin too hard. I wouldn't have been able to recall Darius's fake name if Jack hadn't just used it.

"It'll just take a few minutes, I promise." He flipped open a narrow paper pad.

"What happened at the diner?" Delaying was always a good thing, and I wanted to know. I figured that not hearing a large explosion was a good thing.

"It's still under investigation." He gave me a stern look. "Now, the last time you saw your cousin?"

"When I found his dead body. Did the two people in the street kill each other?" I'd either find something out or annoy him so much that he retreated.

"Still investigating. Before seeing him dead, when was the last time you saw him? Alive."

"Years ago, couldn't even tell you." I phrased it carefully, but still felt a slight tightening of my throat. I could tell Jack exactly when I last saw Darius. He left me in our apartment and said he'd be right back.

"And where was that?" Jack had his bored cop voice now.

"At the family home. In Charatian, a small village. He was already bad news and had problems with drugs and booze." Not a lie. The town name was a stretch. "Were the explosives the same as what was dumped here?"

Jack gave a polite smile. "No, different completely. And a bonus answer if you promise to stop asking more questions—" He paused, waiting for my nod. "They were on an extremely defective dead man's switch. It should have exploded the moment the man holding it died, but it didn't. Can I continue?"

I sighed and nodded. I'd gotten little information, but to ask more would just piss him off. He wasn't giving up on this.

"Thank you. You had no contact with him after that?"

"None at all. He was pure trouble, and the only ones looking for him were other drug dealers and thugs. His side of the family considered him dead." I almost added that I hated him for things he'd done. Not a good idea unless I wanted to go back on the suspect list.

"You had no idea what business he'd been in?"

"Not a single one. If the contents of his shipping box so far are any indication, he was trying to run scams with cheap junk he'd bought in various places." I watched Jack's face carefully. I hoped that by giving him a bit about the shipping container, he wouldn't want to see what had been in it. But he appeared to be thinking things over.

"Good to know. After you've taken any personal family belongings, we'd like to go through the rest. If you don't mind, of course."

There was a request there. I didn't have to agree. But, considering the number of dead bodies around me, it would be good to keep the cops more or less on my side. The problem was that so far, there was only a small amount of junk they could safely have.

"I think so, yes. I'll want to make sure the rest of the family has a say. And it'll be a while before I go through the rest of the boxes. With the opening and all." I waved around the room when his brows started to furrow.

"Of course." He closed his notepad and got to his feet. "I need to get back to my work on our primary investigation. I'll call you if I have any more questions. And when we find your cousin's body."

He was halfway out the door before I got to my feet. "Thanks, bye."

He gave me a sharp nod and strode to his car.

"That was interesting. Who would want Darius's body?" Lucie stretched and stood up. "And the paperwork?"

"I have a feeling someone from home took them. But why not do it immediately? They couldn't have known there would be an office mix-up." I watched Jack drive away. It was curious that he just came around today to ask questions about this.

Lucie flounced to the door. "Anyway, I was going to go hunt down Keith and tell him to get his ass here to get rid of those seeds in the back. The frozen ones can wait a bit, but we don't want the weather to get warm and sunny with all of those tiny plant time bombs out there." He tilted his head toward the door handle. "We also really should have him put in a cat door down the line."

I wasn't going to remind him that cats shouldn't be in food-serving locations. I'd been saying it for the past two months. I did tell him that Keith might still be at Martha's house and opened the door. He ran off without so much as a thank you.

I went to the linen closet and brought out two tablecloths and assorted napkins. I knew this teahouse was nothing more than something to show the Eltrisian higher-ups that I could be a functioning member of society, but it was still fun to set the table with my new linens. Then the silver, tea warmers, and tea pots. I put out one per person, as I had no idea what everyone would want, and I had a lot of tea.

I took three of the tiered stands into the kitchen and started warming up the oven. The sausage rolls would be easy—Betsy already made a bunch and froze them. But she said she had a lot more in her freezer. Which sort of scared me. I made sure to relocate all of the rolls in the second freezer to the counter or the first freezer. Today, there shouldn't be anything anyone would need in the second freezer, but I hung a sign on it as well. It was having trouble and shouldn't be opened. Plus, it would explain why I relocated the rest of the sausage rolls.

I knew Betsy would be bringing more food, but I wanted to get things ready. I'd just dragged out the individual containers for jam, curd, and clotted cream when a knock came from the front.

I peeked out; it was Keith. Already? "Thanks for coming. Lucie found you?"

Keith darted in. I noticed his van wasn't in sight. "Yes, but Betsy saw him and is rushing to get them over here sooner. Laxiun weed? You're sure?"

"Lucie is. I've never seen it. And it's not something I want to look up on the infinity web." Like Earth's internet, users could be tracked on it. "Come on." I led him to the kitchen and moved my barricade.

Keith carefully opened the kitchen door, swore a lot, then shut it. "How did they get all over?"

I explained about the jars being hidden in the spice side of my teahouse. That the one outside started to hiss, and my ill-advised attempt to throw it away. From the doorway. I could admit that I'd been a bit freaked out.

"The other jars are in the freezer? Good thinking. But we have got to get those seedlings in the back out of here and neutralized."

I nodded and waited for his grand plan. "And?" I finally said when he just kept glaring at the kitchen door. "Can't you magic them? Or something?" Honestly, I had no idea what spell could work against those seeds. I'd never encountered anything like them when I still had access to my magic.

"I'm thinking. If we can get them back into a glass jar and put them in your freezer, we'd have more time to sort it out. I need to talk to my sources."

Those sources were starting to irritate me. I understood keeping people secret from each other. I was trusting Keith to keep who I was secret from them. But it still bugged me.

"I have plenty of empty jars, but how are we going to get them all? The one I touched is trying to settle in and take out this place right now."

One of his eyebrows raised. "Touched? I thought you said you kicked it?"

"Fine, yes, I kicked it. They weren't hissing anymore, but that was weird. Seeds shouldn't hiss."

"The laxiun seeds need frenetic energy to sprout. The hissing was just their waking up; they would have stayed seeds if they had remained in the jar. And weren't thrown at a trash can."

I raised my hands. "How was I to know? Funny thing, strange and deadly Eltrisphere plants weren't part of my gladiator training. Nor my Earth information course."

"Sorry. Do you have a broom? Preferably wood with natural bristles?"

I reached into the broom closet and brought one out. I'd picked the natural ones because I felt they fit with the teahouse feel.

"Okay, Betsy, Martha, and Jamie should be coming soon; they had so much stuff that Ralph had to rent a moving truck. Put the barricade back up in here. When I finish, I'll climb over the fence and come in the front door. I parked out of sight." He looked around. "Do you have a small cooler and ice packs?"

I dug a red cooler out from the storage closet and gave it to him, along with some ice packs from the freezer and an empty spice jar.

He darted out the back, and I resecured my note and wall of stuff in front of the door.

I finished prepping things, even brought out a pack of fancy cookies I'd bought. We'd be serving fresh ones once the tearoom opened, but this way the ladies could take the edge off before the real food.

I heard something at the front door. Still a bit paranoid, I looked out the narrow side window by the door, but nothing was there. I heard the scratching again, and this time I flung the door open.

To find five black and tan puppies covered in dirt. And each holding a suspicious-looking dead vine in their mouth.

# Chapter Twenty-Three

"That's so not good." I wanted to move away from the door, but that might make them come inside. Shutting the door on their faces didn't seem like a great idea either. The puppies seemed extremely proud of their finds.

Maybe those were the dead laxiun vines buried by whoever kidnapped my friends and ransacked their homes. Or, they could just be common Earth weeds.

The laughter in my head pointed out that my luck didn't go that way.

"Hi, puppies. What do you have there?" I didn't expect one of them to drop their dead vine and start talking in Sihlia.

"Gifts. You. Nice lady."

So bad on so many levels. "That's sweet. Where did you find them?"

"That way." The puppy raised a paw in the general direction of the cliffs over the ocean. There were a lot of buildings, streets, houses, and a forest between us and there. I needed them to take those things away. If Keith wasn't wrangling the seeds in the back, I'd ask him to do it. But he was, and I wasn't sure how the puppies would react to him anyway.

"Have you shown them to your mother?" Brutus didn't seem concerned about where her puppies went; at least they seemed to have free range of the town. She might recognize the vines, though. I hoped that being dead meant the vines weren't still dangerous, but that wasn't a chance I could take.

Not to mention that since there was a good chance these were some of the ones stolen from Betsy, Martha, and Jamie, they couldn't be here when the ladies arrived.

I crouched closer to the puppies and spoke softly in Sihlia, "I think your mother would like to see them. She might even want you to keep them with her. I love that you brought me these, but she needs to see them. Okay?" I'd put a few test sausage rolls in the oven, and heard the ding. "Would you like a reward? Snacks?"

All five little tails wagged so hard I was surprised they were still able to stand.

"You need to stay here, though. I'll give them to you, but you need to sit."

Five puppy butts dropped to the ground.

That was a good sign. I ran to the kitchen and grabbed my test sausage rolls. They were only about two bites big, so I cut them in half and put them on paper plates.

That they were probably still hot didn't slow down the puppies. They dropped their vines and started stomping and whimpering until I put the paper plates in front of them.

I didn't think Lucie normally used his magic to eat before he was cut off from it, but these five inhaled the sausage rolls in a moment and looked to me for more.

"Sorry, babies. That was it. Now, can you take the plants to your mom for me? Don't bring them back here. Or to my house. Keep them with your mom." At least Brutus could keep them from everyone else.

"Nice lady," they said in Sihlia. Then the puppies picked up their dead killer vines and trotted off into the hedge across from Tiberius's enclosure.

I was just shutting the door when a rustle came from the side. Luckily, it was Keith.

"Where are the seeds?" I stepped back to let him inside.

"In your cooler. I left it in the back in a shady spot that should remain that way during the day. We can get them after the tea. Anything I can do to help set up?"

I was shaking my head when a large moving van came trundling down the road to my teahouse. "What the..." My words dropped when Ralph, Betsy's handyman/gardener, waved as he parked. Martha was bouncing in the seat next to him. I could see Betsy and Jamie crammed in there as well.

It was good that Jack had left, and Keith's van was down the street. This truck took up most of my parking spaces.

"Why is it so big?" I'd figured a pickup truck with a shell, or a small U-Haul. This was a moving van, one big enough to move an entire apartment type of U-Haul.

"I found so many wonderful things!" Martha climbed out of the cab. "These belong here! And they are gifts, no need to give them back." She waved her hands as she ran around to the back. "I'm just so glad that they will have a home and be seen."

A brief chill hit me. I hadn't seen anything she brought. The furniture inside her house was lovely, but what if these items were in the attic for a reason? On the scale of what was going on around my life right now, that was an extremely low concern.

But it was nice to briefly worry about something silly.

Betsy, Jamie, and Ralph climbed out of the huge cab and also ran to the back. I shared a look of concern with Keith, then we followed.

"Oh. My." I had never been a fancy lifestyle girl. Being a gladiator meant a traveling life. But what I could see was stunning. I didn't even care if they came with ghosts; they would add ambiance.

There were two short loveseats, a mess of small Victorian side tables, what looked like a full-sized dining table with at least one leaf extension, and six gorgeous Tiffany lamps. "Are you sure? These are amazing." I couldn't stop looking at them, and they weren't even out of the moving van yet.

Martha ran over and hugged me. I was a good four or five inches taller than her, and had kept my physical gladiator fitness training up in my bottle during lock up, but honestly, I didn't know if I could have fought free from that hug.

Martha released me and stepped back. "I don't have children, but you have become as dear to me as Betsy and Jamie. These things were just languishing in the attic and basement. I'm proud that you like them!"

"We couldn't get the fainting couch out yet, but we will." Betsy jumped into the van and handed down a side table to Jamie, who put it to the side.

Ralph picked up the table as Jamie brought over another one. "How about you three get the things out of the van, and Ceian, Keith, and I will move them inside. You can sort them once they're all there."

We quickly got an assembly line in place and moved everything inside. I looked in my tearoom and shook my head. "I know we'll make it all fit, but also a fainting couch? That would be cute, but not sure I want my customers dozing."

Betsy laughed as she jogged up. "It's not that large, and I think we can fit it in that area between the office and kitchen." She waved her phone. "I noted the size, and if you have a measuring tape, I can see if it will work. It's for us on busy days." She winked.

I got the measuring tape, and she scurried off. I kept looking at the new stuff, my old stuff, and back again. Such a difference. My original things didn't say 'linger and enjoy yourself over some tea'. Even just piled up, Martha's stuff said exactly that.

"I was thinking we could move two side tables over into the shop portion, put displays on them, plants, knick-knacks." Martha had a determined look as she wandered around the things she brought over.

Keith and Ralph stood by two side tables and tilted their heads in question.

I nodded. Martha not only gave me this stuff, she seemed to know what she was doing.

We all stepped in, moving my original tables, side tables, loveseats, and lamps in whatever order she gave.

There were a few false starts; the loveseats had to be split up, even though aesthetically they looked charming together. The only corner that would hold them was where the public restrooms were.

Somehow, I didn't envision nice ladies and gentlemen climbing over loveseats to use the facilities.

The smaller of the two, an ornate burgundy tapestry with green and yellow flowers, went to the shop side. Moving the side tables to either side made it fit perfectly under the big window.

The slightly larger loveseat was deep blue with purple and yellow embroidery, and was also nestled near a window, but on the teahouse side. Both looked like they were brand new. "You're certain you don't want these back? People spill things."

The loveseat in the shop would be for sitting only, no food. But Betsy and Martha had already set up a coffee table, complete with doilies, in front of the loveseat in the tearoom.

"Oh, my stars, yes. Furniture needs to be loved as well." Martha was walking on clouds as she distributed her doilies on all of the tables. "Oh, we do need some room for the large table." She walked over to where it sat in the entrance. "How about toward the back, it can seat eight, if need be, with the insert, otherwise it's a lovely six-seater."

Keith and Ralph no longer asked for confirmation, just made the moves Martha said.

After the doilies were laid to her standards, the Tiffany lamps were placed, moved, adjusted, moved again, and eventually plugged in and admired. The large Moroccan lamp looked stunning on the shop side.

"You've created a wonderful place, Martha, thank you. And to all of you for helping move things about. It's just...I don't have words." That was uncommon for me. I often had the wrong words, but I usually had something.

Not this time. My teahouse and shop were amazing, and that was before Martha and Betsy brought in the house plants they'd started talking about. I just wanted something simple that could get me through this parole quicker.

They gave me a dream I didn't know I had.

Betsy, Jamie, and Martha came over for a group hug with tears in their eyes. Then Betsy patted my back. "Let's get a move on!" She and Jamie ran out to the van and came out with trays and a cooler.

"The only thing I'll need to heat up this round will be the mini quiches. But I should do some test baking. Oh! Mini cakes." Her nod was more for herself than any of us, as she and Jamie ran into the kitchen.

Martha relaxed on the loveseat on the tearoom side. "I'll test the service from here, make sure folks can eat here comfortably." Her grin was pure Lucie when he'd done something clever.

"Would you like some tea?" I'd had to move my teapot warmers during the great setup, but I could set one up for her now.

"That would be lovely. Do you have anything like Yorkshire Gold? I know it's not fancy, but I do find it comforting."

"I have Yorkshire Gold itself." I went to the kitchen.

"Why is the backdoor blocked?" Betsy yelled before she realized I was in the kitchen doorway.

"The hinge," Keith stuck his head in. "And a few other issues with the back. No worries, Ralph, I'll take care of this one." Ralph was already on his way to the kitchen.

Keith was faster than I. Ralph was a handyman extraordinaire; of course, he'd offer to fix things. Granted, Keith had hopefully gathered all of the vine seeds, but we couldn't take that chance.

Ralph shrugged and went back into the tearoom and sat next to Martha.

I leaned out of the door. "Would you like some tea, Ralph?"

"I recommend Yorkshire Gold," Martha said.

"Sign me up for that, please."

I pulled down two teapots, scooped out the tea into the strainers, and hit my hot water boiler. The thing was massive. There was no way we would ever run out of hot water during a single day.

"Oh! You did get it!" Betsy had been focusing on batter for the mini cakes, unwrapping fresh bread, and sorting the little quiches and sausage rolls from my freezer on trays. She pursed her lips and peered closer at the hot water boiler. "We may want to paint it something pretty down the line."

I set up the pot warmers, lit the tea lights, and put out the teapots and cups, saucers, three types of sugar, cream, and tiny spoons in front of Ralph and Martha.

I knew the feeling wouldn't last for long, but just setting it up was far cooler than I thought it would be.

"Oh!" I ran back into the kitchen, grabbed two tall glasses, and filled them with infused water from a dispenser on the counter. Not as large as the hot water boiler, but it was big enough, and cute. "Here we go." I sat them down in front of Martha and Ralph. Right now, even the cucumber and lemon water was exciting.

It didn't take much to find excitement after a hundred years in my bottle. A jinn's bottle was similar to the booth on that TV show, the one with the blue Police box. It was much larger on the inside. But unlike the TARDIS, it couldn't take me to distant planets or drifting around outer space. Unfortunately.

Martha served herself and Ralph their tea as Jamie helped Betsy in the kitchen.

Keith roamed around the shop side, pulling out jars and nodding, as if he were looking for something.

I thought all the remaining jars were mine, but he might be a better judge. It wouldn't be good if some Eltrisphere spice was bought by a local.

"Oh!" I ran back to the kitchen, dodged around Betsy, grabbed my fancy box of cookies, and put a few on a China plate. I'd just sat them down for Martha and Ralph when there was a knock at the door.

Even though it wasn't one o'clock yet, I wasn't surprised to see Hannah.

"I was going to apologize for being early, but I'm not the only one." She grinned and handed me a bouquet and a berry pie. "I do come bearing gifts, however." She waved hello to Ralph and Martha.

"Thank you so much! We just finished setting things up, Martha donated the lovely furniture, and Betsy and Jamie are getting the food set up."

Keith came out of the shop and took the flowers and pie. "Welcome, Hannah. Let me get these in water." He flashed a frown my way when Hannah looked away. I wasn't sure if he'd found something bad or just hadn't finished searching the jars.

"Can I give you the tour?" My place wasn't large, but I was proud of it.

Hannah smiled. "Tour away."

I started on the shop side, and Hannah oohed and aahed over the loveseat and the jar display. "I'll have to place some spice and tea orders for the diner. Perhaps after the tea, I can see what you have."

"That would be wonderful. Keith has been helping with my stock." I raised my voice

enough to hopefully reach Keith.

"Gladly!" He came out of the kitchen with two more tea warmers. "I've been recruited. Be careful going into the kitchen, those two are fast!"

He set the tea warmers down on tables and went back for more.

"Maybe we'll do the kitchen last." I waved my arms around the tearoom. "This is the tearoom, as you saw. There are two public bathrooms back there...which I now realize needs a sign."

Martha had been sipping tea, but her hand shot up. "I'm on it! I'll create the perfect one before the opening."

"Thank you!" I turned Hannah toward the back. "This is my office and extra storage. Martha's giving us a Victorian fainting couch that Betsy assures me will fit right here." I waved at the space.

"That's a wonderful idea! I might need one of those for busy days." Hannah winked. "If I can keep my staff off of it."

I smacked myself in the head. "I completely forgot. Is the diner open now?"

"Open and busy. Everyone who missed us this morning came in. I think we're getting crowds because they're all hoping for a scoop on what happened. Sadly, we haven't been told anything."

I wasn't going to tell her about the failed dead man's switch on the bomber. Jack could break that news. "I'm so glad everything's okay." I took us through the tearoom and into the kitchen.

"The kitchen is even adorable." Hannah waved to Betsy and Jamie.

"Go sit! Food's coming!" Betsy paused. "Okay, not Ceian. We need these trays loaded and tea served."

I hustled into the kitchen and helped fill the tea trays with far more food than our group warranted. Might have to remind Betsy to reduce the servings once we were open for business.

We spread out over two tables, with Martha and Ralph remaining on the loveseat.

The food looked lovely, smelled wonderful, and everything went great for the first half hour.

Then the kitchen exploded.

# Chapter Twenty-Four

It said a lot that Betsy, Jamie, and Hannah ran toward the kitchen when the explosion happened. Martha and Ralph, who were partially blocked by the coffee table in front of their loveseat, fought their way out as well.

I feared the worst as I slammed open the swinging kitchen door. Yes, I should have felt for heat first, but I didn't smell fire. And I was seriously freaking out. Had the failed bombers from before come back?

I had to keep moving with my friends piling up behind me, but the kitchen looked fine. Like a cooking and baking whirlwind had been here, but nothing exploded.

But the items I'd put against the back door had fallen.

Keith rushed past me. "I think it came from the back. The rest of you should go out front and wait." He turned to Hannah. "Please?"

Betsy and Hannah were both take-charge people, but Hannah did it at a professional level.

"Come on, folks, they've got it. Grab a cookie on the way out." She nodded and pushed everyone else out the front door.

That none of them hesitated said a lot about how much they respected Hannah.

I kept the kitchen door open to make sure they'd left. I thought about locking the front, but Keith was ahead of me. The lock clicked magically.

"I think they would stay out, but they are nosy."

"Agreed. How are we going to handle this? Was that explosion the cooler?" Now that I realized my kitchen hadn't been blown up a few days before my delayed grand opening, I admitted it wasn't a huge explosion. Just startling and not something to expect when having a lovely tea.

"I don't think so. If those seeds had blown up, this kitchen would be gone." He tested the door and then the handle. "No heat. But let me go first."

I nodded. In times of possibly deadly exploding magical seeds, always let the magic user go first.

He cracked open the door, looked around, then scowled and opened it wider. When he went out, I followed.

Everything looked like it had the last time I'd seen it. Minus the killer vine seeds. Although my trash can was smoking. The cooler looked fine.

"Were there seeds still in the trash?"

"There weren't when I finished." He pushed open the lid and revealed a small, blown-out hole in it. "This wasn't here either."

"What happened?" I stalked over, carefully avoiding the cooler sitting peacefully in the shade. Yup, something had been tossed into my trash can. Something explodey but small.

"Kids." Keith looked at the fence. "Probably figured no one was here. It looks like the remains of one of those illegal little firecrackers. You can get a new trash can easily enough. Just show them this one."

I glared at the can. "It's a good thing that I have two more." Forgotten Hollow was consistent with most places that I'd lived in the Eltrisphere; the government moved glacially.

Keith paused as he looked closer at the damaged lid.

"What?" I was getting better at spotting his 'something is wrong' looks.

He dropped the lid. "Nothing. We should bring the others back inside. But give me a few minutes to break the door hinge."

"First, that wasn't a nothing look, secondly, what?"

"I'm going to break it magically. I should have done it before, but I'm still not used to using magic much. And fine, yes, there was a hint of an old magic spell when I looked in the trash. The wrapper from a cracker was also there. But something else."

"Okay, do your thing. No more secrets, though, okay?" We returned to the kitchen.

"I'll try." He created a spell to make the door appear broken. He was good; it looked broken, like it had been forced open and shut again. Perfect.

I left when he piled stuff around it again.

My guests were waiting out front, but mostly peering in the windows.

"False alarm, some kid tossed a mini firework in my trash can. Keith's re-securing the door."

Ralph stepped forward. "Are you sure I can't help? I have my tools in the moving van."

"Keith's pretty determined to fix this; I don't want to take it from him." I aimed a pleading smile at Ralph. "But I'll have plenty of work down the line, if Betsy is up for sharing."

"We can work something out." Betsy smiled as she resumed her tea.

The rest of the tea went smoothly, with Hannah's fresh olallieberry pie sealing the deal.

We'd planned on talking about what was going on and bringing Hannah into our fold, but I wasn't certain about Ralph.

He resolved the issue by getting to his feet and picking up his plates.

"Sir, this is a full-service tea. Please leave your plates." I got to my feet as well. "Do you have to leave now?" Yes, I'd just been thinking about that, but it seemed rude to chase him out.

"Thank you. But yes, I should have plausible deniability in certain events. Thank you for the lovely tea." He nodded to Betsy.

"Keith has already said he will make sure we get home."

"Thank you for getting the van and bringing the stuff over. And moving it around. I'll make sure to pay for the moving van, just send me the bill." I was so grateful for the furniture help, I'd pay triple what had been charged.

"Pish." Martha cut in with a wave of her hand. "I already paid for it. I'm a full-service furniture and decoration provider. Thank you, Ralph."

Ralph said his goodbyes and left.

Hannah grinned and leaned forward. "So, who's behind everything? It's those black suits, isn't it? I have never trusted them."

I looked at Betsy; she would be better at telling things. She hesitated, then filled Hannah in on what had happened two months ago.

"No black suits at that time, obviously." Hannah's eyes grew rounder as the story grew. "But that's what happened to Old Man Clapper? Did they ever find his hand?"

That was a good point and one I hadn't thought about. As far as I knew, it hadn't been found. Hopefully, it wasn't around here.

Betsy leaned forward, looked around slowly, and dropped her voice. "No. It never turned up."

Hannah smiled and shook her head at Betsy's melodramatics. "I can't believe that about Tommy the contractor. He was going to do some work on the diner for me. Before he went into the big house. Did the specs and everything. He seemed so nice."

"He wasn't." Keith had continued eating as Betsy told her tale, but shook his head now. "Seriously, I know a lot of people liked him, but he tried too hard. I never trusted him."

I watched Keith carefully. I didn't know him when all of that happened, but did he know something important about the entire event? Something to ask him privately. I was having to make way too many sub-sections of my brain trying to sort out what could be said to whom.

"Does this tie into what happened recently? You all being kidnapped?" Hannah's humor at Betsy trying to make Clapper's hand sound ghostly vanished. Kidnapping wasn't something to joke about, even though it had turned out okay.

I knew it could have been much worse, especially since it looked like people from the Eltrisphere were involved. Some nefarious ones.

"Not that we can find." Jamie frowned. "I've been trying to hack into the Black Suits' website, but it's sealed tight. Extremely tight."

Betsy nodded. "None of us have many memories of what happened, but we all saw multiple people when they grabbed us at the hollow. I don't see how it could be connected to events of two months ago."

"Not that the cops believed us about multiple kidnappers." Martha shook her head. "Alice seemed to, but not the rest. And they still haven't figured out how we were knocked out. The chemical vanished." She folded her arms and sat back with a nod as if that resolved the issue.

Hannah looked around at all three. "Why were you out there again?"

I sat back on this one. There was no reason to believe that there was a connection between stolen and dumped junk mail and the kidnappings. Not to mention that Lucie and Tiberius had no connection to the mail in any form, yet they were also taken.

My thoughts, which I didn't want to share, were that the connecting element to everything so far was me. Until I knew what that connection actually was, I was staying mum.

I finished off a few more cookies, the last of the olallieberry pie, and another full pot of Darjeeling as Betsy, Jamie, and Martha told the tale of the stolen junk mail.

Even Keith, whom I was fairly sure was sweet on Betsy, hid his looks of incredulousness at the tale.

The thought that Betsy would make an incredible storyteller on the circuit in the Eltrisphere was now reinforced. Storytelling was considered an art in the jinn worlds of the Eltrisphere, and she could make excellent money.

I still didn't understand why the three ladies had been so obsessed with stolen junk mail.

"Did you find out if people were missing non-junk mail?" Keith finally weighed in. "Taking and burying junk mail is fairly odd. Unless it's tied to a bigger theft."

"We tried, but the cops weren't helpful. And no one's mentioned it to the post office." Betsy sighed. "It has to be connected. They lured us out to the Old Hollow and grabbed us. Why else?"

"Maybe they'd seen you tracking the junk mail and used it to get you alone to kidnap you for other reasons?" I wanted to pull back the words the moment they came out. So much for segmenting my brain.

"But what would be the reason?" Hannah asked. "Is it connected to what happened two months ago? Were there accomplices who suspected your involvement and wanted revenge?"

Hannah was good. That was something I hadn't thought of. I'd figured that Tommy was just an opportunistic leech taking advantage of me being new to town. That he might have been a part of something bigger was a worrisome thought. Although that could explain the apparent ties to me.

I didn't need them to decide to go investigate the drop point with that weird pentia spell still hanging out. Keith helped block it, but it was still there.

"Have any of you had weird dreams since you came back?" Keith was still eating but paying attention. Too carefully, in my opinion. He thought the spell in the barn might have affected them. Which meant that there could be a connection between whoever cast that spell and whoever took my friends.

"Damn it." I looked up at my outburst, which I thought was in my head. "Sorry, just bit the side of my tongue."

That pulled them away from the barn issue as they all commiserated. Hopefully, away from any possible magic-induced nightmares, too.

That lasted less than five minutes.

"I did have some strange dreams," Martha said. "I just figured it was from whatever they used to knock us out. And keep us out. We were gone almost twenty-four hours, and none of us recalls a thing."

"Me too." Jamie frowned. "I normally don't remember much about my dreams, but these stuck in my head." She took a long sip of tea. "Last night was the first time I didn't have them."

Betsy and Martha nodded. That couldn't be good.

"Mine were extremely specific." Betsy started, but Hannah cut her off with a frown.

"Have you three discussed them with each other?"

They all shrugged, but shook their heads.

"No, just never thought about it until Keith brought it up just now," Betsy said.

"Ceian? Do you have any notepaper? Hannah asked as she pulled three pens from her purse. "Hazard of work." She gave one to each of the other three.

"I'm sure I do." I went to my tiny office and fished around until I found a new lined notebook, then came back out. "How many pages do you each want?"

Hannah was watching them. "Give them each ten. Write everything you recall, and draw things too."

I gave them the paper, but Hannah wasn't done.

"Split up. It's too easy to be influenced by others unintentionally. Martha can stay on the loveseat, but Jamie and Betsy should move so no one can see what the other is writing."

"You're good at this." I wouldn't have thought about them being separated, but it made sense. Dreams were difficult to catch and recall, even in the best situation. That they might not be natural, my thinking, based on Keith's asking them about it, could make it worse.

"Thanks. I used to teach Psychology down in the valley at the local college," Hannah said. "Running a diner is far more relaxing."

I smiled. I'd never been interested in being a teacher, but I admired those who could do it. "Before you get started, does anyone else need some more tea? Snacks?"

Two requests for more tea and two for snacks, and they settled in to work on their dreams. Hannah watched them carefully over her tea.

Keith motioned toward the kitchen. "I can get started on fixing the back door, but let me show you something."

Since I knew he could fix the "broken" back door with a simple spell, I figured we needed to talk.

He waved me to the far end of the kitchen, further away from the tearoom, and kept his voice low. "I think they were drugged with svila leaf when they were grabbed. It vanishes into the victim quickly. It links the victims together, including shared dreams, until a counteragent is applied. It also makes them malleable."

It was probably too much excitement and caffeine, but it took me a few blinks to sort his connection. "The way they were affected when you were all up at the Grasshopper."

"Yes. It explains why they were, and the hotel employees weren't. My exclusion would have been because I'm not human. But it was bugging me why they were affected. Then I thought to ask them about their dreams." He shrugged. "I could be wrong; they might have no similarities in their dreams." The tone of his voice indicated he seriously doubted that. "I can do a quick check of what they're writing and determine if it was svila leaf."

I nodded. I didn't know much about herbs, aside from recovery ones, for when I'd hurt myself in the arena. But I'd heard of svila leaf. It was a class ten mind-altering substance and illegal on most worlds. "How do we get it out of their systems? And I thought we didn't think the black suits were from the Eltrisphere?"

He shook his head. "I'm not sure about Earth remedies. I'll need to look into it. But until we figure out who's behind this, we might not want to." He waved me off when I started to shake my head. "Think about it. Whoever, black suits or not, is behind all of this, believes they have some level of control over those three. Even if the black suits are human, someone with them probably isn't."

"If we remove the effects of the svila leaf, they'll know we're onto them." I shrugged. "I normally don't sleep a lot, so I watch cop shows. But is it safe to leave them like this?" The idea that whoever was behind this might be able to control my friends was terrifying.

He sighed and looked toward the tearoom. "As long as we keep them away from the Grasshopper long enough for me to find an Earth counteragent. Which won't be easy with those three."

"You're right. Oh, you might want to make some noise."

Keith nodded, and the sounds of hammering and low-level swearing were heard.

I started to head back to the tearoom but spun around. "What about the jars? Did you search them all?" I was proud of my collection of spices, herbs, and teas in bulk. I didn't want to have to be constantly worrying about them exploding.

"I didn't get through all of them, but I will before Hannah gets an order in. We don't need Eltrisphere spices or seeds in her diner." He sent another low-level general noise sound spell.

"Thanks." The three ladies were still writing and sketching, but it seemed to me they were slowing down. I sat next to Hannah to wait.

"I'm done." Betsy put down her pen and dove into some of the remaining tea sandwiches. "That was harder than I would have thought. I'd write something, and a bunch more thoughts came tumbling out." She handed the papers and pen to Hannah. "Here ya go, teach."

"Thank the stars, I'm done too." Martha shook out her hand. "That was painful." She walked to Hannah, dropped off the paper and pen, snagged a few sandwiches as well, and went back to the loveseat.

Jamie just muttered under her breath, turned in her papers and pen, grabbed a bunch of cookies, and stumbled back to her chair.

Hannah looked at me and held up the papers. "Do you want to go through them?" She folded each group of papers in half so she kept each person's notes separate.

"Keith said he would. I'm still going through my cousin's things." I nodded to the three ladies. "That is, if none of you mind?"

"Thank you, I can't speak for the other two, but they weren't those types of dreams." Betsy winked and kept eating.

"The cousin who died here? Have you thought of having a séance in your teahouse?" Hannah looked far too excited about that.

"Oh! That would be thrilling!" Martha recovered from her exhaustion immediately.

I started to point out that séances don't work on this planet, but caught myself. "But he was only found on this lot. The police said it was a body dump, nothing more. Wouldn't his spirit be cruising around where he was killed?" I'd never gotten into watching shows with ghosts, so I wasn't sure of the protocol.

"Not necessarily." Hannah peered closely at me. "But waiting might be a better thing."

I doubted séances would work here, but if they did and Darius came back? Things would get ugly fast. At least for me.

Keith came in through the front door. "I think I fixed it, but I had to oil the hinges, so don't use the door for a bit. Mind if I go shopping through the rest of your bulk spices and teas?"

Hannah handed him the dream reports. "Mind if I join you? I'd like to see what Ceian has."

I was worried, but a glance at Keith showed that he wasn't. He also wasn't concerned about anyone going into the backyard. Most likely, he'd searched for vine seed stragglers and moved the cooler. And figured he could stop Hannah from buying anything that looked dicey.

"By all means, go right ahead. I can make smaller jars of most of them if you want."

A half hour later, Hannah had three jars of different loose-leaf teas and brought them to my register. "Your first sale! I'm honored."

I grinned and rang it up, putting them in one of the nice, fancy big shop bags I'd bought. Yeah, it was more thrilling than it probably should be.

She shoved a bunch of money into my hand.

I sorted it, but she took a step back. "You gave me too much. By a lot." I tried to hand back a few extra bills.

"No. It is considered good luck to pay extra cash on the first sale. Both for the business and the customer." Hannah's smile was so wide that I couldn't say no.

"Well, thank you." I finished the sale.

That prompted everyone else to buy at least a jar of tea or spices. Keith bought two of them after a prolonged search. He must not have found any questionable ones, as the ones he bought had my handwriting.

"I think we're heading back now. We're trying to see if the plant-nappers dumped the vines they stole in the woods somewhere." Betsy headed for the door.

Keith, Hannah, and I all shouted "no" at the same time.

I wasn't sure why Hannah did it, but I knew why Keith and I did. Hannah just probably knew in general that snooping around out in the woods might be a bad idea for these three.

"We established that it wasn't a single person who kidnapped you three, and only one body of a possible kidnapper was found." Hannah was a few years younger than the other three, but she looked like a kind but stern grandmother explaining why there was no candy. "Going around town is one thing, but until everyone has been found out and taken care of, you shouldn't wander in the woods."

"Not to mention, why would they dump plants they specifically stole?" I didn't want those three roaming around either, but Hannah already put it better than I could. Hopefully, the puppies had found all of them.

"Good points. I suppose we can continue looking into the mail situation. In town." Betsy sounded a little defeated, but I wasn't sure I believed her.

Neither did Hannah. "That would be wonderful! Can I tag along as well? The diner's well-staffed, and they'll call if there's an emergency."

"That would be superb." Betsy spun to me. "Thank you again for a wonderful tea. I'll pop by tomorrow and we can make a specific list of new supplies for the grand opening."

"Oh! We didn't talk about that. We need a grand opening plan." Martha looked ready to sit again.

I needed to clean up, then get back to those cursed boxes.

"How about samples?" Hannah said. "I did that with cinnamon buns and coffee when I opened the diner. Mini versions of both, but folks loved it. You don't want to go broke, but a little free goes a long way in Forgotten Hollow."

"That's a great idea." I hadn't given it much thought. Okay, if I were honest, no thought. I'd never run a business in my life, let alone a food-based one. "Maybe a cookie and a mini sausage roll with a disposable cup of hot tea? I have three hot dispensers, so we could offer three different types?" I knew not everyone liked tea, but those people weren't my customers.

"Brilliant! Any more brainstorming can be at Hannah's for breakfast tomorrow." Betsy hugged me, as did the rest of the ladies.

Keith waited until they were outside. "I'll get them where they're going, then meet at your place?"

For a few moments, I'd forgotten about the boxes of magical mayhem in my house. It was nice while it lasted.

"Thank you. I still have a lot to go through, and what I've found so far is weird." I peeked outside. Hannah was taking my bike out of her car and waved as she put it in the bike stand for me.

Keith left with the ladies, and I finished cleaning everything. Right now, washing the fancy dishes, cups, and stands was fun. I knew that feeling wouldn't last long at all. I might need to look at hiring more help down the line.

The bike ride home was quiet. Or mostly so. I was approaching the hill toward my cottage when a black SUV sped past me. A glance back caused me to pull completely off the road.

Six more black SUVs were racing to get out of Forgotten Hollow.

# Chapter Twenty-Five

I waited until the last black SUV was out of sight, heading toward the freeway in the distance. No other traffic of any sort was coming this way, so I resumed my trip home. They were supposedly staying longer, but instead were leaving early? I doubted that was all of them, even if each SUV was full, but seven cars were a lot.

Maybe they were on a field trip. I slowly continued down to my driveway as that thought bounced around. Part of me would love for them to leave early, and we could shove all this weirdness behind us until next year. If I was still on Earth.

The other part of me felt we needed to resolve this now, not a year from now. The black suits themselves might be from Earth, but someone in their organization wasn't.

Lucie was sitting on the fence between my yard and the puppies' lot. He jumped down and sauntered over.

Never trust a sauntering cat.

"Good to see you're back. I'm heading out on patrol." He sat down in front of me and gave his version of an innocent look.

"Too bad, Keith and I are going to be going over Darius's things. Thought you might want to see what else he had."

The immediately flapping tail pointed out that Lucie hadn't thought of that. "Oh, yeah. I probably should. There might be some of my things in there that I want back."

He hadn't mentioned that earlier, but he had said Darius hadn't let him bring most of his stuff back from India. And I wouldn't know if anything was his or not.

He probably made that connection while I was gone. Giving Lucie too long to think wasn't a great idea.

"True." I got off my bike and we walked to the house. "Where's Tiberius?"

"Out on the side of the barn. He likes it there and feels that if he changes back into himself when asleep, no one will see him." Lucie gave a brief, sympathetic glance toward the barn. Even he was concerned about Tiberius changing into a goat permanently.

My phone rang as we approached the door. Camfield's number.

"Hi, Camfield." I didn't have to fake being happy about his call, just friends or not, I was looking forward to a nice, lovely dinner with him in a few hours.

"Ceian, I am so sorry. I'm having to fly home for a brief trip, an emergency meeting in LA. Can I get a rain check for dinner?"

I kept my disappointment out of my voice. "Sure, things happen. Have a safe trip."

"Thanks. Oops, at the airport now. I'll come by when I'm back." He hung up.

"Date canceled? Didn't know you had one," Lucie asked.

"Just friends, but yeah, postponed." I left my bike against the cottage and unlocked the front door.

"We did...what happened?" Lucie darted inside, then froze, arched his back, and puffed his tail.

I wanted to do the same when I pushed the door completely open. My house was ransacked. Swearing under my breath, I went through and straightened things.

"Doesn't look like anything is broken or missing, hopefully." The front room was hit the hardest. The door to the guest room, and Darius's things, remained locked.

Lucie was wandering and sniffing everything, but stopped and hissed on the bottom shelf under the landscape painting.

Right where my bottle had been.

I did what any self-respecting jinn would do when her bottle, the heart of who and what she was, had been stolen.

I passed out.

***

I felt a paw tapping my face, but I couldn't figure out who it was, or why they were in my bedroom.

"Come on, I know you're freaked out, but Keith is pulling into the driveway."

Lucie. Telling me about Keith. I was on the floor because...my eyes flew open, and I scrambled over to the bottom shelf of my bookcase.

My bottle couldn't be gone. Maybe it fell behind something. Knocked over. Rolled away under the refrigerator.

Not that it would fit, but all options had to be explored.

"It's not here. I checked while you were out. I'm sorry." Lucie even went so far as to lick my hand in a sign of comfort.

I started hyperventilating. I'd heard so many horrible tales of jinn losing their bottles when I was a kid that the concept itself just kept bashing around my skull.

"Hello? Anyone home?" The sofa blocked Lucie and me on the floor from the open door. I waved my hand over my head limply.

"Why are you down there? Are you okay?" Keith walked around the sofa.

I flailed my hand where my bottle had been and silently opened and closed my mouth.

Lucie finally spoke. "The house was broken into when I was next door, Tiberius was asleep, and you were all having tea. They took her bottle."

"Oh no." Keith dropped next to me and peered into my eyes. "Come on, Ceian, you're stronger than this. You'll be fine."

That wasn't what I'd expected, but then again, Keith wasn't a jinn. Still, he should understand something of bottle protocol.

"No, I won't." Tears started falling. Not nice, lady-like ones, but huge, ugly ones. Jinn didn't cry often, but when we did, it was never pretty. "Bottle...it's who I...am!" I grabbed Lucie and started sobbing all over his fur. Granted, after my one hundred years of jail time, I was a bit tired of it. But it was still *my* bottle.

Jinn were assigned their bottles within their first year of life and only received new ones in extreme cases. We spent so much time in them that they became an extension of who we were.

The fact that Lucie didn't twist away as I continued hugging him spoke a lot about how screwed I was. At least the cat understood.

Keith gently lifted my face and wiped away a few tears. "You'll be fine. Everything you are is inside you. I know. I *was* married to a jinn for many years. She was always losing her bottle. Sometimes for years at a time."

Curiosity stomped on my sobbing. "I didn't know you were married."

Lucie took the distraction to jump out of my arms and headbutt a box of tissues over.

"I was. She was amazing and older than I. She was almost three thousand years old when she passed. I started wandering after she left." There was an old sorrow there, but happiness as well. He'd had a wonderful life with her.

Three thousand was an older jinn. "How old are you?" Thinking about him and his late wife made me able to ignore the hole in my heart where my bottle had been.

"I'm one thousand and three." He mugged to show off his face, which looked like a healthy human in his late sixties.

"And you don't look a day over eight hundred. Fair enough, I'm five hundred and eighty-seven."

"I would have suspected much less than that. You understand now why I said the loss of your bottle, while horrible, is not the end of you?"

I gave a huge sigh. I didn't know when the horrors that my family had told me would happen were coming, but I didn't feel different.

Then the chime from the landscape painting went off.

Keith's eyes went wide, and he rushed into the hall, out of sight from the screen. Lucie went to his cat tower and glared as Xieth's face appeared.

"Why are you down there?" Xieth scowled down at me, and I fought not to laugh at the distortion of his face because of the angle.

I scrambled up to sit on the sofa. "I was picking up things." I almost told him about my bottle, but Keith shook his head from the hall. I'd find out why later. "We were hit again. They ransacked the place, but I'm still checking to see what's missing." It was the truth. Lying by omission, unless directly and specifically asked, wouldn't choke me.

The odds of Xieth asking where my bottle was were extremely slim.

"This isn't good. Did they get into Darius's possessions?"

"No, the door was still locked. If I had some access to my magic, I'd have a better chance of protecting everything." I didn't intend to say that. Yes, I wanted my magic back, especially with my bottle gone, but pushing him wasn't a good idea.

"We're looking into it. Not yet, but situations are changing. And not for the better."

That was unexpected. "Oh. Okay. Thanks."

"I just called to see how things are going with the tea business. You are being watched closely, you know."

"We're right on target. Meeting with my local business women tomorrow to plan our grand opening." I shrugged when his already beady eyes narrowed to slits. "It's a thing here. Brings in new customers so they like your product and want more." I gave a slow nod as if I'd totally heard of this before today.

"Earthlings are odd. Go ahead, but keep me updated on it. Also, report on anything you find of interest in that miscreant's belongings." He raised his voice. "And stay out of trouble, cat." With a glare over my head in the direction of Lucie's cat tower, the landscape reappeared.

I felt a brief twinge at seeing my bottle in the middle of it, but took a deep breath and relaxed.

Keith better be right about my bottle.

Keith remained in the hall, so I went to join him. He raised a finger to his lips and counted down on his watch.

"We're good now. I can't remove the delay when he logs off, not yet anyway. There's a chance anyone calling in could still hear you for a full minute after they shut down the screen."

"Thanks for the warning. Shall we start with Darius's stuff?" The words were barely out of my mouth when Lucie was off his cat tower and winding around my legs.

"I'll help, of course." He moved over to circle Keith's legs as well.

I shrugged. Cats were cats. I unlocked the door and let out a sigh when nothing was disturbed. I'd intended to check just in case the thieves had relocked the door when they left. The loss of my bottle had derailed that thought.

"This pile over here are the ones I'm concerned about. There's the collection of cast-off clothing that I think can go to a charity when we're done." I paused. "After the cops go through it. Jack wants to see anything that's not personal to our family."

"Let's see what else is in a few of these before I start poking around magically." He reached for a box cutter, then turned to me. "I was surprised that Xieth is considering giving you access to your magic. Even just a part of it. He's too much of a jerk to do something helpful for anyone else. There's something big going on. And I believe that spell in the barn was part of it."

"My thoughts as well." Lucie hopped up to the top box to watch. "Good thing you didn't mention it to the cherub. We need to figure out what it is and who did it. Oh, unrelated, Brutus sends her regards and thanks you for the snack. She hasn't had those in years."

I quickly filled Keith in.

"Those were most likely the ones stolen from Betsy and the others. But why steal them and then dump them?"

I shrugged. There was enough unconnected weirdness going on that I wasn't going to speculate on bad guy behavior. "Maybe they weren't what the thieves thought they were? But why go through all of that work if you weren't sure what you were stealing?"

"Unless they removed a chemical or component from the vines before discarding them." Keith looked up at Lucie. "Brutus ate them all?"

Lucie had been washing his face but stopped to nod. "She loved them."

"That supports her being a hoxien wolf; they can digest anything."

"Maybe the puppies will find more leftover ones?" I wasn't going to blame myself for destroying potentially useful dead weeds. There was no way for me to know they might be helpful, and I figured Brutus would know what to do with them.

One handy tip I learned on the gladiator circuit of my youth—holding self-blame could get you killed.

Or at least seriously mangled.

"You never know." Keith started to slice open the box in front of him when my brain decided to wake up from its earlier shock about my bottle. "Oh, on my way home, seven black SUVs passed me. They were heading toward the freeway."

"What? I heard confirmation that they were staying an extra week from the hotel staff just a few hours ago." He shrugged. "Before our tea, I made a quick check at the Grasshopper. That entire group has been booked and paid for through the end of next week."

"That just makes it weirder if those cars don't come back. Good idea to go up there without the ladies. At least until we get that svila leaf out of them. There are too many elements of mayhem floating around."

Keith nodded. "Indeed. Let's see if we can get some of them resolved." He continued to cut open the box, lifted the flaps, swore like a sailor, and jumped away.

# Chapter Twenty-Six

"What?!" I yelled as I stepped back as well, and Lucie looked ready to find a way to fly over the boxes blocking him from the door.

"I'm not sure." Keith's grip on the box cutter was tight enough to turn his knuckles white.

"How can you have that kind of reaction without being sure?" Lucie hadn't jumped yet, but his tail was about to fly off his butt.

"I know what I think I saw. If it is that, we're more screwed than I could have imagined. If it's not, we're still probably screwed." Keith now looked a lot closer to his one thousand years of age.

"If you don't tell me now, I'm pushing you out of the way. What could—" My words were cut off as Lucie launched himself at the open box, not over it.

He stayed there for less than a second before screaming like he'd been burned and shooting off down the hall.

"Oh, dren." I ran after Lucie, but he was on his tower, looking pissed but not injured. I came back, shoved Keith aside, and pulled open the flaps.

Inside was a silver-etched black lacquer box about the size of a box of cereal. Part of me wanted to touch it, and the other part screamed to run away.

Rather, it was Keith, grabbing my collar and yanking me back when I reached out for it.

"Don't touch it! It's a mob spell box."

Extremely not good. Every mob kept its most deadly information, mostly on other mobs, in a specialized family box. It should never be out of that mob's home base.

Ever.

I'd heard the spells on most of them could destroy half a planet, or a small moon, if they were triggered incorrectly or forced open.

"What in the was Darius doing with *that*?" I leaned closer but kept my feet where they were. "Which mob?" I really hoped it wasn't the Xlontg-Firesti.

Keith glared at the box. "The Pasken. They were destroyed about twenty years ago. Their entire compound was obliterated."

"And this should have been blown up with it." I still wasn't going to touch it. A glance in the living room showed that Lucie was furiously cleaning his paw pads.

"It should have been." Keith had the torn look of wanting to touch it, but not wanting to.

"And that idiot Darius got it how?" Lucie stopped cleaning long enough to yell from his cat tower. "There's no way he could take down a one-armed drunken cherub, let alone be involved in destroying a mob."

"Rumors at the time were that it was a hit from the Xlontg-Firesti mob," Keith said. "Never proven, of course."

My brain was still rattled from my bottle shock, but it hit a nasty conclusion eventually. "The Xlontg-Firesti were after Darius. Darius somehow had that box, which most likely has some nasty information about the Xlontg-Firesti." I started pacing. "They paid him to get it, he did, but never gave it to them. What's the best way to burn a cottage to the ground with no one catching you?" I could start over. I could hide somewhere else on this planet, give up all plans of ever going home.

"Easy there. I don't think you have to destroy everything. This is actually helpful, now we know why you're such a focus of attention."

I glared at the stupid shiny black box. "Can we destroy it?" Yes, whatever secrets that were in it were worth billions of gold coins if sold to the right person. It was the lack of living long enough to enjoy the lifestyle that was gibbering in my brain. I never took any paid fight dives when I was in the arena because they were all associated with mobs.

"You or I couldn't, even if you got all of your magic back. And unless we could nuke it from space, human weapons won't work. I can put a shield around it to block their search. There was one on it long ago, but it was damaged at some point. The current one won't hold if someone looking for it gets on this property." At my nod, Keith settled a light spell over the entire box. He then carefully folded the flaps back in place and taped them shut.

He used so much tape that it was nothing but a lumpy blob. I wasn't sure how much protection packing tape provided to evil boxes, but at least no one would accidentally open it.

Keith nodded to the tape blob. "We need to put this in the barn. Not over the sigil, but in a corner. I'll look for a locked trunk for it tomorrow."

I grabbed the tape-covered box. "Lead the way." I didn't feel anything coming from the box, which said a lot more about Keith's abilities than anything else.

Magic users became stronger as they aged, and at over a thousand, Keith was strong. He was currently having some issues because he hadn't used his magic for forty years.

He and Lucie led me out to the barn. Keith unlocked and held open the door.

"Far left corner?" There was still a bunch of junk over there, so hopefully this wouldn't stand out.

"Sounds good."

An electric shock of pain, terror, and anger hit me as I crossed the threshold into the barn. I screamed and bounced back out. The pain stopped, but the residual lingered.

I almost dropped the box, but luckily, the survival part of my brain panicked and held on to it tighter.

Keith and Lucie ran to me. A sharp braying came from the other side of the barn, and a groggy-looking Tiberius came charging out. "Intruders!" He skidded to a halt when he saw the three of us near the open barn door. "I thought we weren't coming into the barn right now? And why did you scream?"

"I needed to put one of Darius's boxes outside. The box didn't like the barn." Adrenaline was keeping me upright, but that was going to end soon.

Tiberius's eyes narrowed, and he stepped forward to sniff the box. Then his eyes flew open, and a look of sheer horror filled his face. "Why is that here! They'll kill us all!"

Tiberius was a centurion. Big, fierce, a fighter for justice as he saw it. I'd never heard the level of fear in his voice that he had right now.

Then he gave a weird bleat and fell over with all four legs sticking up stiffly.

"He's a fainting goat? That was cruel of the council." Keith walked over to Tiberius. "Explains the name of your teahouse and shop, though."

A few seconds later, Tiberius snorted and scrambled to his feet, flustered but calmer than before. "It was extremely cruel. I hate it when that happens! By the way, I can hear you when I have my little problem." His glare at all three of us was extremely Tiberius-like. "Now, why is something like that on this planet? Who does it belong to?" He aimed his glare exclusively at me this time, but carefully didn't look at the box.

"It's not my fault; I didn't ask for this to be in Darius's stuff. And no, I'm not saying who out here." I adjusted the box in my arms. It wasn't large but much heavier than it looked. "Where can we put this?" The reaction to entering the barn meant it couldn't go there.

Keith frowned and looked out into my yard.

Lucie jumped in before Keith could come up with an idea. "You have shovels and he has magic, right? I bet if we asked nicely, Brutus would let us bury it in her yard. No one from Earth or the Eltrisphere would mess with a mother hoxien wolf, even though the humans don't know what she is."

"Good idea. The humans aren't who we're worried about." Brutus and I were friends of a sort. And she still scared the heck out of me.

Tiberius scowled. "I don't know what *exactly* is in that box, but you're thinking of hiding it in an empty lot? We know it's not empty, but the humans think it is. What are you going to do when someone buys that place?" He knew the box was dangerous, and that was enough for him.

I hadn't thought about that. I didn't want neighbors, regardless. "That's a really good point. Maybe my yard, but near their fence?"

Keith shook his head. "There is a bigger point than that. No one has claimed that lot, and from what you told me, the cherubs who were working with Darius lived there. But did they own it? Not just for this situation, but I think you having immediate neighbors is a bad thing. Given everything that keeps happening."

The other side of my fenced-in yard was an open field and a small side road. There really weren't any houses adjacent to me.

Probably why the council picked it.

"I seriously doubt that Xieth is going to give me money to buy the other lot. And I need to set this down somewhere." I was strong, but holding a heavy object got old fast. My adrenaline was fading.

"I can do it." Keith's voice was low as he looked over to Brutus' yard. "I'll buy it under a company I own that would be extremely hard to connect to me."

All three of us looked at Keith. The guy drove a fixed-up Vanagon and he was rich? I'd never seen where he lived, but I didn't think it was in a rich part of town.

Forgotten Hollow didn't really have one, just a few larger Victorians like Martha's.

He turned to us. "Yes, the company I own is successful, stable, and has an exceedingly well-hidden ownership. Please don't tell Betsy or the others." He blushed. He was embarrassed about being well off. I was too grateful for it to do anything but nod in agreement.

"Thank you." The box started slipping. "Seriously, where can I put this?"

Tiberius nudged the wheelbarrow toward me.

"Thanks." My arms were shaking so badly, I wrapped them around myself after I set the box in the wheelbarrow.

"First, let me talk to Brutus; we've built a rapport." Lucie wandered across the yard, then turned back. "You might want to close and lock the barn, and wheel that box back into the guest room. The fuzz is here." He twitched his tail and jogged across the grass to the other lot.

Two cop cars. They could be having a slow crime day, or there was worse to be dumped on me.

"I'll lock things up here. You go hide the box." Keith plastered a smile on and waved to the cars as they turned into the drive.

I nodded and rolled the wheelbarrow a few more feet, then grabbed the box and ran inside the house. They wouldn't have seen me yet, but the first car was pulling up behind Keith's van.

I ran to the guest room, shoved the box in the back corner of the closet, locked the door, and jogged back out.

Keith was chatting with Jack, Alice, and Officer Jones. None of them looked stressed or worried, but there was still time. I knew that usually, Forgotten Hollow's criminal activity was low, but sending three cops over just to chat seemed odd.

"Ceian, look who just arrived." Keith looked up.

I nodded hello to everyone and tried to keep my suspicions from showing on my face. The other two smiled, but Jack did not.

I was getting tired of that look.

He was still disturbingly attractive, even when frowning, but it wasn't fun to be on the other side of it.

"We just wanted to go over some new details from the diner this morning. Do you mind if we talk inside?" Jack's voice was completely neutral, and he even dropped the scowl.

Not good.

# Chapter Twenty-Seven

At least he didn't ask to go into the barn.

I forced a smile. "Sure. The place is a bit messy, but there are places to sit." Since whoever broke into my house this time was most likely from the Eltrisphere, I didn't want to report it. Not to mention explaining that the only thing stolen was my bottle would be weird.

Then a tiny voice in my head pointed out that if the cops found my bottle somewhere, they'd have no idea who it belonged to unless I reported it.

I sighed as I swung open my door for them. "Someone broke into my house while I was either at the diner or at my teahouse." I shrugged as Officer Jones pulled out his notepad. "They were searching for something, but nothing was broken, and only one thing was stolen. An old family bottle." I gave him a long description of it, but a cough from Keith stopped me before I started going on about the inside.

*That* would have been weird.

"I'm sorry for your loss and the intrusion." Jones flipped his pad open and smiled. "But we'll keep an eye out for it."

"Was it valuable?" Jack asked as they all sat. "Aside from personally. Was it a money-based theft?"

I refrained from asking if he thought I looked like I had expensive things sitting around and shook my head. "Not valuable to anyone outside of my family." Not a lie, and it triggered a thought.

If whoever stole it was a jinn, they might be able to go inside it if they had enough magic. They could have thought I had valuable belongings hidden in there. Such as a mob family box or the fabled Stone of Zalianthia

"Did you just think of something else?" Jack jumped on that too fast. What was he expecting?

I gave my most reassuring smile. "No, I just flashed back on some memories of that bottle in our family. It's in that landscape painting." They all took photos of it. I should have thought of that before giving them that long description, but my brain was seriously crashing toward overload.

And my arms still ached from holding that vile box. I wanted a long bath, a pile of food, and no one in my house. Darius's stuff could wait another day.

"What can we help you with?" Keith asked Jack after a glance at me.

My impending brain tilt must have been showing.

Jack didn't comment, but powered on. "They finished the autopsies of the bodies outside the diner. Nothing helpful has been found yet about their deaths." He paused and watched me. "However, one of the men had your name, address, and location of your teahouse in his pocket. It also said when you'd be at the diner this morning."

Jack was stoic, but a flash of real concern crossed his face.

"What? Can I see the note? Can I see a picture of the man who had it? Who was he? Why was he coming after me?" I wasn't proud of the way my voice started getting in the 'too high for humans to hear' range, but this just tipped things over. If my bottle were here, I'd be sorely tempted to dive in. Regardless of the witnesses.

"I was hoping you could tell me who he was." Jack was back to neutral as he pulled out his phone, selected some images, and handed the phone to me.

The first was a dead, pale blond man who, for a moment, I feared was Camfield. A closer look revealed he was much older. I couldn't tell if he was in a black suit because the photo was probably taken in the morgue, and he didn't have a shirt on. I swiped to the second. Same lack of shirt, but this man was younger, had a darker skin tone, and thick black hair.

"Neither of them looks familiar. Were they wearing black suits?"

"No black jackets. But they both had white shirts and black dress pants." Alice answered when Jack paused. "Sorry, detective, but she needs to know. You even said it yourself, aside from their different color jackets, they were dressed like the Grasshopper crowd."

Jack nodded. "True. It's worrying that neither is familiar to Ceian. They had been arguing right before they died, according to a witness down the street, so they might not have been on the same side."

The next image on his phone was the note. Disturbing to see, even though I knew what it said. Who, aside from my friends, knew where I'd be earlier?

"Does the writing look familiar?" Jack asked as I handed him back his phone.

"No. Which one had the bombs and which had the note?" I was hoping they weren't the same person. If they'd been arguing, maybe the note holder was trying to stop the bomber.

"The blond man. We don't have either of their names, nor has anyone recognized them. Since this is a second bombing attempt, the feds are trying to ID them for us."

"He had both?" Maybe I'd misheard.

"Yes. The other man was trying to pull him out of the lot when they both dropped dead."

"Did you find out why the dead man's switch didn't work?" More details weren't making me feel better, but I couldn't help asking. "Oh, did you know seven black SUVs like the black suit people drive raced out of town?" I glanced at the time on my phone. "About an hour ago."

"Still searching on the switch, something fused it at the time both men died. They both had old-school pagers on them, and they were fried. Maybe they were connected to something. Which way were the SUVs headed?"

"Toward the freeway. I don't know if they came back. I was cleaning up what happened to my house."

"Um hm." Jack was even more neutral than before, but got to his feet. "Thank you for looking at the pictures. If you think of any time you might have seen those two, or who else might have known your agenda, call me."

Alice flashed me a sympathetic smile as she and Jones got up as well. "I hope your grand opening goes well. I saw one of the flyers in town."

I thanked her, but waited until they had pulled away before swearing. "What flyers?"

Keith shrugged. "I have a feeling Betsy and the others decided not to go hunting for more missing mail and found another task. I saw one up at A Lotta Joe's on my way over here, but I figured you knew."

"Not a word. And we were just with them a short time ago. I appreciate all the help, I do. But it's overwhelming to keep track of life and death situations mixed in with what color napkins to get." I dropped to the sofa and plopped my head in my hands.

"If you don't mind, I'm going to run a few spells over the entire barn before I go, just to make sure that box didn't trigger something."

I sighed and lifted my head. "Thank you. We can finish the boxes tomorrow. And the box of evil can wait. I'm worried about burying it at this point." I was sliding into overwhelm and exhaustion.

Keith nodded and went out to the barn.

I stretched out on the sofa. There were too many things racing around my head. But one thing I could at least send a text about. I stayed on the sofa for a few more minutes, then got my phone and texted Betsy asking if she could send me a copy of the flyer. I added that I was busy, so not to come by.

I adored her and the others, but I didn't need any more visitors.

I was starting to doze off when my cellphone rang. I answered it without looking at the number; I didn't even open my eyes. I figured it was Betsy confirming that she didn't need to come over. Probably while she was on the way over. "Hey."

"Where is the Stone of Zalianthia?" The voice was creepy and sounded like someone was using one of those toy voice changers the knick-knack shop sold.

"Who is this? I'm working with the police; they will find you." I was now extremely awake. Thinking that the man found dead in my barn a few days ago wasn't the only one behind the kidnappings was one thing. It was annoying to have it confirmed. And that these people still thought they could get the stone, which I didn't have, even though their leverage was gone.

"We will get the Stone. You will regret betraying us, *Darius*." The call clicked off.

I stared blankly at my phone. They thought I was Darius? Jinn can disguise themselves, but I didn't look remotely like him. And when I found him, he looked more or less like I recalled. Of course, I'd spent a lot of my bottle time envisioning him dead, so there was some distortion.

Why did this person, or persons, think that Darius had the Stone of Zalianthia? If he'd had that, he wouldn't have been hiding on a backwater planet like Earth. He'd sell it fast and live the high life on one of the rich luxury worlds.

I glanced toward the locked guest door. I could call Keith back, but I needed to not be around people for a bit. Those one hundred years in my bottle had left me not used to being around people. I'd been adjusting to being around my friends and coping with things until life kept pulling the rug out from under me.

Which left me to sort this out for now. What if, along with that mob box, that rat Darius had somehow found the Stone of Zalianthia but didn't realize what it was? What if the thing was *inside* the mob box? I longingly looked at the space where my bottle had been. I never thought that I'd miss it so much so soon.

That call drove away any exhaustion I felt. I needed to do something.

I wasn't going to dive into the mob box, no matter what. Keith's level of taping was terrifying. But I could at least dig into some of the other boxes.

I opened the outside door to see if the animals wanted in, but neither was in sight. Lucie definitely proved his toughness by socializing with Brutus. But if we were going to be neighbors for a while once Keith bought that lot, it was good that there was a connection.

I shut and double-locked the door. Not that it had proven helpful against whoever stole my bottle. Unlike the first time, no windows or the door were damaged.

I added some lighter-weight gardening gloves, just in case there was something else in those boxes that shouldn't be touched. Then, I entered the guest room.

I grabbed the box cutter and made my first swipe in the next box in the pile, when a scratching came from the front. I went out to the front room and peeked out the window.

Yup, Lucie and Tiberius were both there. They kept looking at the sky and moving closer to the door.

The weather had been decent when I was dealing with the mob box, but it wasn't now. Strong winds were cruising through, and the clouds were heavy and dark.

"It's freezing out there!" Lucie darted in before I finished opening the door. Tiberius waited mostly because he was big enough that he had to. The gust of freezing air that followed him made me wish I had a jacket on.

"What happened? The weather was fine before." I glared at the sky, then shut and locked the door again. I'd seen a few storms during my time here, but this one was wicked looking.

"A witch storm." Lucie stomped over to the kitchen and glared at his empty food dish. I normally wouldn't rush feeding them, but the weather was nasty out there, and it made me feel bad they'd been stuck outside.

I filled his dish and replaced his water with a slightly warmed-up version. Then I fed Tiberius and tried to ignore what Lucie said.

I gave up. "It can't be a witch storm, you daft cat. Earth doesn't have them. And, while I will agree that there are more non-humans down here than expected, the power required to create a witch storm is massive."

I closed all the curtains. The storm was freaking me out, even if it couldn't be a witch storm. Witch storms were violent acts of nature that weren't really created by nature. At least not by themselves. Not all planets were susceptible to them, but my home world had been. I went through a ten-day one when I was a kid.

I freaked out so badly after three days, my parents threw a bunch of toys into my bottle and had me stay there. They'd drop in to check on me, hang out, and give me meals. But it was probably a good idea on their part.

"You two will be fine in here? I'm sorting some of the boxes." I wasn't up to debating whether that howling wind was the result of some crazy, powerful Eltrisian or not.

Tiberius looked up, nodded, and went right back into his bowl. He had shelter, comfy blankets, and food. He was good.

Lucie inhaled the rest of his food and raced to the guest room. "I'm on it!"

I followed him in, adjusted my gloves, and resumed cutting the first box. "More trinkets. Great." I pulled out what looked like knockoffs of ancient Egyptian jewelry. "He paid to bring these here? What for?"

Lucie sniffed them and hissed. "They're fakes, alright, but they have something weird baked into the clay. I don't know what it is, but you probably don't want drug dogs sniffing them." Lucie often stayed up with me watching the cop shows. I secretly thought he wished he were a police dog.

"In the faience? That stuff they use to make fakes?" I held the necklace closer. I couldn't tell if they had drugs baked into the ceramics or not.

Lucie snorted. "Darius was sure he was going to get rich selling Earth artifacts in the Eltrisphere, fake or not. The drug smuggling must have been a way for him to hedge his bets."

"How would he know which Earth drugs would impact people from the Eltrisphere?" I shook my head before Lucie could respond. "Never mind, I don't want to know." I pulled out all of the jewelry, valuable or not, Darius hadn't helped matters by just cramming it all in the box. "I need to repack these with coffee grounds, just in case." According to my cop show obsession, I needed used and dried grounds to break the scent. I didn't have those. Unused grounds should at least do something. My focus had been on Eltrisphere people, but human cops could cause issues, too.

Lucie watched me as I shoved coffee grounds from my kitchen into the box, then sealed it and added it to the bad box corner.

I still only had two boxes of clothing to turn over to Jack. I let my annoyance at thinking about him come out, and got a little rough in the tape slicing on the next box. Lucie wasn't near me, but he jumped back anyway.

I knew Jack and I hadn't started great. He showed up the night of Tiberius's and my arrival, investigating a disturbance on my new property.

That disturbance happened to be Tiberius and me arriving. He found us both in a dark barn, which was certainly a unique way to meet. Then all the bodies kept popping up. Ones that I couldn't be blamed for. And I knew Jack didn't believe that at all.

"I think you're done. Unless you're planning to slice up those books." Lucie came closer again, but remained above me on the pile of boxes.

"What? Oh." Thinking of Jack, and my feelings about him, which I kept telling myself were simply that I didn't want someone thinking badly of me, I had kind of thrashed the top of the box. If I wanted to keep these books, I'd have to find a new box to put them in. "You could have stopped me sooner."

"You're armed; I'm not going up against a gladiator jinn with a blade." His tail swished rapidly, and he kept an eye on my box cutter.

"*Former* gladiator. That was a few lifetimes ago." I sighed and picked up the top book. No scratches on the cover. At least nothing I did. It wasn't in bad shape, but it was old. Not as old as me, but that wasn't uncommon on this planet. "The Meaning of Man." I flipped open to the first page. "Printed in 1856, London." I leafed through the pages, skimming the words as I went. "It's as dry as it sounds." I put it aside and took the next one. "Treatise of Crops and Waterways of Southeast Asia. Also, from the 1800's same publisher." There were ten books in the box, all from the same era and publisher. All of them were as exciting as the first two. They were in decent shape for being as old as they were, but there was no way any of them would have had value as collectibles. Anywhere.

I was putting them back inside when I noticed the box was deeper than they were. Took them back out and found a false bottom.

Two more books. I wouldn't have opened them even if I could. Both were clearly high-end Eltrisian spell books. And sealed tighter than a cherub's purse.

"I hate that man."

"Darius, I presume? Even from here, I can tell those books are dusty, old, and boring. I never saw them before today, by the way." Lucie settled down to watch the next opening, but was clearly becoming bored. And he also couldn't see the two spell books from where he sat. Something I didn't want him to see anyway. I quickly put them back inside and put the Earth books on top. Then sealed the box and shoved it to the keep side.

"Yes. He was a jerk, but he had to have had a reason for getting these books and shipping them halfway around the world. I'll save them and sort them out later." I had been hoping that these stupid boxes would give me information, closure, or some nice extra bit of money—legally. So far, that wasn't happening.

There was no way I was dealing with spell books without magic.

I hit three more boxes. The good thing was that I found three more random clothes boxes, also filled with mundane household stuff that even Lucie didn't want, and other safe items to give to Jack. The bad thing was there was nothing useful, helpful, or interesting. Nor any sign of the Stone of Zalianthia. To be honest, I wasn't certain I knew what the thing looked like. But nothing was coming close to any vague description of it in those three boxes. I shoved the three clothes boxes into the "give to Jack" corner and sighed.

Fatigue caught up to me again. Or it was just boredom from the boxes I'd gone through. "I'm done. It's been a long, weird day, and we're making progress on these." I looked at the ten or so boxes still waiting. Part of me figured that since I'd opened a bunch of boxes so far and nothing magical had attacked me, I was probably due.

Which meant that waiting for Keith, and for me not being exhausted, would be the best idea.

Lucie shrugged and jumped down from his perch on the boxes. He'd spent the day cruising around, sleeping, and hanging out with the hoxien wolf family; he wasn't tired.

After locking up the guest room, I sorted out an exciting frozen dinner and settled in for some tube time.

"What happened today?" Tiberius pulled his blanket over to the sofa and snuggled in.

I expected him to ask which mob family's box was in the closet, but it appeared he'd rethought about knowing.

I filled both of them in on the dead guys at the diner, the bombs, and the vine seeds being in the teahouse. I knew he wasn't asking how our tea went. If Tiberius didn't already have a cranky goat face, he did now.

"None of that is good." Tiberius scowled. "Why are there so many things connected to this town? I sat in on the consideration panels for your parole. Forgotten Hollow was the first choice and was brought up by a few people. The council was anxious for it to be used, but they'd never had a parolee here before. Not in the two hundred years they've been using Earth. I didn't think it was odd at the time."

"But you do now." I started swearing. The council did nothing fast, unless it was a pay increase for themselves. "That is bad. Especially when combined with whatever weirdness is going on with Xieth." I looked at the landscape painting. I was grateful that Keith had been able to block any unwanted listening.

"Darius knew about Forgotten Hollow before you were paroled here." Lucie was sitting on the sofa, cleaning, but looked up. "He had this as his primary destination when we escaped the salt mines in Laxtunius."

"But he spent time in other lands?" Tiberius narrowed his eyes as the centurion part of his brain kicked in.

I was glad to see it. As a centurion, Tiberius was a pain in my ass. But I didn't want him to fade into a goat forever.

Now, had Darius still been alive and turning into a goat or worm, I'd say that would be an improvement.

"Yeah, claimed he needed special items for his operation." Lucie snorted. "I'm thinking he meant the coffee one, but it could have been something else. We didn't chat much."

"Where did he get those Fholovian beans?" They had been part of the madness that happened when I first got here. They're extremely rare, even in the Eltrisphere, illegal to own, and could control minds. Darius thought they'd improve the coffee of Forgotten Hollow.

"No idea." Lucie shrugged. "I didn't even know he had them until you found them."

I needed a murder board like some of the cop shows used. One that no one else could see, though. Just my list from yesterday had freaked me out. I grabbed my notepad and jotted down a few things, but kept them non-specific and hopefully understandable for me. I could set up a closed file within the infinity web, but honestly, if I needed to do anything more today, including thinking, I was going to scream.

We discussed the day's issues a bit more, but neither of us had any ideas. Lucie did say that Brutus was fine with me digging and burying the mob box on her lot. But at this point, I wanted to make sure Keith could buy that lot quickly before I risked it.

That was braining for tomorrow. I was even too exhausted for a cop show. I clicked on the channel for my new favorite guilty TV pleasure, I Dream of Jeannie. The episodes were goofy, fun, and aside from me sometimes wearing an outfit similar to hers, it was hot in some areas of my home world after all, not at all true. Perfect mind candy.

I fell asleep in the middle of Major Nelson chastising Jeannie about something and woke up to Xieth yelling at me.

# Chapter Twenty-Eight

"Ceian! What are you doing down there?!"

That was not a good way to wake up, and from the annoyance in his voice and the lack of Lucie or Tiberius in the room, he'd probably been yelling for a while. The lack of light coming in through the curtain gap in the front window told me morning was still thinking about making an appearance. My phone flashed with messages. And I had a furious cherub screaming at me.

"I was sleeping, that's what people do at night." I took a few deep breaths to calm down before the snarky tone in my voice got worse. "Sorry, yesterday was a long day." I bit my lip when the words came out. I didn't want him asking about it.

"Ah, yes. Setting up your business. That still is no excuse for calling a witch storm. Not to mention, how in the seven levels of the abyss did you do it? Those bands are still on, right? They show as active. The council had approved releasing some of your magic, but they're taking it back after that stunt."

I needed coffee, tea, anything with large amounts of caffeine. "What? I...how could I?" I held up my wrists to show the silver bands I still wore. "*Why* would I?" My brain panicked as it chased the words he said around a bit. "They approved it?" If I needed more proof of things going horribly wrong in Xieth's end of reality, I just got it. I was surprised at him saying he would talk to them about it. That they had already reviewed it and agreed was freaky.

"Yes, just a few hours ago. Not all of your magic, obviously, but a little to help you blend in there and go through the items Darius had quickly. However, there were reports of an unauthorized witch storm in your area last night. Its focus was your neighborhood. No damage that I can tell, it vanished as quickly as it came. As for how you did it with your magic blocked, that's something they'd like to know. So would I."

My jaw dropped. Xieth looked hurt. I'd disappointed him. I recognized it from seeing it on my parents', aunties', uncles', and various cousins' faces growing up.

I'd never seen, nor expected to see, it on Xieth's face.

"If I could do something magical, why would I pull down a killer storm on my home? Why would I do it at all?" My brain was really too squished right now to sort this out. I desperately needed caffeine and extravagant carbs.

"The current council theory is that you were so furious at whoever tried to destroy your teahouse and kidnapped your friends that you managed to fight through the bands. You pulled up the spell in order to smite your enemies, then changed your mind and snuffed it." Xieth calmed down. "I personally think it's all a bunch of hogwash. I knew you couldn't break the bands, and if you could, you wouldn't have pulled that storm back."

I opened my mouth to defend myself, but he beat me.

"If you knew who took your friends, and you *could* pull a witch storm on them?" He folded his chubby arms and raised a massive eyebrow.

He was right. Old me was fairly hot-tempered. I'd mellowed in my hundred years of bottle time. "Okay, I'm pretty upset about a few things going on, granted. But the fact is, I still have the bracelets on." I almost said I can't access my magic. But twice so far, weird things indicated that might not be the case. And somewhere inside, I believed that it had happened enough that I started to choke when I was going to say I couldn't access it.

There was no way I could let Xieth have a hint that I'd worked magic through the bracelets. Unintentionally.

There was a slim chance, no matter how unrealistic, that the bug fumigation tent had caught a stray wind and taken off on its own.

Without any wind around at the time.

"That. You had a thought right there. What was it?" Xieth leaned forward as if he could crawl out of the frame and pry my secrets out in person.

That was a disturbing mental image. Although if it were anyone other than Xieth, I'd be insulted that the idea of my having a thought was so shocking.

"I just thought about the wind that tore off that tent over my teahouse. But there hadn't been a wind around at the time. At least not before it happened." I had to watch how I said it, as there was a good chance that one was mine. I was hoping that if I could connect it to the witch storm from last night, which I knew wasn't me, then it would take suspicion off of me.

Xieth sat back in his chair. "There could be a windmage hiding down there. One of them would be able to do both of those. The witch storm was so short that the spell buoys around Earth barely had time to register it. Something like a wee tent wouldn't have registered at all."

"I don't recall hearing about spell buoys?" I shouldn't be nosy, but I *hadn't* heard anything about them. If I couldn't get the witch storm issue cleaned up, and my magic continued to leak despite the bracelets, I needed to know what to watch for.

"They were installed after we found out that Darius had been down there doing who knows what. Don't worry, if the council does re-approve your magic being partially released, you won't trigger it. Unless you decide to do something like a witch storm." He laughed hysterically at his joke of my having enough power to pull in a witch storm.

"Thank you. Like I said, still wearing the bracelets. But I have an unrelated question: the police here say that Darius's body has gone missing along with all of his files. That wasn't an Eltrisian cleanup, was it?" If it wasn't, and someone else stole the body, we had a bigger issue. His body would not appear human in an autopsy.

Xieth's eyes widened a tiny bit at my question, then he shook his head. "I'll have to look into it; more operations are going on down there than I'd originally been told. It's completely missing?"

I kept my internal eye roll off my face. As opposed to partially? I forced a serious nod. "Yes, as next of kin, they notified me. There was a mishap that was only recently discovered."

"They lost a body? They can't have that many lying around in that town. I'll look into it." He sat up and straightened his hair, such as it was. "Keep me updated on all of these items. Continue to look into Darius's belongings. Make sure your teahouse opens without a hitch." He smiled. "Nice flyer by the way." Then clicked off.

I wanted to ask him how he got a copy of the flyer when I hadn't. Did he have actual physical spies down here?

I sighed and checked the time. He'd called me at five-thirty am? That was beyond rude. Time was different between us, obviously, but he'd made it a point to be aware of my local time before. He might have just been worried about me pulling a witch storm. Or more things were going on. He seemed relieved and already distracted when he cut the call.

"You two can come out now." Neither Tiberius nor Lucie was in the front room. Unless they were hiding under something. Xieth never spoke to them much, and they wanted to keep it that way.

My bedroom door opened wider, and they came out looking sheepish.

"He was really pissed this time, Ceian. Yelling the moment the screen went live. You slept through a lot." Lucie stalked over to his food bowl as if they'd been apart for weeks.

"Indeed. Very annoyed." Tiberius walked to his corner but continued to watch the screen with narrowed eyes.

Lucie looked up from his nearly empty bowl with a smug smile. "I told you that was a witch storm." He'd probably been sitting on that 'I told you so' for hours.

"Fine, it was. You win. Do you know who did it and if it was targeted at us? Because that would be helpful."

"She has a good point." Tiberius shifted direction and went to the door. "I'd like to go out."

I let him out, and Lucie remained silent.

"I didn't do it." I jangled my bracelets at him. "Any more than you did." I wasn't sure how powerful a magic user Lucie was, but that shiny silver collar he wore should stop all magic.

"I know. But I wonder if someone wanted it to look like you did it. That storm came up fast and was right on our place. There's something bad going on." He jumped on his cat tower. Usually, he went out first thing in the morning, but he was worried.

I couldn't sort out cat behavior, nor was going back to sleep now an option. I poured some cereal and sat down with my phone to check if Betsy messaged me when I was asleep.

She'd texted back at half after ten, then five minutes later. Then, ten minutes later. I checked for calls; my phone had been near me, and any call coming in should have woken me up. No calls from anyone, just fifteen texts that stopped after an hour.

"Not good." I pulled up the text collection and went to the earliest one.

The text was an image of the flyer, with a note that every store and restaurant in town had them, and people were excited.

I didn't need that additional stressor before a grand opening tea. I glanced at the flyer; it looked fine, and moved on to the next message. Betsy, Martha, and Jamie had gone investigating after their computer arts and crafts flyer creation. The next clump of texts was her telling me to come out to the Old Hollow. They weren't there, but there were weird lights. Then they were there, then not. The texts were short and didn't make a lot of sense.

The last one was that they had gone into the store. I read it five times. All of this build-up, and they went to a store? Which store? I knew all of them usually got up early, but calling at five-thirty in the morning wasn't a nice thing to do to anyone.

Even though I wouldn't call this early, it didn't mean I wouldn't text. I hit both Betsy and Keith, asking her where she was and him if he'd heard from them.

Then I ran for the shower. I was dressed and running out the door, after having to let Lucie out and back in three times with him finally remaining out, when my phone rang. I checked the number before answering; it was Betsy.

"Ceian? Where are you? We're waiting."

I held the phone away from my ear. It was her number and almost sounded like her, but not completely. My magic might or might not be blocked by the silver bracelets, but my jinn senses weren't. And right now, they were tingling.

"Where are you? Who's with you?"

"In the Old Hollow. The ladies, the ladies are with me." That was definitely not Betsy. Not even Betsy when drunk.

"Be there in a flash." I hung up the phone and grabbed a power bar and a bottle of tea.

I ran to my bike. Racing to the Old Hollow was a horrible idea. It was clearly a trap.

And I didn't have a choice.

Brutus stood near our fence and nodded. Her puppies were rolling in the tall grass near the fence. "Hi, Brutus," I said in Sihlia. "Could you keep an eye on my house for a bit?"

"No, thank you." Also in Sihlia. "I am going with you. The babies will protect your home." She reached down into the grass and pulled out a leash. She still wore the collar that Old Man Clapper had on her when she escaped. "This makes humans happier."

I thought about it for a moment, then nodded. "Can you run alongside my bike?"

Brutus's grin was extremely toothy. "You'll have to keep up with me." She brought me the leash, and I attached it to her collar. I had wanted backup. A hoxien wolf was pretty good backup.

"Can your babies tell Lucie and Tiberius where we went? We have to go to the Old Hollow." Neither cat nor goat was in sight.

Brutus nodded and barked a few times. The puppies were running into my yard in a moment. "Done."

"Great." I climbed on my bike, still holding on to her leash. "Don't go too fast, I'm a bit rusty in the speed department." As far as I knew, no one had claimed to have found Brutus since she escaped from Old Man Clapper's house.

If she wasn't worried about being identified, I wasn't.

I could tell she was holding back as we went down the trail along the cliffs. Few things could outrun a hoxien wolf when they were hunting.

My phone rang when we were about halfway there. I almost let it go to voicemail, but I grabbed it. Keith.

"Ceian? Where are you?"

I held the phone away from my ear. It was his number. Had whoever was behind this grabbed Keith, too?

I almost said I was looking for Betsy and the other two, but if this was a trap, likely, and this wasn't Keith, possible, I didn't need to tell them more than they needed to know. "Where are you?"

"I'm at Betsy's. Ralph is worried; she didn't make it home last night. I just saw your text. Sorry for the delay."

Sihlia was more common among jinn than most other races, but I knew the real Keith knew it. I shoved aside the fact that so did the person who left the dead black suit man in my barn.

"What is a hoxien wolf doing on the farm?" It was an old and stupid joke, and made a little more sense in Sihlia.

He didn't pause but also responded in Sihlia, "Whatever she wants to."

"Okay, we're running to the Old Hollow. On the Fern Trail now."

"I'm on my way." He clicked off, and I hoped that I hadn't just made a huge mistake.

I'd slowed down while on the phone. Brutus politely waited until I put my phone away, then picked up speed again. She wasn't going as fast as I was sure she could, but we were still moving faster than a human on a bike with her dog should be able to.

Luckily, I spotted the hikers ahead of us on the trail before they heard us and turned around.

Brutus and I dropped to a normal pace as we caught up to them.

"Great day for a hike." I forced a cheerful smile as we passed.

"It is! Nice dog!" One of them yelled, the others just raised their steel coffee holders in salute.

"Thanks, she's wonderful!" I waved again as we turned around the bend.

"Thank you," Brutus responded in Sihlia, but she obviously understood English.

"Just the truth." I peddled faster to keep up with her. Having a hoxien wolf on my side wasn't a bad thing.

The forest grew denser and darker until it appeared more like the end of a day, rather than the beginning.

No sign of Keith yet.

Officially, the Fern Trail ended in another mile or so, then I'd need to turn even further into the woods to get to the Old Hollow.

We both slowed. I wanted to get there quickly, but while having Brutus was extremely handy, having Keith as well would increase our odds.

Especially if the people on Betsy's phone still believed that I was by myself. I slowed us down more as we approached a cross path.

A dark shape quickly walked toward us, and I lifted my hand to wave. I'd never seen Keith in a cloak and hood, let alone all black. I dropped my hand when Brutus started growling.

# Chapter Twenty-Nine

Aside from Brutus, and my speed and ability to physically fight, which was a bit rusty, I had to admit, I didn't have any weapons.

That cloak could be covering anything.

The person stopped as Brutus's growls turned to snarls. Smart move. I hoped whoever they were didn't decide to run.

The tall being shifted on their feet, and I released my hold on Brutus's leash. Leash laws were important, but it was more important not to be dragged off my bike and through the woods by a pissed off hoxien wolf chasing prey.

The person shoved back their hood and then raised their hands. "Hey, don't let your dog come after me. I'm just heading for a LARP, no live steel." He pushed back his cloak. He had a duct-taped, wrapped pole about the size of a sword hanging from his belt.

He was also about sixteen. A tall and skinny sixteen at that. And so terrified that I was afraid he was going to pee his pants.

I had no idea what a LARP was, but I had seen flyers for something called a Renaissance Faire in a few months. Judging by his attire, now that I could see him better, he looked like someone from the flyer.

"Sorry, you scared us. My dog doesn't like cloaks." I didn't know what else to say.

"That's cool." He lowered his hands and took a long breath. "What's his name?" He didn't come closer.

Brutus barked but also said a word in Sihlia at the same time. "Hadari." It meant friend.

"Her name is Hadari. I'm sure she feels bad about startling you." I was going to say scared, but egos at that age in males were fragile. Dressed like he was, he was obviously trying to project a fierceness he didn't actually have. "I'm Ceian."

"That's a lovely name. Both of them." He flushed. "You're the one with the new teahouse. Great flyer. My friends and I are planning on dropping by for the grand opening." He still didn't move forward. "I'm Jeff. I live in Forgotten Hollow." He slapped his head. "Durh, we all do. The three of us here, that is."

Someone was coming down the side trail in a section of forest not far behind him. I grabbed Brutus's leash, or Hadari's, if that was what she preferred. It might be her real name. The name Brutus was given to her by Old Man Clapper.

This time it *was* Keith.

"Jeff! Good to see you. You coming to my art class in two weeks?" Keith sounded and looked like himself; that was good.

Brutus/Hadari wagged her tail as he came toward us. She liked Keith.

"I'm hoping to. We've got a LARP going on out here today."

"At the Old Hollow? I promised to show Ceian it. She's been in town a few months and still hasn't seen it."

"Naw, we're a bit past that. More room in the witch's clearing out near the cliffs. We have a full troop this time. Folks even came in from Orick."

"Sounds fun, have a great time. Don't take any wooden spell coins." Keith winked and shook Jeff's hand.

I would have missed the moment if I hadn't been watching them closely. Keith slipped Jeff a spell of some kind. Jeff froze for a moment, still grinning, then blinked and released Keith's hand.

"Thanks." He turned to me. "It was nice to meet you and Hadari. I'm looking forward to the teahouse opening." Whistling, he continued on the trail he'd been on. Hadari even gave him a friendly woof as he passed.

Keith came closer and petted Hadari. "Your real name is lovely. Thank you for not eating the scared high school student."

"I have to say, she wasn't the only one freaked out by that kid." I got off my bike and walked alongside it as we followed the trail to the Old Hollow. "What's a LARP?"

"Live action role playing. They create worlds and adventures to inhabit. Jeff's a good kid, and a talented artist if I could get him to practice more. Can I read the texts you got from Betsy?"

I handed him my phone. "All except the last one, which was a phone call. I caught it live." I wished I hadn't, so I could play it for him. If someone were trying to pretend they were Betsy, they did a bad job.

He quickly scanned through the messages, then handed the phone back. "Not even close to her normal wording. Did the phone call say anything about the Stone of Zalianthia?"

"No, because for some reason, the person thought they had convinced me they were Betsy. Like those text messages, it didn't sound like her."

Hadari didn't pull on her leash, but she seemed to be enjoying being out here. She might have escaped from the animal catchers two months ago, but she probably knew she was still on their wanted list and had been staying out of sight.

Maybe I just inherited a dog, and she now had a way not to need to hide.

"Did it sound sort of like her?" Like Hadari, Keith was watching the trees around us.

"A little? But it was more like someone trying to copy her voice when she was drunk." I'd only seen the three ladies drunk once; it was a scary enough event that I didn't need to repeat it.

"It has to be gomblers."

"Are they about three feet high, with goofy big eyes, big feet, and orange skin?" I'd heard of them, and Keith had brought them up before, but I had never seen one. Until now.

Keith was looking at me, but turned at my question. There were four little orange beings about twenty feet ahead of us. All of whom looked way too happy to see us.

"Stop. Don't come any closer." Keith held his hand up to them.

Hadari tugged on her leash, but sat down next to me when I didn't move. The gomblers looked too innocent to be anything except evil.

Hadari was drooling with the need to chomp them.

"Play. Now." That sounded closer to Betsy's voice than it had when they called earlier.

"Where are our friends?" I debated releasing Hadari's leash, but figured if we couldn't find the other three inside the Old Hollow, we needed these things alive to tell us what they did with them.

"Dancing! Play, now!" The gombler speaking took a few steps closer, then suddenly jumped at me.

Hadari was smarter and faster than the gombler was. She leaped, grabbed the weird orange thing in her jaws, and flung it into the trees. High into the trees. Then she grimaced and spat a few times.

"Sorry, girl. They taste awful." Keith patted her head.

"How do you know what they taste like?" That was almost more disturbing than the three orange creatures facing us.

"My old hunting dogs used to tell me." He grinned and turned back. The three gomblers were no longer smiling and kept glancing up into the trees for their friend. "Even if you don't recognize a hoxien wolf, you've now seen what she can do. She could also rip you apart as easily as she threw your companion into the treetops. Where are our friends?"

"And who brought you to this planet?" Jeff's voice coming from behind us wasn't expected. He shrugged when we both turned. "I thought maybe you were on some sort of quest. Those three are definitely aliens."

Too many catastrophic disasters going through my head at the same instant shorted me out. Maybe Keith could use magic to make Jeff forget what he saw.

"We're nowhere near the witch's clearing." Keith wasn't smiling, and his voice was low as he cast a spell.

Jeff's eyes went wide, then he fell backward and began snoring.

"What...nope, don't want to know. That will keep him from remembering, right?" Hadari and I kept watching the gomblers.

"I don't know. He's extremely creative, and those are the most difficult to spell. He should be out for a few hours, and hopefully, we can convince him he didn't see anything."

"Good. Okay, little orange things, tell us where our friends are and who brought you here, or I will let her go." Hadari did a fake lunge against her leash.

"Ick. Peoples back there. The dumb ones brought us. We show—" The gombler's words were swallowed as they all vanished. A similar flash in the trees above us indicated the fourth had been taken as well.

I started shaking. "That looked like the transfer beam used to bring Tiberius and me down here." Granted, I only saw the transfer from the inside when I was shipped that way. But there had been a few prisoner movements being done before mine.

That technology was so highly guarded that only the high council had access. And even then, only the highest of them.

"It was. This is extremely not good." Keith went to Jeff and hauled him to the base of a tree. Then pulled over a fallen tree branch and arranged it to look like it had fallen from that tree and hit him. "His friends will find him. We need to rescue Betsy and the others."

I unhooked Hadari's leash; she was in the mood to run, and having the leash drag behind her wasn't a good idea. "Find them, please."

Hadari gave a low bark and shot off down the trail.

"Shall we? I'm not as fast as a jinn, but I should be able to keep up." Keith grinned.

"Let's go." I hid my bike in some bushes. It was better to run without it, and riding would slow me down in the dense trees.

Running full out was freeing, but this time it was tinged with fear for my friends.

Hadari swerved to head off-trail, and I barely avoided slamming into a tree.

"I see them!" Keith obviously had better eyesight than I did. Hadari stayed ahead of us, running toward something, but I couldn't see what the something was. "They're tied up."

As we ran closer, I saw the three ladies piled up against a massive tree, sleeping. Hadari wasn't barking, but she also remained ten feet away from the tree and sat down.

"What's surrounding them?" The shield around them was so perfect, I only noticed it because of Hadari's behavior and a brief, random sunbeam that flashed it iridescent for a moment.

"A tulil shield. Strong, but not long-lasting. Often given to non-magic-using minions. It's about to drop."

I saw the shield as it fell, but didn't feel it. Shields were tricky, and while I'd heard of a tulil shield, I'd never seen one. I was never a powerful or interested magic user before I got locked up. And a hundred years of no magic, only to lose it again, really didn't help.

Not surprising to me, Keith ran to Betsy first, even though she was the furthest. I went to Jamie and Martha.

None of them looked roughed up, and the bands on their hands vanished when the shield fell. Smart. Right now, we had no evidence to help us find out who was behind the gomblers.

Jamie recovered first and started swatting around her. Nothing was there, and she didn't even open her eyes.

"Jamie, wake up, you're okay." I dodged her flailing hands.

"What?" Her eyes popped open, and she looked around. "Why am I out here? *How* am I out here? Where are Betsy and Martha?" She made a face. "And do you have a water bottle? I feel like something gross died in my mouth."

"They're here too, but I have no idea how or why you three are here." I was about to say I didn't have any water, but Keith handed me two bottles.

He was using a lot of magic for someone who wasn't supposed to be here. I knew he had an unrequited thing for Betsy, but he'd never get to see her if he got caught and taken off planet.

Jamie gladly took the water bottle as I switched to waking up Martha.

Martha rolled over and snuggled into the tree roots. "Not now, having a good dream."

I shook her again. "Martha? You're in the woods."

"I'm what? We were at The Drunken Toad Pub...not sure why. Betsy said something about the mail robberies?" She looked at the bottle in my hand. "Oh, water? Thank you!" She quickly chugged it down.

That Keith was still working on Betsy was concerning.

Betsy waking up screaming and yelling about aliens was worse.

# Chapter Thirty

K eith grabbed Betsy's hands as she started hitting him.

"It's me, Keith. No aliens, I promise." His magically augmented voice probably soothed everyone within ten miles.

Betsy settled immediately, and she drank the bottle of water he gave her.

She finished it, then shook her head. "I still don't know where we are or why."

Jamie got to her feet and brushed herself off. "Just outside of the Old Hollow, I'd guess. We're off the trail, so it's hard to tell."

Martha was the first to spot Hadari, who had remained still as we woke them up. "Is that Old Man Clapper's dog, Brutus?" She seemed torn between not wanting to pet a potentially dangerous dog and really wanting to pet the dog anyway.

"No, she's a new addition to my family. Her name is Hadari." I tried to think of a quick way to explain how I suddenly added a dog and five puppies when Forgotten Hollow didn't have any pet rescues or pet stores.

Keith stepped in. "I picked up Hadari and her puppies from a rescue out of town for Ceian when she mentioned wanting more security. Hadari already gets along great with Tiberius and Lucie." He nodded to Martha. "She's friendly to friends of Ceian."

Martha squealed and ran forward to hug, pet, and scritch Hadari.

At first, Hadari froze, then I saw her relax into it. I might have six new dogs, but Hadari found a new best friend.

"So, if they weren't aliens, who were the little orange guys who took my phone?" Betsy sounded calm, but she also seemed certain of what she saw.

"Aliens?" Jamie shook her head. "What are you talking about? You had a new tip that The Drunken Toad Pub was up to some nefarious business involving mail fraud. So, we all went out for drinks. Then we ended up here. I have no memory or clue as to why or how." She was the most no-nonsense of the three, and she needed answers.

"That's what I recall as well," Martha said between cooing at Hadari.

If I weren't a jinn and from her actual home system, I think Hadari would leave me and live with Martha. I'd be fine with shared custody. I just wanted her safe.

I had no idea what we were going to do with Betsy claiming she saw aliens.

Keith dropped his voice, but we could all hear him. He also had a serious look. "There was an experiment out here, one that they didn't want anyone to know about. And that shouldn't have been on public lands." He raised his hands before the ladies could question him. None of them looked terribly alarmed. "You can't speak of it to anyone."

Jamie stepped closer and narrowed her eyes. "But what were they? Why didn't Martha and I see anything? Were they AI? Projection screens? Betsy, did they speak to you?"

Keith shook his head slowly and put his finger over his lips. "No one. Not to me, Ceian, each other. I wouldn't even talk about it to yourself."

I knew what had really happened, and the tone of Keith's voice and his intensity still had me freaked out. Then I realized he was backing everything up with an emotional nudge. Emotive magic wasn't a strong one for me, but I knew that it could leave a slight psychic trail when used. Keith was taking a risk the more he used it.

Especially since it was clear now, if it hadn't been already, that there were other members of the Eltrisphere down here.

Jamie paused for a bit, then shrugged. "I'm cool with that. Can we get some food? Either we didn't eat last night, or I forgot it. Either way, I'm starving."

Betsy and Martha nodded.

"I could eat," Betsy said as she stretched. "Can we swing by Pop's Liquor afterward? I'll need to get another phone. I lost mine somewhere."

Either Keith was still sending calming mojo at Betsy, and I wasn't feeling it, or Betsy and the other two were getting far too used to being kidnapped and having weird things happen to them.

"Aren't you worried about your lost phone?" I hadn't intended to ask that at all. Especially since I knew what probably had her phone right now. Wherever the gomblers went when they were zapped out of here, the phone probably went with them.

Martha responded first with a wave of her hand. "Pish, Betsy has a frequent buyer plan at the phone stand inside Pop's."

"She goes through a lot of phones," Jamie added.

Betsy pulled herself up to her full five feet one inch height. "All in the line of duty, I'll have you know." She held an imperious glare for a few moments, then dropped it with a shrug. "Food now?"

I looked at Hadari. "I need to take Hadari home first. Meet you all at Hannah's?" I also needed to go back and get my bike.

Keith petted Hadari. "Good idea, see you in a bit." The four of them went in the general direction of the main trail, but I noticed he was veering away from it a bit. Good idea if Jeff was still passed out against that tree.

I had no idea how well Jeff and Betsy knew each other, but having them talk to each other about supposed aliens wouldn't be good.

I waited until they were out of sight before Hadari and I ran to where I had left my bike. I quickly got on it and started riding at jinn speed. Whoever was stalking me through my friends was getting on my nerves. I might not have magic at the moment, but my gladiator skills were only a little rusty. I wouldn't mind physically hurting people if that was what was needed to keep my friends safe.

Our speed kept increasing, and Hadari seemed to be having fun. I knew she could still go much faster than I, but we were making excellent time.

We were just one hill away from home when Hadari gave a low bark and slowed down rapidly. I was still lost in my thoughts and almost didn't brake fast enough to avoid being yanked off my bike.

Hadari came to a complete stop a few feet away from the top of the hill.

I stopped as well and swung down off my bike. "What is it?" I spoke in English since I knew she understood that, and I had no idea if someone was close enough to hear me.

She narrowed her eyes and spoke softly in Sihlia. As before, her words came out under a low growl.

"Bad people on the other side." She lifted her head, sniffled, then growled again.

Anyone who Hadari called bad was someone I didn't need to meet. I looked around. We'd gone off the trail and onto the narrow access road meant primarily for first responders. But unless I wanted to backtrack a half mile, all the while wondering who was ahead of us and possibly heading toward my house, I needed to go forward.

"How many?" I leaned toward her but continued to watch the top of the hill. I doubted that a hoxien wolf would allow bad people to sneak up on her, but better to be safe than sorry.

"Four and truck. Pretending to fix things."

"I think we need to go past them and just act like we're going home after a ride. They're too close to *our* home." I assumed that Hadari and her puppies would be joining us, but her doggy grin told me she agreed.

"I will behave."

"Thank you. And I will have a loose grip on your leash in case things go bad. Don't attack unless we don't have a choice."

"Good idea, too close to home." Again, the doggy grin.

I started whistling to give whoever was ahead of us a warning as we resumed walking. I remained off my bike, and Hadari walked alongside me. We crested the hill and saw a utility truck parked to the far left of the access road. I didn't see anyone near it and was about to drop Hadari's leash and let her go find them when two men came out from the rear of the truck. They didn't seem concerned about us, but there were still two missing. Not to mention the truck had a small cab, four men would have had a hard time fitting inside. The back appeared to be for storage of their supplies, but obviously, if they weren't really utility workers, that could be empty, and where they rode.

And a perfect place to carry kidnapped victims. Like a woman and her dog. We hadn't taken this road on the way out, so I had no idea how long they'd been here. They could have been involved in kidnapping Betsy and the others.

I almost jumped a foot when the man closest to me said, "Good morning." I recovered and smiled. Then fought hard to school my face and keep it smiling.

He was one of the fake bug tent men, but not the one I'd spoken to.

"Good morning." I kept my voice lighter than normal and added a bit of a southern twang to it. I pulled the brim of my baseball cap a bit lower and slightly picked up my pace.

"Nice dog, is he friendly?" A third one came out from the field that the truck was parked next to as we passed.

Hadari gave a low, but extremely clear, growl.

"Sadly, no, he's not. Have a great day." I gave a jaunty wave, got back on my bike, and pedaled away. Hadari shot them one final growl and loped alongside me.

"Are they still looking?" I kept my voice low and spoke in Sihlia.

She glanced over her shoulder. "Yes, no, now they are not. I think we interrupted something; all four are in the road now, and they're packing up."

I went faster as we tore down the dirt road and around to the main road and my driveway. I definitely needed to close it off. I was surprised that more cars didn't accidentally turn down it, thinking it was a side road.

The puppies and Lucie were playing a game between the fence posts. Tiberius was in the middle of my yard, soaking up the sun.

I rode to the front of my house and jumped off the bike. The fake utility truck had been pointed my way, but they could just be heading out.

Unless they were looking for me.

# Chapter Thirty-One

**"I** need everyone inside the house, now!" I unlocked the door and kept an eye on the access road as I shoved my bike inside. "Come on, everyone. Dogs, cat, and goat get in there now." I kept my voice low but continued to frantically wave them toward me.

Hadari led her puppies, and Tiberius trotted after them. Lucie took his sweet time striding across the yard.

"Now. Or I leave you out here." As far as I knew, those men hadn't seen Lucie, but I didn't want to take a chance. I'd also figured they'd left town.

Lucie paused. He was as curious as an Earth cat, but he also knew there was some weird stuff going on. He raced for the door. "In!"

I shut and locked the door and pulled the heavy curtains over the window. "Okay, folks, move away from the door and window. Tiberius and Lucie, Hadari and I saw some of the men from the teahouse bug tent attack. Yes, that's her real name; she and the puppies are with us now."

The entire group, even the puppies, moved to the far end of the room or into the hall. I remained near the door as I heard the crunch of tires on the driveway. Whenever I got it closed off, I was keeping that gravel for a warning system. Maybe all the way to the front door.

I held my breath as I listened for the sound of anyone walking to my door. I heard low voices, but they weren't close. After a few minutes, I heard tires on gravel again.

I waited a few more minutes, then grabbed my cell phone and called the police station to report seeing the fake bug men. Jack and Alice were both out, but Officer Jones took my description of the men and the fake utility truck.

I was going to tell him they'd come to my driveway, but there was still a slim chance it was someone else just getting lost. Instead, I thanked him and ended the call.

"Okay, you can come out." I looked at my phone. No messages, but even if Keith took the long way to his car, the others would be at Hannah's soon. And my stomach growled to remind me I'd never eaten the protein bar.

I opened the front door but turned back to the menagerie. "I have to leave again, but if anyone comes down that drive who you don't recognize, you *all* need to hide. That means you, too, Lucie."

"There are many hiding places in my lot. If they come back, we can all hide over there. Even the centurion." Hadari grinned as she winked at Tiberius.

I didn't know if all other Eltrisphere beings could sense what he really was, or if it was just that extremely acute hoxien wolf nose. But she obviously wasn't concerned about him. Size-wise, they would currently stand shoulder to shoulder.

"Thank you." After all the animals trotted out, I pulled out my bike, locked the house, and took off. I had a feeling, although they were much smaller than their mother, the hoxien wolf babies could defend themselves.

I took the walking/bike path like I did this morning. Most likely, those fake utility guys were gone, but better not to take that chance. It was late enough that I heard a few hikers as I rode and slowed down. But they were on a different trail.

I slowed down again as I pedaled to the bike rack near the diner. No remnants from yesterday, which I wasn't too surprised at. Keith's van was in the lot, and they'd just been seated as I walked in. Their waiter waved me over.

I glanced around for Hannah or the black suit crowd, but they weren't in sight. The waiter took our drink orders, then scurried off.

"I didn't know Hannah took days off?" She hadn't said anything about it at yesterday's tea, but she was new to our group.

Betsy frowned toward the kitchen door. "She rarely does. She'll stay home when she's sick, but aside from that, she's usually here every morning." She nodded to our waiter, visiting another table. Chuck said she called in sick this morning."

"And you don't think she is?" I didn't need more people to worry about. Eltrisphere issues might not be behind everything that was going weird as of late, but I couldn't help but feel guilty about it all.

Not that I had a choice about moving here, setting up the tea-house, or what I was.

"I think it's mighty suspicious. We get kidnapped, again, mind you, and at the same time, Hannah calls out sick? Chuck was the one who got her call, and he said she didn't sound like herself and cut off the call quickly." Betsy folded her arms. "I think someone grabbed her."

My concern must have shown on my face as Keith forced a smile. "I'm sure she's fine. After we eat, we can visit her to make sure she's doing okay."

Chuck came back with our drinks, took our food order, and scurried back to the kitchen.

I looked around the diner, but there were only two couples and a family seated. And they weren't near us. I'd debated not telling Betsy and the ladies about the fake utility truck. But if those men weren't involved with some Eltrisphere attack, they should probably know about my seeing them.

I took a deep breath and spilled it out as fast as I could. I didn't want to be talking about it when Chuck came back. Hannah was part of us now, but he wasn't.

"I'm so glad you had Hadari with you!" Martha looked ready to swoon. "You could have been attacked!"

Jamie nodded. "I agree, but could they have been coming back from dropping us off? We have no idea how long we'd been there."

"The same men who targeted Ceian's teahouse might have been the ones after us as well?" Betsy scowled, then turned to me and patted my hand. "I am so sorry. Whatever mess we've gotten ourselves into, they've drawn you in as well."

That wasn't the connection that I was guessing, but unless I was willing to risk their lives by telling them what I really was, and that I was indirectly the target, I couldn't say anything.

"It's not your fault." I smiled at all of them. "It's whoever is behind this mess's fault. And I haven't been kidnapped."

"But that could have been because Hadari was with you." Martha looked ready to cry. "I feel bad about you living so far away from the rest of us, even with Hadari."

I forced a grin. It was sweet, and while I appeared in my early thirties, at over five hundred years old, I could take care of myself. Most of the time. "We'll be fine. Tiberius and Lucie are fierce as well." I refrained from reminding them that both had also been kidnapped.

Chuck and the busboy came out with our food in a show of excellent timing.

I almost ate as much as Keith. Again. I would have been more worried about it, eating like that only happened to me when I was using a lot of magic or fighting in the arena, but the food was too good to think about it.

"Did Officer Jones say anything about needing a sketch artist for what you saw?" Keith drank some tea after tearing through his food.

"No, but he sounded distracted. Jack and Alice were both out on a call."

"Ohh! What was it? Bank robbery? Murder?" Martha leaned forward just as two cop cars pulled up.

"I think we're about to find out. Or maybe they got hungry?" There was a chance that those weren't Jack and Alice pulling up in the two cop cars that just arrived.

Then a familiar, tall, handsome, and annoying man got out of the first car. Alice in the second car was good to see, Jack, not so much.

My sigh was louder than I'd intended. They headed directly to our corner.

"Officers! So lovely to see you both. To what do we owe the honor?" Betsy bounced to her feet as they approached.

I had been worried that if the three ladies reported being kidnapped again, we might have problems. Not to mention that while the first kidnapping could have been by someone from the Eltrisphere, I knew for certain that this one was.

Humans didn't have magical shields or control little orange gomblers.

But from the same grin plastered on Martha and Jamie's faces, there wasn't a plan to do that. Riding over with Keith might have helped.

"Just stopping by to do a wellness check." Jack forced a smile, which would be handsome if it didn't look like it was painful to do.

Alice laughed. "We were so glad to find you here, all three of you. Ralph reported Betsy missing early this morning. No one answered at Jamie's, and Martha's staff said that you hadn't come home last night either. We're glad to see you all."

Betsy dropped back into her chair with a sigh that was almost as loud as mine had been. "I'm so sorry. I meant to borrow a phone and call Ralph last night. I decided that it would be fun to have a late-night campout in the forest, you know, see if any spooks came out. But I lost another phone, probably at The Drunken Toad."

She turned to Jamie and Martha. "You two were right, we should have gone back there."

Jack's smile vanished. "Where's your camping gear? Ralph didn't say anything about it being missing."

Jamie's hand popped up. "We used mine, I have enough for a lot of folks. Former scout leader." And she had no one who could claim otherwise about it being used.

"It's in my van. They called Ceian and me to come get them." Keith tagged onto Jamie's statement.

"Ah." Alice waited for Jack to respond further.

"Yes. I guess then everything is fine." Jack started to turn to walk out, then spun back and glared at me. "I did get an interesting call from Officer Jones about you being accosted by the men who had the fake bug tent?"

I had no idea why Jack Lanclin distrusted me so much. Okay, there was the bodies issue, but still. The look he gave me was that I was hiding something major.

Which I was, but not what he thought.

"Yes, have you seen the utility van anywhere? It looks normal until you see it closer." I gave my best smile and chuckled. "I wasn't accosted. Once I recognized that at least one of them was from the tent debacle, I passed through quickly."

"And she had Hadari to protect her." Martha nodded with a huge smile. "No one would mess with Hadari."

"Hadari? I thought your goat's name began with a T?" Sadly, those stunning, rich brown eyes of Jack's were narrowed and squinty again.

I had hoped to ease Hadari into the world of Forgotten Hollow as my dog. Not too many people ever saw Brutus, as Clapper had used her to guard his home from the inside. I was hoping to build up more people who knew her as Hadari before I sprung her on the cops.

Brutus was a wanted dog after all.

"Ceian was concerned about the safety of her home. I was down in Summerville on a quick trip yesterday and adopted Hadari and her puppies for Ceian."

"Puppies? Ooo! I missed the part about the puppies!" If Martha wasn't trapped in the curved booth seat by others, she would have run out by now. And probably all the way to my house.

"What kind of dog is she?" Unlike Jack, Alice was genuinely interested.

"A mutt," Keith said before I could respond.

Martha bobbed her head a few times. "I'd say she looks like a cross between a Rottweiler and an English Mastiff. Not as jowly as them, though." She clapped her hands and turned to me. "Do the babies look like her? How many?"

"They do, and there are five." I wasn't up on Earth dog breeds, so I'd take Martha's word for it.

"Like Clapper's missing dog, Brutus?" Jack was back on the hunt for whatever shenanigans I was up to.

He needed a better hobby.

"From what I heard, yes? I am bad with dog breeds." I looked to Martha for confirmation.

"I'd seen that poor dog Old Man Clapper had. Hadari is much prettier, larger, and a mother. Similar, but Brutus wasn't part Mastiff." Martha spoke with such authority that Jack shrugged and backed off.

"Thank you. And Betsy, please keep Ralph updated on where you are if you stay out. Keith? Can you do a few sketches of what Ceian saw? They probably left town or dumped the fake truck, but you never know."

Betsy nodded enthusiastically, and Keith did normally. I wanted to ask Betsy what she was excited about once the cops left. Although she could just have had too much tea.

This took longer than I wanted, as Jack and Alice stopped to say hi to the other diner patrons. Jack was positively chatty now.

Maybe that was the real him, and I just brought out the cranky and suspicious side.

Once they were gone, Betsy almost exploded. "He knows something. Jack has a secret and was fishing for answers."

"What? How can you tell? And what is it?" I told myself I didn't need to know. I needed to steer clear of him, do my time, and get off this crazy planet.

"I don't know what it is, but it's something centered around you." Betsy was beaming like she'd just cracked the secret of the Sphinx.

Keith laughed. "I think he has a crush on Ceian, but doesn't want to. He gets tense when he's around her."

I narrowed my eyes as I turned to him. Was that a casual observation or one made because of him being a slanaigh?

He simply gave me an unhelpful smile.

"Oh, the detective likes our girl!" Martha was bouncing again. She also needed to back off the caffeine.

"I think he's still upset about the way we met and the ongoing issues with bodies on my property. He'll get over it eventually." I turned to Keith, mentally willing him to back off. "I have things to do, still going through Darius's possessions and all. Keith? Can we do the sketches here?" I didn't want to have to go to the station, not with whatever Jack was hunting for about me.

"Sure, let me get my sketch kit from my van." His grin said he found my discomfort funny. Slanaighs manipulated emotions, and they could also sense them.

I stared at his back as he left. He'd better be staying out of my head. And Jack's, for that matter.

I turned back to Betsy. "You got excited because you think Jack's hiding something other than having a crush on me." It wasn't a question, and the resulting grin on Betsy's face indicated that I was right.

"Yes. Keith is a dear man, he really is. But he does work for the cops sometimes. I'm not sure how much we can trust him. Which sounds bad, I know."

Martha and Jamie shared a look but kept quiet. Like me, they'd noticed that Keith had his own crush. On Betsy.

And super sleuth Betsy was clueless.

"I think he's trustworthy, but what was it?"

Keith was too fast and already striding toward the table with his artist kit.

"Later." Betsy nodded and tightly shut her lips.

I adored Betsy, but there were times when her secrecy was frustrating.

# Chapter Thirty-Two

As much as I wanted to find out Betsy's true suspicions, I also would love to get those fake bug tent guys locked up. It was a slim chance, but if doing sketches would help with that, I was all for it.

Keith set up his sketch pad, and we started.

Unlike the first time, I recalled three of the men that I saw and their van very well. My naturally suspicious character was reasserting itself. It paid more attention to details instead of freaking out.

"Those are great sketches." Jamie sat next to Keith and watched him closely.

"Thank you." Keith grinned. "Ceian gave good descriptions. I can tell you that's one thing that hurts in battling crime, when victims and witnesses forget details."

He slid them over to me to check.

"Looks good. I'm sorry I didn't see the fourth guy up close, but I didn't think sticking around was a good idea."

Keith packed the sketches away, and Martha grabbed my hand.

"How did Hadari react to them? I bet she realized they were bad." Keeping Martha away from my dogs might prove extremely difficult, judging by her swoony eyes. If they were normal Earth dogs, it wouldn't be an issue.

"She growled." I smiled. It had been satisfying to watch the looks on the men's faces. And it was telling. I doubted they were Eltrisphere after the attack on the teahouse and figured they were hired thugs. But seeing them back in town had me question it.

They had been worried about Hadari; she was a huge animal, but if they'd recognized a hoxien wolf, they would have raced off as soon as we crested the hill.

"I'd say she knew they were bad." Betsy grinned. "Good dog!"

I got up. "Keep me updated on anything that comes up. And nice work on the flyer." I'd originally intended to ask them to run things by me first, but there were too many issues going on. And it looked better than anything I would have made. If I'd thought of it. "I've got to get back to my cousin's things. I don't want Detective Lanclin accusing me of dawdling. He asked that anything the family didn't want be sent back to the police."

"I could come help with the puppies while you work." Martha's grin was huge. "Keep them out of your hair."

Betsy took Martha's hand with a serious look. "We need to have a major sorting of last night after I get my new phone." Her bright blue eyes were earnest. At least until she winked at me as Martha turned away. She knew Martha might try to camp in my yard with the dogs.

"Thank you for the offer, Martha. We're still getting settled. I want to get all of the animals used to the new situation." And work out how to keep the dogs' true selves secret. They might

look like a Rottweiler and an English Mastiff mix, but they definitely weren't. I squirreled away that description in case anyone else asked.

I scooted for the door while they debated their order of operations.

I probably should have found out why they were at The Drunken Toad Pub, but I didn't think the mail fraud caper was connected to anything else.

The ride home was smooth, quick, and no weird trucks, cars, or people were on the road.

I rode up to my front door, expecting to see some of the animals, but nope. Leaning my bike against the house, I jogged over to reassure myself that the barn was still locked. So much had been going on, I hadn't had a chance to find out what Keith was planning for the spell in the barn or to make sure Tiberius remained his true centurion self.

The lock and chain on the barn were intact, but no animals were around. I wouldn't be worried, except for all the problems that had been taking place around here.

I went to the side of the barn to find them. Nope. Glancing over to Hadari's lot didn't show them either, but there were a lot of hiding places there. I ran over and called, but kept my voice low.

Tiberius's head popped up in the middle of a massive bunch of giant weeds. He was blinking hard. "What? Are we under attack?"

"Just wondering where everyone was." I had always prided myself on not making deep connections to others. Not worrying about other people made things easier when you moved around a lot. Now I was worried about a goat. And a cat, and six dogs. Not to mention a few humans. "Are the others here too?"

"Here, boss." Lucie twisted around my legs, and I hadn't seen him even come up. "The doggos are in the shelter in the back of their yard. You going into those boxes again?" There was more than a little greed in those orange-gold eyes.

While saying no might be the better answer, even if I could lie, I probably still wouldn't do it. I might need Lucie, depending on what was in those remaining boxes. I just wanted them out of my life. The mob box still needed to be buried, but I didn't want to do it in full daylight. Not to mention, I doubted that Keith had had a chance to buy Hadari's lot yet.

"Come on, Lucie. Tiberius, have a good nap."

Tiberius nodded and sank back into his weed mountain. Lucie was at the front door of the cottage before I could turn around.

"Why were you guys over there?" Lucie wouldn't be noticeable lurking about, but Tiberius normally would be. Unless he was asleep in a huge clump of weeds. Although I didn't think anyone knew that Hadari and her puppies had been living there for the last few months.

"Just seemed like a more comfortable place to go. When are we getting our barn back?" He jogged to the kitchen the minute I opened the door. His bowl of kibble was still good, so he chomped away while looking at me for the right answer.

"No idea, but hopefully soon. All of you need to be careful in that lot until it belongs to Keith."

"Eh, Tiberius is the biggest issue. Hadari says she can teach him to hide, though. The side of the barn isn't enough for our group." He trotted to the guest room door. "Don't we have work to do?"

I sighed and followed him. I unlocked the door and swore. The boxes were where I'd left them.

However, my bottle was sitting right on top of the pile.

I froze.

Lucie jumped up and sniffed around it. He pushed forward a note that had been behind it. "Smells like yours, and there's no trap under it or the note."

I hadn't thought of my bottle being on top of something explosive. I was going to have to increase the viewings of my cop shows.

I grabbed the note.

That it was in Sihlia wasn't shocking, although whoever was behind this most likely could also read and write English. The good thing about using Sihlia was that if the note fell into human hands, they couldn't read it. The bad thing about using it was that if it did fall into human hands, it could bring unwelcome attention.

Keith had been able to change the previous note before showing it to the cops, but he wasn't here.

The writing was pristine, and it seemed to be similar to the previous note.

They addressed me by my shortened real name, Ceianthia Da Hithjan; something no one on this planet should know. The letter said they rescued my bottle at great personal risk and knew of its important significance to a jinn. They hoped they could be of service again in the future and wished nothing but to protect me.

I flattened the note and held it for Lucie to read.

"This person didn't steal my bottle, yet they broke into my house, leaving nothing to indicate they'd done so, and broke into this room, just to bring it back. How are so many people breaking into this place?"

Lucie finished the note and looked up. "Unless it's all the same person and they're crazy. They kidnapped us, then brought us back to impress you, but didn't say who they were. Now, someone breaks in, only steals the bottle, which would be what I'd steal if I were stalking a jinn, and now it's back again. Returned at great risk to curry favor. Seems shifty to me."

"You do have more of a criminal mind than I do. And it is odd about the exceptionally clean break in both times." I scowled at the pile of boxes. What I should do would be to ignore the note for now and focus on the boxes.

What I *wanted* to do was make a murder board like they had in cop shows. Granted, I was more interested in finding out who kidnapped and returned my friends, and who stole and returned my bottle, than in murder. But there had been some dead bodies as of late as well.

I envied those glass boards used on some of the cop shows, but those and even the much cheaper dry-erase ones were out of my budget and accessibility. Also, I seriously doubted that the Yarn Bucket craft supply had them in their warehouse.

But I had paper, tape, and a nice empty wall in this room. I grabbed the supplies and brought them in.

"Aren't we looking inside the boxes? We really should get them finished." Lucie lashed his tail. He was nosy, like Earth cats everywhere. It was one of the similarities between the species.

"We should, but I also need to figure out what's going on. You could be right about the same person who was behind the kidnapping return, and the bottle theft being the same. I don't think they're crazy, though. They're trying to get themselves on my side. I just don't know why."

Lucie sighed and looked longingly at the boxes, then perked up. "Maybe they want to ask for their three wishes?"

"Ha, ha, ha. A jinn joke. You know, that was a brief time in our history, a few thousand years ago. Trapping people in their bottles and only releasing them if the jinn agreed to use magic for them wasn't funny." Every once in a while, some smart ass in an arena fight would pin my arms and try to get me to give them wishes.

Everyone who tried it lost the fight. Painfully.

"Do you have writer's block?" Lucie finally asked after I stood staring at the blank wall for a full five minutes. "Maybe opening a few more boxes would move that along." Only the tip of his tail twitched as he tried not to be impatient.

"I'm fine. Just deciding where to start." There was so much space. And what if I forgot something important? I sighed. "Maybe I should work on the boxes to get things moving. Or at least a few."

A knock at my front door caught me before I opened the first box. "Sorry. You wanna stay in here?" I wasn't expecting anyone. Keith, Betsy, and the others should still be doing their breakdown of what they recalled before they were kidnapped from the pub.

In cop shows, they'd be looking at cameras from nearby storefronts to catch the evildoers.

Forgotten Hollow hadn't gotten that far in technology or the need for it yet.

If anyone in town had noticed people carrying out the three women, they would have stopped them.

Lucie scooted out of the guest room and jumped into his cat tower. He obviously wanted to see who was calling, but remained far enough away from them if they were up to no good. I shut and locked the guest room, then went to the front door.

I slowly opened the door, again reminding myself I needed to get a peephole put in.

It was Camfield. His blond hair was tousled, and for the first time, he wasn't dressed in business attire. It definitely raised his attractiveness level, especially when combined with his accent.

"Ceian! I am so glad that you're home. I just got home for a quick turnaround and a flight to New York this time. We still need to set a dinner time for us when things settle down. I wanted to beg a favor." His smile was charming, and I nodded before I even thought to invite him inside.

"Could my goats come over here for a few days? My goat watcher is also out of town, and I'm having some work done at my house, so the goats can't stay there. I can even bring you a temporary pen and shelter; it works great."

That had not been something I was even remotely expecting. "Um, sure? I won't be home much with the grand opening and all." I'd sort of hoped that he would be planning to attend.

"I know, and I am heartbroken at missing it. There are only six goats now. I sold some off."

"When are you leaving?" I was planning on spending the rest of the day at home, but tomorrow I would be focusing on the teahouse and food shopping for the grand opening.

"In an hour." He winced. "I am terribly sorry. I was hoping to put off doing the repairs, and a neighbor was just going to pop by to make sure the goats were okay. But the kitchen pipe burst."

I was set to say no until the pipe situation. "Sure. When are you bringing them over?" I hadn't heard a goat until that moment, but then I heard a few of them out of sight.

"Now? Again, I do apologize. We will have our dinner at Chez Champion, I promise! I borrowed a truck and have the goats and the collapsible pen in the back."

I shot Lucie a look to stay, then slipped out the door and locked it. If Camfield noticed, he didn't say anything. I knew we were going to be in my yard, and I had no reason not to trust him. But at this point, my trust had been pushed too far.

Six mildly annoyed goats and a huge bunch of fencing sat in the back of the large pickup. I glanced at Hadari's yard, but Tiberius and the dogs weren't in sight.

Hopefully, they stayed that way.

Camfield was stronger than he looked and navigated the odd fencing collection down after moving the truck further into my yard. The best spot was on the far side of my yard, but I made sure it didn't block access to the side of the barn.

If I didn't know that there was no magic on Earth, I would have thought Camfield's pen was a magical device. A few tugs and pulls, and it unfolded, and he locked it into place. Then he went and retrieved an equally easy-to-set-up shelter and collapsible water trough.

"That's great." I had no intention of getting more goats, and Tiberius wouldn't agree to being penned, but it was still cool.

His goats trotted down the ramp he put at the back of the truck and into the pen. They made enough noise that I kept watching the empty lot for anyone popping up.

"Thank you so much for being understanding and helping me out, Ceian. I have a few bags of goat chow for them. We can just put them in your barn?"

I almost nodded, then stopped myself. I needed to not be so distracted by attractive men. That was what landed me in my bottle for a hundred years, thanks to Darius. "We can leave them on the side of the barn; Tiberius won't disturb them. Unfortunately, the barn is still being treated for a few problems." I couldn't lie, but it *was* being treated for a spell infestation.

"Ah, maybe when I get back, I can help you as repayment. And Tiberius is welcome to have some of the goat kibble I brought. My vet recommended it." He jogged to the truck. "And don't forget I still owe you dinner!" He waved and drove off.

Tiberius and Hadari both came out of the tall grass on the empty lot after a few minutes.

"That was odd." Tiberius sniffed toward the goats, but didn't approach them. "These aren't the ones he had before."

"He said he'd sold some off, so maybe those were the ones that followed you before." I looked at the goats for a few moments, then went over and filled the giant water trough for them. "Hadari? Could you check out the goats?" Tiberius had a good sniffer; Hadari was a hoxien wolf. One of the reasons they were so feared was their ability to track anything for miles and miles.

Along with what they could do to you once they caught you.

"I can," Hadari said in English. It was rough, but the words were clear.

Judging by the way Tiberius was grinning next to her, I guessed who had been coaching her.

The goats gave a few inquisitive baas when she approached, but didn't appear afraid. Again, a good sign that they weren't odd Eltrisphere beings in disguise.

She sniffed them carefully as she walked around the pen. Then came trotting back to us. "Earth, they're from here." That was in English. "There are no changes in them." That was in Sihlia. But she was getting there. Not that she would be able to speak to many people in either language while we were here.

"Thank you. And you as well, Tiberius." A cat's yowl from the house cut off anything else I was going to say. Lucie didn't sound hurt, just annoyed. I ran over, unlocked the door, and stepped out of the way just in time to avoid being plowed over by an orange streak.

He slowed and walked into the pen and sniffed each goat in turn. "Nice goats. Not the same ones who were here before. You could have said no, you know." He left the pen and rolled in a patch of sun-filled dirt.

"I didn't want him to leave them somewhere unsafe. They're fine here and not really a bother." I looked up to see Tiberius coming out from the side of the barn, dragging out one of Camfield's bags of goat kibble. It wasn't a brand he liked, so I thought he'd leave it alone.

"I couldn't let Camfield see the barn floor, so I just told him to dump it there. You have plenty of your own kibble." Camfield said I could give some to Tiberius, but he didn't need more food. I unlocked the barn door to toss the bags inside.

He dropped the bag. "It smells odd."

Hadari jogged over, sniffed it, and pulled back with a snarl. "Poisoned."

The bag appeared to still be factory sealed, but I brought over the second bag. "What about this?"

She took a step closer to it, then again pulled back. No snarl this time, but she wasn't happy. "That one too."

I looked over both bags, but couldn't find any place where they'd been opened or punctured. "Who would try to poison goats? And why?"

Before anyone could try to respond, Jack Lanclin pulled up my road and into my driveway. As usual, he didn't look happy.

# Chapter Thirty-Three

"Where'd Camfield go?" The words almost beat him out of the car as he got out and glared at me.

I folded my arms. This wasn't a good way to start a discussion. "Why?" Was Jack watching my house? Or was he just randomly out looking for Camfield and decided that he came here? Neither made me happy. I was getting a little annoyed at Jack's ongoing distrust and suspicions.

"I need to talk to him." He folded his arms in reaction to mine. He appeared to be bracing himself for a fight.

"Have you tried his house?" I asked as sweetly as I could to annoy him. He wanted a fight? There were many ways to battle.

"He left home a short time ago with instructions to his repair folks that he'd be gone for over a week. You have his goats. And I just saw him race out of here and toward the freeway."

*That* was his issue; Camfield was too far ahead of him and on the freeway before Jack could catch him. I had a feeling that if he'd been closer to Camfield, Jack would have chased him on the freeway. Although I wasn't sure what the point was.

"What's so important that you're all worked up about?" So much for me being sweet. I liked Jack when he wasn't being a jerk. Something he'd been far too much lately.

"It's police business. Nothing for you to worry about. Where was Camfield going?"

I really wanted to string him along, but I had enough complications in my life right now, and he could be useful if more attacks happened down the line. Rather, when they happened. "I think he said New York. He showed up a few minutes ago, asked me to watch his goats, set up their pen, and took off. It was a business emergency of some sort." I wanted to look behind me to see if Hadari was still in sight, but if Jack hadn't noticed her, that would cause him to do so.

I wasn't going to hide her and her puppies forever, but right now, I thought it was still for the best.

"Where does he work?" Jack leaned in with a glare.

"I have no idea. I've only spoken to him a few times. Mostly about his goats."

"Really? I thought you two were dating?"

That was an odd question. I supposed that, if Camfield and I were dating, and he was up to something nefarious, I could be part of it. "No clue as to where you got that idea, but no. We were going to meet for dinner last night, as friends, but he had to cancel. I can assure you that I have no idea what he does for a living. Why are you looking for him?"

I knew he probably wouldn't answer, but there was always a chance.

"Nothing that concerns you. If you were dating, I might be able to include you."

I almost laughed at the awkward way he said it. No cop would be talking to a girlfriend or boyfriend about the details of their loved one.

Unless the cop was setting a trap.

Maybe this was a technique he recently learned. To get me to admit to being Camfield's girlfriend. If so, he needed to go back to detective school.

"Yup, too bad. Maybe we'll start dating when he gets back. He seems like such a nice, charming, and handsome man." This time, my smile was so sweet it could cause cavities at ten paces.

Jack had tan skin, but the flush on his face was obvious and short-lived.

"You do that. If you hear anything, please let me know immediately." He looked past me. "Is that your new dog sitting by the goats? She does look like the one Old Man Clapper had."

I glanced back. Hadari and Tiberius were near the goats, but blocking the bags of goat feed from sight. Odd, but they had their reasons, I was sure. I knew Jack was astute, but I doubted he could spot poisoned goat chow this far away.

"Betsy said the similarity was there, but Hadari is larger. And *she* has puppies." I added the last as five black and tan fuzzballs raced to Hadari and started jumping on her.

Hopefully, if I kept telling people that Hadari was bigger than Brutus, and obviously a female, they'd believe it and leave the dogs alone.

"Ah. Nice looking dogs. You might want to fence in your driveway with all of your animals." That was normal Jack, and he smiled at the dogs.

"Next on my list, right after the grand opening. Will you be going?" That last bit slipped out against my intention.

He started to shake his head, then stopped. "I hope to, thanks." He looked ready to add something, then gave an awkward smile. "I'd best get back out there. Jones said Keith dropped off the sketches of those men and their van; we're getting them out to other agencies. Just ask Camfield to stop by the station when he comes back to collect his goats." Again, the nicer, less suspicious side was showing.

"Will do." I felt like I'd just met a cute boy at one of the clan dances. I held up fine against snarky Jack, but nice Jack was dangerous. Luckily, he nodded, got in his car, and left.

"That was smooth. Not. Let me guess, you didn't date much?" Lucie washed his face from where he sat near the goats. "Aside from your ill-fated love affair with Darius, anyway. Actually, it might be safer if you didn't date with that track record."

"Ha. I wasn't trying to be smooth or impress him. I wanted to know why he was after Camfield. There's a lot of weird stuff going on around here, but I don't think Camfield is involved."

"Then what was he doing with poisoned goat food?" Lucie paused cleaning again. "Maybe the rest of his goats weren't sold, but killed and buried on his property."

"What? Why? And maybe someone else was trying to kill his goats and doctored those bags? That makes more sense."

Camfield's goats were looking at the bags longingly. I wasn't sure what I was going to do with the poisoned goat food, but they couldn't have it.

"Tiberius, I'm going to have to borrow that extra bag of your food from the barn." I raised my hands when he started to object. "I promise, I'll replace it before you run out. They obviously can't eat this." I usually fed Tiberius inside the cottage, and I'd just opened a new bag in there. He had enough to last two weeks.

He gave a long-suffering sigh. "Fine."

I'd already unlocked the barn, but hadn't opened the doors. Until Keith took care of the pentia spell, I didn't want anyone inside.

Tiberius's bag was right inside the door. I grabbed it, then dragged over the two poisoned bags and locked them inside the barn.

"Hadari? Can you check out this bag?" Tiberius's food was from a different company, but better to be safe. Maybe there was an attack on goats in town.

She trotted over with her puppies tumbling along behind her. After a few long sniffs, she shook her head. "It smells awful, but not poisoned. How eat?" A combination of English and Sihlia.

"It tastes good if you're a goat." Tiberius gave an insulted sniff.

"Everything tastes good if you're a goat." Lucie was behind me. "I'm going on patrol. Don't worry, I won't let anyone grab me." He flashed his claws and ran off before I could stop him.

Who was I kidding? Unless I kept him locked up in the cottage all the time, I couldn't stop him.

I put out food for Camfield's goats, then went back inside. I'd lost the mental momentum for working on my crime board list, so I went to the guest room to work on the boxes.

Lucie could play catch-up if I found anything odd or questionable in them.

The first box was a bunch of chimes. Again. I was going to be annoyed if there was nothing new in these boxes. I dutifully took them all out, without letting them jangle, then carefully put them back, sealed them up, and added to the bad pile. Yes, on Earth, chimes were innocent, but they could be something far more if magically imbued in the Eltrisphere, and I had no idea if Darius had messed with either box of them.

Or why he had them. It seemed as if he'd been working on establishing a magical coffee connection on Earth and planned on staying. Yet, he had a lot of human trinkets that were clearly for the Eltrisphere market. Which implied he was planning on leaving. Maybe these were his emergency back-ups.

The next box was cooking implements. Without my magic, I couldn't be sure, but they looked just like what they probably were. Junk he'd picked up on his Earth travels. They and two more boxes of clothing joined the collection for Jack. At least the collection looked more substantial. I hoped Jack had to go through each box himself.

With a sigh, I cut open the last box. Packing paper. Lots of it. What I thought was the bottom was another box.

An extremely well-sealed box. And filled with still more tissue paper. A third box about the size of my fist was settled inside the second one.

This one wasn't sealed, and the box seemed extremely old. Very expensive. And not from Earth.

The lump in my gut tried to convince me to wrap it back up until Keith and his magic were with me.

My hands betrayed me and kept twitching toward the box. There was no way I could let whatever was in there just wait until Keith could drop everything and come over. What could be dangerous in such a small size? Even keeping that question in my head sounded like a setup for a disaster.

I lifted the little box out, ignoring the I-was-sure-imagined tingling in my fingertips as I moved it.

Then lifted the lid. More packing paper. Unlike the rest, this wasn't from Earth. I recognized the spell symbols on the paper. But they were dull and lifeless; they had no power.

I still tried to talk myself out of unwrapping the surprisingly light item.

Two deep breaths, and I folded away the former spell paper.

# Chapter Thirty-Four

Peeling back the paper revealed a key. An old, battered Earth key, probably from a train station locker. If my TV watching held true.

I wasn't bummed about not blowing up, being cursed, or triggering a bunch of armed Eltrisian guards, but this was extremely anticlimactic.

There wasn't a train station in Forgotten Hollow; the nearest one was in Ghoston down the mountain. I wasn't sure if it was less than twenty miles from here, but that was as far as I could go under the rules of my parole.

Too bad Xieth and his cronies hadn't moved up to mobile parole anklets like they had on TV.

I pulled out my phone and looked up the map app. According to it, I was just inside the range. A half a mile short of twenty miles.

I'd have to ask Keith to drive, and hope the map app was right. I wasn't completely clear what would happen if I went outside my range, but the implication had been that it wouldn't be good.

Sending Keith alone to get whatever was in the locker briefly crossed my mind, but while I trusted him, I'd only known him a few days. Depending on whatever Darius had squirreled away in the locker, I wasn't sure I trusted myself to open it, let alone anyone else.

I wanted to call Keith right now and head down. But it had already been a long morning on little sleep and a rude awakening from a cranky cherub. As the adrenaline from opening the box slowly died, I realized I was hungry and tired. Regardless of the massive amount of food I had at breakfast.

I locked the guest room again and went in search of lunch. I didn't have much. I could have ridden into town and eaten out, but it felt so good to be in my cottage and alone that I ended up foraging for sustenance in my kitchen.

Bonus was a half loaf of Betsy's banana bread still in my fridge. That was one thing I needed to go over before the grand opening—Betsy's bread options. She would do the sausage rolls as well, but her quick breads were famous.

I wanted people to realize they'd be part of the tea service, so I planned to add a slice to each grand opening plate. Not only did I need to prove I was a functioning member of this society in order to run through my parole and leave, but I also hated doing things halfway.

If you step into the arena, you better plan on winning.

I took my odd collection of food and dropped onto my sofa. It was almost too quiet without Lucie or Tiberius, but not enough to see if they wanted to come in.

Lucie was most likely still on patrol, and Tiberius and the dogs were probably napping. I switched on the TV. Another round of I Dream of Jeannie sounded nice, but a cop show might give me helpful information.

I settled on one of the never-ending streams of cop shows, and while interesting, it wasn't informative unless we had a case of more bodies with missing body parts.

Unfortunately, I ate all of my food and fell asleep in front of the TV again.

And was shouted awake by a cranky cherub, again.

"This is what you do all day? You have a bedroom, right? A real bed was provided, I believe. Yet, you sleep out here with that mindless racket."

Calling in twice in one day was a bit excessive for Xieth. I hit the remote and turned off the TV. At least I hadn't fallen to the floor this time.

"Sorry, I didn't get much sleep last night." I wasn't going to answer his other questions. "I've been working on the grand opening." Hopefully, linking the two close together would imply I'd been staying up late working the past few days.

"Hmmm. See that it goes perfectly. No screw ups. How goes searching Darius's things?"

"Just finished an hour ago. He had a lot of contraband that he clearly was planning on selling, but that was about it." Again, another skirt of the truth.

"You'll have to keep everything a bit longer; there's a concern he might have set traps on them."

I forced myself not to glare, but that would have been something good to let me know before I started opening them. "I didn't find anything explosive." I hoped.

With my luck, there was something in there and I'd put it back without noticing. The barn might be a better storage location. If there wasn't a pentia spell lingering there. But maybe if I didn't cross the spell lines, I could shove the boxes in the far back.

"Good, good, good. Just checking on you, you were a bit out of things this morning. Oh, and dump any plain human junk you find; we won't need those. Try sleeping in your bed sometime, and not in the middle of the day." He ended the call before I could respond.

I stared at the landscape painting for a few moments longer than necessary. He called this time just to see if I'd blown up yet. Great.

I'd gotten about a half-hour nap before Xieth's call, better than nothing. I now wanted to get those boxes, all of them, potentially dangerous or not, out of my cottage. My fear of the spell in the barn was overwhelmed by my hatred and now fear of the boxes.

Aside from the mob box, which I didn't trust anywhere that wasn't buried six feet deep, and the weird key box. Okay, the book box stayed as well. Most of the books had seemed to be plain, old Earth books—but those two Eltrisian spell books made the entire collection suspect in my mind.

I went outside to unlock the barn and get my wheelbarrow. Hadari, her puppies, and Tiberius were gone. Most likely, she felt more comfortable in the tall grasses and ruined house of her lot. Note to self, once Keith's acquisition of that property went through, I wasn't going to cut back any plants. At least not without asking her.

I knew I'd eventually have to tell Xieth about the six hoxien wolves, but after his stunt of checking to see if I'd blown up yet, I didn't want to tell him anything he didn't need to know at the moment.

The barn looked the same, still with straw covering the spell on the floor. I was sure I imagined the chill that went through my spine as I walked briefly inside to get the wheelbarrow.

I'd make sure to pile the boxes far from the spell in the center of the barn.

Unless...if I put them on the spell and they exploded, I could be rid of both. I'd check with Keith on that.

I called him as I walked back to the cottage with my wheelbarrow. No answer. Once I got inside, I left a brief message mentioning nothing important. I believed his phone was secure, but with my luck, he'd listen to it on speaker. There wasn't much I could say that could be heard by others, so I ended my ramblings, asked for a ride to Ghoston sometime, and told him to call me.

I worked on the potentially exploding boxes, like the chimes, first, but left the mob box, key box, and book box shoved in the guest room closet. It took three trips, but I got them into the barn.

I chickened out on placing them in the spell circle and kept them between it and the wall. Then brought out the boxes that the police could have. I could have called the station and asked them to send someone out to get them, but even though our conversation had ended on an okay note, I was still annoyed with how Jack started it. He could wait a bit longer.

I was just locking the barn back up when the ground shook with an explosion, and a plume of smoke came from the coast. The smoke was thin, but seemed to be growing.

I figured the fire department was already on it, but I called them anyway as I ran for my bike.

I had no idea what I could do, but Jeff and his LARP buddies were in the general area of the smoke. As soon as I was sure no one could see me, I went into full jinn speed. It felt faster than this morning.

My speed increased as a shadow raced alongside me.

Hadari. Her tongue was hanging out, and she looked to be having a great time. And wasn't even running hard, although I was probably hitting about eighty miles per hour. I slowed down, and she adjusted her pace to keep up. She gave a sharp nod and blinked as she slowed, and I saw she now had her leash in her mouth.

Many animals in the Eltrisphere had magic, but I was used to Lucie being blocked like I was. Obviously, Hadari had it, and it wasn't blocked. Which made sense as I had no idea who brought her down here, but it probably wasn't authorized.

Although her being out here with a leash was a good idea, she and I needed to talk. Soon. I also needed to know if the puppies had magic.

A shudder went through me at that thought.

There were a few people ahead, all coming from the car park at the edge of the forest. No sirens yet. A moment later, that changed.

I parked my bike, fixed Hadari's leash, and we jogged toward the smoke. It hadn't gotten larger, but it also hadn't stopped.

And while concerned people were running toward it, there was no one running out.

A weird fog hit as we got closer to the smoke, but it wasn't from the smoke.

"Ceian? Is that you?" A tall shape came out from the mist. It was Jeff, and he bent down to pet Hadari. "What are you two doing out here again?"

"There was an explosion? Smoke? This weird mist?" I was way more confused than he was.

"Oh, sorry, that was us." He looked around as if just noticing the fog for the first time. "Not sure about this mist stuff. But our alchemists were up to something. The sylia explosion was to scare them, and the eternal flame was to keep them back."

It took my brain a few moments to catch up to those words. They weren't human terms; they were Eltrisphere terms. I forced a smile to cover my panic, and Hadari head butted Jeff for more pets as a distraction.

"That's interesting, but I think the authorities aren't going to be happy about whatever happened out here." I needed to find out where Jeff and his friends heard those terms, let alone found a way to use them. Unfortunately, not with more people running up as we spoke.

"Yeah, I'll get our captain, let him explain it. Bye, Hadari." He grinned and ran back into the fog.

"Ceian?" Betsy came running up and stopped next to me. "Can you believe this? I bet someone was trying to destroy the evidence." She peered into the fog, but didn't appear to want to go in.

I didn't blame her; whatever was causing it was getting thicker.

"What evidence? And where are the others?" She was supposed to be with Keith, Jamie, and Martha. But that had been a few hours ago.

"Evidence of the mail caper. They knew we were onto them!" She looked behind her and put her hands on her hips. "They were behind me. Well, Martha and Jamie were. Keith had to go to the police station. He dropped us off after we checked in on Hannah.

Poor thing has a horrible cold! All bundled up and could barely talk. Now, where did those two silly geese go? We have to put out the fire and save the mail!" She reached down and scratched Hadari behind the ears.

"I'm not sure there is a fire, and isn't saving junk mail a bit odd? Don't most people destroy it?"

"Oh, that's what they want us to think!" Betsy put her hands on her hips and tried to peer through the fog. "Which way is the fire?"

"There you are, Betsy!" Jamie came running up. Then noticed me. "Hi Ceian, did Betsy call you?"

Martha came up behind her. She wasn't running, but walking extremely briskly. "Hadari!" She dropped down to give Hadari attention.

"I came here because there was an explosion and then smoke." I knew that Forgotten Hollow folks were a bit different about how they reacted to things, but I seemed to be the only one concerned about the current situation.

"Oh, it was those kids," Jamie said. "They get carried away with their playing."

"They've exploded things out here before?" Granted, Jeff hadn't seemed worried, but still. I could see the column of smoke still making its way through the fog. And he'd used Eltrisphere terms.

"Come on! The fog is thinning; we need that mail!" Betsy raced off before she finished shouting.

Martha rose, and she and Jamie dutifully took after her.

I turned to Hadari, but she gave a dog shrug and tugged on her leash. "Fine. We should probably make sure they stay out of trouble." I knew that was a fairly useless idea, those three hunted trouble better than a hoxien wolf, but I had to try. We still didn't know who the other two men who'd kidnapped them had been.

I hated to think badly of the dead, but I hoped they were the two as yet unidentified bodies who'd been found in front of Hannah's diner.

Betsy was right about the fog; a few feet in, it began to clear. The stream of smoke looked even more unnatural now that I could see it better.

Hadari's low growl as we got closer wasn't reassuring either.

I called to Betsy, but she, Jamie, Martha, Jeff, and at least a dozen people were all standing around the column of smoke. And none of them were even blinking.

# Chapter Thirty-Five

Hadari rubbed against Betsy's leg, and I touched her arm. She startled, blinked, and stepped back. No one else moved.

"What happened?"

"I don't know. You didn't answer when I called your name." Hadari moved to Jamie. Was she breaking some kind of spell? Another rub and another startled reaction.

That wasn't good; it confirmed that whatever the people working with Jeff's group had done, they'd managed to channel real magic.

Or one of them was another escaped Eltrisian.

I distracted Betsy while Hadari quickly released everyone, then returned to me. She wasn't growling anymore, but her eyes were narrowed as she faced the column of smoke.

I stepped closer to see what was causing it, but it just seemed to be coming from the ground.

"The mail! It must be completely burned by now." Betsy joined Hadari in glaring at the smoke.

"There's no fire." I wasn't sure how Betsy or any of the rest of the formerly transfixed people missed that. It wasn't hard to see that the smoke came from plain, unburned dirt.

"Yes, there is, right there at the base." Jamie pointed to where the smoke met the non-fiery ground.

I wasn't going to question whatever she thought she saw. "Ah, yes, maybe the mail wasn't in there. Jeff said his people made it."

The rest of the people around me were throwing sand, dirt, and water from water bottles onto the non-existent fire. Then, a small golf-cart-sized fire truck came up. I'd never seen the vehicle before, but it was a good size for the forest. A group of firefighters ran behind it.

I waited to see if they froze or saw the non-existent fire as well. They immediately drenched the base of the smoke column. Maybe their normal reaction to a supposed fire blocked the spell from stunning them? Or had Hadari not only freed the others, but cut that spell off?

The smoke vanished as Jeff and about fifteen similarly garbed teenagers came across the clearing.

"Sorry about that." Jeff nodded to the lead firefighter and ran his hand nervously through his hair. "Marcus, our captain for this adventure, said it wouldn't be noticeable."

"Which one of you is Marcus?" The firefighter looked around as his people made sure nothing was burning. They also stopped Betsy from running to the center.

"He left a while ago." A tall girl dressed as a medieval scribe answered. "He said he was getting help." The tone of her voice said that she was having serious second thoughts about this Marcus person.

"What's his full name? The police will need to speak to all of you." The firefighter nodded to where Jack, Officer Jones, and two other uniformed police officers were walking up.

"Tandi, I think. He keeps his persona mysterious and his real life too." The girl looked around at her friends and shrugged. "Mages can be weird. He showed up during one of our games a few months ago and showed us some cool books. They were unlike anything we had and looked really old. He said he was a gamemaster and could create some intense LARPs for us."

Jack nodded to the other officers with him. "We'll need to interview all of you. You know open fires aren't allowed in the forest."

All of the kids nodded and went off to the side to be interviewed.

"Where are the books?" I hadn't meant to say that, and that feeling was reinforced by the glare Jack gave me as he followed the kids. "Sorry, my uncle was a rare book collector. Someone could have done this if they were trying to steal this person's books." That was an extreme stretch, but it might be plausible. If the books they'd used were related to the Eltrisphere magic books that Darius had in with the boring Earth books, they were also seriously dangerous. Somehow, I didn't think there was any point in bringing that up.

"He must have taken them with him; they weren't in his tent in camp." A short teenage boy answered.

Jack let a long sigh out through his nose. "We'd better see your camp, and we can interview you all there." He looked around at the rest of us. "The rest of you are free to go." The words were polite, but the tone wasn't.

"But the mail..." Betsy cut herself off at a glare from Jack. "Wasn't here, I'm sure of that. Let's go, ladies. Hannah might need some soup."

I knew that Betsy wouldn't give up that easily. Jack was a delay, nothing more. They'd be back.

"What caused the explosion sound?" Tim, one of the baristas at A Lotta Joe's, asked. He was massive and looked like he'd been spending a lot of time at the new gym.

"Good question." I'd expected Jack to brush Tim off, but instead he turned to Jeff.

Who held up his hands. "It wasn't us. I don't think. Nothing we were doing should have done that. It sounded to us like something out at sea." His friends nodded anxiously around him.

"Once we find out, we promise to let people know. It might take some time. Thank you all for coming to help." Again, a not-so-subtle nudge from Jack to move us along.

I'd planned to follow Betsy, Jamie, and Martha, but Hadari pulled me further north into thicker woods and away from them.

"Tell Hannah I said hello," I said as Hadari and I left. "Hadari has some more walking to do."

All three waved goodbye, although Martha appeared torn between going with her friends and remaining with Hadari. With a call from Betsy, she stuck with her friends.

"What do you smell?" A hoxien wolf's nose was more sensitive than any animal on Earth.

"Bad things." She was using Sihlia again, and her voice was low.

I really hoped bad things didn't involve bodies. Jack was going to put me on cottage arrest if I kept stumbling around them. Regardless of the fact that I hadn't killed anyone.

We were soon out of sight and sound of the people in the clearing behind us. The forest was denser and wilder on this side. Thru-hikers would sometimes come this way as a detour, according to Betsy. There was access to the massive Pacific Coast Trail via Seiad Valley that could be reached from a smaller series of trails here, but most folks didn't casually come out here.

Hadari froze, her normally floppy ears perked up as she sampled the wind for something.

I released her leash, and she tore off. I doubted anyone was here to notice, and while I was fast, I wasn't hoxien wolf on a trail fast.

Luckily, she didn't have to go far. I caught up to find her whining and digging at the base of a tree.

"What did you find?" I didn't have a shovel or magic, so hopefully whatever it was, it wasn't deep.

"Eltrisphere. It smells like home. Not in a good way." Mostly in Sihlia, the last sentence was in English. Her upper lip rolled up in a snarl.

I also hoped that whatever was there wasn't big if we were going to have to carry it out. We were a good distance from my bike and even further from my cottage.

"Maybe we should come back with tools."

Hadari doubled down on her digging. "No, person not far enough away."

Very not good. I assumed she meant that Marcus person. If there was a chance these were items from the Eltrisphere, we couldn't leave them behind. I dropped down next to her and joined in digging. The ground was softer than I'd thought; whoever buried this had done so recently.

Hadari pulled on something in the ground and started walking backward. It was a backpack, an old one, but intact. Once she freed it, I unzipped it slightly. The good news was that no dirt had gotten inside, but the bad news was that the first item was an ancient Eltrisian spell book.

I kept up a steady, low-volume litany of every swear word I knew, both English and Eltrisian languages, as I looked at the rest of the books. Yup, four books from various cultures in the Eltrisphere. And very similar to the two smaller ones I found in Darius's box.

"I hate Darius."

"Many did." Hadari gave a doggy grin, then dropped it. "These can't stay here. Earthers could find."

"I have a feeling they already did. Most likely, Darius sold them to Marcus." I dusted off the backpack as best I could, then put it on. "I wish I could disguise this; if any of Marcus's friends see it, they'll probably know who it belongs to."

Hadari went behind me and rose on her back legs. I almost fell forward as she nudged the backpack.

"Perception spell. No one knows what they see, if they see anything." She came around to face me. "It won't last long."

"Thank you." She and I really needed that long talk. Perception spells weren't casual magic.

I let her lead us out. I had no idea which direction to go, and this time she moved at a jinn's fast speed, not a hoxien wolf's fast speed.

The clearing we'd been in before was empty. The cops could have still been with the kids at their camp, but the firefighters and local folks were gone. Which was good. Not that I didn't trust Hadari's spell, but perception spells were tricky. I was trying to help by not moving as if I had four heavy books on my back, but I knew I looked odd.

My bike was right where I left it. Getting on it with the full backpack wasn't easy, but after a few unsteady gaffs, we were off down the trail. The backpack was hard to balance, but we kept up a decent pace.

There was no one at my cottage, aside from Camfield's goats, Tiberius, Lucie, and five passed-out puppies. Everyone seemed to be in nap mode.

Hadari walked with me up to the cottage door, and I invited her in.

These books were her find after all.

I shoved papers off my coffee table; it would be easier for Hadari to see them there than on my kitchen table, and slid out the books. Part of me had hoped that Hadari and I were wrong, that they weren't ancient, forbidden, and not just on Earth, spell books.

I heard the universe laughing in my head. For some reason, it always sounded like Xieth.

# Chapter Thirty-Six

Sadly, I could only open one of the books. The other three wouldn't budge, even when I put them on the floor and let Hadari try.

"Too strong of magics," she said, then went to the door. "Nap time for puppies."

I got off the floor and opened the door to let her out. I wasn't going to point out that the puppies had been napping when we came back. Moms knew what needed to be done.

"Thank you for your help, I wouldn't have found those books without you."

She gave a doggy grin, head-butted my hip, then jogged out. The puppies hadn't moved when we came home, but they all bounded to their feet, jumped over Tiberius, and raced for their lot next door.

I hoped that Keith would be able to buy it soon.

I'd just hidden the new books in the back of the closet of my guest room when a soft knocking came from my door. Tiberius could knock with his horns, but it was never soft.

Keith was there with some sandwiches and snacks from Hannah's diner. "Really late lunch, or very early dinner. I brought plenty to share." He came in and looked around. "Where are Betsy and the others? They were supposed to meet me here after dropping by Hannah's again. They brought her soup."

"I just got back from the woods, and all three of them were there. Hadari and I went to see what happened." I glanced outside. I hadn't seen three little old ladies in my yard, but they could be tricky. Rather, Betsy could be, and the others followed. "They didn't say anything about coming here, though."

Keith sighed and put down the food. "Was there mail involved? That distracts her. I was at the police station."

I nodded and told him about the event in the woods, Jeff's mentor, Marcus, and the words Jeff used. Then I told him about Hadari tracking the four Eltrisian spell books.

"I can't say I've heard of someone named Marcus around here. Do you think he's from the Eltrisphere?"

"How else could he have understood the words of that spell?"

"Good point. Luckily, he's either a failed mage or just stumbled into the right pronunciation. If those two spells you mentioned had opened correctly, we'd be in a mess right now." He looked out the window. "Actually, we wouldn't be here right now. This entire area would be in the ocean."

I knew enough to recognize the terms Jeff used, but not what they meant. I was glad I hadn't realized how dangerous they were at the time.

I brought out the four books, but Keith couldn't open the other three either. He swore and shook his head at the one we could open. "This was taken out of a Naomth Sanctuary. If he wasn't dead already, Darius would have a lot to answer for." He glanced through it, but then closed it quickly. "We need to find this Marcus person and get answers."

I was about to put the books away when Betsy called.

"Hey, I thought you were all coming here?"

"Help! Hannah is a monster!" Then the call ended. I'd say it was another trap, but this definitely sounded like Betsy.

I frantically tried calling her back, but it went to a busy signal, and the same with calling Jamie and Martha.

Keith also tried all three on his phone, but got the same result.

"Let's go to Hannah's house." Keith helped me shove the food into my fridge and lock the books back up in the guest room closet.

I jogged over to Tiberius and his new goat buddies; Lucie had taken off again. "We have to check on something. When Lucie returns, I want you to go into Hadari's lot. Run there if anyone comes here before that." If Lucie had been here too, I would have tried to lock them both up. Then again, they'd been grabbed from inside my house before. Hadari could protect them better.

Tiberius looked at Camfield's goats but then nodded his head.

Keith's Vanagon was faster than it looked, and within ten minutes, we were in front of a cute green house. Betsy came running out the front door as we pulled up, and the door slammed shut right behind her.

"Help! Oh, do help! Hannah is a monster, and she has Martha and Jamie trapped!" Betsy didn't get scared easily, but her clear blue eyes were wide with terror.

Keith got to her first and took her hands. "It's okay, we're here and we will take care of this."

I felt his emotional nudge. I wasn't sure how I felt about him using it on humans so much, but Betsy calmed down immediately.

"What happened?" I watched the house as Keith focused on Betsy.

"We came to bring her some soup after stopping by the Old Hollow. She didn't answer at first, then the front door popped open." Betsy pulled her hands away from Keith and waved them around, although neither Keith nor I said anything. "I know! That should have tipped us off. We missed it."

"Why? You had no idea something was up." Still no movement from the house. The upstairs windows had sheer curtains, but they didn't budge or show anything.

"True, but still, a good investigator is never caught off guard. Anyway, we went inside after a short debate. When we were here this morning, Hannah had been bundled up on her sofa. This time, the blankets were there, but no Hannah." Even without looking at her, I knew she was wide-eyed and doing her slow nod. Betsy would make such a great living on the storyteller circuit.

"After searching the ground floor, we went upstairs, calling her as we went. Then we found her." That was said so strongly, I turned to her almost against my will.

"And?" I might have spoken louder than necessary when her pause went too long.

"There was *a thing* in the upstairs hall. That's the only word I can use. About Hannah's height, but covered in moss, branches, leaves, and dirt. It attacked me! I fought back and grabbed my phone to call you. I thought Martha and Jamie were behind me. But as I ran down the stairs, the bedroom door slammed shut, and I couldn't open it. Martha and Jamie were gone! That's when I saw Keith's van. We must rescue them."

I had borrowed Hadari a lot today, and right now I wished I had her with us. Whatever was there didn't sound like Hannah. Or anything from Earth.

"We will. But we need you to stay with the van." Keith sent another emotional push when she opened her mouth to argue. "We can't lose the van. What if whoever is in there sneaks out with Jamie and Martha and escapes in my van?"

It didn't make a lot of sense to me, but Keith's magic mojo wasn't aimed at me.

"You're right. I'll stay here. Do you have a club or a tire iron I could use? Just in case."

Keith paled but nodded to the small tire iron inside the van. "Now, stay here. No matter what you hear, stay here. If we don't come out in fifteen minutes, call the police."

She probably should have called them before calling me initially, but if this was some non-Earth monster, it was better that she hadn't.

Betsy nodded and flashed me a brave smile, then climbed into the van.

Keith and I walked to the front door.

"Any idea what the thing is that she described?" I kept my voice low. I didn't know all of the life forms in the Eltrisphere, but that didn't sound familiar at all.

"No. And that worries me. Actually, it sounds like a comic character some kids were working on in my art class. Three friends of Jeff's showed up for one class a few weeks ago. A variation of a swamp monster, apparently."

"Did you know them?" He'd said he didn't have a kid named Marcus in his class, but maybe he didn't know.

"No. I'm fine with kids dropping in; the class is funded by the school on weekends. I do require a sign-in if they come more than once. You're thinking of that Marcus person."

"I am. And I'd think you would have noticed if he were an adult." Not to say that there couldn't be a teenage person from the Eltrisphere down here. But the odds were low.

"I would have." He nodded to the door, twisted the handle, but it didn't budge. "You ready?"

"As much as I'll ever be." Even if I'd had my magic, I couldn't have popped that lock as cleanly as he did. I probably would have shattered the door.

The house was eerily silent as we did a quick search of the ground floor. Keith nodded and pointed up the stairs. I was a trained fighter, but he had magic. I let him lead.

The only door that was shut upstairs had some muffled yells coming from it. I had a feeling that was the room we were looking for.

Keith stood near the handle and waited until I stood on the other side and nodded. The door opened before Keith could do it, and a running pile of moss, leaves, and vines charged at us.

Keith moved at jinn speed and grabbed the creature in a tackle. Three forms were on the bed, all tied up with an odd variety of bedsheets, towels, and shirts.

Hannah, Jamie, and Martha. All of them were uninjured but furious, as I quickly untied them.

"That monster! Keith, be careful!" Hannah jumped to her feet, grabbed a floor lamp, and ran to help him.

"It's okay, just a kid. Probably on something he shouldn't have taken." Keith stood up and held up a costume of vines and leaves.

Hannah and I both narrowed our eyes. We knew what we'd seen, and that looked like a cheap costume from a costume shop. Jamie and Martha were rolled off the bed.

On the floor, looking confused and worse for wear, was a short teenager.

"Why am I here? Where am I?"

"Marcus, I presume?" I'd have to wait until we were alone to find out what had really taken place, but the red flush on the kid's face said my instincts were right. How did a human teenager turn into whatever it was he'd turned into?

"Yeah, you've heard of me?" His confusion vanished as he smiled.

"The police would like to speak to you, actually." Keith dropped the costume on the floor and grabbed the boy before he could run. "I work for them, and you don't want to test me. Or my friend. You took something bad, flipped out, and hurt my friends."

Marcus's smile faded, and he rubbed the side of his head. "I don't know where that costume came from, or how I got here. But I don't do drugs. Honest. The last thing I recall was hiding some D&D books in the forest and taking off. Things went weird out there."

"Books? You set off a fire in the forest. The fire department wants to speak to you, too." I was mostly going to let Keith handle the kid; less chance of my trying to avoid any lying that way.

"I didn't....Okay, I did that one. But no drugs. And I've never seen that costume thing in my life." He looked at Hannah, Jamie, and Martha. "I'm sorry if I scared you. I didn't hurt anyone, did I?"

Hannah put down her lamp. "You need to get your life together, kid. Whatever caused you to do this wasn't good." She turned to the other two. "Come on, ladies, we should go to the kitchen."

I had no idea how long Hannah had been tied up. But she recovered amazingly fast.

I glanced at Keith as the three ladies went out, Jamie phoning Betsy to come back inside. He shook his head. He hadn't nudged Hannah along. She was as strong as she seemed.

"Do you really have to call the cops? My folks will ground me for years."

Keith pulled his phone out. "Yup. Actions have consequences. Something you did led to this." He called it in, then the three of us, with me carrying the fake costume, trooped downstairs.

# Chapter Thirty-Seven

Betsy came rushing in, hugged everyone, aside from Marcus, then joined the other three in a glass of wine. She positioned herself to glare at Marcus until I almost felt sorry for him.

I knew he hadn't taken drugs, but most likely triggered something in that one book he'd gotten open. How Keith removed the spell and created that fake costume, I wasn't sure.

They didn't have lights or sirens on, but the police showed up quickly. Alice and Officer Jones knocked, then came in to hear the story.

Alice flipped her notebook shut once they finished. "We will have to give you a drug test and take you in for fingerprinting. The easier you make this, the less time you'll spend with us."

"I understand." Marcus looked around the room with a heavy sigh. "Again, I am so sorry."

Hannah walked with him and the cops to the door. Officer Jones dropped the fake costume into an evidence bag. I didn't hear what Hannah said as they reached the door, but it stopped the other three in their tracks. She laughed and looked pointedly at Marcus.

He nodded rapidly, then he and the cops left.

"What was that about?" Keith worked his way through a formerly full package of sandwich cookies.

"I'm hiring him as a new busboy. We could use an extra one, and he needs something to sort out his life. I'm all about creativity, but something went extremely wrong with that boy."

All of us had the same questioning looks, but Hannah had faced the worst of what happened, and it was her diner. If that was what she wanted, that was what she was doing.

Wine and cookies finished, we left Hannah to clean up her house. Her part of the story had been short; she'd had a bad headache, the diner was already well-staffed, so she called out sick. A short time ago, a knock came at the door, and she didn't recall much of anything after that until Keith and I showed up.

Her recovery plan was to heat the soup the others had brought and watch murder mysteries for the evening.

The rest of us went to Keith's van. "I still have food at Ceian's if folks want more than wine and cookies for an early dinner." Keith looked to me in confirmation; he needed to tell me what Marcus had really done, or become, and this would delay that.

But my friends were safe again, and I could wait. With my nod, Martha, Jamie, and I climbed into the back of the van, Betsy took the passenger seat up front, and Keith took off.

Tiberius was dozing near Camfield's goats, and Lucie, Hadari, and the puppies were nowhere to be seen.

I looked over to the lot. I wasn't sure how to explain the dogs not being here.

"Where is Hadari? Do she and the puppies stay in the barn?" Martha almost jumped out of the van and looked around.

"Actually, she's probably next door," Keith said faster than I could come up with something. "I just bought that lot as an investment this morning, and Ceian has been gracious enough to let Hadari and her puppies act as guards. They go back and forth. Tiberius and Lucie as well."

All three of the ladies gasped and congratulated him.

"Maybe we should go inside to further discuss this new acquisition and the possibilities." Betsy's gleam in her eye made me nervous. I was glad Keith had been able to get the lot, and for his quick thinking, but Betsy had an "idea". Those were often dangerous.

The food Keith brought earlier was cold sandwiches and sides, so nothing needed to be heated up. We spread out and ate as Betsy mentally went through whatever plan she'd just hatched.

I was enjoying the light chatter, but whatever Betsy was thinking was making me edgy. Hopefully, Keith wasn't smitten enough with Betsy to have missed it. He and I hadn't decided what the official story of the lot was going to be, so I didn't know how we would deal with Betsy.

"Oh!" Jamie waved her sandwich. "We didn't get a chance to tell you; seven black SUVs came racing toward the Grasshopper while we were on our way to Hannah's. No way to tell if they were full or not, but I think those were the ones that left before."

I had really been hoping that at least those specific black suits were out of the picture. There was a chance someone with them wasn't human, but I had a feeling most of them were. Getting them to leave until next year would be wonderful.

The topic snapped Betsy out of her plans for world domination—or at least empty lot domination. "Now, where did they go? What are they up to, really? Maybe we should do another recon. I can't shake the feeling that they are connected to the mail issue." She gave one of her slow nods. "The timing is suspicious."

"You might be right. Maybe they were the ones who stole our vines as well!" Martha said. "Think about it, they could have some powerful medicinal properties. No one knows for sure what the company the black suits are from does."

I looked around. "No one knows what they do?" That seemed more than a little odd.

From the worried look on Keith's face, even though he'd been here the entire time the black suits had been coming to Forgotten Hollow, he hadn't thought about what they did for work.

The three women looked at each other with wrinkled brows.

"That's a good question." Betsy stalled by taking a long sip of tea.

"It is." Martha nibbled on a piece of her sandwich.

"Indeed." Jamie finished her sandwich, folded her arms, and sat back.

"Oh! I see Hadari coming into the yard!" Martha jumped to her feet and ran out the door before I even knew she'd turned to the window.

Jamie and Betsy got up as well and followed her.

I had a feeling the excitement for Martha was real, especially if the puppies were there, but the other two were doing so because questioning about something that had clearly been magicked made them uncomfortable.

Then Keith got up as well.

"You too?" I didn't think Keith was in any way obsessed with hoxien wolf puppies.

No matter how adorable they were.

He kept his voice low. "No, but I am worried that whatever the black suits might have been using to confuse people in town might have hit me, too. I'm wondering if we never noticed those questions about the black suits, or the memories were messed up recently. Whatever it was, it's very subtle." Both of us watched the landscape painting. Thanks to Keith's additions, Xieth couldn't eavesdrop unless he fully opened the screen, but I noticed that Keith always took a seat where, if that happened, he couldn't be seen.

"We should probably go make sure Martha isn't stealing the puppies." I got up with a glance at the painting, then we followed the ladies out. I paused and looked around for Lucie while Keith joined them

Hadari was lounging and watching proudly as Martha, Betsy, and Jamie played with the five roly-poly puppies while they chatted with Keith.

"Oh, I'm sorry, ladies," Keith's voice was loud enough to catch my attention. "I can't join you on your mail search this afternoon. I promised Ceian that I'd run her down to the train station in Ghoston. I can give you a lift back to town before we leave, though."

That was news to me, which was probably why he spoke so loudly. I just wanted to do it soon.

The ladies conferenced for a few minutes, then came over to me,

"It looks like we're going to head into town, one more clue before night falls." Jamie shrugged. "Betsy wants to walk this time, so it's a good thing we ate already."

I hugged her and the other two. I wasn't a big hugging person, but I had leftover anxiety from my fear that they'd been taken again this morning.

"Just be careful near that hotel, we don't know what those black suits are up to, especially at night." I wanted to check that train station locker, but I really didn't want those three out at night right now.

"Oh, not going near them. Yet." Betsy gave her infamous slow nod. "I want evidence first." She sighed and raised both hands when Keith and I opened our mouths. "I promise we won't go near them until you both are back and we can make a solid plan. However, since they're only here for a few more days, we'll need to move fairly quickly if we want to get to the bottom of this." Betsy smiled far too broadly and led her friends down the road.

I waited until they were out of sight. "Am I the only one who felt a chill at her words?" It was amazing that those three hadn't had anything serious happen to them before I came along.

"Nope." Keith sighed.

"Thanks for offering to take me down there so soon," I said as we walked back into my cottage for the locker key, and a question hit me. "I don't understand how something in a public locker could still be there after however long ago Darius put it there. He's been dead for two months; wouldn't they just break it open and dump the stuff?" I knew things worked differently on Earth, but I couldn't imagine it being so in this case.

Lucie darted inside when I opened the door but silently went for more food. Never mind that he still had some outside.

"Without magic, yes. But Darius probably left a spell of some sort on it." Keith glanced over to me as I came back from the guest room with the key in my jeans pocket. "And whatever is inside the locker might also be actively helping avoid discovery."

"Lucie, you have no idea what Darius could have locked up?" I petted him as I gave him more food.

"Nope. Seriously, if I hadn't been locked up on that prison planet by mistake, I never would have hooked up with a scum like him." He turned to me. "Unlike you."

"I was young...er, and stupid. I fully admit that I fell hard for an absolute jerk." I stopped petting Lucie. There was no way I wasn't giving myself grief for my horrible taste in men. It had been a lifelong career until my bottle prison time. Now I was done.

The laughter in my head this time sounded like me.

We were just pulling out of my driveway when Keith's phone rang. He swore and turned off his car when he saw the caller.

"Hey, Jack, anything wrong?" He held the phone so I could hear the response as well.

"Yeah, that kid, Marcus. We let him go with his parents after interviewing him, but he said Cyber Kondle sold him some magic books a few months ago, and he thinks they were what caused him to have his blackout, or whatever happened at Hannah's house. He's coming back tomorrow. Could you see if you can get sketches of the books? He says he lost them in the woods, but we didn't find anything."

"I can be there. We were just running down to Ghoston. Ceian has a friend coming in at the train station."

"That's nice. Where are they coming from?" Jack's voice sounded suspicious.

"Cincinnati, wasn't it?" Keith was fast.

I forced a smile even though Jack couldn't see it and raised my voice. "Yes, a dear old friend. I do hope she can make it." A slight tightening of my throat.

"Lovely. Keith? Do you mind if I hitch a ride? I need to pick up something down there. My car's been acting up."

Jack had no idea what was happening, but he knew something was wrong. If it didn't possibly mean my death or imprisonment, and at least that for him, I would tell him everything just to get him to back off.

No one had been specific during my short briefing before being sent down here, but letting humans know about us was extremely forbidden. The outcome wouldn't be good for anyone.

"By all means." Keith didn't look any happier than I, but his voice didn't show it. "Pick you up at the station?"

"I can come to you, just don't want to take the car out of town right now.  No Betsy this trip?"

Keith blushed and scowled at the phone. Everyone seemed to know except for the object of his affection.

"I find her charming, yes. But no, she's not going on this trip." The clipped tone of his voice said that was all he was going to say.

Jack sounded like he was walking now. "How long have you known your friend, Ceian? What's their name?" He might have been trying to sound friendly, but it felt like an inquisition.

"Chrisabelle and I have known each other since we were kids. Haven't seen her in forever." True—I did have a friend named Chrisabelle when I was young. And hadn't seen her. That she wasn't human hadn't been asked.

Jack swore over the phone as his walkie-talkie crackled. "Detective Lanclin here." His voice tensed. "Call the alarm company and send a car out. I'll be there in a few minutes."

"Sorry, Keith, thanks anyway. Alarms are going off at The Drunken Toad Pub and A Lotta Joe's Coffee. No idea why, and they can't shut them off. I'll have to pass on the trip to Ghoston."

Keith looked like he was holding his breath until the call ended. "I've used more magic in the last week than in the forty years prior. That one hurt." He rubbed his forehead.

"What did you do?" I stood back as Lucie ran up and jumped into the van.

"I called a spell into both businesses to trigger the alarms and keep them going. Child's play to do when I was younger, although the technology was far different back home. I hoped Jack would be called in. We couldn't have him come with us."

"I'm so glad you said that. I was afraid you were switching sides." I laughed. "Not really, but it did freak me out."

"I knew that if we said no, or changed our plans, Jack would just be more suspicious." He looked over to me as he started the van again. "I do think he has feelings for you, but I don't know that they're all good. He doesn't trust you."

I wasn't sure if it being confirmed was better or worse. Forgotten Hollow wasn't large enough to avoid him completely. "I need to stay away from dead bodies and potentially deadly problems. Maybe then he'll leave me alone."

Keith's look wasn't hopeful. "I wouldn't count on that. I do think he's also intrigued by you. There are too many emotions about you in his head to easily sort out without doing an intrusive spell. Let's get out of town before he shuts down those alarms."

# Chapter Thirty-Eight

I hadn't been outside of Forgotten Hollow yet, so I felt a thrill of excitement as Keith pulled us onto the freeway.

"Are you sure you're ok to drive with what you just did?" Not that I could do much about it if he weren't. I had no idea how to drive a car and figured that since the council hadn't provided one for me, nor had the skills to drive one been transferred into my head, Xieth and his cohorts didn't want me doing it.

Keith looked better, but he'd been fairly when the call ended with Jack.

"I feel fine now, I think it was just over-spending my magic. I was paranoid about being found when I first came to this planet, so I never kept in shape with magic practice. After forty years, I'm rusty."

"I hear ya. After a hundred years in that bottle, I have no idea what will happen when these things come off." I raised my wrists to jingle the bracelets. "Have you sorted out how to see if I did magically slip in town that day with the tent?"

"I tried scanning for traces, but those bracelets are blocking it. I've also been looking into the witch storm and that spell in your barn." The scowl on his face wasn't good.

"You think the two are connected?" I felt better about him not being able to tell if I slipped magically or not. If a magic user right next to me couldn't tell, hopefully Xieth wouldn't be able to either.

"I think the pentia spell in the barn might have drawn the witch storm in unintentionally. I doubt that it created the witch storm, though. The same magic user could have been involved with both, though. We need to remove that spell on the floor of your barn, but I'm afraid to alert whoever set it by using magic on it. The fact that it was cast and set before you were stationed here isn't good and implies the council's involvement. Or at least awareness."

"There must be something we can do that doesn't involve using magic." One of the more annoying late-night commercials popped into my mind. It was a cleanser, one that could remove just about anything. Graffiti, paint, strip furniture in seconds. "Could we break the spell by lots of cleaning? Goopbegone seems pretty tough."

Keith shook his head until I said the name. "That stuff is vile. Horrible. Shouldn't even be made." He paused. "But it might work. We'd need to take out three of the spell lines completely to make the spell defunct."

That made me feel better. It wasn't fixed, but there was a plan. I was becoming adept at ignoring issues.

I leaned back in my seat with a sigh and watched the cars around us as the afternoon grew later. "It's interesting out here." We were still in the mountains, but the thick trees of Forgotten Hollow were gone. The freeway was four lanes across and mostly surrounded by tree farms.

Keith laughed. "I forgot, this is your first time out. Did they say anything about you not leaving Forgotten Hollow? I should have asked before we left."

"I have a twenty-mile limit, but Ghoston's train station is inside of it. Barely. So as long as we don't go past there, I'm fine. As far as I know, there aren't any other parolees near here, but they didn't want me roaming." Which wasn't bad now, but could be depending on how long I was down here. Tiberius had also been kept in the dark, but he had no idea he was being sent down here until it happened.

A laugh escaped before I could catch it.

"What was that?" Keith took an off-ramp, and we went into a small town. Ghoston, if I had to guess.

"Just thinking that my situation isn't good, but Tiberius's really sucks. He was clueless about what the council planned."

"How badly disgraced was he? Centurions are normally treated well. Or were when I lived in the Eltrisphere."

I shrugged. "No idea. I thought it was only because he'd been instrumental in my capture, which appeared to have been a mistake. One they won't completely admit to. Now I'm wondering if there was something else." There was a massive dose of overkill in what the council did to him.

"It does seem suspicious. And the spell in the barn was targeted primarily at him. Have there been any more times when he hasn't been like himself? More of remaining sleeping as a goat?" We drove into a train station parking lot. I'd never been near a train station, but had seen plenty through the magic of TV. This one looked like them, albeit a bit smaller.

"Not that I've noticed, but to be honest, I haven't been paying enough attention. Unfortunately. I'll feel better once we break that spell on the barn floor."

"Me too." He parked and we walked inside.

I panicked when I didn't see any lockers, but Keith nodded off to the left. A small area of lockers with red keys similar to the one in my pocket was in a corner.

I stuck my hand in my pocket, trying hard not to look suspicious. What if this was a trap? What if we couldn't find the right locker? I was a stronger magic user than Darius had been; he tricked me because he was ruthless, and I thought I loved him. But what if he had a stronger magic user spell the locker?

"We're fine." Keith gave me a kind, grandfatherly look. Probably one of the few people on this planet who could do it, based on our ages.

"Sure." I let out a long breath and nodded. "Any idea how to find a magically hidden locker? If it were easy to find, someone would have cleared it out by now." I wasn't sure if I was more freaked out about finding whatever was there or not finding it. The chaos that could happen if a human found an Eltrisphere weapon of some sort had already been hinted at by Marcus and the effects of Darius's books.

"I promise we'll find the locker." Keith picked up speed. "I'm magically blocking the station cameras, but can't hold them for long."

The bank of lockers seemed larger once we got to them. Probably because I was face-to-face with them. "There are only ten or so without keys. Do we try them? How do you tell them apart?" I knew logically that the one we wanted would be hidden, but logic wasn't playing fair right now in my head.

The fear of finding that locker and whatever was inside it was hitting me harder. I clutched the key in my pocket.

Keith froze and looked at me closely. "I apologize; I didn't think about a spell on that key. I think you're going to pass out now."

I really didn't think that Keith knocked me out. But his timing was perfect. The world went black.

The next I knew, I was on the floor, and Keith was holding me up. And Darius was laughing in my head.

"Get out!" I yelled. The voice didn't stop, and Keith rocked back a bit. From what I could see, no one in the station noticed.

"Ceian? Are you okay?" Keith's voice was low.

"I think so. I might be losing my mind." I focused on the laugh inside my head. I couldn't make it stop, but I got the volume down. I waved a hand and pushed myself up. "I'm okay. I think Darius left a trap spell on the locker and the key. He dropped me with fear and won't stop laughing in my head." Jinn didn't deal with death magic, but when I was back to my full self, I was going to find a way to get Darius back.

However he had died the first time; it had been far too easy.

Keith helped me to my feet, then swore and stepped back.

"What?" He was looking at me as if I'd grown two heads and scales.

I patted my shoulders just to be sure.

"You're burning up." He held up his hand that he'd helped me to my feet with, and a flash of red faded as I watched. "You don't feel anything?"

"Annoyance at the still laughing moron in my head. And a slight headache, probably from said moron. But that's it." I held out my arms. Nope, no scales or red burning skin.

Yay me.

"Where's the key?"

I took it out of my pocket. "Looks normal to me." Granted, before this, I'd never seen a train locker key in person.

"It does." Keith scowled as he reached for the key and hit my hand instead. "What the...can you hand me the key?" He finally asked after two more tries.

"That's weird. It feels like it's there, but then it's your hand. Here." Keith held out his hand, and I dumped the key into it. But nothing came out. I turned my palm toward me, and it was hanging from my hand.

"What did that idiot do?" I could pick up the key, but the moment I put it into Keith's hand, it vanished and popped right back into my hand.

"He hired someone for this spell. I avoided him as much as possible, but Darius wasn't this powerful. That key's spell was most likely triggered by proximity to the locker."

"Which should mean that if I hold the key out, I should be able to feel where the locker is. In theory." First good news in a while.

Keith was pointedly looking back at the rest of the station. "I'm holding a spell against the humans as well as the station cameras. Both are beginning to fall. We have less than fifteen minutes."

It became a game as Keith's spell fell, and Darius's purchased spell finally decided I might be okay.

The laughing was less mocking now.

I found the hidden lockers in twelve minutes and thirty seconds. A strip of lockers, faded as if they weren't in this reality, finally appeared adjacent to the last wall. Keith didn't see them, but I did.

*"Pick correctly or die."*

# Chapter Thirty-Nine

The words weren't good, and that they were in Darius's voice made them worse. Five train station lockers and I had one shot. And from the increasingly worried look on Keith's face, we were on the edge of being discovered and videotaped.

Channeling my annoyance for Darius, and everything he'd put me through, into the hand holding the key, I slowly passed it in front of each locker. I had no idea what I was expecting to happen, but hopefully something would kick in. The first four did nothing.

The final locker gave a soft click when my hand reached it, and the laughing in my head stopped. I waited another few seconds, then put the key in the keyhole and held my breath.

Another click, and I pulled open the door, grabbed a cloth-wrapped bundle, and shoved it in my canvas bag. I stepped away, and the mystery row of lockers, along with the key, vanished.

"Good timing, my spells just fell, and there's an odd pressure building in here. We probably want to leave. Now." Keith was looking around us as if we were about to be swarmed by attackers.

I didn't feel what he did, but I agreed with his assessment. People were now looking at us. Which meant the cameras were able to see us, too.

I doubted that anyone was looking for non-humans doing magic, but there was a certain cop who might try to get station videos. He hadn't wanted to come with us just to run errands. Even without my addiction to late-night cop shows, I would have figured that one out. He was trying to find out what I was really up to.

I wouldn't put it past him to borrow the video officially from the train station.

"Hold on a second." I clutched my bag closer to me, then acted as if I'd received a call. I even went so far as to talk silently into the phone. And looked extremely sad as I pretended to hang up and put the phone back in my bag.

"Christabelle couldn't make it. Her granddad is sick." Both were true as far as I knew. I refrained from smiling at the camera. If Jack could be tricky, so could I. And if I'd been wrong about him pulling the tapes, then I'd just done that charade for nothing.

I was fine with that.

"Oh, I'm sorry." Keith's stomach loudly grumbled. "I know we just ate, but can we pick up some food on the way home?" Keith was turned toward the cameras.

I shrugged and nodded. I was a little hungry, which was weird but probably caused by whatever Darius just put me through. But I hadn't been doing magic like Keith had.

"You think Jack will take those recordings, too, don't you?" I asked once we got outside the train station. Keith and Jack worked together and seemed friendly enough, but that didn't mean complete trust.

"Possibly. I didn't think of it until your phone stunt, but as I said, the feelings I pick up from him are mixed. Now, which fast food? Going Bonkers Burgers or The Dogger?" He unlocked the van door, and I climbed in, keeping my bag close to me. No idea what was inside, but it was heavier than I would have suspected from the size.

And I wasn't even going to think about seeing what it was until I was home and behind locked doors. "We don't need to stop."

"Yes, we both do. There was a magic drain in that station. That's what wore down my spells. And you were using something magical as you found the hidden lockers. I felt it."

"I didn't feel anything. But aside from some rage, I didn't notice anything when I might have thrown that striped bug tent last week, either. So, I'm somehow leaking magic?" Even though the thought had been lurking in my mind, this seemed to make it more real.

It made me sick to my stomach.

"I'm voting for the burgers; they have more variety." Keith gave me that kindly grandfather look again. "As for leaking magic? I'm honestly not sure. The tests we'd need to prove or disprove it for sure would raise too many red flags for Xieth and the council."

I frowned and clutched the canvas bag tighter.

I would have sworn that I was too upset to eat. Until we pulled up to the drive-thru, and the smell of fatty food filled the air.

"I'm starving." Whether that magic in the train station came from me or somehow through me, I had no idea. But I was ravenous.

Keith ordered enough food for five people, maybe ten. And two drinks.

If the kid at the window thought it was odd, she didn't say a thing. Just took Keith's money and started shoving out bags of food through the window.

"Do you mind if I eat in your van?" I asked to be polite, but I was about to start chewing on the bags.

"It's fine, just hand me a burger."

We'd each finished a massive burger and fries before the ten minutes it took to reach the freeway on-ramp.

"It was weird that Darius had spells set up with the key and the lockers, right? Maybe that's what pulled in my magic." I handed Keith a second burger and opened one for myself.

"Maybe." He didn't sound optimistic about it. "I'll pick up some Goopbegone from the hardware store down here. I think we need to get that pentia spell removed."

"Thanks. Do you want to come see whatever this is?" I patted my bag. Keith had been interested in Darius's boxes, but he seemed to be avoiding my canvas bag.

"I don't think I should. There's a repulse spell on it. A strong one. I avoided Darius when he moved here, but I know that level of magic was out of his league." He shuddered as he glanced at the bag.

"Great. You don't think it's going to explode on me, do you?" I would be more worried, and I should be, but the food overload was hitting me hard. It was a good thing that I apparently wasn't the sort to fall asleep in a car, or I'd be drooling against the window right now.

He laughed. "Probably not, most likely it would have blown us both up when you opened the locker door." His smile fell as he looked in his rearview mirror. "That isn't good. We have two black SUVs following us."

I glanced back, but could only see one; the second must be directly on the first one's tail. "Where did they come from?"

"A side street right before the freeway on-ramp. It might be nothing; the black suits are still lodging in Forgotten Hollow, and these could be returning. Or they might be government agents of some sort."

It was sad that I wasn't sure which one would be worse. The black suits were weird and disturbing, but aside from one showing up dead in my barn and possibly having been involved with kidnapping my friends, they mostly seemed to ignore everyone.

Tailgating this close wasn't ignoring anything.

If the feds were following us, it could just be mistaken identity. Even though Lucie wasn't with us, the laugh in my head at that thought sounded alarmingly like him.

"Can we lose them?" I didn't know how to drive a car, so I wasn't certain what was involved in shaking a tail. But I'd seen it on TV shows many times.

"We might if I take an off-ramp before we get closer to home. But they don't seem to care if we notice they're following us."

Any chance to say more came out in a squeak as I frantically hung on to the food and the canvas bag when Keith raced across three freeway lanes to an off-ramp.

"Sorry, I had to try. And they were probably expecting it. Or at least the second car was."

I looked back. I'd take his word for that being the second car; it looked like the one I'd seen before. And it was directly behind us.

Keith went down a few residential streets before pulling over. "I've had enough." He parked and stomped out of the van before I could ask if I should stay put or not.

I crawled out from under the food, clutched my canvas bag tight, and followed.

Two men, neither in black suits, but both looking alarmingly bland anyway, were getting out of the SUV.

Keith stood behind his van, arms folded, and with a glare I'd never seen before. He was a pissed grandfather to the ultimate degree.

"Why are you following us? We've done nothing wrong."

Both men pulled out their badges. Even at this distance, I saw the big FBI letters.

"Are you Keith Casinta? We've been trying to contact you."

"I am. Why?" His arms folded tighter, and I swore that the tip of his braid twitched.

"Is this your...daughter?" The second man seemed ready to say something else, and I added my glare to the fight.

"Friends. We're friends. I don't drive, so Keith offered to take me into town."

"That's fine. Maybe you can help. We're investigating a group staying in Forgotten Hollow. Getting people to talk to us in town doesn't seem to work. The group is staying at the Grasshopper and represents the Skyharp Company."

"The black suits?" I tightened the hold on my bag as I shut my mouth. At least now I knew the name of their company.

"What is your name?" The first man narrowed his eyes in my direction.

"Ceian Lasinaria. Newly moved into Forgotten Hollow. Non-driver."

The second FBI agent tilted his head. "The Fainting Goat Tea and Spice? I saw that brief. Did Lanclin ever find out who was behind the bombing attempt?"

"That's me and my teahouse. And if he has, he hasn't shared that with me." It was petty, but I didn't know if Jack would tell me anything useful at this point.

"He will. He's a good cop." He paused and stepped back at a look from the first agent.

"We believe they often do wear black suits. They've never caused notice before; having company retreats across state lines isn't a crime. But there have been some odd reports lately. And three of them have turned up dead." He turned to me. "I believe one was found in your barn?"

"I guess? The body was wearing a black suit, but I didn't know who he was. I didn't kill him or leave him there." Not a lie. But things could get bad if they continued asking me things. I should have stayed in the van. Hopefully, the FBI hadn't looked into me enough to see my earlier run-ins with dead bodies.

"Have either of you ever noticed odd behavior from them? Anything to do with mail?"

I was grateful that neither agent was looking at me at the moment, as I was pretty sure all of the blood draining from my face at his words would be noticeable.

"Mail? Like what?" Keith relaxed his arms.

"We believe they might be smuggling stolen government or corporate secrets out via junk mail. And they're doing it when they're on their retreats. I think they usually only stay for one week?"

"Yes, I believe they extended it this time," Keith said.

"I told you they were on to us." The second agent shook his head and handed each of us a card. "Thank you both for your assistance. If you think of anything related to them, at any time, call this line. Thank you."

The two agents nodded and spun back to their SUV.

Keith waited until they drove off before relaxing. "That's not good. If Betsy and the ladies are investigating the mail issue..." He turned and ran for the driver's seat. I was buckled into the passenger's seat before he started the engine.

# Chapter Forty

As soon as we were on the freeway, I started calling Betsy, Jamie, and Martha. None of them answered. "Maybe we need to track their phones. Put some sort of locator inside the casing or something." Before Keith could respond, I called Hannah. It was doubtful she'd gone with them, but they might have circled back over to her house after they left mine.

And they all were so busy having a great time that none of them answered their phones. Right. This planet was phone addicted.

Hannah answered just as I was about to hang up. "Ceian? What's up?"

"Are Betsy and the others with you?" I noticed that Keith's speed kept increasing. He was worried about them as well.

"No. They swung by again to make sure I was still recovering after my adventure, but left, oh, about a half hour ago? Betsy got a phone call, said, 'we have them now,' and they ran out."

Keith heard her and sped up even more. He also started swearing in a variety of languages under his breath.

"Do you know where they went?" I wanted to lower the speaker volume so Keith didn't crash us into something, but I was afraid that his not hearing anything might make things worse.

He really needed to address his crush on Betsy.

"Yeah. They said there was some mail out behind the Grasshopper. It sounded like Betsy had recruited some of the high school kids to help look for it."

"Do you know who called her?" I'd been thinking Marcus was just an overexcited geek, and not intended for anything bad to happen. But if others in his group were leading Betsy and the others astray, all bets were off.

"No. It was male, but not that Marcus kid."

"Thanks, call me if you hear from them, and keep your doors locked."

She paused. "Okay, but I expect you all at the diner tomorrow to fill me in. All doors and windows are locked. Stay safe." She clicked off before I could respond.

"Someone tricked them. Again. They need to stay away from the Grasshopper and that twice-cursed stolen mail." Keith continued swearing as he took the exit for Forgotten Hollow at a much faster speed than felt safe.

"We'll get them back. We have to." I hadn't cared about anyone during my hundred-year lock-up. Now all these feelings were smacking me around.

Keith took a long, deep breath, then released it slowly. He repeated it a few times before we crossed the lights into Forgotten Hollow proper. "You're right, we will. Betsy has always been a loose cannon, but most of their adventures were harmless in the past."

"Until I arrived." I raised my left hand to stop him. "Don't think I haven't thought of it. I show up, and those three get dropped into murder investigations. And it just keeps getting worse."

"Hey, the black suits, or rather the employees from the Sky-harp Company, have been coming here for years. I seriously doubt the FBI would be tracking them if they hadn't been causing concern for far longer than you've been on Earth. It's not your fault. Besides, Betsy would be pissed if you took the credit for her being kidnapped."

I couldn't help but laugh. "You're right, she probably would be, she likes having the 'street cred' as she puts it. But let's find them and make sure they're safe."

"You read my mind." Keith slowed down after his mad dash, but was still going faster than the posted speeds up the hills to the Grasshopper. We parked down the road a bit from the hotel, near where he'd parked when we were on recon the first time.

"Do you think the call was a trap?" I was glad it wasn't Marcus; he was already in serious trouble, but Jeff and the other kids with him had seemed fine.

"I don't know. Betsy swore she'd be more careful about things like that after they were kidnapped the first time. I honestly have no idea what to do with her."

I took his arm as we walked along to the back of the hotel. Night was falling, but the hotel had plenty of outside lighting. The Grasshopper was built on a cliffside, but for the most part, it wasn't a steep drop to the ocean. "There's not much we can do, aside from trying to rescue her." I'd just finished speaking when a loud dog bark and a high-pitched scream came from ahead of us.

"I know that bark!" I released Keith and ran up the slope. Hadari hadn't been in my life for long, but she had a distinctive bark. The scream wasn't familiar, though. It was female, but didn't sound like any of the three we were looking for.

We ran around the back of the hotel. Keith had much longer legs than I did, but he let me lead. Clearly, I wasn't the only one who recognized a hoxien wolf bark.

Hadari was barking, growling, and snarling at two of the black suits. A man and a woman.

"Easy girl, who are you guarding?" Hadari's stance was full defense mode, but until we came fully around the corner, I couldn't see what she was protecting.

Keith started swearing before I did.

Betsy, Jamie, and Martha were out cold, again, and tied up against the wall of the hotel. I didn't see any blood, but they could have other injuries. Three times being knocked out in a week? If I thought any of them would listen, I'd drag them to the hospital to have their heads examined.

"If you've hurt them in any way." Keith's swearing vanished as he stalked toward the two black suits.

That he was obviously known by Hadari made the man and woman take a few steps away from him.

The cliff behind them wasn't steep, but they could still fall to their deaths if they weren't careful. Something they weren't focusing on right now. Hadari had them spooked.

"What did you do to our friends?" I walked forward and petted Hadari. She stopped growling for a moment, turned to me with a doggie grin, then resumed growling.

"We didn't do anything. We came back here...for reasons." The woman glanced at the man, then continued. "We found them like that. Then your dog came along and tried to eat us. It needs to be locked up."

I ruffled the fur around Hadari's collar. "Oh, she was. Some-times animals get loose. She wouldn't have reacted to you un-less she also thinks you hurt her friends."

"We didn't do anything." The woman's voice was calmer now, and the man stopped hunching. "You don't even know what's going on, do you? There are powers outside of this world. Powers that we will control. Is your dog going to protect you from that?"

Keith subtly walked behind the two as we talked. They still should have noticed him moving closer. Which meant two things: he was using magic to hide, and these two weren't from the Eltrisphere.

Keith simply said "boo" to them, hit them with a spell, then grinned as they collapsed.

"Keith? Why am I on the ground?" Betsy struggled to sit up, but she and the other two were tied together.

Keith ran to them, and he and I worked on untying them.

Jamie shook her head in disgust. "I'm not sure how we got here, but someone has no idea how to tie up their victims." She twisted a bit, then slid out of the ropes. "Morons."

With her help, Martha was also freed. I let Keith finish untying Betsy. The last few days, I'd seen Keith's heart in his face when he dealt with Betsy. This was the first time I saw it on hers as well.

And she seemed surprised at her own reaction.

"What were you three doing here?" Keith and Betsy were having a brief heart-in-eyes staring match, so I directed my question at the other two.

"Betsy got a call, one of the high school kids she's pulled in to help us with the great mail caper." Martha scowled at the area they'd been lying in when we arrived. "We came back here to meet her friend. But no one was here. Then everything went blank." She sighed and rubbed the side of her head. "They snuck up on us and knocked us out. Again. Didn't they? You know it can't be good to have it happen so many times in one week. We could be losing brain cells each time."

"I doubt that, but it's really pissing me off." Jamie's fists were tight, and she was eyeing the unconscious black suits. "Did they do it?"

Jamie was quieter than the other two, but more of a fighter at heart. Right now, she wanted to punch someone.

"We're not sure. Hadari must have followed you three or some-how knew you were here. When we arrived, she was growling at them and protecting you." I looked over to the two still uncon-scious people. Depending on the magic Keith had used, they might be out for a day or so.

Not helpful for us, but he had been pissed and scared. I wouldn't blame him if he hit them with more magic than was needed.

Hadari walked forward and sniffed the man and woman black suits. She stepped back and briefly shook her head. She didn't believe they were behind the attack on Betsy, Martha, and Jamie. Unfortunately, her speaking in either English or Sihlia right now wouldn't be a great idea.

"You didn't find any mail?" I continued watching Keith and Betsy as well as our unconscious black suits in case that changed. But Hadari was close enough that if they were faking their continued unconsciousness, she'd notice.

"We did, actually. See? Whatever they keep using to knock us out *is* scrambling my brains." Martha's round and kindly face looked odd in the full scowl she shot at the two unconscious black suits. "Like I said, we got here, Betsy's contact, or whoever called us pretending to be someone she knew, was a no-show. We looked around on our own. Found a huge collection of discarded junk mail off the side of the cliff. We were debating the best way to pull it up when whatever knocked us out happened." She paused. "I think."

Jamie beat Martha and me to the cliff, and Betsy and Keith followed. Betsy kept her swearing low, but it was there.

"I can't believe I forgot that! It was the biggest haul ever, right there for the taking." She dropped to her knees and pointed at the extremely bare cliffside. The lights from the hotel reached it as well, but there was nothing there. "And whoever knocked us out took it."

Keith had exceptional eyesight, even better than mine, so he spotted the trail down the cliff first. "Or, whoever got you three pushed it into the ocean."

We were up high enough that even with advanced eyesight, seeing anything in the water way below us was almost impossible. But when I squinted, I saw a few brightly colored bits of junk mail way down the slope.

"We have to go down there! There's a beach nearby; the mail might have been washed ashore."

Keith took Betsy's shoulders gently. "Maybe a piece or two will eventually float to land. But they won't be in any state to give us any information. And it's a long and dangerous hike to Stalo Beach. I tried it once when I first moved here, in the daytime, not at night. I was forty years younger at the time and couldn't make it." He looked around and dropped his voice. "And there's important information we need to tell you about the mail."

I hadn't been sure if Keith was going to tell Betsy and the others about the FBI, but I agreed that this wasn't the place for it.

Betsy still had her fighting face on and looked ready to go without him. Or any of us.

Hadari came forward and put her head under Betsy's clenched fist.

"You're telling me not to be stupid, aren't you, girl?" Betsy relaxed. "Thank you for protecting us. I do wish you could tell us who did this."

Hadari gave one of her tongue-rolling doggie grins, trotted to a corner of the building, and started digging. She tugged out a tattered advertisement.

"Oh, you clever girl!" Martha ran forward to hug and pet Hadari. Betsy and Jamie ran forward to help pull up the rest of the hidden mail collection.

Keith and I stood back and shared a look of concern. The ladies needed to back out of this, but telling them that without divulging the FBI involvement wouldn't work.

Even once those three knew about the FBI, they still might not back down.

All of us turned when a car pulled up behind us, and we could hear two people coming our way. Hadari ran to me, and Keith dropped back to stand in front of Betsy, Martha, and Jamie.

No one was getting knocked out this time.

# Chapter Forty-One

I held my breath, hoping this didn't come to a fight, but balancing on the balls of my feet as I would for an arena match.

Two familiar FBI agents came around the corner. "Good work, we thought those two were up to something." The lead agent said as he walked past us to the two crumbled black suits. "Lovely dog." He smiled at Hadari as he passed her.

She turned to me, but didn't appear threatened by them.

That was good, I guess.

"Did you find them unconscious?" The second agent stopped in front of me, but watched Keith and the ladies behind me. He was really asking if we'd done it.

Keith came forward before I screwed things up with a bad attempt at not lying. "They were that way when we got here. Also, our friends were tied up when we arrived. Another friend told us where they were going based on a suspicious phone call."

I hoped that when he knocked the two black suits out, he'd also managed to scramble their memories a bit. They might not have a clue as to what hit them, but they definitely saw Keith and me.

"And whose dog is this?" The second agent smiled. I figured he probably already knew since he knew who I was.

"She's with me. Her name is Hadari. She got loose this afternoon when we went down to Ghoston."

"What are the feds doing here?" Betsy stomped forward but didn't pass me or Keith.

"We're on a case, and that's all you need to know." The second agent looked over Betsy's head to Jamie and Martha with a sigh. "But please, all of you, stop trying to find discarded junk mail. It's part of a federal investigation."

The collective gasp from all three ladies had probably been heard back at Hannah's diner. The good news was that Keith and I didn't have to tell them. Bad news, it still probably wouldn't stop them.

"I knew something was going on!" Betsy jumped up and down. "It's the black suits, isn't it?"

The first agent came back from checking the unconscious man and woman. "We can't discuss the case. We would like to get detailed information concerning your last few hours. But not here."

A second car pulled up, and I knew before the man and woman arrived; they were more feds. The original two nodded to the new ones. The new ones motioned to Betsy, Jamie, and Martha, but waved off Keith and me when we also stepped forward. "Just those three right now. We'll come find you if we have any questions for you. Have a nice night."

Jamie was ready to fight, Martha looked a little frightened, and Betsy appeared intrigued.

The two original agents went back to the unconscious black suits, but nodded toward Keith and me. "We know where you both live; we'll find you if we have questions." He gave a sharp nod, and he and his partner crouched down by the unconscious man and woman.

I really wanted to grab that pile of mail that Hadari had unburied, but it was too far away to do it without being seen.

Given that it was the focus of a full investigation, I was surprised that the FBI agents hadn't seen it.

Until I glanced to the corner and didn't see any mail.

Hadari gave one of her doggie grins and led the way out. Hoxien wolves had their own type of magic, but I wasn't sure what they could do.

Keith and I quickly followed her to Keith's van. I waited for us to be inside before asking Hadari about the mail. I knew the FBI wouldn't let us hang around here long, but I was beginning to think the mail had some important clues.

"What happened to the mail?" Keith got out before I could.

"I reburied it as they walked up," Hadari said in her odd mixture of Sihlia and English.

She was using more English now.

I nodded. "Excellent. I think we need it." Both Keith and Hadari gave me confused looks.

"We need to get Betsy and the others out of this, not make it worse with new mail." Keith started the van and drove down the hill and through town.

"Agreed. They shouldn't be near it. Bad." This was all in Sihlia from Hadari.

"They shouldn't, but I don't know how much I trust the FBI. They've been tracking these people for how long? Yet waited for them to come to our town to grab them? I think they don't care what happens to the people of Forgotten Hollow. As long as they solve their case. We need to solve it first."

Keith glanced over at me a few times as we made our way to my side of town. "I think those three are a bad influence on you. No offense, but even my late wife was fond of pointing out that jinn rarely have a strong attachment to a single place."

I felt my face grow red. "It's not that. These people don't deserve to go through whatever this is. Not to mention, if bad things happen to Forgotten Hollow, I might have to go back into my bottle." It wasn't a lie, and I didn't choke. There was more to it than that. I *was* becoming attached to people here.

"Agreed. I don't want to leave here." Hadari was back to mostly English. "My babies love it."

"Let's deal with this in the morning," Keith finally said as we pulled down my street. "Do you want a ride to the diner tomorrow?"

I slid open the van door when he stopped, and Hadari raced out and into the empty lot.

"Thanks, but I need to do final, final checks for the grand opening. With all that's been going on, I lost focus. I'll take my bike down." Granted, I wasn't as excited about my teahouse right now as I had been, but I was sure the feelings would come back.

"Okay, see ya then. We'll keep each other updated if the ladies contact us, right?"

"Or the feds. Have a good night." I patted my canvas bag as Keith drove off. If the FBI agents thought my extreme closeness with a canvas bag was odd, they hadn't given any indication.

But now that the latest Betsy crisis was hopefully resolving, I wanted to know what Darius had cursed me with this time.

Hadari gave a soft woof and ran over to her lot.

Tiberius and Lucie were near the front door, and Camfield's goats were sleeping in their pen. I checked their water, added some more goat chow to their dish, and let them sleep. I think I missed Camfield more than they did.

"Took you long enough." Lucie huffed himself up and shoved past Tiberius to go inside first. "We could have starved out there."

I seriously doubted that. Tiberius paused at the open door, then gave me a head bob and came inside.

"Have a good day?" I glanced around the dark yard before shutting and locking the door.

Lucie was already head down in his bowl. Tiberius gave me a head tilt, goat snort, and went to his blankets in the corner.

That was odd, and something I wished Lucie had seen. "Anything weird happen while I was gone?"

Tiberius gave another goat snort and picked up a corner of one of his blankets. It wasn't like him not to want to eat, but he could have been eating outside.

Then he looked at me with his eerie gold goat eyes and calmly began chewing on the blanket.

"Tiberius?" I didn't yell, but normally that tone would cause him to give me a smartass response, or at least a sharpened glare my way.

He just continued eating his blanket and glancing around the living room for dessert.

"Lucie? When was the last time Tiberius said something?" I kept my voice low and moved slowly toward the extremely goatish Tiberius. There was nothing behind those eyes aside from moving toward the knitted blanket on my couch.

He didn't seem too concerned when I snatched the knitted blanket out of his reach.

Lucie was still inhaling his food but glanced up. "What? Dunno. An hour or two ago? I just got back right before you did. Hey Tiberius. Beat up any criminals lately?"

Tiberius didn't look toward either of us but quietly continued eating his blanket. "This is bad. We have to get him outside and chain him to something. That isn't Tiberius right now." I'd been happy that we might have a way to break the spell in the barn, but had it come too late? The feds following us, and concern about what Betsy and the others had gotten into, had cut off our planned side trip for the Goopbegone.

Lucie and I had almost gotten Tiberius to the door when the landscape painting chimed, and an annoyed cherub face took over the screen. "Who triggered a force three spell alarm down there this afternoon? And where were you?"

Lucie kept poking Tiberius to go out the door, and they both fled. I had a feeling Lucie was more motivated by avoiding Xieth than getting the goat back outside.

Force three spells were stronger than average spells, and few magic users could call them. Keith could probably create one. But before my lock-up, I knew that I couldn't have.

"I was working on things." I felt a tug at my throat on that one. I wasn't vague enough. "As for who did it, I have no idea, Xieth." I raised my wrists to emphasize the bracelets. "No magic, remember? And my fellow townsfolk appear to be human." That nice 'appear' let me skate without choking me. Keith appeared to be completely human. I wasn't saying everyone here *was* human.

"True. I thought maybe you would have noticed something." Xieth was hopeful, but his steam about the issue was fading fast.

"I've been occupied with the teahouse, but I can't believe we had a force three spell here."

"It actually wasn't in your town, but you might have still felt the edge of it. About twenty minutes south of you. There's a large vehicle transit area there."

I did some breathing exercises before answering. "I didn't notice anything up here. Maybe it was too far away." Meanwhile, my brain was having a breakdown. Had I triggered a force three spell even with the magic blocking bracelets and hadn't been aware of it? This was bad, bad, bad. Almost worse than Tiberius turning full goat.

I fought to keep my face neutral.

"Tomorrow, when you go into town, bring up that you heard about an earthquake down south, and see if anyone felt it." He watched me expectantly, so I nodded and forced a smile.

"I'll report back anything I hear on anyone who felt that."

"Very good, carry on." He gave me a nod before the landscape reappeared, but from the look on his face, he was already moving on to the next crisis.

I waited a moment to make sure he wasn't coming back, then grabbed the canvas bag again and ran out the front door.

I had no idea if Tiberius would wander off if he was all goat, but he wasn't moving away from the side of the pen. He also seemed to be enraptured with one of Camfield's goats.

While I wasn't an expert on goat expressions, it seemed she returned the interest.

That would be horrific for too many reasons to think about. Luckily, the pen was high and designed for goats.

Lucie watched the drama, but remained motionless aside from the tip of his tail. I had a feeling that if Tiberius tried to make a new goat girlfriend, Lucie was going to stop it with his claws.

Neither would admit it, but Tiberius and Lucie had a grudging friendship.

A dark blob ran toward us, but then quickly separated into Hadari and her puppies.

She sniffed Tiberius, then backed away. "He's changed." Her English was becoming clearer.

"Yeah, he has." I quickly told her about the curse on the floor of my barn.

"You two will also be affected?" She looked between Lucie and me.

"It looks like it. We might have a way to stop it. I just hope it's not too late."

"Put him on a leash, a metal one, then bring him to my area and stake him in the center of the yard. He's still inside there, but it's fading. The other goats are influencing him."

I wasn't going to argue about that. I found a heavy metal chain and then connected it to Tiberius's collar. Even though Tiberius wasn't a magic user, they'd slapped a magic breaker on his neck like they had Lucie.

It was supposed to keep other magics from getting to him. Same with my bracelets. But then, how did that pentia spell on the barn work?

I needed to sort that out, just not right now.

We got Tiberius set up in Hadari's yard. He'd be hard to spot in the dark, and he couldn't see the other goats at all. I knew he could still smell them, but Hadari and the puppies kept distracting him.

With a nod to Hadari, I went back to my cottage. Still clutching my canvas bag.

"You going to lock us in or just stand there?" Lucie paused just inside the living room. "And what's in that bag? I didn't see it before."

I quickly locked up the cottage and pulled the heavy curtains tight. Not good. No one else had seen the canvas bag in the past few hours? Keith might have dropped an object spell on it when we were at the train station, but I doubted he wouldn't have told me. I dropped my voice to a whisper. "It's what was in Darius's locker." I hadn't meant to tell Lucie until I'd had a chance to see what it was. But I was feeling a little out of sorts. I glared at the landscape painting.

In theory, Xieth couldn't spy on me. I trusted Keith's magic, but I wasn't sure I trusted the Universe's sense of humor. She could be a capricious beast.

"Come help me sort the stuff we're going to give away." I quickly went down the hall and held the door open to the guest room. Those boxes were all in the barn, but Xieth wouldn't know that.

"Good idea." Lucie licked his whiskers as he stared at the canvas bag. "What is it? Riches? We're splitting the big things, right?"

"I don't know. I didn't think it would be a good idea to open it in front of anyone." I looked down at the bag. Whereas before I wanted to keep whatever was inside for me alone, I was now reluctant to open the bag.

"Agreed." Lucie leaned back. "But should you try to get a hold of Keith and tell him about Tiberius? Maybe he can do something." That sentence appeared to have hurt him to say. He loved seeing what was in bags. Or boxes. Especially if there might be riches involved. Suggesting a delay was uncat-like.

I looked at my phone; it was only seven o'clock, but it seemed later. "Good idea." I tucked the straps of the canvas bag over my shoulder, went to the living room to grab my phone, then marched back into the guest room.

Lucie simply remained on the desk.

It took three rings before Keith answered. Honestly, I figured he would have caught it on one.

"Any news?" From his short breath, he'd had to run for the phone.

"Not about Betsy and the other two. But we have a problem." I told him about Tiberius first, then about Xieth telling me there was a force three spell cast in Ghoston a short time ago.

"What? There's no way that you or I wouldn't have felt that. But we'll deal with that after Tiberius. Thanks to the feds, I didn't get the compound to try on the pentia spell, but I think I've put something together with what I have. I'll be there soon. I doubt there's going to be much time before we lose him forever. And you and Lucie will be next."

People needed to stop reminding me of that fun tidbit. Since, unlike Tiberius, Lucie and I were already in our natural forms. I had no idea what that curse in the barn would do to us. "I know. Thanks, see you soon."

"There we go. Now, about the bag?" If Lucie could rub his paws together like hands right now, he would. It wasn't that he didn't care about Tiberius, but in his mind, that issue was being taken care of.

"I don't know." I didn't want to have to keep carrying the thing around, but I was also getting wary of opening strange things.

"Do you want to be carrying an unknown, probably magic, object with you while Keith tries to purge a powerful spell? Cause I don't think you do."

I hated it when a con cat was more rational than I was. "Fine, but I might still need to carry it anyway." I opened the bag and lifted the object out. "It feels like a bowling ball. What was Darius up to?"

Lucie leaned forward, sniffing. "Nope, no bowling ball. Besides, Darius hated those shoes. Open it." This time, the licking was probably to address his drooling.

"Fine." There was tissue, then heavier wrapping paper, then more tissue. And what looked like a black leather-covered box with creepy writing on it. "This is in Ugani. In the extremely old magic language Ugani." I started to cover it back up. Ugani was a dark language from an even darker class of magic users. They had their own world that was technically on the edge of the Eltrisphere, and did what they wanted without repercussions from any officials.

Whatever was in that box was staying there until I could pack it with that mob box, cover them in cement, and charter a boat to take them and me out to sea. Far out.

"Pish, they can't be that bad. Myths and rumors most likely." Lucie narrowed his eyes when I shoved the box back into my bag and continued to refill it with paper.

Too bad about the bag, but it was going into the sea as well.

"What if it's something that could harm humans? Something called in a force three spell, maybe it was that thing." Dang manipulative cat.

I shook my head and looked for something to put the now overstuffed bag into. Too bad I didn't have a safe of some kind. "No. There's more danger to everyone, particularly you and me, if we open it. You agreed about not opening the mob box, why not this?"

"Because we knew what kinds of things were in the mob box, a bunch of stuff to get us killed. If no one knows about that thing being down here, we're fine."

I knew Keith would be here soon, and I'd rather not open it in front of him. Just in case it exploded or froze Lucie and me in a spell. Someone had to save us. "Fine. But you're moving closer to me. If I blow up, we both go." I'd make him open it if he had opposable digits.

He moved closer to the small table I had the bag on. "Annnnd open it, now?"

"There are times I really don't like you, do you know that?"

"You say the sweetest things." His grin showed his fangs.

Never try to insult a cat; they enjoy it.

I dug all of the papers back out, put on gloves, and lifted the box out of the bag. If I were lucky, the box would be magically sealed, and I wouldn't be able to open it. I was fine with destroying some horrific object of doom without knowing exactly what it was.

Sadly, my luck stunk a lot of times.

At first, the lid wouldn't budge. Then I slid my hands along the sides and heard two clicks. I'll admit I screamed. But it was just the lid releasing.

More paper, old and mostly crumbling, but it appeared to be from Earth. The little pink elephants with baby rattles on a few sheets were a big tip-off. Darius had wrapped it.

"What. Is. It? Seriously, if you move any slower, I'll think a mini-gorgon is in there and is spelling you." Lucie's nose was at the edge of the box.

"Fine." I pulled off the final sheets and swore in every single language I knew. I'd never seen this thing, aside from a few images of rare, deadly, and most likely mythological objects. "It's the Stone of Zalianthia."

# Chapter Forty-Two

I couldn't move, but I hoped that was just my own fear response and not something that evil stone was doing.

It wasn't bowling ball size, but only a little smaller. A hundred faceted edges gleamed a rainbow of colors, and I swore there were faces, screaming ones, inside of them. I dropped a tissue over it to hide the faces.

Lucie hissed, puffed his tail, and then he scrambled to the furthest end of the room. "Someone down here knows you have it, that's why they wanted it for ransom payment. Or they thought you did, when you didn't, but you do now. I wouldn't want to be you." He was trying to sound tough, but there was terror in those orange eyes.

"Nope. You were here. Those faces saw you, too." Dealing with Lucie gave me the strength to put the stone back into its box, cover it in more baby shower tissue, and close the lid. "We're both doomed." I was being surprisingly calm.

"Faces? What faces? How can it be my fault that *you* have that?"

"There were screaming faces inside the facets. Couldn't tell who or what they were, and I'm not opening that box again." I wrapped the box in the last of the paper, put it back inside the canvas bag, found another box to cram the entire thing into, then buried it in the back of the closet. I'd debated moving it to my bedroom, but I didn't want that thing any nearer to me than it had to be.

Entire worlds had been destroyed by people fighting over that nasty thing. Somehow, Darius found it, and now it was my disaster.

I shoved a few more odds and ends into the closet, then slid the door shut and pulled over the desk and chair to block it, when there was a knock on my front door. I locked the guest room door as I went to answer it. It was probably Keith, but the way my life had been going, who knew *what* was on the other side of that door?

"Hey...Jack. What brings you out here?" I glanced into the darkness behind him, but no sign of Keith's van. I'd had more visits from Jack today than I'd had in two months. Probably not a good thing.

He didn't smile and had his notepad out. "I wanted to ask you and Keith about your trip to the Ghoston train station. There was an incident there this afternoon."

I forced my face to remain calm and motioned for him to come in. "Keith isn't here. He was going to do some work on the barn, but had to get supplies from his house."

"If he doesn't make it back, I'll find him at work tomorrow. I also heard that you and he met two FBI agents." Jack went to the kitchen table and sat; he rarely went to my comfortable furniture unless other people were with him.

Maybe he thought that might imply friendship of a sort.

"Yes. They said they knew you and asked us about a mail issue up here." It was easier to skim the truth with someone like Jack, who had no idea what my coughing, twinging, or choking would relate to. People who knew what that meant for a jinn were harder to fool.

"Nothing else?"

What had I missed? Jack looked like he was waiting for me to screw something up. "Not really. They were mostly talking to Keith. If they said they spoke to us about the incident at the train station, they were lying. They didn't even mention that anything had happened there. Was anyone hurt? What happened?" I was going to fling more questions at him, but Jack held up his hand.

Just as someone knocked at the door again. I had no idea where Lucie had gone, but I doubted one of the animals was knocking.

"It's probably Keith." I swung open the door, and Betsy, with Jamie and Martha, came charging in.

"Ceian!  Sorry, it's late, but the feds just sprung us, you wouldn't believe what they said about our junk mail!" Betsy froze, with the other two bumping into her, when she saw Jack at my dining table.

"Oh! I hope we didn't interrupt anything! We'll catch you up in the morning, Ceian. Hannah's again?" Betsy tried backing up, but neither Jamie nor Martha was moving.

Jack got to his feet before Betsy could shove the other two back out the door. "Good evening, ladies. I was going to call on you tomorrow. Thank you for saving me the extra trips. Maybe we'd be more comfortable in the living room?"

Sure, he was gracious and considerate with those three.

"Actually, I did leave a pot on the stove..." Betsy hovered in front of the sofa.

"Before or after you spoke to the FBI agents who just released you?" Jack's voice was far more pleasant than when he'd been speaking to me, but there was an edge of steel under it.

Betsy sighed and dropped to the sofa. Jamie and Martha remained silent but joined her. Jack took the chair, so I brought around one from my dining room table.

"Thank you, ladies. I assume the agents told you not to speak to anyone about their case?" He shot me a look at that. Like it was my fault that Betsy immediately came here with the intent to disclose everything.

"Oh yes." Martha bobbed her head and gave her best grandmotherly smile. "We had been chatting with Ceian when they brought us in, so we just wanted to make sure she was okay."

Jack's smile for her dropped as he turned to me. "Why were you up at the Grasshopper?"

Obviously, those FBI folks had done their fair share of talking to Jack after the fact. Although judging by his annoyance, Jack might have known where Betsy, Jamie, and Martha had been picked up, but he hadn't been told that Keith, Hadari, or I had been there too.

Interesting.

"Hadari got out. Someone said they saw her on the other side of town, heading up the hill to the Grasshopper. Keith was still with me after our trip, so he took me there." The term someone was vague enough to keep me choke-free. I assumed that if the FBI folks had told Jack details, they told him about the three older ladies being tied up and knocked out again.

"Interesting." He echoed my internal thoughts completely. "What did you find there?"

I had no idea what the feds knew, what they told him, or what was going to get me out of this without being locked up or choking to death.

"She found us. Rather, she and Keith did." Jamie leaned forward and glared at Jack. "We told your fed friends everything; what happened to us up there, the lost mail, Hadari, Ceian, and Keith saving us. If they didn't share that with you, I believe we shouldn't be giving you any further details." She folded her arms and leaned back.

I was proud of her. Of course, she just told Jack pretty much everything except for a few specifics, but she implied there was more she wasn't telling.

Jack's jaw clenched, then he relaxed and nodded. "Fair enough. Ladies, I apologize. I shouldn't have been so aggressive in my questioning. It's been a long day. Thank you, Ceian, for helping to rescue them. All the mail went off the cliff, you say?"

The smile he flashed me was a real one, and it was a doozy. Too bad he thought I was the mastermind of some nefarious plot rooted here in Forgotten Hollow; he was a gorgeous guy when he let himself be.

Betsy decided that whether she told it to the feds or not, the mail information was public domain and immediately launched into finding the stash, then being attacked and losing it. "I think we were almost going to crack the case wide open."

"It went over a cliff? All of it?" He wasn't glaring but did watch all four of us.

"As far as we know. Betsy wanted to go down to the beach, but fortunately, Keith talked her out of it." Jamie responded first.

"That's what it looked like." I cautiously threw in as his look lingered a bit too long on me.

"Hmmm." He jotted far more down in his pad than he said. "Do you want the ladies here when I ask you and Keith about the train station?"

"Oh! Keith's coming over?" Betsy's grin was wide. It had taken her a while to realize how Keith felt about her, and that she returned it, but she was like a schoolgirl now.

"Yeah, he was doing some quick work on my barn and said he'd be back." I frowned. He should have been here by now.

"We didn't see his van, but there was a light coming from your barn when we drove up." Martha nodded.

"What?" Panic made me jump to my feet. It might be Keith, but why didn't he come to the house? "That tricky guy. I'd better go make sure he doesn't need anything. Be right back." I had my hand on the door handle when Jack got to his feet.

"We should all go, see if there's anything we can do to help with this emergency repair." His tone indicated that he'd love to know what it was, but wouldn't push in front of Betsy and the others.

Good.

"Sure, as long as we stay out of his way. There was a dangerous crack in the barn floor." Not a lie, that curse had etched a bunch of cracks in it. Ones I really hoped weren't visible or active now.

Lucie had been hiding under the sofa and shot out as soon as I opened the door. There was no sign of Hadari, the puppies, or Tiberius as we crossed the yard to the barn.

"Still have Camfield's goats? How long is he gone for again?" Betsy peered at the resting goats as we passed.

"He said about a week. Something for work." Yup, there was a light coming out from the top and bottom of the closed barn doors. As we walked, I thought extremely hard about who was with me and hoped Keith was paying attention. His people weren't telepathic, but there was emotion attached to the people with me that he might pick up on. The door slid open before we got there, and Lucie darted inside.

Hopefully, he went there to warn Keith and not just to be nosy.

Keith pushed open the barn door the rest of the way as we approached. He had goggles on and looked filthy. Lucie was at his feet, looking smug. "Hi, everyone. I wouldn't go in here right now. I was able to make the repairs, but some of the stuff was toxic. It should run through in a few minutes." I peered in the door, but the curse wasn't visible. A nice, clean barn floor with a repaired crack was all I saw.

Probably an illusion, but hopefully he did enough to destroy the curse.

I turned back to him when a wave of magic slammed into me, and I collapsed.

# Chapter Forty-Three

I felt myself drifting in nothingness, and my wrists felt on fire. Then there was yelling around me and someone lifting me. They were running with me. The combination of drifting, being carried, and the world screaming at me was odd. But I couldn't open my eyes.

"Someone pick up her cat, too. He also collapsed." I felt and heard Jack as he yelled that. He was the one carrying me. I must look bad; he sounded freaked out.

The rest of the voices sorted themselves out, and soon I felt being placed on my sofa.

"I've got Lucie, he's breathing, but looks a bit crispy around the whiskers." That was Martha. "His collar is gone."

Strong, cool hands picked up mine carefully. "So are Ceian's bracelets. It looks like there are burn marks on her wrists." Jack again. Still sounded worried.

I managed to open my eyes. "What's happened?" The world was blurry, and it took a lot to get those words out. I felt like the one time I stupidly accepted an arena fight with a giantess. I lost and spent a week feeling like pulp.

Jack was crouching in front of the sofa with a worried frown.

Keith, who was standing behind the sofa, was the first to speak.

"I'm not sure, but it seems that the chemicals I used reacted badly with your bracelets and Lucie's collar. They exploded. How do you feel?"

I could sort of see Keith's face, and what I saw worried me more than Jack's. Keith was covering something bad, but no chemical should have blown off my bracelets. Or Lucie's collar.

"How's Lucie?"

"Still unconscious, but he's breathing better." Martha was petting him.

"What were the collar and bracelets made of?" Jack was more concerned than suspicious right now, but there was still a bit of cop tone in his voice.

I started to shake my head; even if I could explain it, I wouldn't. Nothing in those bracelets or Lucie's collar was from Earth.

"Those pieces were ancient," Keith said. "I'd guess something volatile and not used at all anymore was inside them. You could hear a slight movement inside them before the explosion. I'm just glad neither of you was hurt worse." *You were seriously injured, and I'm not certain what my spell did. Stay down until they leave.*

That last part was in my head. I had thought he wasn't a true telepath, but he did it somehow.

Betsy came over with a damp cloth. "Do you need a doctor? How many fingers am I holding up?"

"Three. My vision is coming back. But I think I need to stay prone for a bit. If I'm still feeling off tomorrow, I'll go down to the clinic."

Jack shook his head. "You shouldn't wait; head injuries can be bad. You fell hard."

That was a problem. He had a good point, but while I appeared human, I wasn't. A medical check would point that out immediately.

"Actually, she landed on her right arm; her head didn't hit the ground," Keith said. "It was easier to see from my side."

I winced and rotated my right arm. "It's stiff, but nothing broken." I might or might not have landed on my arm, but that excuse worked.

"You need medical advice." Jack's jaw got that stubborn set.

I knew he and I could argue until morning, so I changed tactics. "What happened at the train station? You wanted to talk to Keith and me about it; we're here now. And I'm not going anywhere."

Keith still looked a little freaked, but pulled over the rest of the dining room chairs for everyone else. "This would probably be the best time, if Ceian's feeling up to it."

"You can't question them! Ceian is hurt; she needs to go to sleep." Betsy practically growled at Jack.

Even he looked reluctant and hadn't brought his pen or notepad out.

"I'll be fine, thank you, Betsy. I don't have much to say, and I'd like this over and done with. We do have a grand opening coming up."

"Well? What did you want to ask us?" Keith schooled his face, but he wanted Jack out of here even more than I did. Something scary had happened in that barn. Something powerful enough to destroy the magic shields on both Lucie and me.

Jack watched me carefully for a few moments, but when I didn't pass out, grab my head, or scream in pain, he sighed and got out his notepad and pen. "Earlier today, the Ghoston train station suffered an earthquake, a windstorm, and a minor flood. Inside and all at once. We pulled the videos, and you two were seen leaving ten minutes before."

I waited for something else, but nothing was forthcoming.

Betsy deepened her scowl. "I'd think that a lot of people probably left during that same time frame, the station is always busy. Do you really think Keith and Ceian could do those things? Maybe you're the one who needs to go to a doctor." She had moved her chair closer to me, but looked ready to jump to her feet and fight off Jack if he tried anything.

"Was anyone hurt?" That was my worry. Xieth might have tried to nail me for casting a force three spell down there, but there was no way Jack could have thought that Keith or I could do those things.

"Surprisingly, nothing serious. The train station personnel got everyone out quickly, and the entire incident was cleaned up in a few hours."

"Even the flooding?" Martha looked up from petting Lucie at that one.

I was pretty sure Lucie was awake by now. He was just enjoying the attention.

"Yes, the water wasn't as heavy as the initial reports." Jack's brow furrowed. Something about the incident was worrying him. "The videos didn't show you picking up your friend." With that, concerned Jack was gone, replaced by suspicious Jack.

"She called to say her work got swamped and she couldn't come out," Keith answered before I could. "Do you need a signed affidavit from her? I'm sure she'd send one to Ceian if needed."

It had been a long day, and I was stressed, bruised, and as I recovered, felt off. Probably from the loss of the bracelets. But Xieth had been thorough in explaining that even if I busted them off, it would be weeks before my magic came back.

I wasn't sure that I was feeling my magic, but something was funky. My skin felt on fire from the inside.

"That won't be necessary. No one really believed that you two did anything." Jack sighed and ran his fingers through his hair. "I was asked to see if either of you noticed anything strange while you were there. The feds hoped that you'd seen something. It's believed to be a concentrated attack; they just have no idea what the goal was. Or how it was done." He got to his feet and watched Keith and me. "Just call me if you recall anything odd, anything at all. And Ceian, promise me you'll go to the doctor if you feel worse." Concerned Jack made a brief return, then he shut down and gave a tight nod.

Betsy bounced to her feet and escorted Jack to the door. "I promise to keep an eye on her, Detective. Have a lovely night."

Jack paused at the door. He had to know Betsy and the others were now going to tell us everything that had happened with the FBI, but he just sighed and left.

Betsy didn't shut the door until Jack got in his car and pulled away.

"Nosy coppers! Now, about the feds." Betsy bustled back into the living room, ready to burst.

I felt worse and wanted everyone to leave. Honestly, I was surprised that Xieth hadn't called my landline to get me to make everyone leave so he could call me out on the busted bracelets.

Then another knock at the door.

I doubted Xieth was going to send enforcers down here, but he had for those cherubs who knocked off Darius. This might turn horrible quickly.

Betsy was closest and grabbed the door before I could say anything.

"I got it! Maybe Jack forgot something." She swung open the door and screamed.

Keith raced to the door, with Jamie and Martha behind him.

A low voice, one I'd hoped to hear again, responded before I could crawl off my sofa.

"Ceian, we have a problem."

Lucie jumped to his feet, but it was too late; Betsy, Jamie, and Martha were screaming. Then, as one, all fainted.

I couldn't blame them. A seven-foot-tall, blue jinn with a pair of massive wings peeking over his back would make most humans scream and faint.

"Sorry. I saw the cop leave and thought it was only Keith in here." Tiberius held out his blue hands. "What happened to me?"

"Come in, Tiberius. Keith? What can we do about them?" The only way humans who knew about the Eltrisphere would be dealt with would be to be forcibly removed and locked up on some planet far from here. Or far worse. I couldn't let that happen to my friends.

Tiberius was too big currently to comfortably fit in my cottage door; this was made worse by the three passed-out women collapsed in front of it. He made it, but not gracefully.

"Good to hear you again, my friend," Lucie said as he moved to his cat tree. "You looked better as a goat, though."

Keith bent down to check on all three women. "I didn't have a choice; I had to knock them out. But they all got a great look at Tiberius."

"Sorry, I was dreaming about really being a goat. Then I felt burning metal around my neck, and I woke up like this in Hadari's yard." Tiberius looked around for a seat, then sat on the floor. His size made it difficult to sit; those wings made it impossible on human furniture.

Then my landline rang.

"Keith, you have got to get these three out of here; that has to be Xieth." I kept my voice down even though Keith's blocking should be working. Like Jack, Xieth was contacting me far too much today.

Keith nodded, lifted all three ladies about a foot in the air with a spell, then, with strain clearly showing on his lean face, left the cottage with the three unconscious bodies bobbing behind him.

I was worried about his magic overload, and I didn't even know if he'd used magic in the barn. But the phone had to be answered.

"Yes?" I stalled a bit as Tiberius crawled out of sight down the hallway.

"Ceian? What is going on down there? Another force three spell! This one was on your property! Hold on, let me switch." He abruptly hung up, then appeared as the landscape painting vanished. "What happened?"

I tugged my sleeves down to cover my bare wrists, glad that Lucie had ducked out of sight with Tiberius. "I'm not sure what happened before. You wouldn't tell me." I was hoping that Xieth was so worked up that he'd keep flinging vague, open questions at me. If he directly asked if Keith, whom he didn't know about, had somehow broken the magic blockers on the three of us, I'd have to tell him.

Jinn weren't fond of people being specific.

"No one knows! Two force three spells, and no one knows! The council is furious and worried. In both cases now, it's as if whatever caused the problems blew out the ability for our scanners to determine what it was." His already beady eyes narrowed to slits. "You didn't notice *anything*?" That last word was loaded with a lot of possibly painful implications.

"There was an odd pressure a short time ago. I fell, but I'm fine." My throat twinged at that, but I didn't choke. "How can someone down here, a planet filled with magicless humans, block the spell buoys the council installed?"

Xieth started to answer, then shut his mouth and nodded. "Good point. You're alone?"

"No humans are in here; it's getting late." Not a lie, also not what he asked.

"There are rumors that the council is having problems. Big ones. Some groups are trying to take them out. And those groups might have a person or two down on that rock of yours."

"But not in Forgotten Hollow, right? I'm the only prisoner?"

"Yous the onlys prisoner, but yous mights not be the onlys Eltrisian. Things are goings on. Big ones." He'd seemed fine a moment ago, but he was slurring and listing as we spoke. It was as if he were getting drunk as I watched—without anything to drink.

"Are you okay?"

"I'ms fines, completely…fines." His eyes rolled back into his head, and he slid off whatever he'd been sitting on. The screen reverted to the landscape painting.

Lucie started to come out, but I waved him off until the painting was secure.

"Was he drinking? He sounded drunk at the end." Lucie marched over to his food bowl for more kibbles.

"I didn't see anything or anyone with him, and he didn't eat or drink while on screen with me. He had no idea that our magic blockers were gone, yet knew a big spell had hit here." I wished that I hadn't sent Keith away; he might have an idea of what just happened.

"This is bad. If I don't change back to a goat in the morning, what's going to happen? I can't stay in the barn forever." Tiberius resumed his seat on the floor.

"How did this happen? Keith was trying to shut down the pentia spell that was turning you into a goat." I waved my hand when Tiberius tried to cut me off. "Trust us, for most of today, you weren't you. That spell was destroying you."

"You were even getting moony about one of those goats out there." Lucie smirked. "It wasn't pretty."

"What? I didn't do anything, right?"

That was something I'd never seen before, Tiberius in full centurion blue glory, looking terrified.

I'd like it more if it weren't because he was fully visible here on Earth.

"Nothing happened, but we had to chain you in Hadari's yard. Where is she, by the way?" I still felt off; that magic wave had hit me hard. And regardless of what Keith had told Jack, I did hit my head. I started for the kitchen, and the refrigerator door opened when I was still a foot away from the handle.

"You just used magic." Lucie waved his tail, and the container of kibble wobbled about and awkwardly refilled his bowl. "We're free!"

I shakily closed the refrigerator door with my hand. I'd hoped that since Xieth hadn't picked up on our blockers being broken, we might still not be able to use magic. I'd wanted my magic back; unless I did something in front of someone, humans wouldn't be able to sense it. But I didn't want it back this way. "We're screwed."

"Hey, Xieth didn't notice, did he? We're fine." Lucie proceeded to chortle, then inhale more kibble.

"Has the cat always been that stupid?" Tiberius's glare toward Lucie was lost when the cat wouldn't look up. "They will eventually sort out that our bands are gone, you heard Xieth, something is going on with the council and their spell buoys. But when they do, it's going to look like we willfully took them off."

"They'll have to catch me!" Lucie ran for the door.

"You're going to live the rest of your life as a stray Earth cat? You can't use magic if you go on the lam; they'll find you." I understood Lucie's need to be free to use magic again. I only had access to my magic for less than a day when I first came down here. In my bottle, I had been magically blocked. But the risk in this case was far too high.

Lucie sighed and walked away from the door. "You're right. I've become a cat of leisure. The wild life isn't for me. But don't you think we should see what was done to the barn? It might be Tiberius's new home after all."

"He could be right." Tiberius shook his head, but didn't get to his feet.

I grabbed the flashlight and opened the front door. I hadn't heard Keith's van leave, but he said he'd parked on the other side of my cottage. Betsy's car being in the driveway wasn't surprising.

But all four of them lying sprawled out in the yard was.

# Chapter Forty-Four

We ran to them. Keith spelled Betsy, Jamie, and Martha when they inadvertently saw Tiberius in jinn form, but I didn't know who knocked Keith out.

I gently turned him over. Yup, my flashlight showed me what I didn't want to see; Keith's face was gray and pinched. Sure sign of magic over-drain. He knocked himself out. It spoke a lot about his abilities that the three people he spelled remained that way even when he collapsed. Whether he'd destroyed his access to magic permanently or not remained to be seen.

"This isn't good. What shall we do with them?" Tiberius glanced at Betsy's car. "And their vehicles?"

My first instinct was to put them all in the barn and hope no one noticed they were missing.

There might be a better way. "We need to bring them all into the cottage. Tiberius, can you help? I don't want to use my magic unless I have to." Keith's Xieth spying blocking spell on my cottage was tied into a loop; therefore, it wasn't dependent on his magic to keep running. But Xieth wouldn't have to spy to pick up magic. Once he recovered, anyway.

Tiberius shrugged and picked up Betsy. "Where in the cottage?"

"On the sofa, sitting up. I have an idea."

I had him bring in the four of them and stage them as if they'd passed out while sitting. Then found a bottle of whisky in the back cabinet, pulled out five glasses, swirled a bit of whisky in them, and then sadly poured most of it down the drain. Massive waste, but it was sacrificed for the greater good.

I took both Betsy's and Keith's car keys, tucked blankets around the four of them, and turned out the living room lights.

"You're leaving them there?" Even Lucie wasn't happy with it. Of course, they were already snoring, and he often slept in his cat tower.

"You can sleep in my room. It's the best I can come up with. Tiberius, I'm going to have to lock you in the barn to make sure no one opens it."

"Sure." He went to the kitchen, grabbed an armful of packaged food and some water, then followed me out.

I took what was left of his blankets, and we made a bed of straw for him. The barn no longer smelled odd, and the cement floor under the straw was still clear. The pentia spell wasn't just marred by the chemicals; it was gone.

"Eh, not worse than centurion basecamp. Thanks."

I left him a flashlight before putting the chain and lock back on the outer door.

I went back into my cottage, ignored the snoring and spelled people in the front room, and finally went to bed.

***

I couldn't have been asleep for long when I heard pounding from the front door. Even through my bedroom door.

"You gonna get that?" Lucie asked from the foot of my bed. "I can't."

I grumbled as I got out of bed, put on my robe, grabbed my phone, and stumbled to the door. From the sounds, my four guests were still passed out. A glance at my phone indicated it was four twenty-five in the morning.

I waited to see if maybe they'd go away, and again promised myself to put in one of those peepholes in my door.

Another round of knocks indicated it was wishful thinking.

I opened the door to find Camfield.

I wasn't sure who I'd been expecting, but this disheveled, handsome man was not it. Not to mention, he was still supposed to be out of town.

"Where are they, Ceian?" He started to push his way in, but I'd had the presence of mind to put my foot up to block the door from opening.

"Who? Do you know what time it is?" My question was echoed by a chorus of snores behind me.

"Who's in there? Are my goats inside?"

"What? No. There was a celebration last night, and none of my friends were fit to drive home, if you must know. Your goats are in their pen." I peeked past him, but it was still too dark to see the pen. "They were there when I went to sleep."

"They're not there now. Your male goat took them, didn't he? Broke them out somehow." He was far more worked up than a few missing goats should warrant.

"Tiberius is in the barn. Alone. He wasn't feeling well, so I had to quarantine him. And unless he picked the lock from the inside, grabbed your goats, and locked it back up, he's in there alone."

"Let me see."

I was pissed now. Camfield had been a fun diversion, and he was good-looking, but this was ridiculous.

"No. He is quarantined. Your goats aren't there. They probably broke out and ran home." I held up my cell phone. "Now get off my property before I call the police."

"I'm going home, then *I'm* calling the police. I need to see your goat." He stomped off before I caught up to his words.

He was more upset about Tiberius than his missing goats. I grabbed another flashlight and looked over to the pen. It was empty and one side was gone. Those goats made a run for it and were probably home right now.

Why was Camfield worried about Tiberius?

"Ceian?" Betsy's soft voice came from behind me.

I shut the front door and hit the kitchen lights. She was awake but hadn't moved. The other three were still out.

"Are we having a rave? Or orgy? Was it fun? Oh, my head is killing me." She was between Jamie and Martha, both of whom were still snoring. "I had the oddest dreams."

"Stay there, I'll get some tea. There was a lot of celebrating last night."

"What were we celebrating?" She leaned forward and sniffed the glass on the coffee table in front of her. "Oh, gods, whisky?" She flopped back in between her friends. "Tea, me, please."

I got out my biggest teapot; the others would be awake soon. Things were going to get tricky when Martha and Jamie woke up. I had a feeling Betsy's dream was about a giant blue man. One weird dream was one thing; three would be hard to cover up.

The others were stirring when I set the teapot and cups at the dining table. I wasn't going to trust scalding hot liquid with a bunch of magic-slammed people. Not all spells left this kind of hangover, but it was lucky for me that this one did.

All three ladies, quietly, aside from mutterings under their breaths, dragged over the chairs, sat at the table, and sipped their tea. I didn't want to wake Keith; I hadn't had a magic over-drain since I was a teen, but I remember how nasty it had been.

"I hope we had fun before we passed out. I feel hideous. And had weird dreams." Jamie had almost crawled into her teacup, then pushed it forward for more.

"Me too. Weird things about goats and some big blue guy." Martha also pushed her teacup toward me.

"Yes, the blue guy. He was weird." Betsy reached over and took a cookie from the plate I'd put out. That was a good sign.

Jamie pulled herself out of her cup. "We all had the same dream? What are the odds?"

"Pretty good since we were drinking whisky, celebrating your cracking the mail case, and Ceian had that Aladdin movie on." Keith stumbled to the table and collapsed into a chair. "Betsy thought it was hilarious and had us watch it a few times."

Keith was good. He looked awful, like all of those thousand-plus years of living had slammed into him at once. But he'd covered us for both the drinking and seeing a giant, blue, winged man.

Although I didn't think the genie in Aladdin had wings. I'd taken it upon myself to track down all movies with jinn, or genies, when I'd first arrived here. Funny, none of them got it right aside from our bottles. But even that varied. Tiberius's people were from a distant mountain region. They were jinn, but few had magic, and almost none of them had bottles. Luckily, it had been dark, and Tiberius's wings weren't extended at the time.

"Oh, I love that movie!" Martha smiled and rubbed her forehead. "My headache seems to be fading. Any chance for a ride home for a shower and change, then to Hannah's for breakfast?"

I was surprised, but the other three nodded. Keith still had lines around his eyes that he hadn't had before, but I wasn't sure how bad of a magic drain he'd had. For someone who hadn't used much, if any, magic for forty years, he'd been using a lot lately.

Betsy finished the last of her tea and got to her feet. "I can take Jamie, if Keith can take Martha. She's closer to his house. I feel better, but I wish I recalled what we'd sorted out about the mail caper." She winced. "Maybe I won't think about it too hard for now." She patted down her pockets. "Where did I put my keys?"

"Oh! Sorry. I didn't want any of you taking off." I handed Betsy and Keith their keys back. "I'll meet you there in an hour?"

The group headed for the door with murmurs of agreement. The sun was just doing its early dawn move, and although it had been an awfully short night, I admired the beauty.

Lucie came out and wandered into the yard as both cars left. "That was close. Hey, where are the goats?"

"They escaped as far as I can tell. Camfield was the one who knocked. Did you actually go back to sleep when I got up?" I shut the door as Lucie and I went to the barn. Centurion or goat, Tiberius needed to have some freedom.

I expected Tiberius to be there waiting; there weren't that many places in the barn someone his size could hide. But I didn't see him anywhere.

"Um, Ceian? I think he escaped, too." Lucie was all the way in the back of the barn, behind the pile of abandoned farm equipment.

# Chapter Forty-Five

I swore under my breath as I looked at the hole in the side of the barn. The good thing was that I doubted anyone had broken in and grabbed him, judging by the wood being shattered outward. Not to mention that at his full size, Tiberius was a serious fighter.

The bad thing was that the shape was at least seven feet tall. I had hoped that he'd resume his goat form, with him still intact mentally, and we could carry on like before.

"Why would he have done that? He was fine with being locked in." I glared at the broken pieces of wood when they didn't answer me.

Lucie gave the cat equivalent of a shrug. "Maybe he had to pee?"

Before I could stop him, he shot out through the hole. I could fit through the hole, but I wasn't sure that was a great idea in my robe and slippers. I ran through the barn and along the side where that wall led.

No Lucie and no Tiberius.

"What's wrong?" Hadari walked up behind me quietly and spoke softly.

I screamed as I jumped.

"Sorry." I quickly told her what happened to Tiberius and that he'd broken out while in jinn form as we walked back to the cottage. "I need to shower and change. Could you help Lucie? I think he's looking for Tiberius."

"We'll find him." She gave a sharp bark, and five puppies came tumbling across the yard. If those five grew into their massive paws, they were going to be bigger than their impressive mom.

I shuddered at the disasters that would ensue.

A few more barks, and all of them took off around the side of my barn. I'd be worried about the puppies running around loose if they had been Earth dogs. But I knew that even as cute and roly poly as they were, hoxien wolf pups could defend themselves extremely well.

I thought about trying to reach Xieth after whatever happened to him last night, but he could take care of himself, too.

I showered, changed clothes, and locked up the house, but still no sign of Tiberius, Lucie, or the hoxien wolves. I called a few times, but they could be anywhere. Lucie and the dogs all had much better abilities to track things than I did without resorting to magic.

I got on my bike to head into town. Hopefully, Keith could help me figure out a way to find Tiberius without magic from either of us. I was worried about how Keith's magic was doing and if it was safe to use mine. If it was even really back. I didn't feel different; the refrigerator door could have been a fluke.

I didn't think testing it right now was a good idea.

Camfield's house should probably be avoided. He *had* threatened to call the cops on me, after all. Not to mention it wasn't on my direct path into town.

So, of course, I rode my bike in that direction. I planned on staying back and just doing a quick ride past his street to see if his goats were there. Besides, if they were there and Tiberius had changed back into his mindless goat self, he might have gone to find his girlfriends.

Camfield's house was only one house away from the corner, so I figured I could see something just by remaining on the cross street.

No goats of any kind were inside the large pen on the side of his house. Unfortunately, his car was in the driveway, so I couldn't go closer.

Swearing at all of these problems popping up right before I was about to open my teahouse, I changed direction and rode downhill into town.

Keith's van was in the lot already, and Hannah waved at me from the kitchen door and pointed to what was becoming our corner.

Keith, Betsy, Jamie, and Martha were chatting as I came up to the table. No black suits in sight this time. Maybe they were getting ready to leave. A small part of me had briefly wanted to know what they'd been up to, but at this point, I just wanted them gone. I still wasn't certain if any of them were Eltrisian or not, but someone else could sort that out.

"I already got you a tea, you look about like I feel." Betsy patted the chair next to her.

"Thanks. How are you all doing? I didn't drink much last night, but didn't sleep well."

"Feeling a lot better, thanks. I have a feeling it might hit after we do the final prep for tomorrow's grand opening, though." Martha bounced in her seat. "I'm so excited!"

I forced a grin. I would be excited, too, if there weren't so many bits of random mischief and mayhem floating around. Also, I was a bit nervous. I'd never owned a business before, and while I was used to crowds, it was in an arena setting. I didn't have to pay attention to anyone but my opponent.

Slightly different than trying to encourage people to love my teahouse and spice shop.

"I made and froze a ton more sausage rolls last week. Scones too. Bread and mini cupcakes have been baked." Betsy smiled. "It feels great to be a part of this. Sadly, I still don't recall what great connection I made about the mail caper."

Jamie frowned. "And I doubt the feds will tell us."

Hannah bustled over. "Okay, what'll you all have? I'm taking a break after I get your orders in so that we can finalize things for tomorrow. And everyone can quietly fill me in on the recent adventures." Her wink indicated she knew something was afoot. Good guess with this crew.

We ordered, and Hannah was almost back to the swinging kitchen doors when a mass of black suits marched through the door. They didn't wait to be seated but moved toward their normal area. Never mind that there had to be almost thirty of them.

"Oh no, they don't," Hannah turned and yelled into the kitchen. Two massive men, both dressed like cooks from a prison movie, came out.

We all got up from our table as well. Those two men were impressive, but there were a lot of black suits.

Hannah charged up to the leader of the pack. "I can't serve a group this large right now. You should have called ahead."

"We have plenty of space. Just needed to get out of the conference rooms for a bit." The man was actually smiling as he spoke.

I'd figured it had been bred out of them.

He motioned to his people wandering around the empty tables. "See? No fuss, no bother, we have it all set up."

His grin was frightening now. None of the other black suits looked up as they pushed tables and chairs together. A family seated nearby looked at Hannah in concern.

Hannah stomped closer to the black suit with her two bouncer-cooks right behind her.

I knew they were good chefs; the food here was amazing. But those two looked like boxing buddies rather than cooks.

The busboy came running over and helped relocate the family away from the black suits. I didn't think the suits were going to be able to stay, but being away from it all would make for a better breakfast for the family.

"I don't have the staff here this morning to serve you all." Hannah's jaw popped as she leaned forward and snarled. "*You will have to leave.*"

The door chimed, and Jack, Alice, and Officer Jones came in. From the annoyed look on Jack's face, they weren't coming in for breakfast. I also doubted that any of Hannah's people had time to call them to come over and help get rid of the black suits.

I started toward the police, no idea what I'd done now, but Jack just gave me a curt nod and kept going. Alice and Officer Jones both smiled as they passed, so I must be okay.

For now.

Until my seven-foot-tall, blue jinn-former-goat showed up somewhere, anyway.

"Mr. Ditmyer, I believe you were told to keep your people in line. We have two, a Ms. Quila and a Mr. Houlth, in our holding area. They are being charged with, and I quote, 'goat wrangling'."

I put my hand over my mouth and fought to keep my face neutral. I'm sure there were probably other farms with goats in the area, but Camfield's were missing. I'd add Tiberius, but I wasn't sure if he had gone back to being a goat or not.

"What? That's preposterous. Why would they do that?" The formerly calm Mr. Ditmyer's façade began to crumble. The rest of the black suits stopped moving furniture in order to watch what was going on.

"They wouldn't tell our officers. I advise you to stop whatever it is that you're doing and go speak to your people. You'll probably need a lawyer. They stole Camfield's goats, and he's already lawyering up with charges against your entire organization."

I got the idea that Jack didn't like Camfield. But the tone in his voice, along with the slight smirk, indicated he disliked the black suits even more.

"But..." Mr. Ditmyer took a few deep breaths, then turned to the rest of his people. "Return to the Grasshopper and tell the boss what happened. And if any of you know why Quila and Houlth took the action they did, please inform him and our lawyers. I'll be going to the police station." He gave a tight nod to Hannah and her bouncers, then followed the cops out.

The rest of the black suits looked at all of us, as if debating disobeying him. Then they streamed out the front door.

"Those people keep getting weirder." Betsy shook her head as the last one left. "Seriously, a lot weirder."

Hannah smiled. "Hopefully, that will be the last we see of them. If they come back, *any* of them, I'm denying them service. Thank you, boys." She smiled at the cooks and the busboy.

Keith hung back and walked with me as the other three took the lead back to our table. "How are you feeling?" He kept his voice low and glanced at my wrists even though I'd worn long sleeves again.

"Tired, but okay. I haven't tested *anything*." The incident in my kitchen could have been a fluke. I needed to talk to him about Tiberius and Xieth, but it would have to wait. We'd dodged a dagger with the three ladies seeing Tiberius, but then not recalling it, thanks to Keith and the movie, Aladdin. We needed to keep them away from this mess.

Speculation about the ongoing shenanigans with the black suits bantered around the table for a bit, then the food arrived.

Hannah joined us with her cup of tea and breakfast sandwich, and we finalized plans for tomorrow.

"You really don't have to make all those sandwiches." I tried telling Hannah again.

"Pish, I want to help, and Jamie and Martha don't have the kitchen I have here. Even just doing small sampler plates to give out would be too much for you and them alone. Trust me, I think most of the town is planning on stopping by."

Jamie and Martha had taken over sandwich duty, but Hannah offered to help. The food would still be what we'd be serving on our regular tea menu, just made in massive amounts.

"Thank you, all of you." It was going to be hard to leave here when the time came.

Betsy took my hand. "Ceian? Are you okay?" Her bright blue eyes were full of concern.

"I'm fine." I forced a smile. "Just nervous about tomorrow." No choking on those words. They weren't the biggest worry in my life right now, but I was concerned.

"Not a worry." Hannah grinned. "I've recruited some crowd control and general assistance personnel." She pointed toward the door where Jeff, Marcus, and about a dozen more teenagers came striding in. All were in their garb from their medieval event. Two of the girls drifted to the tables with customers, curtsied, said a few words, and left flyers on each table.

Jeff led the rest to us, where he bowed to me. "Lady Ceian, we are honored to be in thy service for the morrow. May chance we be allowed to decorate the outer area of your fair establishment as well? And hold a small fighting demonstration during the event in your pen?"

I looked at the earnest faces, even Marcus. "I would be quite honored. Thank you, all."

"Thank ye!" Having greeted the customers and dropping off a pile of flyers on the hostess stand after a grin and nod from Hannah, the group left.

"Was this your idea, Hannah?" Keith's smile was closer to its normal level.

"It was Marcus's, actually. Well, probably Jeff's. He's taken over as the leader of their group. I thought, if everyone is coming to The Fainting Goat Tea and Spice, we should provide a spectacle worthy of the masses."

# ChapterForty-Six

The meeting at the diner was mostly a bunch of chatting about what was going on with the black suits. And why two of them had supposedly stolen Camfield's goats.

Hannah had been facing the front door and smiled. "I think someone might be looking for Ceian? Maybe to wish you luck for tomorrow?"

I was not expecting Camfield to be looking around the diner with a massive bouquet in his hands.

Especially after our last interaction a few hours ago.

His face lit up as he spotted me, and he ran over. "Hi everyone, do you mind if I steal Ceian for a moment? It won't take long. I have a call with New York in a bit."

Everyone nodded, and I slowly got to my feet. I was still annoyed at him for falsely accusing me of goat-napping, but it was hard to say no to that accent and smile.

We walked outside and out of view of the windows.

"I am so sorry that I accused you of stealing my goats. I couldn't have thought of who might, but I shouldn't have let my wild accusations fly." He handed me the flowers. "These are a small thank you, but I would love to take you out tonight to Chez Champion. I know we keep trying to get there, but I will make it happen this time."

"The flowers are gorgeous, thank you. Your goats came back?" I'd figured since he'd been the one to tell Jack about the black suits stealing them, that they'd been returned.

"Not yet. But Officer Jones called and said they are closing in on their location." He shook his head. "There are so many places for them to hide in the woods. Sadly, the black suits aren't talking yet. My lawyers will be here soon; they'll take care of this." He turned up the charm, and the smile increased a few watts. "Dinner? Please? I owe you so much more, but this will be the start. Would six-thirty be too early? I want to have a nice long dinner and get to know this amazing woman better."

I was pretty sure my smile was completely simpering idiot at this point. "I'd like that."

"Excellent, I'll pick you up then." He took one of my hands free of the bouquet, kissed it, and gave a small bow. "Until tonight."

I almost walked into the glass door as I waved goodbye. I'd been attracted to Camfield, at least until he accused me of goat theft, but I felt like a schoolgirl with my first crush.

"Those are stunning!" Betsy gushed. "I'm thinking those are not congratulations about the teahouse flowers?"

"No, we have a date." I was going to tell them about his accusations and apology, but just didn't want to bother. Who cared why? I had a date with a charming man. "Shall we go set up what we can for tomorrow's grand event?"

We bundled into Keith's van. I was going to ride my bike over, but the flowers were too big.

"You are swooning, my girl." Betsy turned around from the front seat. "Well, and seriously hooked. He is such a nice man. And British!"

"He's wonderful. We're going to Chez Champion."

Keith glanced back as he parked on the street near my teahouse. But unlike the three ladies, his eyes were concerned.

I ignored him. Maybe he just didn't want me to fall for the wrong guy.

We went in, and I put the flowers in a vase. They looked great in the pass-through between the kitchen and the front room. Some of my giddiness faded, but I blamed it on the weird night.

We worked on setting up the teahouse. Unlike the original plan, no one would be coming inside during the grand opening; that idea died when so many people indicated they were attending. Ralph showed up with a trailer and eight good-sized wooden picnic tables he'd borrowed from various sources. We set them up in the small parking lot.

We were winding down after two hours, and I was about to call it quits until tomorrow, when two things happened.

Betsy stopped in mid-step as she walked back inside, her eyes went wide, and she yelled, "I know what I told the feds!"

And the ground shook strongly enough to rattle the windows.

"What was that?" I knew what earthquakes were, but that wasn't it.

Everyone ran outside, and Keith pointed to a plume of smoke out in the woods.

"Is that the Old Hollow? Again?" Jamie sized up the distance with her hand.

"That's what it looks like. We need to go out there," Betsy swore. "And I again forgot what I told the feds. I don't forget things, why this?"

I wasn't sure if she forgot because the memory was too close to Keith's spell when Tiberius, in all his jinn glory, showed up last night. Or something more nefarious.

We still had no idea who was behind the witch storm and the force three spell alerts. What if what Betsy discovered had to do with an Eltrisian?

Keith smiled and took her arm as we walked to the van. "You've had a lot of things going on lately; it'll come back."

I wasn't sure if her relaxing about the missing memories was because of Keith himself or if he'd just used magic on her. Considering he'd collapsed last night from magic overuse, I hoped it wasn't magic.

More things to bring up whenever Keith and I had more time to talk alone.

"This is so exciting!" Jamie was almost bouncing in her seat, something I wouldn't have expected from her.

"What is? Someone trying to blow things up there again?" I doubted it was Jeff and Marcus's people; I'd seen them frolicking around town, handing out flyers.

"After the last situation up there and the results, I contacted a friend of mine who looks into these things. He thinks that we may have a mystery spot of our own." She put a lot of weight on those last words, but I still didn't have a clue.

Jamie elaborated for me. "It's a gravitational abnormality. They pop up in places all over the world. There's the Mystery Spot down in Santa Cruz, the Oregon Vortex up in Gold Hill, Oregon, and lots more. They're amazing."

"I went to one once, and it gave me a day-long headache." Martha looked ready to climb out of the van.

"It's the magnets." Jamie shrugged. "Or something. Who knows, but they're really fun."

"How could one just pop up?" I'd have to look these things up after my life settled down. I wouldn't be concerned, but something was going on out there that had non-humans all over it.

Keith pulled into the lot, and Jamie hopped out of the van.

"I think someone is creating it. Come on! It's still smoking!"

We walked briskly toward the Old Hollow, although Martha hung back a bit. I thought I saw Tiberius in goat form in the woods near us, but he was gone before I could call him.

Yup, same spot. Same smoke. No teenagers.

But three people in black suits took off running as we got closer.

"They were digging? You can't make a gravitational anomaly like that." Jamie stalked around as we all scooped dirt onto the small, but very real, fire near the hole.

"Those black suits are out of control. Can the mayor ban them from coming here next year?" Betsy found one of their shovels, and we quickly got the fire out.

"But the fire shouldn't have caused an explosion, right?" I peered into the hole; it was deeper than I'd expected, but it just looked like a hole. One that, after finding two more discarded shovels, my friends were filling back up. "And shouldn't the fire department be here?" Those words had just left my mouth when we heard sirens, and the fire crew came out.

They said they were delayed by a false fire alarm at the Grasshopper.

We told them who we saw running away, but since we'd only seen their backs, there wasn't a lot to describe. Two men, one woman, black suits.

We left the fire crew, and Jamie, who said she wanted to do some exploring, and Keith dropped me off at the diner for my bike before taking Betsy and Martha home.

"Have a lovely date." Betsy winked as they drove off.

I smiled all the way home. There had been a lot of weirdness, but Camfield and I were fine, and we were going to have a lovely dinner.

No animals were in sight, even in Hadari's yard. I unlocked the barn in case someone went back inside through the Tiberius-sized hole. Nope, still empty. Luckily, the spell on the floor hadn't returned either.

My cottage was quiet and unmolested, a nice change. I actually flopped on the sofa and grabbed the remote for some mindless TV time before I needed to get ready for my date. But after an hour, I kept looking at the landscape painting.

Something had been wrong with Xieth last night. He could be a complete jerk, but drinking on the job wasn't his style. As annoying as he was, I could have ended up much worse off.

I should check on him.

With a sigh, I rolled off my sofa and tapped the side of the frame of the painting.

A distracted female cherub with way too much makeup blinked owlishly at me. "What?"

She might be Xieth's sister.

"I'm trying to reach Xieth." There was no way I was telling anyone about whatever happened to him last night. "I might have missed one of his calls."

She shook her head and looked down at something on her desk. "No. You haven't. He's been in meetings all day."

Doubtful. "Okay, good. Um, could you leave a message for him to contact me when he can?"

"Sure." Then the landscape painting snapped back into place.

This was bad. There was no way Xieth wouldn't want to call and bug me the day before his teahouse project had its grand opening. The success of it wasn't just important for me, but for him, too.

There was an odd scratching at my door. Sounded too high up for Lucie.

I opened the door. "Hadari, where are the puppies?"

She came in. "I sent them to sleep in our yard. We never found Tiberius, but we avoided any areas where those humans in the black clothes were. They seem to be everywhere in the woods. Lucie was with us for a while, but he had his own agenda and left us a short time ago. Saying he won't be home tonight. I can go back out if you'd like. The puppies will be safe where they are."

It was already close to five, and I didn't want anyone running into the black suits. Betsy was right, they were getting weirder.

"Thank you, but no. I'm going out tonight. Could you keep an eye on things here?"

She gave me one of her hoxien wolf grins. "Gladly. Have a nice evening." She trotted back to their yard.

I needed to get ready.

Camfield showed up right on time, with another bouquet. "I saw these and knew you needed them."

"Thank you." I put them away in the kitchen and came back to the front as he looked around the yard.

"Your goat got taken, too? And your cat?"

"Tiberius is resting." I shrugged and locked the door. "Lucie is out being a cat for the night."

We walked to his car.

The restaurant was wonderful. At least that was the overwhelming feeling I had. Like this morning, I felt a little giddy around Camfield almost immediately, even though I only had one glass of wine. I couldn't even say what we had to eat, but it was wonderful. Camfield was charming, and everything was delightful.

Our drive home was peaceful and relaxing. Camfield chatted about a merger his company was doing with another one, something that would bring a lot of new business in.

I couldn't recall the specifics. I just kept watching his mouth as he spoke, wondering when he would kiss me.

He walked me to my door, then slid his hands down my arms to my wrists and leaned forward to kiss me.

I fully responded. Yes, getting involved with a human wasn't the best idea. But right now, I didn't care about the rules.

The kiss was amazing. "Would you like to come in for a drink?" Also, probably not a great idea. Still not caring.

"I would love to." His smile lit up the night, and I fumbled for the lock.

"Maybe you should sit a bit, let me get the drink for you." He led me to the sofa and gave me another intense kiss.

I almost swooned into the sofa as I dropped down.

# Chapter Forty-Seven

A loud scratching sound echoed through my dreams, and I swung my arm out to hit wherever it was coming from.

And flung myself off my sofa.

If I was going to keep falling asleep out here, I needed a wider sofa and maybe some cushions on the floor.

I was dressed up, and I still had my high heels on. Until I kicked them off as I went to the door.

Lucie was scratching furiously, but stopped as I opened the door.

"Ooo, hot date?" He sauntered past me as I squinted around the yard. I thought I'd only had one glass of wine, but I felt hungover.

"Camfield took me out for an apology dinner. They found who took his goats."

Lucie looked up from his leftover kibble. "And? He's not still here, is he? If so, why are you still dressed?"

"I fell asleep out here after he left. It was a lovely night, and he was a perfect gentleman. Meanwhile, did you find Tiberius?"

"Fresh kibble, first."

I poured more into the bowl.

"Nope. Something is going on in the woods, but nothing I could find. No goat-jinn either."

"Okay, I'm going to go shower and get ready for our grand opening." I paused at the landline phone. "Right after I check if Xieth called."

Lucie nodded and went back to eating.

There were no missed calls on the landline. I was getting worried that Xieth hadn't contacted me. Not returning my call wasn't that surprising; he didn't like being told when to address things. But given the amount of chaos taking place down here and how he'd been when I last saw him, a bit of concern was in place.

Or would be if there weren't so many other issues to worry about. Tiberius and Camfield's goats were still missing, the mysterious black suits, the feds, and something weird in the center of the Old Hollow. Jamie texted me last night that she was calling it the Forgotten Hollow Mystery Spot and was trying to figure out how to market it. Maybe tie it into the teahouse.

I kept thinking about the issues while I showered and then dug through every bit of clothing in my closet.

"Aren't you ready yet? Seriously." Lucie finally yelled from the kitchen.

"I'm working on it! Go out and look for Tiberius." At this point, my fear had shifted from someone spotting a seven-foot-tall blue jinn to a former jinn being turned back into a mindless goat.

Even in goat form, I knew Tiberius could take care of himself, but only if he was still mentally Tiberius.

"Why is the guest room door open?" Lucie had given up yelling from the kitchen and was in front of my bedroom door.

"What?" I swung open my door. "It can't be, I checked last night..." I ran to shove open the formerly locked door. Books were tossed all over the place, and the closet door was open.

"No, no, no." The Pasken mob box was still there; obviously, even a thief wasn't stupid enough to want that. But the sealed-up box that held the Stone of Zalianthia was gone.

I started shaking and dropped to the floor. "That's it. Everything's done. They took it, Lucie. It could be traced to me. You should escape while you can." I started sobbing as everything from the past week slammed into me. "I won't let the council know you knew about it. Tiberius either. If he's not a goat-brain now." My sobs grew impressive, great, huge, ugly ones.

I felt Lucie's fur brush against my folded knees and thought maybe he was trying to comfort me.

Instead, I felt a paw smack me across the face a few times.

No claws, luckily. But he still had far more force behind those swings than an animal his size should have.

"Snap out of it!" He was raising his paw for another round when I grabbed it.

"You can't stay here. I can't defend you. Besides, whoever took the stone probably knows you knew about it. They all might be looking for you, the council, the black suits, the feds, who knows? You have to leave."

Lucie ignored me and went into the closet sniffing. "Camfield."

"What? He and I made up." I stopped sobbing and wiped my face. Good thing I'd decided to put on my makeup after I figured out my clothes.

Not that it mattered now.

"Did you make up inside the closet? Because I'm smelling him all over here." He came out and started doing a hunting dog impersonation. "Yup. Down the hall. In your bedroom, but only a few steps inside." He stopped in front of my bottle. "His scent is all over your bottle. But it's not new." His tail puffed as he glared at a toy mouse not far from him. It burst into a ball of smoke. "I'd say my magic is completely back, probably yours as well. Camfield is an Eltrisian and hid his magic from us because he knew we didn't have magic. He's the one who took your bottle last week. Probably the person who orchestrated the kidnapping of Tiberius and me, too." He shook his head. "First, Darius, now whatever Camfield is? You might want to look into taking up vows and joining a convent. Just saying."

I started shaking. Too many emotions and not enough sleep to deal with them. I stalked over to the kitchen. Whoever created this cottage setup bought two sets of dishes. One I liked, the other I hated and kept way in the back of the cabinet.

I dragged the ugly ones out and, one by one, smashed them on the floor. All the while shouting the vilest swear words in Sihlia I could think of.

Lucie jumped on the back of the sofa when broken shards started flying. "You probably have your full magic back. Wouldn't using it be less messy?"

"Possibly, but not as satisfying. Not to mention, we don't want to attract unwanted attention." I glanced at the landscape, but it hadn't moved. "I can't believe that I fell for his pretty lies!" I paused mid-plate-smashing. "You said you could tell his scent on the bottle wasn't new. Can you tell how long ago the other scents were?"

Lucie shrugged, judged the distance between his sofa and the hallway, then leaped over the collection of shattered plates and trotted into the guest room. I got out the broom and swept my mess up. It was childish, but safer than using magic, and it made me feel better.

Not as much as imagining doing serious damage to Camfield did, but still a bit more like myself.

"You're not going to like this." Lucie came out with his ears slightly back. "Those scents are from last night. Tiberius wasn't here; I wasn't here. He knocked you out and stole our stone."

"That..." a few more Sihlia swear words colored the air. "Those kisses last night. I felt different, he *spelled* me." He wouldn't have been able to do it if I'd still had my magic-blocking bracelets on. He'd taken my wrists to pull me closer when we were talking, felt they were gone, and zapped me with a passionate kiss. "I'm going to kill him. Very, very, slowly."

As in so much of my life recently, my thoughts of revenge were interrupted by a knock at my door.

Betsy, Martha, and Jamie. All looking lovely and ready for a teahouse grand opening.

"That's an interesting outfit choice." Betsy tilted her head as she took in my mismatched clothing. I'd been mid-change when Lucie called me about the guest room door.

"Sorry, things have been hectic this morning." I was grateful that I'd swept up the broken plates at least. "Come on in, I'll just be a minute."

"Have you been crying?" Martha asked as she passed me. "Is everything okay with the dogs? I didn't see them next door."

I knew Hadari and her puppies had returned last night without finding Tiberius or the missing goats. They must have gone out again.

"They're fine. I'm just stressed out and slept oddly." I'd almost said slept badly, but the fact was, I'd slept great.

Thanks to that poisoned kiss Camfield gave me. My fists tightened at the thought.

"I told Betsy we were too early. I wanted to run some tests on our mystery spot from yesterday. Did you know that land isn't owned by anyone, officially anyway?" Jamie's grin was huge.

I wasn't sure what made the Old Hollow weird, but it might keep the three out of trouble for a bit.

"I didn't know that. Actually, you all being here now is great. Could I get a ride into town?"

"Sure, but what about the goat? Isn't he supposed to be there?" Martha asked.

"I don't think Tiberius is feeling like himself today. Jeff and his group can run their show in the pen as long as they want."

I ran into my bedroom, after a detour to shut and lock the guest room, and put together a decent outfit. Billowing pants and a flowing shirt, both of green and blue. Added some jewelry, including bracelets that almost looked like my exploded ones, and darted out.

Betsy got us to the teahouse in record time. It was only half after eight, but there were already a few people outside the door. I freaked out until I realized it was Hannah and her two bodyguard cooks.

Along with Jeff and two others in garb and a bunch of cases and boxes waiting near the picnic tables in the former parking lot.

Betsy parked around the corner, and we brought in food and supplies.

"Is there anything we can do?" Jeff leaned into the doorway. "We'll have the decorations up shortly."

"No, I think we're good." I dodged out of the way as a few more piles of food came in.

"Then we'll set up in the pen? No goat today?"

"He's sitting this one out. The pen is all yours, thank you."

Hannah brought in a few hundred smallish but sturdy paper plates.

"Where'd those come from?" I had some, but they were cheap. These were heavier and cuter.

"My diner. We bought them for a town BBQ a few years ago, which got rained out. Figured this was a good use for them." She patted the pile and darted off to set up folding tables for plate assembly in the shop.

Looking around at the mountains of food, teapots, plates, cute napkins, and other supplies, it almost pushed aside my Camfield fury.

Almost. This was a nice distraction, and would hopefully secure my ability for the council to let me stay here until I finished my parole, but Camfield was going to have to pay. And we had to get that cursed stone back.

Hannah sent her cooks back to the diner, and Keith showed up. He still looked paler than normal, and while he already was a slender guy, he was starting to look skinny. Over-taxing magic didn't do good things for the body.

Betsy took one look at him, grabbed a bunch of Hannah's tiny sandwiches, dropped them on a plate, and then put them on a table. "Sit. Eat. What kind of tea do you want?" There was no messing with her with that tone of voice, so Keith surrendered and sat. "I'm serious." Her eyes narrowed.

Keith grabbed two tiny sandwiches and held up his hands. "Thank you, I'll eat. Just Yorkshire Gold today, thanks." He grinned after Betsy nodded and stomped off to start his tea.

Soon, the kitchen chaos settled down, my massive water tank was heating up, assorted teapots were at the ready, and Hannah finished setting up the assembly line for the food plates.

We planned to greet guests just inside the door, hand them a plate with a tiny sandwich, a mini scone, a mini sausage roll, a mini cupcake, and a slice of Betsy's bread. Right past the door outside would be the tea station with disposable cups of tea, along with apple juice for non-tea drinkers.

Martha set up a donation bottle for homeless animals on the tea table. She'd wanted to bring Hadari and the puppies to represent, but I said it would be too hard on them.

Not to mention, Hadari had magic; I had no idea when that might kick in for the puppies.

She understood, but I had a feeling there would need to be serious puppy cuddle time sometime soon. And if folks were willing to help out rescue animals because of free food, I was all for it. Xieth covered the costs of everything for the teahouse start-up, including this event. Even though they didn't want to, I made both Hannah and Betsy take money for the food and supplies they brought in.

The sounds of shouting through the currently closed front door marred the comforting feeling settling in. I ran to the door with most of my friends on my heels.

It was Jeff and Marcus in the pen. With swords drawn. Real ones.

# ChapterForty-Eight

Had we misjudged Marcus? Both guys looked serious as they circled each other. They weren't using rapiers, but heavier swords like those from The Lord of the Rings movies. Some arena fighters used swords. I didn't use them often, but I could tell that Jeff and Marcus were familiar with the weapons.

"What are you boys doing?" Betsy yelled from behind me. I was surprised that she could see around me blocking her. But if something was going on, she'd see it.

"Practicing losing. So far, I can beat both of them." There were now about ten more garbed teenagers watching from the sides. The one who responded to Betsy's yell was a tall, athletic-looking blonde girl in fighting leathers.

Jeff and Marcus nodded to each other and stopped fighting.

"You're going to use live steel?" Keith asked from over Betsy's head.

"Only for part of the demonstration. Right when you first open up." Marcus looked much younger now.

Camfield had probably been behind what happened to him, too. My theory was that Darius hooked Marcus up with the books originally, but Camfield seemed to be taking over everything Darius started.

"What was that?" Jamie turned to me.

"What was what?" I waved at the teenagers to go back to fighting.

"I swore I heard a growl."

It had been me thinking about Camfield and Darius. I hadn't noticed I'd growled until she said something. "That's weird, I didn't hear anything. We should get the plates ready."

The grand opening was only going to last four hours, from eleven to three. To me, it looked like we had enough food to easily cover a few days.

However, Betsy and Hannah were scowling as we got our assembly line going.

"We might need to get emergency supplies. This doesn't look to be enough." Betsy was a tiny general as she marched around the piles of food.

"Not enough at all." Hannah nodded as she walked behind Betsy with her arms behind her back.

"We could put less on each plate?" We'd just started the line, but could easily redo them at this point. None of the plates had even gotten to the covering area. Hannah brought a professional-sized roll of plastic wrap to cover the plates. The small parking lot had eight picnic tables, but most folks would have to walk a block over to the small town park to sit down.

"Nope. This is when you will be the belle of the town. We will feed them all!" Hannah laughed a bit manically as she took her phone out of her pocket. "Boyos? I need you to bring in the backups. Plus, any cakes we have fresh. Thanks." She grinned with a shrug. "Always have more than you need.

"Agreed." Betsy already had her phone out. "Ralph? Hit the freezer in the garage, bring everything in."

"You two are amazing. Scary, but amazing." I looked around the room. "You all are. Thank you so much. I know that's not enough, but thank you." I kept blinking my eyes to keep from crying. I didn't cry once when I was in my bottle for a hundred years, but today I was all over the place.

Maybe humans caused crying.

Everyone came forward for hugs, then darted back to their stations.

"We've got this covered. You go sit in your kitchen, have something to eat, and drink some tea. There will be enough going on today to wear everyone out," Hannah said as she and Betsy went outside to wait for their deliveries.

I did what Hannah ordered. Poured a cup of tea, grabbed a few tiny sandwiches, and sat on one of the kitchen stools.

The scratching at the back door wasn't loud, but it was clearly not just a random branch. I popped open the door to find Lucie raising his paws for more scratching. He didn't come inside, but he looked frazzled. "Is your thing over yet?" His tail lashed furiously, and he kept looking over at the fence behind him.

"It starts in half an hour, what's wrong? Is Tiberius back?" Lucie never came to me with his personal problems, but he was more freaked out than I'd ever seen.

"No, our goat-jinn is still missing. There's something up with those humans in black suits. I don't know what, but it's not good. I overheard a group of them in town as they headed out to the woods. And they mentioned Camfield by name. I couldn't get close enough to hear more."

"Ceian? Clear space in there, we've brought reinforcements." It was a good thing Betsy shouted before she and Hannah came in. Lucie had time to hide behind the trash can outside, and I shut the door.

"We'll get these ready, but keep them in here for if we run low." Betsy directed Ralph to set down about a million mini sausage rolls on the counter.

"Congratulations on the opening, Ceian." Ralph nodded. "If you don't mind, I thought I could help with traffic control out front. You're already getting a line down the street."

I broke away from looking at the mountain of food. "What? Oh, wow. Thank you for bringing these, and by all means, traffic away, I'd appreciate it. Jeff and crew out front offered to help as well when they're not performing."

Hannah and her cooks were next with extra sandwiches, cakes, and what looked like a bunch of mini quiches. I thanked them all as well.

"Is there really a line out there?" I was suddenly nervous. What if this failed? Xieth implied that they'd reconsider my parole, but if someone had taken him out, maybe they'd just lock me back up.

"Yes, there is, and you need to take a few deep breaths." Betsy had her hands on her hips as she glared up at me.

"Sorry, just freaking out." I did take the breaths, though.

The three of us went to the front. There was a truly terrifying number of small, plastic-wrapped plates filling every surface in my teahouse.

"Martha and Jamie are taking care of the drinks out front. I think we're ready." While Keith still looked tired, his smile was genuine.

Trumpets weren't part of my plans, but that's what I heard. I opened the front door to see Jeff turn off a disc player and climb up on a wooden box. "Welcome, lords and ladies, to the grandest opening of The Fainting Goat Tea and Spice! We have some demonstrations now whilst you wait for the amazing food. There is some seating in the lot, and more tables have been prepared in the park. Enjoy!" With a flair I wouldn't have expected from him, Jeff jumped off the wooden box, kicked it out of the pen, and drew his sword.

It wasn't Marcus who faced him but the tall blonde girl from before. Just seeing her first moves, my money was on her.

"I believe that's our cue." Betsy waved to the first person in line. "Welcome!"

I took my place, thanked people for coming, and handed them a filled plate and napkin.

Everyone seemed almost alarmingly glad to be there. And happy my teahouse was opening up in town.

Time fled. We were about to close up, and the line was down to stragglers and a few repeats when three people in black suits walked up.

They stepped out of the line and waved a few more repeaters ahead of them. When there was no one else, I figured we'd fed most of the town, they stepped forward.

"We still have plates." Betsy's smile was brittle, but at least she had one, which was better than mine. I was trying not to growl.

"No...well, yeah, thank you." The first one was a tall man with short red hair. He looked a little worse for wear up close. Like he'd been roughing it. While wearing his expensive black suit.

The other two, another man and a woman, looked the same. All three took their plates with gratitude. Something I hadn't seen on the faces of any of their crew in the past two weeks.

The tables in the parking lot had cleared out, so once they got something to drink, the three black suits sat down. All of them ate, but they kept glancing at me.

"I think we're good to shut down, right?" It was three-thirty already. "I'm going to go chat with our friends." I forced a smile. Maybe my magic was working, or maybe I was picking up on something beyond them being scuffed up, but there was something wrong.

Keith said something to the ladies and came forward before I shut the door. "I'll just even the odds a bit." He nodded to Ralph, who moved away from watching Jeff and crew pack up, and focused on the black suits with folded arms and a glare.

"How did you like the food?" It was hard to be mad at these three; they really looked like life had kicked them in the teeth.

Regardless of what I felt about the black suits.

"Thank you, it's great." The tall red-haired man responded. "You're Ceian, right? And he's Keith?"

Keith remained a few feet to the side of me, but we both nodded.

"We're in trouble," the woman said after she wiped her mouth. "There's something wrong up at the hotel. We escaped last night, but they're getting worse."

"Who's getting worse?" Keith stepped closer.

"The bosses." The third man was short and stocky. "We three are relatively new to the company, and this was our first retreat. It was great to start with, but the last few days have been weird."

The red-haired man nodded. "We all went out to some place in the woods last night, no idea where. They just kept walking in what felt like circles. The three of us took off when we had the chance, but I think the rest are back there."

"There in the woods, or the hotel?" I wasn't completely sure that these three weren't up to no good.

"Some might have been sent back to the hotel. They said something, or did something the bosses didn't like." The woman shook her head. "We took off and hid."

"They wouldn't tell us what it was, but they were looking for something out in the woods." The stocky man ran his fingers through his hair. "I've only worked for them for a few months, but that is a messed-up company. I just want to get back to New York and leave this job."

Before I could ask more, like if they knew Camfield, all three started beeping. Rather, the old-fashioned pagers they had on did. Each person paused, took the small black box out, looked at the tiny screen, then got to their feet.

"Thank you for the food and tea."

"We have to go now."

"Have a nice day."

Whereas all three had appeared exhausted and worried a moment before, they now seemed recovered and had no emotion on their faces as they turned and walked away.

# ChapterForty-Nine

Ralph started to block the black suits, but I shook my head to let them pass.

"That was weird, even for them." Keith came closer and kept his voice low. "Those pagers changed them completely."

"Like mind control. Could those laxiun vines have been involved?" We'd never had a chance to examine them, but anything mind control-ish wasn't good.

"You think the people behind this used the vines and connected them to those pagers?" He watched the black suits turn the corner. "You could be right."

"What was with those three? I know those people are strange, but they acted like they didn't even see me." Ralph shook his head. "I'm off then, thank you for letting me help, this was fun." With a final glare in the direction of the black suits, Ralph walked to his truck.

I saw Lucie jump out over the back fence. He glanced at me, but took off in the opposite direction from the black suits.

None of this was good.

"We need to find out what's happening. Without including the others. I need to tell you about Camfield." I kept my voice low; Betsy and the others were still inside, but I knew that wouldn't last long.

"We do, but if we just take off, they'll follow us."

I tried to think of anything that would keep them here, or at least not at the Grasshopper or the woods. Nope. Not a single thing. Betsy was the worst, but the other three weren't far behind.

"Only one way. Betsy can't be in peril anymore." Keith strode into my teahouse without telling me his plan, so I followed behind.

"Ladies? Can we ask you all a question?"

I had a bad feeling about what his plan was, but the four of them were already close by, so he spelled them before I could stop him.

Betsy, Martha, Jamie, and Hannah froze in place.

Keith leaned against a table in exhaustion but focused on the four women. "Ceian and I had to go back to Ghoston station, where we left a package for her friend. Everything's fine. Have a relaxing afternoon. Do not go to the Grasshopper or the Old Hollow. Or anywhere in the woods."

I grabbed his arm as he sank lower.

"They'll wake up in about ten minutes, but the planted memory should hold for an hour or more. Let's hit the Grasshopper first." He didn't try to pull away as I supported him.

"You can't keep using your magic, you've already collapsed once." I forced him into a chair and brought over three plates of sandwiches. "Eat. Now." I did my best Betsy glare, and poured him tea and a big glass of water.

He started to get up, and I pushed him back down with one hand. Jinn were stronger than humans, but so were slanaigh. Right now, Martha could beat him in an arm-wrestling match.

He shrugged and inhaled the sandwiches and tea in record time. "I'm fine."

"Nope, you're not." I waved my hand in front of all four women's eyes. Not a single blink. I had to hope the spell would hold. "Let's go."

Grumbling to himself, but bringing along another full plate, Keith went to his van.

He ate the entire way over to the hotel, and I filled him in on Camfield.

Keith parked a bit away from the Grasshopper, but there was no one in sight. No staff, gardeners, guests, no one.

I shuddered as a chill went up my back. "Something is seriously wrong." Again, not sure if it was my magic making itself known or just too many scary movies when I ran out of cop shows for my late-night viewing.

I'd never been bothered by them, but they must have settled in my psyche.

Keith already looked better, but he needed to stay off magic for a bit. "Let's try the hotel lobby first." From the tight look on his face, he was sensing the disturbance too.

Points for it being a magic vibe, not a scary movie vibe.

The lobby door was unlocked, and three employees were passed out on the floor.

Maybe some scary movie vibe.

We checked, but all three were simply asleep.

Back to magic.

"They weren't attacked directly; this is residual." Keith led the way toward the conference center. The door didn't want to open at first as if something was holding it closed, but not as if it were locked. I stepped forward and shoved it open.

"Sorry, have a lot of pent-up energy today." Truth was, I was stronger than Keith. Especially right now. Two black suits were slumped against the door, also asleep. About twenty more of them were collapsed around the seats.

"We have to break what did this." Keith jogged up to the dais. He grabbed a bowl from a small table. "This is full of laxiun vines; there had been water in here. And a magic fire. Whatever the others are up to, they didn't want these to join."

"Which means that we do. How can we wake them?" None of the unconscious black suits seemed to be in pain; they might be when they woke up from sleeping in such odd positions, but not now.

Keith didn't answer, but glared at the bowl in his hands. A wave of magic flowed away from it, and then it exploded.

I ran forward, but he just shook out his hands. "Messier than I'd hoped, but it wasn't complicated."

"You can't keep using magic." He looked better than he had after the teahouse, but that was the food and caffeine.

"Our choices were slim. You can't risk letting anyone know your bracelets are off."

Before I could respond, the black suits started sitting up. I didn't see the three who had come to us, so these might have been here since last night.

I dropped near the two by the door as they moved. "Are you okay? We found you unconscious."

"I'm going to kill them."

"Excuse me?" I pulled back, but he shook his head.

"Sorry, we were drugged or something. Those *bosses* didn't think we were going along with their twisted program, so they brought us here and drugged us." He took a deep breath and got to his feet, then helped the man next to him.

Soon, twenty-two pissed off black suits were on their feet and looking for blood. One of the odd things about the black suits was that there were rarely signs of emotion. Unless utter disdain for everyone else counted. It was snapping back into place now.

"Do you know where they went?" I had no idea what was going on, but I knew it wasn't good. And they were somewhere in the woods.

One of them looked at a pager and swore. "The clearing." He paused as his expression went blank. The call had hit them when they were unconscious, but it was still active now.

Keith grabbed the nearest pager, stomped on it, and dropped it into a trash can. "Destroy your pagers, that's how they're controlling you."

Only the one near me looked at his, but the others shrugged and listened to Keith.

I grabbed the one from the guy next to me and destroyed it.

He blinked but still slowly walked toward the open doors.

"Stop him!" A woman from the back yelled.

"Follow him!" Keith yelled back. "You want payback? Follow that man."

The man picked up speed as he cleared the conference center, but none of us had trouble keeping up with him as he marched into the woods.

I stopped briefly as I thought I saw Tiberius, as a goat, and a few other goats in the woods, but he was too far away to be sure.

"We don't have weapons. We should have weapons." The man leading was chanting to himself, but Keith looked at me.

"Are you ready to fight?"

I grinned and shook out my arms as we walked. "Yes, I need a good workout." If Camfield were there, I could deal with him. If not, I could just imagine all of the bad people were him. Or Darius. I'd had a lot of great workout sessions in my bottle doing that.

I'd expected to be heading toward the Old Hollow, based on Lucie's brief message, but we were heading toward a clearing not that far from the parking lot for the trails.

"Wait a minute." Keith held back the rest of the black suits as the one we were following went into the clearing. He seemingly vanished into thin air.

"We have to shatter it, *without magic*." I kept my voice low as I tried to sort out a way to break a cloak spell before us.

Here I was terrified about the slightest bit of magic showing, and someone was using massive spells around humans.

Keith closed his eyes, and suddenly the clearing was full of black suits. Some were unconscious; in fact, a lot of them were. The awake ones were clustered around a distant blond person.

"Camfield." I knew growled that time.

# ChapterFifty

K eith put his hands up to stop me from running forward.

Probably a good idea.

"Let me wake the others first, I know how the spell works now. It won't take much magic at all. I'll be fine. If they're out like the ones at the hotel, they might be on our side."

I didn't like the 'might' comment at all; there were a lot of people knocked out here if they ended up not being on our side. But he already cast his spell.

The ones closest to us moved first, and the ones that came in with us helped them to their feet.

Then Camfield spotted us.

"Defend me! They want to take everything away from us!" He was holding onto straps that held something to his back, but distanced himself as his minions ran toward us.

Luckily, the ones that were waking up joined in the fight against the ones under Camfield's control. Keith and I fought as well.

Hadari and her puppies came racing into the clearing from the same direction we'd come in. None of them barked, but the controlled black suits ran away from them. They might be under mind control, but they weren't stupid.

I grinned and punched a black suit who stupidly tried to run past me. It had been a long time since I'd fought in an arena, and this was different. But it still felt great.

Keith was holding his own well, but I noticed he wasn't using magic this time.

Our side was slowly disabling the attacking black suits. We were all trying not to hurt them too badly, but we had to stop this.

Then I spotted their pagers flashing red on their waists. "Destroy the pagers!"

That helped. Every one of the bad ones who lost their pager passed out, and the evil black suits who remained standing stumbled back as Camfield continued yelling.

That didn't last more than a moment or two, and the black suits with us started dragging their friends out of the middle of the fight.

The remaining evil black suits, I needed them to have hats or something to tell them apart, rallied and continued the fight against us.

Camfield sent a spell of some sort, and three of the black suits on our side froze, then turned to fight against their friends next to them.

Even without the pagers or the vines, Camfield was using mind control over them.

Xieth might have arrested the two evil cherubs originally behind this mess after they'd bumped off Darius, but he hadn't killed the plan they began.

Camfield was far sneakier than anyone I knew. He was like Darius, but with brains and a fake British accent.

Lucie was right, my taste in men completely sucked.

Hadari started barking; currently, her puppies were harassing a pair of black suits they'd managed to tree. But Hadari's barking wasn't about them; she sounded happy.

Over the hill came Betsy, Jamie, Martha, Hannah, and Ralph. They were escorted by Jeff and Marcus's troop. Granted, the teenagers were armed with duct tape-covered poles instead of swords, but I'd seen what those things could do. I'd been impressed by their short live steel demonstration this morning, but was grateful there was none of it in sight.

Keith's spell on the four women not only fell before it should have, but it also led them where we didn't want them.

Their appearance startled the remaining evil black suits, and I saw most from both side collapse unconscious. Keith looked paler again, so he must have snuck in a spell when the evil ones' concentration blinked for a moment.

The remaining evil black suits froze; there were only ten now, but then they turned and ran toward the Old Hollow. Jeff, Marcus, all of their people, along with Betsy, Jamie, Hannah, and Ralph, yelled and raced after them.

"That was too fast for me." Martha jogged over to us and shook her head as she caught her breath. "Sorry it took us so long to sort out where you went. There was some miscommunication. Are you both okay?" Her concern was focused on Keith.

"I'm fine." Keith didn't look or sound fine, or look fine, but he smiled. "Really. Just my age catching up to me."

Considering that he was over a thousand years old, that was a lot of age.

Hadari and her puppies came running over to Martha and distracted her from Keith.

Camfield faded back into the trees when our reinforcements showed up, and his black suited minions took off. He might have been involved with corrupting the black suits, or just taken advantage of what the evil cherubs and Darius started. But he was involved now. He turned to run into the deeper part of the woods.

He'd fashioned a backpack out of my canvas bag for the box with the Stone of Zalianthia in it. He used those laxiun vines to hold it all together. They might have simply been convenient for his pack, or they were doing something else evil. We had to get the stone away from him. We had no idea what was going on in the Old Hollow, but a chill went up my back. We didn't want that evil stone near that weird thing in the center of the Old Hollow. I ran toward him.

I wasn't the only one trying to stop Camfield, though.

A flock of goats, led by Tiberius, blocked Camfield's way from the rest of the forest in a growing circle and kept walking forward. Far more goats than only Camfield's herd. Tiberius must have freed animals all over Forgotten Hollow.

Camfield snarled as he moved backward, away from the goats. "Tiberius. Why couldn't you have eaten the damn goat kibble I left for you?"

Lucie, leading a gang of cats, joined the goats and helped force Camfield back toward us faster. Camfield wasn't going easily and got a swipe across his shin when he tried to push past the cats. His magic might be limited, or he'd overtaxed it badly.

I didn't know that Lucie had made cat friends, or even that Eltrisian cats could understand Earth cats, but I was grateful they could.

I figured Keith and I didn't have much time to get the information we needed from Camfield about all that he'd done, and take back the Stone of Zalianthia, before the cops showed up. Someone would have reported the current mess to them by now.

Hadari nudged her puppies toward Martha, then spun and ran to Camfield. He screamed, but had nowhere to run. Hadari stopped before she hit him, but growled as she stalked forward.

"I'll call her off if you drop the pack." Like I could control Hadari's actions, something Camfield most likely knew. No one controlled a hoxien wolf.

But Hadari just kept stepping forward with Tiberius and Lucie bringing up their groups at the same pace.

"Here! Here! Keep that monster away from me!" Camfield's scream was so loud they probably heard him back in town.

A lot of things happened at once.

Camfield threw the pack over Hadari's head. I heard sirens and a loudspeaker from the parking area. Two Eltrisian jinn centurion enforcers of the same species as Tiberius appeared out of thin air, grabbed Camfield, and vanished.

Martha passed out.

Then the ground shook, and there was an explosion from the direction of the Old Hollow.

# ChapterFifty-One

Jack, Alice, Officer Jones, three other cops, and a bunch of what had to be FBI agents based on their suits came running into the clearing with guns drawn.

"What happened here?" Jack looked around at Martha and the collapsed black suits. Hadari's puppies started licking Martha's face.

I glanced over, but Lucie and his cats, as well as Tiberius and the goats, had vanished.

At least that was good. This was going to be hard enough to explain. Too late, I thought about Camfield's backpack. Neither the cops nor the FBI could have that.

It was right in the middle of everything. Before I could take a chance on using magic to hopefully hide it, a sloppy copy of Camfield, a gombler, would be my guess, appeared, grabbed the pack, and vanished in a flash of light. It was too short to be Camfield, but hopefully close enough to fool the humans.

"Was that Camfield? Where did he go?" Jack swung around, looking.

"I have no idea where he went, or how," Keith answered.

"He was behind all of this," I added. "He got some of the black suits to help him, not these; they were trying to help us until Camfield knocked them out with something." I skirted through that one without choking, as it was essentially true.

"Great timing." The tall blonde girl in leather from Jeff's group yelled to Jack as she ran up. "Something blew up in the Old Hollow. Come quick!" She didn't wait for Jack or the FBI folks to respond; she just took off back toward the Old Hollow.

"We've got this. Stay here and make sure everyone's all right." The lead FBI agent brushed off Jack.

"This is my town. I'm going with you." Jack turned to Officer Jones, Alice, and the other three cops. "Call for ambulances and make sure everyone is okay." At their nods, he raced after the FBI agents.

Part of me wanted to know what happened at the Old Hollow, but Betsy would tell us later. Not to mention, I'd noticed that Hadari had taken off in the same direction.

She'd make sure there wasn't an Eltrisphere-related problem.

Alice called the EMTs as Officer Jones and the other three started checking on the unconscious black suits. They appeared to be waking up, but slower this time.

I went to help Martha as she tried to sit up. "What happened?" She looked confused but automatically started petting the puppies bouncing around her.

Keith joined me and frowned. "You were trying to help catch Camfield, but you fell backward and hit your head pretty hard."

I didn't think Keith was up to doing magic at this point. I was surprised that he hadn't collapsed yet, but something in his words made Martha wince and rub the back of her head. "I think you're right."

Alice joined us after she ended the call with the hospital. "You should go to the hospital; head injuries aren't something to be messed with." She looked around. "Everyone here should go in, even if they wake up before the ambulances get here. There are only three vehicles, so it'll take a while to take everyone in." She looked at Keith and me.

He shook his head. "Ceian and I are fine. We were trying to stop Camfield from taking off, but aside from some tussling with those black suits who fled, we're fine. Just tired." He gave her his kind grandfatherly smile.

Alice narrowed her eyes as she looked between us. Finally, she relented. "Fine. But if either of you collapses, I'm saying I told you so for a long time." She grinned. "Officer Jones has delayed his retirement, and he and I are now stationed in Forgotten Hollow for good. Sorry, I missed your grand opening."

"Not a worry, it's been an odd day. We can bring over the leftovers to the station if you'd like?"

"That would be great." She left to organize the most injured to head out first.

"What really happened?" Martha was still on the ground, but it was mostly because of the puppies.

"What do you mean?" My heart went into my throat. Had Keith's spell failed?

"To you and Camfield. I thought you two were going to be a couple. I guess we're back to working on Jack." She sighed and shook her head.

"Working on me, what?" Jack had appeared so silently that I yelped. He had two handcuffed black suits who didn't look in the least bit spelled. They did look pissed, however. Most likely, truly evil ones who were working with Camfield.

"Working on getting you to relax. You are far too tense." Martha flashed her best smile. "I assume that you and the feds stopped the evil doers?"

Jack glanced at me, then back at her. "Most of them. There are APBs out for the rest." He watched us all for a few moments, shook his head, and walked his two prisoners to the parking lot.

Alice showed up with an EMT team and a gurney and stole Martha away. Then came back a minute later with a puppy Martha had tried to smuggle out.

Eventually, everyone came back from the Old Hollow, but Betsy looked disappointed. Jamie was bouncing on her feet, but clearly didn't want to talk until it was just us. Jeff, Marcus, and their group were way too amped up as they came back, waved good-bye, and detoured to another part of the forest.

I just wanted to go to sleep for a week.

Hadari called her puppies to her, and they followed us down to the lot.

"I know we just served a massive tea, but I didn't eat much. My diner in an hour?" Hannah looked pleased but kept shaking out her right fist and grinned. "I haven't cold-cocked anyone in years. Good times."

Betsy looked around to make sure it was only us. Then dropped her voice anyway. "Turns out the feds think your cousin was behind a scam with the coffee industry and got looped into working with the black suits before he died. They'd been running government secrets, not military, but financial, out to other countries through a series of junk mailers."

"Why did the mail come here?" I wasn't surprised about Darius or the black suits, but that still didn't make sense.

"That's where Camfield came in. He had also worked with the black suits before on some nefarious deals. He saw an opportunity to use the junk mail to send codes somewhere else." She frowned. "I think the feds knew more than was said. Anyway, he was trying to use mind control over the black suits, and then he was going to take over the entire town. We were going to be the guinea pigs! Remember our vines? They can control people." She nodded slowly. "I wish we could find more. I knew there was something special about them."

I fought to keep my reaction from showing. How did the feds, or any humans, know that? I was going to have to tell Xieth. If he was still my guardian, at any rate.

"Interesting. That explains why they broke in and stole them all." Keith nodded but kept his face neutral.

"Yup. The feds think wherever Camfield fled to, he won't be back. They aren't completely sure about the Old Hollow or why forming one of those mystery spots there was part of their plan. But I don't think we'll be seeing any more of that junk mail."

I watched Jamie and Hannah, but they nodded in agreement. "They told you all of this?"

Betsy flushed. "Maybe not directly. I might have been spying." She fluttered her hands. "But we needed to know!"

I adored Betsy and the rest, I did. They were the family I always wanted. But she kind of scared me.

After a few minutes of chatter, we all agreed that a shower and a change of clothes would be great, then split up. Betsy offered to give Keith and me a ride back to the Grasshopper, and Hadari and her puppies took off on their own.

Tiberius was back home when Keith dropped me off, along with Camfield's goats. Luckily, he wasn't interested in them at all.

"Good to see you back. You are still you, aren't you?" I unlocked the front door as Camfield's goats roamed around the busted pen. I would need to fix it or get the yard fenced off, since it looked like they were mine now. But they didn't look like they intended to leave.

"Funny. Yes, I'm me. And you're welcome for helping you. I need goat kibble."

Lucie came into the yard but found some sun-dappled ground and flopped down in it.

I was feeding Tiberius when the landscape painting chimed.

"Where have you been?"

I heard Xieth before his image completely appeared.

"My grand opening?" I might need to eventually share what happened with him, but I didn't have the energy right now.

"That's tomorrow, not today." Xieth chomped on a cigar, and I swore he growled. Maybe it was going around.

"No. Today. I just had it."

"How did you…" He peered past me to Tiberius. "Speak to me, centurion. Where was she?"

"At her teahouse. Pretty much the entire town was there. I heard it was a success." He went back to eating his kibble.

"Hrmph. Well, there are new problems. That Camfield person was behind the kidnapping and return of your friends; he was trying to play multiple sides, and the council isn't pleased. Someone tried to open a portal out in your woods. They did something with magnets in an unstable spot. Look into it. Tomorrow. The real tomorrow." He was trying to sound stern, but missing a day was clearly messing with him.

I wasn't going to ask about what happened to him.

"Then I can stay on parole?"

"Of course you can stay. Didn't you hear me? *Things are going on down there.* I need you, the goat, and even that cat to stay on top of them for me. Report back when you find something. Your magic is being temporarily completely released, the cat's, too. Don't make me regret it."

I felt an odd feeling around my wrists, then the landscape painting returned.

"But the bands were already gone?" Tiberius looked up a minute after the screen changed. "I just felt something on my neck." He couldn't do magic, but Xieth must have decided it was safe for the band on Tiberius to be removed.

Not that it mattered really.

I pushed back my sleeves. A faint silver band flared around both wrists, then vanished. Xieth had a spell reserve beneath where the bracelets had been. Like Lucie, I might have been able to do one or two things, but they wouldn't have lasted long. And possibly triggered something, since I was the actual parolee.

I looked at my bottle and tried to lift it magically. It floated in the air.

"I'm back. And we're working for Xieth."

The end for now! New adventures await in Trouble in a Bottle.

# Afterword

Dear Reader,

Thank you for joining me on this NEW adventure!  This series had been bouncing around in my head for a few years. I wrote the novella, Murder in a Bottle, for an anthology, and I always wanted to go back to Ceian and her gang. And here we are!

As always, I appreciate you for coming along on the newest escapade of my worlds.

The next book, Trouble in a Bottle (catching the theme? ) will be out in August 2026. Preorder available now!

Interested in what happened before this book? You can find all the scoop in the Murder in a Bottle novella.

If you want to keep up on the further adventures of new characters and new mayhem, make sure to visit my website and sign up for my mailing list. I keep my emails to a low roar .

You can also sign up on Amazon to follow me and they will keep you updated.

BookBub is also a good place to get updates .

If you enjoyed this book, please spread the word! Positive re-
views and word of mouth are like emotional gold to any writer.
And means more than you know.

Thank you again—and keep reading!

Marie

# About the author

Marie is a multi-award-winning fantasy and science fiction author with a serious reading addiction. If she wasn't writing about all the people in her head, she'd be lurking about coffee shops, annoying total strangers with her stories. So really, writing is a way of saving the masses. She lives in Southern California and spends her days writing and dreaming up more trouble for characters to get into.

She is a member of SFWA (Science Fiction and Fantasy Writers Association) and Novelists, Inc.

When not saving the masses from coffee shop shenanigans, Marie likes to visit the UK and keeps hoping someone will give her a nice summer home in the Forest of Dean or Conwy, Wales.